'How long will you need me?' Annabel asked.

'How long can you remain loyal?'

Furious, she controlled her voice. 'If I give my word I keep it.'

His bear-like manner didn't change. 'Then we'd better give it twelve months. I don't want a reluctant partner. But I need an administrator I can trust for at least the beginning—and I also need a damn good Theatre Sister. Do I take it that you'll agree to twelve months?'

'I agree to that.' She looked straight into his extraordinary eyes.

Gabriel Christie held out his right hand across the table. Annable put down her knife and took it. The handshake was very firm. She knew he believed her, that it was a matter of honour now to stand by their agreement. 'I'll have a contract for you to sign on Monday. You can start on Monday?'

'Yes.' They both went back to the meal. Annabel looked covertly at the top of his leonine mane of blond hair—untameable, she was sure, exactly like the man. This gruff, demanding surgeon had appeared on her horizon in time to save her from unemployment and homelessness. The least she could do would be to try and like him.

Lancashire born, Jenny Ashe read English at Birmingham, returning thence with a BA and RA—the latter being rheumatoid arthritis, which after barrels of various pills, and three operations, led to her becoming almost bionic, with two manmade joints. Married to a junior surgeon in Scotland, who was born in Malaysia, she returned to Liverpool with three Scottish children when her husband went into general practice in 1966. She had written non-stop after that—articles, short stories and radio talks. Her novels just had to be set in a medical environment, which she considers compassionate, fascinating and completely rewarding.

Jenny Ashe has written eleven other Doctor Nurse Romances, the most recent being *The Surgeon from San Agustin, Doctor Rory's Return,* and *Sister Harriet's Heart.*

A HOSPITAL CALLED JACARANTH

BY

JENNY ASHE

MILLS & BOON LIMITED
ETON HOUSE   18-24 PARADISE ROAD
RICHMOND   SURREY   TW9 1SR

*First published in Great Britain 1988
by Mills & Boon Limited*

© *Jenny Ashe 1988*

*Australian copyright 1988
Philippine copyright 1988
This edition 1989*

ISBN 0 263 76317 X

*Set in English Times 10 on 10 pt.
03 – 8901-58734*

Typeset in Great Britain by JCL Graphics, Bristol

Made and Printed in Great Britain

CHAPTER ONE

IT HAD BEEN a fairly normal orthopaedic list—except for one thing. Annabel Browne was Professor Singh's favourite Theatre Sister, and she always enjoyed his sessions—he chatted while he operated, and told the staff jokes. But as they had worked together that sultry Singapore afternoon on the top floor of the Mount Olivia Hospital, Annabel had been acutely conscious of the amber eyes of one of the visiting doctors who always hovered round any of the Professor's sessions. No-one had introduced him. But those piercing eyes over the mask attracted her by their brightness under thick brows, and the uncontrollable fair hair, hardly restrained by the hospital cap, reminded her of a picture of a Viking chieftain she had once seen in a child's story book. She ridiculed herself for thinking of it now, yet as a child of four or five she had been fascinated by that noble face and wild hair—so different from the usual men she met around the streets of sedate, eminently controllable Cheltenham where she had grown up.

Left alone in the empty theatre, she recounted the swabs methodically, tidied away the instruments. The Professor was a sweet man and a clever surgeon—but most untidy. He would throw anything he didn't need again on the floor, leaving his staff to clear away after him. However, it was a small fault in such a big man, and Annabel made no complaint as she cast a final glance round, satisfied that all was well.

The sound of the traffic outside was so familiar that she ignored it—the squeak of brakes as cars slowed down at the junction after coming off the elegant flower-filled East Coast Highway. Annabel left the theatre, wondering idly why the Professor had not introduced the tall fair man by name. Probably because there were three or four extra that day, and he had not remembered all their names. There was a big orthopaedic conference on at the Mount Olivia, and there were bigwigs from many countries who had specially come to watch the Professor operate.

Just then the swing doors were pushed open, and Kenneth Lu Sen, the registrar, wandered back in, idly fingering the keys to his new sleek white Mercedes. 'I was waiting for you, Annabel. What are you doing here alone for so long? Trying to hide from me?'

Annabel smiled rather wearily. Ken had been quite close to her during the last operation, pretending to be very interested in the fusion of an arthritic knee so that he had to press against her back and look closely over her shoulder. 'No, Ken, not really. But anyone who pinches my behind while the Prof. is operating isn't exactly my favourite person.'

He grinned. At least he didn't deny it. He was a personable young man, tall for a Chinese, and, being the son of the man who owned most of the Mount Olivia Hospital, he did not lack female admirers. But Annable disliked his self-confidence, his pleasure in his own charm and attraction. He said, 'I was hoping you would come to Changi with me for a spin—and to admire my new yacht.'

Annabel put her hands on her hips as though telling off a junior. 'Ken, I'm not impressed. It's your father's money, not yours. If I felt like going out with you, it wouldn't matter if you only had a push-bike. I'm a loser OK?'

He shrugged but didn't move from the doorway. 'So? Nobody's perfect.'

'Please, Ken, get out of my way.'

'Come for dinner, then.'

'I'm meeting Celia.'

'How about tomorrow?'

It was her turn to shrug, anxious to get out of the theatre and get changed. 'All right, if you can't find anyone better.'

'Honey, I wish I knew what you have against me.'

Annabel said simply, 'It's nothing personal. I just enjoy my own company.'

'That isn't normal.'

Annabel pulled off her cap and untied the mask from round her neck. She shook down her dark hair and sighed. 'I really can't explain just now—I'm expected at the Club. But—I work hard, you know—I want to be really successful at what I do. And I feel that I don't have time for—er—relationships just now. You wouldn't understand. But I'm reaching out—whatever it is I want, I want to do it all by myself—on my own merit. Does that make any kind of sense?' She smiled. 'Call me in five years or so, when I'll know what it is I'm searching for. I might even have found it!'

He reached out a hand the colour of honey, and touched her hair briefly. 'Keep in touch till then.'

She laughed. 'We're in touch every day.'

'Not the way I'd like it.'

She shied away from that sort of talk. To change the subject she asked, 'Who was that tall man with bushy hair in theatre this afternoon?'

'Pal of the Prof's from Malaysia. Why?'

From Malaysia—a European? 'Just wondered.' And taking advantage of Ken's move from the doorway, she slipped past him, murmured, 'Bye, Ken,' and walked as quickly as she could to the changing room, where she closed the door firmly and leaned on it with a sigh of relief.

A voice said, 'Annabel, what on earth is the matter?' It was Celia Lau, her friend from midwifery. 'You're late for the Club. Martin's been waiting half an hour.'

'You go on. I've just had a bit more hassle from Ken.'

'Lucky girl. His papa owns most of Mount Olivia.'

'So he tells me—several times. Thinks he's God's gift to the nursing profession just because he's got a new Mercedes and his father has bought him a boat.' She waved as she changed into her outdoor clothes. 'You go on, Celia. Catch you later by the pool.'

Celia went to the door, but paused with her hand on
the handle. 'Ken might be able to help you with your
career. You are always saying you want to get on in life.
Why not make friends with people who have already
made it?'

'That's why, you see. I want to be successful all on
my own. I don't want to marry money—or even make
friends with it. The last help I want is from a spoiled
mummy's boy, I can tell you.' She went to the wash
basin and ran some cool water to rinse her face and
hands. Almost to herself, she said, 'I know what I don't
want—but will I recognise what I do want if it turns
up?'

Celia smiled, her almond eyes narrowing with good
humour in her pretty square face. 'I think you will,' she
said. 'See you soon.'

Annabel towelled her face and neck briskly after
Celia has gone, and pinned her hair back. She opened
the door, looked left and right like some sort of spy,
before deciding the corridor was Ken-free and it was
safe to make her way towards the main foyer.

On the way to the imposing front doors, she passed
the pigeon-holes, and noticed a familiar blue air-letter in
the B section. Good—a letter from home. She opened it,
expecting the usual homely chat about family and
friends and her parents's small antiques business. But as
she glanced at the first few lines, she paused and groped
for a seat, where she sat and read the letter through
twice, her face growing very grave. 'The shop is
breaking even. But we had some bad news about the
house.' Their little shop was part of an elegant Georgian
terrace. 'The house next door has some rather dire fault
in their foundations, and we find that we are all affected
to some extent. The Insurance people don't want to
know. Apparently these Regency crescents were
sometimes built with more thought for the style above
ground than the solidity below. You must not worry,
my dear Annabel—we can get a loan to tide us over. But
naturally we must postpone our visit to come out to see

you in Singapore which is a horrid disappointment . . .'

Annabel hardly paused. The hospital bank would still
be open—it didn't keep high street hours. She broke
into a run back along the way she had come—and ran
full-tilt into someone coming the other way round the
corner. 'Well—just look who can't wait to fall into my
arms!' It was Ken Lu Sen, who made the most of the
collision by pulling her more tightly against him.

She held herself stiffly and spoke into the starched
white of his coat 'Ken, this really is very serious. I must
catch the bank before it closes.'

'I'll come with you and force them to stay open!'

'I mean it.' This young man's total assurance galled
her. She stopped struggling, and, gently raising her
foot, she stamped very hard on his toes. Free at once as
he staggered away, she ran into the bank and straight up
to the counter. 'Please, I need to take out fifteen
thousand dollars to sent to the U.K.'

The bank clerk did not bat a svelte painted eyebrow.
She was used to dealing with those with much more
money than Annabel's small life savings. She handed
over the bank draft and Annabel signed it, not
regretting for a moment what she was doing. She had
the money and her parents needed it just now. Annabel
had saved diligently for that special event that she knew
would one day turn up, the moment when she would
know that success was beckoning to her. But she still
had her steady job, and would save again, knowing her
moment would wait for her.

She posted the money, satisfied she had done all she
could, and checked her watch. Celia and Martin would
wonder what she was doing. She quickened her pace
again—only to notice that Ken was waiting at the main
door, leaning idly against a stone lion, twirling his car
keys in his hand. Remembering that inelegant stamp she
had given him, Annabel paused. She was just by
Professor Singh's room—and, without thinking
through her action, she grabbed the handle and let

herself in. She could explain—the Professor was an understanding man. Panting a little, she closed the door behind her and looked round the room. The Professor wasn't in his room. But the tall man was—the man with the shock of fair hair and clear amber eyes . . . She gasped, 'I'm awfully sorry to barge in like this—' Her voice trailed away. In an embarrassed silence the tall man turned away from the window and stared from under those bushy brows at the sight of a dishevelled nurse gasping for breath about to ask for sanctuary. With as much dignity as she could muster, Annabel let go of the doorhandle and tried a gentle smile at this glowering giant.

'It must look a bit strange—' but it was no use. His craggy face did not soften its expression. How dreadfully naïve of her—how unsophisticated. In her distress she knew she had only one course of action—retreat as speedily as possible. Even Ken Lu Sen and his bruised foot would be better than this. Whispering 'Sorry' again, she opened the door, insinuated herself through the tiniest possible crack and closed it behind her, her face glowing with shame. Thank goodness the Prof hadn't been there as well to see his usually competent sister in a most undignified light.

Her composure began to return as she made a clear exit down the steps of the hospital into the lovely witching time that was the city of Singapore at sunset. Above the tall tower blocks, the curved Chinese roofs and fronded palm trees, the sky glowed a gentle red, getting more aflame towards the west. The glorious highway round to the East Coast Park was full of cars and families making for the water sports, the barbecues and the restaurants along the shore. The great heart of business was all around them as they played, the skyscrapers where men never slept, and the huge tankers in the port, still as painted ships on the deep turquoise of the sea.

'Can I drop you anywhere?' It was Ken, still dangling

his car-keys, and he didn't seem angry at having his foot
stamped on.

Hesitantly she said, 'I—I am a bit late for the Club.'

'The Professional? No problem. I'm passing there.'
He was being nice, as his cushy limousine whispered
through the rush hour, cool and comfortable, the
passenger appreciating the airconditioning in the plush
interior. Annabel knew that Ken didn't really care for
her as a woman—he only disliked the fact that she was
unwilling to be swept off her feet, as many of the nurses
had been. However, they said no more that evening. He
dropped her at the gate of the Club, and as she thanked
him he nodded, and said, 'Tomorrow, same time, you
said?'

He was waiting for an answer, disregarding the build-
up of traffic behind him. Was he so very bad? Annabel
said reluctantly. 'All right, Ken. After all, I might have
damaged your foot for life.'

He smiled—there was no doubt about his good looks.
'I accept your apology. I don't mind the pain—at least it
got me a yes from you!' And with a jaunty wave, he
steered out into the stream of traffic and was gone.

Celia and Martin and the others were still in the club
pool. The water was cool and kind, and Annabel soon
joined in, as it splashed and lapped away the tensions
and troubles of the day. Floodlit travellers'-palms
looked down on the swimmers, and a tall frangipani tree
shed its fragrant white flowers like falling stars into the
water. Annabel turned on her back and floated, looking
up at the sky above her, still glowing after the sunset
with the thousands of neon signs that set the entire
horizon on fire. A passing jetliner was making its lazy
approach to Changi Airport, hanging almost stationary
in the warm night sky. How she loved this city. Not even
a pest of a Registrar could spoil the contentment of her
life here.

She lay and waved her hands in the water, propelling
herself gently along, leaving her problems behind as she
swam. Ken would soon tire of her coldness and find

someone more beautiful and more rich. And the tall man in the Prof's office had probably forgotten all about the embarrassed nurse he had seen briefly that evening. He would be shaking his lion's mane and chatting with Professor Singh about much more important matters.

Finally she pulled herself from the water next to Celia, who had ordered two Singapore slings. 'You shook off your tame millionaire, lah?' Celia took the stick of pineapple from the drink and nibbled at it.

'Ken isn't a millionaire—his daddy is. I dislike rich men's sons. They never earned their money, yet they flaunt it for their own glory. Spoiled brats!'

Celia laughed. 'Go on—blow off the steam—that is what your expression is, yes? That's what your friends are for. I'm listening.'

Annabel had known Celia since she first arrived, a total stranger, at the Mount Olivia, and found the Chinese girl kind and helpful. 'Ken isn't the problem. I had a letter from home. That's why I'm late.' She explained what had happened. 'My money will help, of course—but I'd been looking forward to them flying out to see me. I wanted to show them my wonderful Singapore.'

Celia nodded. 'It must be five years since you saw them.'

'Yes. We all thought we'd have enough savings by now. Their business isn't doing all that well—there are so many antique shops in Cheltenham, you see.'

'You wanted to get away from there, I know.'

'Right. I thought a year in Singapore would—open my eyes a bit. How was I to know I'd fall in love with the place?'

'You once said there was a boyfriend there . . .?'

'I don't really count Tony. We just met at amateur dramatics, and he used to take me home sometimes. The trouble with boring steady types is that they can become a habit, and I've seen people drift into marriage with someone who is basically—well, boring!' They both laughed. 'I don't want to make any mistakes like that, you see, so I'm keeping all my relationships at a distance. It's the best way.'

Celia shrugged her slim shoulders, and her pretty eyes turned towards Martin who was just coming along to join them. Clearly Celia wasn't averse to a closer relationship there. Annabel resolved to say no more on that topic. Martin sat down and smoothed back his spiky black hair. Their conversation turned to the past day in the hospital. Martin was a nurse on Orthopaedics. 'The girls in my ward were asking about that tall man with the bushy hair. Did he come up to Theatre with the Prof, Annabel?'

'He did.' She kept her voice steady, though her heart leapt at the memory of that glowering figure. 'But I've no idea who he is.'

'Someone said he comes from Malaysia. Probably K.L. Did you hear his accent?'

'No, I didn't hear him speak. But I certainly know what he looks like when he's cross!' She decided to explain. 'The expression on his face when I barged into the Prof's room was definitely not kind-hearted.'

Martin looked at her as though he knew there was more to her story. But he decided not to pry, turning the whole thing into a joke. 'Has to be kind, Annabel! They all do. This conference is all about orthopaedic help to developing countries. You must admire them for that.'

'From a distance, then.'

The three friends joined the others in the restaurant when they had changed. The Professional Club was expensive to join, but once accepted, the facilities were very cheap and excellent. They sat at a round table, and turned the central revolving shelf to help themselves with chopsticks to fried savouries, tender chicken, Chinese vegetables, huge fresh prawns and sliced squid.

As they sat by the floodlit tennis court later, sipping Chinese tea and watching their more energetic colleagues in the cool of the evening, Celia said with sight hesitation, 'This famous future of yours, Annabel. You think you will ever get to be anything except a good Theatre Sister if you stay at the Mount?'

'Funny you should say that.' Annabel sat up straight. 'I've been buying the *Straits Times* and checking the ads lately. Just for interest, seeing what opportunities there are for trained people.'

Celia nodded. 'I saw the paper in your bag. That ad for the clinic in Malacca, was it? Open at that page.'

'I wasn't going to mention it,' admitted Annabel. 'But it sounded interesting.' And as Martin looked puzzled, she took the paper from her bag and read it out to him. 'I haven't applied or anything. What do you think?' And she found the small print. 'Enterprising GP needs assistant with medical training and a business head, for hard work/discussion/devotion in starting exclusive medical and surgical clinic on Malacca coast.'

'That sounds good!' Martin took it and read it for himself. 'It does not say man or woman. In my opinion a perfect chance for the budding tycoon in you, Annabel.'

'It does sound good. I think I've got some business sense, after working for my father. And it would be good to get in on something like this on the ground floor.'

'Ground floor—how you know?'

'Sorry, Celia—another of my English expressions.' Annabel laughed. 'Anyway, to me there's just one drawback—I don't want to leave Singapore. Now, if the clinic were here—I would have applied for a job already. But who wants to leave this sweet life for the Mosquito Coast?'

Celia said, 'It's worth a try. It would be a gamble— but you know they say we Chinese love a gamble.'

'Speak for yourself,' said Martin. 'I love my steady job. But for you, Annabel—the adventurous type. Why don't you write to this person and tell him you possess all the qualities he is looking for?'

Annabel smiled and finished her tea before saying.

'I'll sleep on it one more time.' And she said goodnight. She knew they would be glad of some time alone together. They had never made her feel unwelcome, but it was plain that Celia and Martin had become closer lately. She hailed a cab at the club gate, and was glad of the thickness of the traffic so that they could go slowly along the bustling streets and she could look around at all the fun and activity that was Singapore. How could she possibly want to make a fresh start in a sleepy little Malaysian job?

Yet—there was the advantage of getting away from Ken Lu Sen. Life at the Mount in the past few weeks had become almost a game of hide and seek with the bumptious young registrar. Yes—she would be glad to get away from him—but not all her other friends, the cheery Professor, the people at the club, and the excitement of being young and free in the brightest city in the world. It didn't take much, on that short drive back to the nurses' flats, to decide Annabel Browne that the job in Malacca, though tempting, was not for her.

Next morning, Annabel had hardly checked the morning's operating list when Ken bounced in, scrubbed up, and demanded her help in tying his gown and pulling on his gloves. 'You look beautiful this morning, Annabel.'

'Good morning.' She kept her eyes averted as she brushed against the honey coloured skin of his neck as she tied the gown.

He ignored her coolness. 'I've booked a table for us at the Goodwood Park Hotel. You like Taiwanese food, don't you?'

She tried not to be impressed. 'Oh yes,' she said, trying to concentrate on how many sterile packs she had taken from stores.

'Then we'll eat there first, perhaps have some champagne. Afterwards, cruise in the Merc along the East Coast Highway, perhaps stop at the Club for a drink—the Yacht Club—I can show you the boat.

Then I thought we could drive round in the moonlight to my father's beach villa at Pasir Ris. We can walk a little, play some music, maybe dance . . .?' He was making the seduction as tempting as possible, his gentle accented English making the offer even more attractive. She knew as well as he that those villas in Pasir Ris were worth over a million dollars— a playground for the very rich . . . Annabel at last looked up at him, and saw his smile of satisfaction—she was just the same as any other woman, fascinated by the high life he could afford her. How she wished she hadn't looked up.

At that moment the door swung open, and the tall fair-haired stranger strode in, striking Annabel dumb. He wished them both good morning in a deep voice with a hint of a Scottish accent. 'Professor Singh has invited me to assist this morning. These gowns are for today?'

Annabel nodded, and went to help him get ready, wondering if by any chance he had recognised the untidy maiden-in-distress who had so unceremoniously interrupted him yesterday. She blushed slightly as the stranger chatted to Ken about the coming list, the latest developments in joint replacement, and the talents of the Professor. He paid no attention to Annabel and she thankfully went on with her routine tasks of preparing the theatre and her nurses and her trays of instruments for maximum efficiency. They were the supporting cast, helping the main actors in this daily drama get on with their vital work unhindered.

The stranger stayed only for the first operation, and as he left he made no sign of knowing Annabel. She relaxed slightly after he had gone, with only the apprehension remaining of her reluctant date that evening with the triumphant Ken Lu Sen. But as she dressed after a cool shower, in her dark green silk pants suit, and brushed her dark hair till it rippled down her back, she wondered what the Viking was doing that night, and whether she would ever see him again.

The white Mercedes was waiting outside the nurses' flats. Ken was leaning on a convenient palm tree, dangling his keys, dressed in casual but expensive slacks and shirt. He was well aware that he was in full view of the flats, and that many envious nurses would be watching who was the lucky lady that night. And they would know, thought Annabel bitterly, that Sister Browne was Dr Lu Sen's latest conquest. She felt the pairs of eyes upon her as she walked up to him in the warm tropical evening, the crickets singing in the grass, and Indian sparrows quarrelling in the branches.

'Hello, my beautiful.' His eyes were approving, but his tone insolent, as though she had already melted into his embrace. 'You make me wait, huh?'

'You know as well as I do what time we left work.' It had been a long day in theatre. 'And to be honest, I'm tired. Let's not be too late back, please?'

He led the way to the limousine, and helped her in. He drove with one hand, his elbow leaning on the window, his eyes constantly turning towards her. 'You know, Annabel, you mustn't believe all the rumours about me. I'm not the naughty boy of the hospital. There are others much naughtier—only they keep their affairs private.' He gave her a lazy smile before turning his eyes back to the road.

She faced him, spoke directly to his handsome profile outlined as it was by the neon of the shop and club signs they were passing. 'This isn't an affair, Ken.'

'Of course not.' His reply was instant. 'This is a nice dinner for two. Nothing more—nothing at all unless you want it.' And he sounded almost sincere.

They arrived at the curved stone staircase that led up to the once colonial hotel, now decorated in blue and white and gold, specialising in Taiwanese cuisine. The crickets chirped in the carpark, and whiffs of expensive perfume drifted among the other sumptuous limousines. Ken held Annabel's elbow as as they went up the staircase, and she was aware that she looked good, escorted attentively by such a well-known Singapore character.

A tall Chinese man in a white tuxedo was coming out

of the hotel, and Ken and he greeted each other with a
hearty handshake. Ken said 'Excuse me, Annabel—this
is an old school friend of mine—'

Annabel shook hands with the friend then, seeing that
the men wanted to exchange a few words, she said, 'I'll
be back in a moment,' and made her way to the
luxurious powder room, to avoid the embarrassment of
standing while her escort chatted to someone else. She
combed her already tidy hair, and inspected her sun-
tanned cheeks before slowly making her way back to the
entrance.

As she returned, the two men saw her. The friend
bowed to her and said goodbye to Ken. As he withdrew,
he called after them in Cantonese, 'Not bad, that one.
You like white girls?'

Annabel felt her skin rise in goose pimples of rage.
Celia had taught her Cantonese, and she could follow
the conversation. Ken replied, 'I think I will like this
one. Like ice—but tonight she is going to find out how I
melt ice!'

'Nice figure—like ripe fruit. Enjoy tonight.'

Ken Lu Sen laughed. 'I will enjoy—and she will be
spoiled for ordinary men after one night with me!'

Annabel's temper snapped. 'Excuse me,' she called
after the man. He turned and took one step back.
Annabel continued in Cantonese. 'You both seem to
have the wrong idea. The night is already over. I see
now that money does not make gentlemen—only
monkeys!' And leaving them both open-mouthed, she
ran lightly down the stone steps, through the carpark
and out on to the main road, where she quickly jumped
into an empty trishaw and drew the curtain. Her heart
was racing, but she had a deep and perfect happiness at
being able to repay Dr Sen so deliciously. He would be
furious at being stood up, and embarrassed—maybe—
by her knowledge of what the real Dr Sen was really
like. He could pretend, make up stories about what
really happened. She paid off the trishaw wallah, and
walked home, buying herself a carton of fresh savoury

noodles—a much better meal than if she had gone with Ken for his expensive evening.

In the morning she was looking forward to telling Celia the whole tale. But as she passed the Professor's room, his secretary was just coming out. 'Oh, Sister—could you spare Professor Singh a moment?'

'Of course.' Professor Singh could restore anyone's loss of faith in human nature, and she smiled as she tapped on his door.

He was sitting behind his desk, and rose as soon as she came in. His face, usually twinkling, was inscrutable. 'I'm afraid I have to tell you—we no longer need your services. On Friday you will receive three months pay and leave.'

'Professor . . .!' Her world tumbled.

He said quickly, 'As you know, our contract can be terminated by either party at any time. There is nothing else to say.'

Annabel took a deep breath. 'What have I done?' But as soon as she said the words, a realisation began to dawn. 'It's Lu Sen, isn't it? His father owns most of the hospital. You know it isn't fair, don't you, sir? You know he's taking personal revenge—that he's—'

The professor sighed, and sat down again. 'Look, Annabel—I don't want to lose you just now—you must know that. But the Jacaranth project has come up—and the Chief has asked for you by name. Have you seen this advertisement in the *Times*?'

The clinic in Malacca! More confused than ever, Annabel stared at him. Why? She took the paper. Beside the ad, the name 'Dr Gabriel Christie' was written. 'Is he someone you know?'

'We studied together. Wonderful man. This new hospital, Annabel, still in the blueprint stage, as far as I know—but with you in there—I know it could lift off, my dear—I feel this is something you must do!'

She stood her ground. 'First you fire me—then you say you recommend me for this job.' The Professor said nothing, but his black eyes were direct and sincere. She picked up the paper again to study the phone number. 'I'll call him, then. As I have no choice.' Her voice was suddenly very subdued.

Her one-time Chief smiled for the first time. 'I knew you could take a challenge! It won't be easy at first. Christie can be brusque with people until he gets to know them . . .'

Annabel swallowed sudden tears. 'A bad-tempered bully.' She paused to catch her breath. 'I don't know why, sir—but I'll do it. I have to.

CHAPTER TWO

THE BUS ride to Malacca was long and uncomfortable, mainly because of the delays on the narrow road, when the temperature and humidity soared, in spite of the air-conditioning. But Annabel, along with the other passengers, mainly Malays, bore the heat stoically, only occasionally wiping the sweat from her damp forehead. She was thoroughly cross when she alighted in the town centre, and asked the way to the beach road, from a seller of coconuts at the side of the road. There were no skyscrapers here. The town was quaint and old-fashioned compared with Singapore, and the driving was atrocious. The coconut-seller scratched his head. 'Long way to coast road from here, *lah*. Better take cab.' He pointed to a row of elderly yellow taxis, the sign at their head reading 'TEKSI'.

Annabel asked the driver how much it would cost, and when he said fifteen ringgit, she shook her head and decided to walk. On the map it didn't seem to be far. Malacca wasn't a large place. The coast road would be cool with breezes from the Straits. Surely there would be no problem finding the hospital. Gabriel Christie's secretary had sent her a sketch map—she sounded nice on the phone, said her name was Phyll. Annabel had yet to hear the voice of her prospective employer, but recalling the Prof's words, she was expecting a gruff oldish man with a bad temper. She amused herself as she walked at a reasonable pace out of the town centre, and towards the north road along the coast, by imagining what Gabriel Christie would look like.

Soon the road was almost right on the sandy shore, and the houses got bigger and more elegant. Her spirits rose. A job in one of these lovely villas would be more like a holiday, with the blue waves crashing on to the white sand, and the palm trees leaning gracefully over the beach, giving welcome shade to the white rocks. Annabel read the names on each grand gatepost. There was nothing called Jacaranth.

She walked on. She was running out of houses, and soon the scenery changed to open paddy fields, with gently grazing water buffalo hardly bothering to turn their heads to see this one lonely walker along the still, dusty road. Ahead was a palm oil plantation, the stocky bushy trees packed close together, their shadows growing longer as the sun began to dip. Annabel realised she was very hungry, and even more thirsty, and her legs were growing tired. She looked around for somewhere to sit down for a while. It was clear she had come too far along the road, and would have to retrace her steps after a rest. She walked down by the side of a field, to the beach, where she sank down gratefully in the shade by a hot grey rock curtained by graceful palms. The waves beat endlessly on the sand, the wind was warm and salty. She leaned her back against the rocks and closed her eyes for a while. The holiday atmosphere had disappeared, and she began to feel sorry for herself, and annoyed that she could have walked right past the hospital without recognising it.

She was awakened by a deep voice, a gentle shake. There was a strong hand on her shoulder, firm and comforting. She opened her eyes, expecting to see a Malay face. Instead, the face was tanned, but not the deep olive of the Malay—and the hair was a wild shock of blond hair like a Viking's in a picture book . . . and amber eyes looked down at her from under bushy brows. At first she thought it was a face from the past. But then she remembered with a rush, and sat up sharply, brushing his hand from her shoulder. It was the man from Professor Singh's room, the tall man she had last seen in the Mount Olivia operating theatre.

'This is no place for a sleep, Sister Browne. There are some very shady characters around her.' His voice was deep as she remembered it, and this time not a bit cross.

'I was looking for Jacaranth. I must have missed it.'

He stood back from her then, and she looked up at the outline of his body, strong and lithe against the pale gold sand and the sparkling waves. He wore cotton trousers and a thin shirt, the sleeves rolled up over the muscular brown arms.

'If I thought you would be daft enough to walk, I would have met you. You should have taken a cab.'

'It didn't seem far.' But then something clicked. 'I say, are you—anyone to do with Gabriel Christie?'

'I am Gabriel Christie.'

Annabel said in a small voice, 'Then I was looking for you.' She scrambled to her feet, smoothing the sand from her dress, conscious of her tangled hair and sweaty face, and conscious too of the indignity of being found asleep and defenceless on the beach. But she knew it was her own fault for not getting more precise directions from Phyll, the soft-spoken secretary. She admitted as much. 'I may have been rather foolish.'

He held out his hand, and they shook hands formally. 'Never mind.' When he smiled, the bushy eyebrows didn't look quite as forbidding. 'I bet you could do with a long cold drink. It isn't far.'

She could think of nothing to say as she walked beside him back along the field and towards the houses. She knew this meeting had not shown her up in a very clear light. He could quite easily refuse to take her on, now that she had proved inept at finding the Jacaranth. She couldn't keep in step with his long legs, as the walked together, with only the whispering of their soft-soled sandals on the hot tarmac of the path. To their left, the rollers dashed on the sand, retreated, gathered momentum again and crashed eternally on the white rocks. She noticed too that the rocks almost dried in between each assault of the waves, so hot was the afternoon sun.

Gabriel Christie broke the silence. 'Here we are.'

She stared in amazement. 'So I walked right past it! But there's no name on the gate.' Indeed, there was no gate, and the house itself was set back from the road, its drive overgrown, and new window-frames being painted in the upper storeys. 'It doesn't really look like a hospital.'

He seemed to take that personally. 'I'm working on it.' He led the way to the front door, where a newly-made alcove housed a small Malay doorman with a beaming smile. 'Percival, this is Sister Brown.' He nodded and beamed again as they left their shoes in a rack in the lofty hall, that smelt of newly cut timber and fresh paint.

'The consulting rooms and offices are on this floor. Come up. Percival's wife Mia is our head cook. Let's find you that old drink.'

'You don't look like a doctor either.'

He stopped on the step above her and looked down. 'What do I look like, then?'

The brows were drawn in a straight line across his forehead, and Annabel knew she had been too bold. She wanted to hide from the keen eyes. 'I'm not sure—just not very—well, medical, that's all.'

He turned back and opened a door on the first floor. 'That makes two of us, then,' he muttered. 'Come into the common room and let's see what we can make of this uninspiring material.'

Annabel flushed hot—she hadn't meant to be rude. He was such a strong personality that she felt uneasy with him, afraid of saying the wrong thing. Yet she did need this job. Just for a while, until she could get back to her beloved Singapore. She looked around the room—furnished with comfortable cane chairs, bright batik cushions and curtains, and an archway through to an alcove where a large fridge held a variety of drinks. 'Oh, this is nice.'

'The decorators have almost finished this floor. Here, try this.' He held out a can of fruit juice, which she poured into the glass he had already put on the table. 'You'll have missed lunch?'

'I'm not hungry.'

'We'll go along to the Club later. You'd like to see the rest of the place first?'

'Please.'

'Singh said you liked a challenge.' The bushy brows were down again as he stared at her while she gave her answer.

'Yes. I'm stubborn about giving in,' she said carefully. 'But a challenge as big as this—as an empty hospital—well, I might be out of my depth.'

'That makes two of us.' He smiled suddenly as he drank from a can of lemonade. 'I wanted a place where I could look after my own patients—a sort of cottage hospital really—a place where they can come and not get ripped off, like some of the private places do. I believe I can make it work. I'm a surgeon as well as having my MRCP. I've got another consultant surgeon, and a gynaecologist—a woman. With a slim but dedicated junior staff and eight nurses to start with, I believe I can make it work,' he repeated. 'What do you think?' And Annabel realised she desperately wanted the approval of this powerful and laconic giant, who had the guts to have a dream and to go right ahead and make it come true.

'I think if everyone also believes that, then it *will* work. It will have to be teamwork.'

'I agree with you, Sister Browne.' It was a simple remark, but it gave her great pleasure. It appeared as though he was ignoring the ignominious way he had found her like a waif at the roadside. She wondered if she worked for him for a hundred years she might lose her awe of him. Perhaps one day they might even be friends?

Then she realised that she didn't want to work for him—because she wanted to go back to Singapore very much. The way Gabriel Christie was speaking, he was expecting total commitment—and that would never do. Malacca was a holiday spot, not somehwere one lived and worked for ever. She turned away from the magnetic face, the bright ambitious eyes—if she weren't

careful, their amber gleam would tie her down by their
sheer force of his personality.

Just then a group of Malay workmen came up the
stairs, their bare feet making flapping noises on the
polished wood. Gabriel Christie said, 'Ah, back from
their siesta. Let's leave them to it, Sister Browne. Time
to inspect the theatre complex.' And he led the way
round the upper floor, and then up to the third storey,
where the flats for resident staff were situated—small
but very neat and well planned, with their own staircase
outside leading to the back garden, and thence to the
white beach.

Annabel said, 'We don't have siestas in Singapore.'

He paused, standing at the window on one of the flats
that looked out on to the sparkling waves and the
distant horizon almost lost in a heat haze. 'We don't get
things done in Malaysia without them. I hope you don't
expect people to work as they do in Singapore—it's a
different world, Sister Browne.'

'It seems very inefficient.'

The tall surgeon smoothed his chin with his hand, still
looking out over the wide Straits. He breathed in rather
deeply, as though dealing with a stubborn child. Then
he said briskly, 'Well now, we've had a look around.
You've missed lunch. I suggest an early dinner at my
club, when you can ask me questions. Then I'll see you
on your bus.'

They drove back into town in his old but fast sports
car, the sea wind riffling Annabel's hair in a rather
delightful way as they neared the old part of the town,
where the ruin of St Paul's Church, which Dr Christie
pointed out up the hill, was once used as a depot for
ammunition when the Dutch fought the Portuguese,
and then the British. Further round the hill was a white
bungalow building, which was the WM Club, or West
Malaysia. 'Most of my colleagues are members here.'

Privately Annabel thought it was rather primitive
compared with her favourite Professional Club in
Singapore. But the view from the verandah was

stunning, and she couldn't help leaning out, gazing at the bright waters, the cheerful children playing on the beach beneath them, the far turquoise waters and the tiny fishing boats dotted about the bay. Dr Christie came and stood beside her. At first he didn't speak, but when she turned to him, she found he was studying her with his unreadable brown eyes. 'Like it?'

She felt herself flush a little under his profound scrutiny. 'It's very beautiful.' Just then a flash of sheet lightning lit up the almost clear sky, and she started, as it was followed in a few seconds by a low menacing growl of thunder. 'A storm is coming.'

'No—the weather is like that here. There are always electric clouds in the Malacca Straits. The lightning is part of the magnificence, I think. As though the gods put on a floor show to entertain the crowds—there's no malice in our thunder.' He took two glasses from a waiter, and said casually, 'You do like lobster, don't you?' They sipped cool mango juice in silence. When the lobster was brought, they sat at a table close to the edge, where the view was uninterrupted. Afteer making sure Annabel's plate was full, he said, 'You'd like to interview me, perhaps?'

'I thought I was the applicant—I applied for the job.'

'Yes, true. But we both have to find out how well sutied you are. This isn't the sort of job you leave after a few months.'

Annabel's heart sank. She needed to work. But she needed work which she could leave as soon as Celia found her another Singapore job. She tried to choose her words carefully. 'You—have paid me a compliment, I think, Dr Christie—you told Professor Singh you thought I would suit you. If I take it on, I'll fulful my contract faithfully. But I have to admit to you that I do want to return to Singapore. I can't see myself ever settling in Malaysia. I love cities and hate—well, the slow pace of life and the acceptance of the second-rate you get in small towns.'

He interrupted then, although he clearly had meant to

let her speak. 'I can't let that go. The Jacaranth is first-
class. I'll not stand for anything less. Is that clear?' he
barked the words, and Annabel was reminded of the
Professor's warning about him being gruff and
brusque. She realised that fate had brought her here.
Financially she had to take the job. If the chief turned
out to be bad-tempered and gruff, she still had no
choice at present.

'I was only being honest with you.' She tried to be
dignified, but was only too well aware that she would
have to take this job an admit it now. She went on,
sounding calmer than she really was, 'How long will you
need me?'

'How long can you remain loyal?'

Furious, she controlled her voice. 'If I give my word I
keep it.'

His bear-like manner didn't change. 'Then we'd
better give it twelve months. I don't want a reluctant
partner. But I need an administrator I can trust for at
least the beginning—and I also need a damn good
Theatre Sister. Do I take it that you'll agree to twelve
months?'

'I agree to that.' She looked straight into his
extraordinary eyes.

Gabriel Christie held out his right hand across the
table. Annabel put down her knife and took it. The
handshake was very firm. She knew he believed her,
that it was a matter of honour now to stand by their
agreement. 'I'll have a contract for you to sign on
Monday. You can start on Monday?'

'Yes.' They both went back to the meal. Annabel
looked covertly at the top of his leonine mane of blond
hair—untameable, she was sure, exactly like the man.
This gruff, demanding surgeon had appeared on her
horizon in time to save her from unemployment and
homelessness. The least she could do would be to try
and like him.

The sun was setting as he walked along with her to the
bus station—and she couldn't help a last admiring look

at the deep rose red of the sky over the palm-fringed beach. If she had to work in a backwater, then she was lucky to have found such a beautiful one. But she didn't confide her thoughts to her new employer—his brows were drawn down over his eyes, and he appeared deep in thought. How could she have even thought of their becoming friends? It was impossible to know this man, let alone like him. She admired his ambition and his integrity. But she had to admit, as the sun sank over the passing scenery of Malaysia, that her enforced stay in this country was not totally to her liking. How she would miss her friends! What would she do in the evenings? Or would they all work so hard that they would be glad to get to sleep at nights—those witching, lightning-filled nights, when the waves crashed on the shore, and the fishermen's lights flickered far out among the tiny islands?

Celia Lau was waiting in her room. 'You've been hours and hours!'

Annabel sat down and took off her sandals. 'I've been to another world. Not one that I'd like to stay in either—but I start on Monday.'

'Is he married? Young?'

Annabel laughed. 'Gabriel Christie is the tall mystery man who was in theatre last week. I couldn't even dare to guess his age—and nobody would marry such a cross-patch . . .' Yet suddenly she was aware of his lithe muscular body outlined against the sparkling sea and her voice tailed off. Physically he was so much of a man—surely he couldn't be celibate. But perhaps he was too much of a workaholic to have time for women—yes, that sounded more like it.

'Where do you stay?'

'A flat on the top floor—with a view of the sea, and a maid to bring me morning tea.'

'Annabel, you've fallen on your toes.'

'On my feet!' They were still working on Celia's grasp of English idiom Annabel said suddenly, 'I'll miss you terribly. You will keep your eyes open for a job for me?

My contract is for a year—then I'll be back, you'll see—just as fast as the express bus can carry me.'

From the moment she set foot inside the Jacaranth the following Monday, she had no time at all to speculate any further about her boss. There were workmen still finishing off, and there were four other doctors to meet and discuss their requirements. There were names of shops to find out, suppliers of theatre equipment, of theatre clothes, of stationery and office furniture.

Running the hospital was not something that frightened Annabel. But the size of the task of getting everything together was more than she had ever done before, and the only conversations for the following week were strictly about the job, and how to make sure everything was completed in time for the Grand Opening. At the same time Gabriel Christie and his co-director, surgeon Amal Malik, had their own patients to see at their old addresses in Malacca town, so Annabel and the senior Sister Cherry Ho had to take decisions alone, with the help of the secretary, Phyll, and the doorman Percival and his pretty plump wife Mia, who carried them all onwards with frequent pots of tea, cold drinks and plates of samosas and curry puffs.

At the beginning of the second week, Annabel was learning her way round Malacca, and the list of tasks still to be done had dwindled slightly. But she had some queries which only Dr Christie of Malik could help her with. She managed to corner Gabriel on his way through from the kitchen with a can of cold beer in his hand. 'Dr Christie?'

'Yes? Oh, it's you, Annabel. You're doing a fine job. First rate.'

'Except that I want to install another room.' She knew that if she didn't say something startling, he would be off to inspect the theatres.

He stopped at once. His eyes shone dangerously. 'Explain,' he barked.

'I feel that the side room next to the consulting rooms could be made into a treatment room for minor cases. Sister could do dressings and injections, instead of all cases having to go up in the lift to the theatre floor or be taking up time in the consulting rooms.'

'Hmm.' He strode round to the room she had mentioned. He issued a few brisk instructions in Malay, then he turned to Annabel. 'Anything else?'

'If you have time——'

'Oh, get on with it. Now's the time to plan, not when everything's done.'

Annabel took a deep breath. 'Hospitality.'

'What?'

'Hospitality for patients' families. They'll need to be fed—and they might want to stay with the patient. Where do you plan for them to wait? And don't say the corridor, because trolleys will have to pass. If you want this to be the perfect hospital, you have to have space for them.'

After a great deal of thought, Gabriel Christie found an outbuilding at the back that could easily be furnished with a couple of couches and chairs. He didn't thank Annabel for the idea—but she didn't mind. All she wanted was to get this hospital safely off the ground and running smoothly. Then perhaps they would let her go. She left him to it, and wandered outside to the back garden, which although still littered with spare timber and paint pots, was beginning to look nice, with palm trees and hibiscus bushes, and a paved area where the staff were to have umbrellas over tables and could relax overlooking the beaches and the rocks and the ever-rolling breakers.

Annabel was suddenly aware that she was not alone, and turning, she saw that Cherry Ho had followed her out. She smiled at the Chinese woman. 'I think we're winning.'

But the other woman's eyes were blank—unfriendly. 'You knew Dr Christie before you come here?'

'No. I applied for the job.'

Cherry shrugged. 'Why for he need another Theatre Sister? I work for him in other hospital, *lah*. My work not good or something?'

Annabel felt worried. If Cherry was qualified, why did Dr Christie make a fuss about needing Annabel? She looked at the other woman, and thought she detected jealousy in her attitude. 'I don't particularly want the job.' She was being honest.

'Maybe you want the doctor, huh?'

'Dr Christie? You must be joking!'

'Then why you come? I well qualified, speak better Malay, know Malacca very well. You know nothing.'

Annabel took a deep breath. Hostility was something she could do without. 'Look, if you want to know why Dr Christie employed me, why don't you ask him? I don't want to stay here any longer than I have to. But I warn you, Cherry—I'll do the job I was employed to do. Then you can have both the doctor and the job. OK?' And she turned and went back inside the hospital. She heard Cherry follow her, and quickly went through to see Dr Malik, who was at last in his room where she could find out if he cared at all about any particular colour scheme.

Dr Malik was thin and earnest-looking. He would have been more at home as a professor. He didn't care about his colours. 'But will you go into Malacca and pick up the stationery I ordered, please? I need to write some letters and we have no headed notepaper yet.'

'All right. Are you sure you want me to go? Percival usually picks up stores.'

Dr Malik nodded curtly. 'You will be doing it when the hospital opens. Better find out where Pagodi's offices are. Take my car.'

So Annabel found herself sitting in Dr Malik's Japanese car, with a list of stock in her purse, and a feeling in her heart that Dr Malik also wasn't all that happy about her appointment. She appeared to have made two enemies in one day. She thought sadly about Celia and Martin, back in Singapore. How she missed

having someone she could chat to! The other nurses
were so far quite nice, but no one she could feel close to.

Amal Malik came up before she had started the car.
'Don't forget to tell that crook that the Grand Opening
is next Wednesday, and we must have everything
delivered before this weekend. That includes a buffet
for fifty—no alcohol, but the usual couple of bottles of
white wine for non-Muslims.'

Annabel was well aware that he was treating her like a
servant on purpose, to make sure she knew her place.
Obviously, here was another person who thought a
Malay ought to have her job. But she tried not to let it
bother her. 'Right, sir. I'll check with Mia later. Don't
worry—we'll be ready by Wednesday.' And she let in
the clutch, allowing the car to coast along the wide drive
towards the road. Unhappiness curled round her heart,
but she resolutely ignored it. She had a job to do.

She had a rough idea where the office of their supplier
was, and was thankful that they drove on the left in
Malaysia, and also that there was a parking space quite
near the ramshackle tin fence that appeared to be the
office of Amir Pagodi. But inside the tin fence was
parked a beautiful sleek limousine, and inside the
wooden office was an even more beautiful Chinese
secretary with exquisite features, and a figure like a
model. 'Can I help you?' Her voice was gentle and
musical. Amir Pagodi evidently was a man of taste.

Annabel handed over the list and gave the message.
The girl laughed at the ultimatum. 'Don't worry,
everything will be on time. Mr Pagodi want to keep the
custom of the new hospital. Is he invited to the
ceremony?'

'Possibly. Phyll will know if you ring her.'

The girl smiled with scarlet lips. 'Delivery will be even
quicker if he is invited.'

Annabel grinned. She was beginning to like the cheek
of Mr Pagodi. 'Then I'm sure I can offer him a personal
invitation. Lunchtime Wednesday.'

'Thank you, Sister Browne.' The girl pencilled in a

desk diary in front of her. 'Deliveries will be tonight. You wish to take the notepaper with you?'

'Fine.' Annabel didn't enjoy being an errand girl, but knew that Dr Malik must not find fault with her. She carried the carton of headed stationery to the car and drove back through the hot sticky streets, glad to get to the coast and the sea breezes.

That evening most of them dined together, the junior doctors who were living in and the radiographer and Mia and Pervival. Mia had several cousins who were all employed as caterers and maids, and they were all more relaxed with Annabel, now that they had worked together for the hardest part of the preparations. It was Percival, distinguished-looking with his white hair and erect figure, and beaming smile, who said what they all thought; 'This time next week, we will have patients in the wards instead of painters.'

Dr Chen said, 'And Malik and Christie will be on the premises, I hope?'

Annabel replied, as the only one who knew. 'They haven't decided. I believe they'll take turns to be on call. I'll be working with Phyll on the timetables.' She added, 'Do they have nice houses?'

The radiographer said, 'The Maliks have a lovely villa not far away. Dr Christie spends more time in his club than at home—he has a flat over his old surgery. Maybe he will live in?'

Annabel walked outside afterwards. The starlit sky was lit up with periodic flashes of lightning that were quite spectacular. She gazed up, and wondered what on earth she was doing in a strange town, where her boss was brusque to the point of rudeness, and two of her colleagues disliked her already. The thunder grumbled, and she felt tears starting. Yet she couldn't cry. Sad though she was, the electricity in the atmosphere gave her a feeling of suppressed excitement—as though something wonderful were about to happen. She sighed. If only that something wonderful could be a transfer back to Singapore!

Next morning she woke early. The sunlight was vivid on the walls of her room, and the crashing breakers outside reminded her that she still felt excited and eager, no longer depressed, but keen to get on with the business of creating the Jacaranth out of the brain of one man. She was living at the seaside—why hadn't she been bathing before? Grabbing her towel, she put her bikini on under a cotton pareo and ran down the outside stairs to the beach, not bothering with shoes. The only person stirring was Percival, who kept a devoted night watch on the clinic and grounds. Wishing him good morning, Annabel ran down to the beach, revelling in the freshening breeze and the exhilarating sound of the waves.

She plunged in to the warm water, but found it impossible to swim. The waves merely caught her like a scrap of seaweed and tossed her back on the beach. For a while it was fun to be thrown bodily about, like playing with a large playful beast. But it was exhausting, and after a while she dragged herself up from the beach, rinsed the sand from her costume in a sea pool, and climbed one of the great rocks to lie and bask for a while in the morning sun. The palms leaned gracefully over the sand, and the water sparkled like diamonds. Annabel closed her eyes, and let the sun and the spray play over her body.

She wasn't sure what made her open her eyes. But as she rolled over on to her front, she spotted her employer, Gabriel Christie, also on his way down to the beach, wearing only cotton shorts. A thin gold chain glinted round his neck, and his hair glowed round his head, whipped by the wind so that he appeared like a wild creature at home with these fierce elements. Annabel felt her heart quicken. Had he seen her? She would be better to slide off the rock and try to make her way in without being seen. But she realised she couldn't get past him. Better to lie where she was, and wait until he had taken his swim and gone back inside again. She was hidden by the overhanging palm trees, and could not be seen if she kept still.

But he did not swim. Instead, he walked slowly along the beach towards the rock. Annabel was just going to call out a cheerful greeting, when a woman's voice called 'Gabriel!' A slim woman appeared, thrusting aside the leaves with a lovely hand. She wore a sarong, and her hair reached her waist, glossy and black. Annabel held her breath. She knew she ought to speak now, but she dared not, having allowed Gabriel to get to close already. She flattened herself against the warm hard rock, and tried not to listen. But so graceful was the woman that she couldn't blame Gabriel for being smitten. She had known in her heart that he must have a lover.

They were talking now, coming even closer to the rock. She heard his voice, gentle and tender now, not curt and unfeeling as Annabel knew it. 'I do see what you mean, Sukeina.'

'You understand. Of course you do.' Her voice was as lovely as her body, soft with a slight accent, and a hint of tears in it too. 'Gabriel, I'm not sleeping. I cannot go on like this, Gabriel. I cannot pretend! You know as I know that both our hearts cry out in desperation. I am a woman of passion—of emotion—you know that as well as anyone, my dear. My life has turned into a prison, and I cannot bear it any longer. Oh help me, Gabriel! Help me, please. You are so noble, so clever at making things—turn out well. I need you so very much.'

Her words were so clear, her diction so fine, that the stunned Annabel thought she must be an actress. Yet the sobs in her voice were sincere enough. Then Gabriel murmured a gentle Scots answer, and Annabel lay against the rock, her eyes closed in desperation at the scene she was witnessing. 'I'm doing my best, Suki. I knew it was ging to be hard at the beginning—while the Jacaranth is still young. But soon, soon, you must—'

'I can't wait, do you not see? It is killing me. It will kill me.'

'My dear, haven't I promised to work something out? I have to go now. You do—?'

The woman moaned, her voice so lost and desolate, 'Not yet, my dear, not yet I couldn't bear it. Don't leave me yet I am so weak and helpless—I am nothing without you!'

'Suki, my poor little thing, I'm here if you need me. I'm glad you came to me. But run along now. Trust me. Trust me.'

There was a silence between them, and Annabel could imagine the impassioned embrace, as the breakers crashed on the sand, and the breeze and the spray enveloped the three of them.

And then there was a rustle as the woman passed the rock very close, and went up the sandy path towards another house. Annabel lay motionless, as though she too had experienced the breathless sadness of the lovers she had overheard. She felt embarrassed— yet it was pity too, for two people in such an unhappy liaison.

After a long time she raised herself from the rock. There was no one there. She slid down like some frightened lizard, picked up her sandy towel, and started to run. Her mind still throbbed with what she had heard. And she needed to get back to reality, to hear her gruff boss speak as she had heard him speak so many times, in charge, not tenderly to an unknown Malaysian beauty.

CHAPTER THREE

ANNABEL paused as she approached the Jacaranth. She could see through the trees that Gabriel was sitting at one of the tables in the back garden. She turned and slipped silently back until she could not be seen. Until he went in, she would take another dip. It seemed the most tactful thing to do. She didn't want to come face to face with her boss, straight after hearing him exchange what sounded like endearments with a beautiful Malay woman. Annabel flung down her towel and pulled off the pareo from round her waist, running violently into the full force of an incoming wave, glad of its might, of having to tussle with it. It helped her forget the power of the emotions roused in her by that whispered conversation by the rock.

Flailing her arms, she tried again and again to swim out into the Straits, and time and again she was picked up like driftwood and flung on to the wet sand. Spluttering and laughing with frustration, she emerged at last, scraping her sodden hair from her face, her eyes still closed.

Then suddenly she found herself caught in two very strong masculine arms, held against a bare and masculine chest. There wasd no doubt who it was, and even as she caught her breath and gasped at the strength of his embrace, she flushed in embarrassment because of the secrets she had so unwittingly overheard. And her body gave an instinctive shiver of pleasure at the closeness of his warm wet body, hard and muscular against her. She managed to say in a husky splutter, 'I'm not drowning, you know.'

Gabriel Christie didn't loose his hold. Annabel looked up through draggled hair into his handsome lean face, the amber eyes never so close before. She could

feel the beating of his heart. Suddenly he lifted her as
though she weighed nothing, and carried her up to the
garden, where he set her down by a chair. She sank into it,
while he returned to fetch her pareo and towel. he threw
them on the table before her. 'These breakers must be
treated with respect. It's my fault, I ought to have warned
you. You don't go charging at them as though this were a
paddling pool at Brighton beach.'

She looked up, trying to be bright and confident.
'I'm not stupid, honestly. I swim well. I can look after
myself.'

And then she saw the expression in his eyes. The amber
had darkened to brown as the brows shadowed them. He
was looking at her with an intensity that unnerved her. She
realised her swimsuit was scanty, and he was looking at her
body as well as her face. He was standing only inches away
from her, and she sensed somehow the warmth of his skin
as he sweated in the morning sun. They seemed to hold
each other's gaze for minutes, yet it could only have been
seconds before he said, his voice even gruffer than usual,
'The waves are nothing—they can only knock you
over—if you strike a rock and lose consciousness. Suppose
you hit a jellyfish and get stung? You know that jellyfish
can kill, Sister Browne, don't you? And the stone fish?'
He took a deep breath. 'You'd better let me know next
time you fancy a swim—I'll take you to the Club.' He
cleared his throat and looked away suddenly, at the small
islands far out in the Strait, and at the flicker of early
lightning against the rising sun.

Annabel said, because she could think of nothing to say,
and the silence was fraught with electricity, 'I didn't see
any jellyfish.'

'Lucky for you,' he snapped.

She stood up slowly, and reached across the table for
her things. 'I'd better go and get dressed.'

He put his hand on the wet towel to prevent her taking
it, caught her glance again with his. With an effort, he
said, 'Just—remember what I said. Take care next time.'

'I will.'

He let the towel go, and she slid it from the table into her hands that were unaccountably trembling. He said, 'I can't afford to lose you now. Not when everything is going so well.'

'With the hospital? You're pleased, then?'

'Didn't I mention it?'

'No.'

He stood upright, allowing her to pass. 'It's going well. Thanks, Annabel.' She walked past him towards the outer stairs, and went up slowly, not trusting herself to run yet. She was too shaken by the morning's events, and especially by the effect her formerly distant boss had on her breathing. As soon as she reached her own rooms, she turned the shower on to full, and stood underneath it, trying to lose herself in the force of the droplets, to calm her body, so suddenly awakened by that unexpectedly close encounter. Even after she had towelled herself and brushed her long hair vigorously, she sat for a long time, listening to the throbbing of her own heart, and trying to forget the words of love spoken by the lovely Malay to Gabriel Christie—the most surprising and disturbing words . . .

The sun was streaming in now, and she shook herself mentally. There was work to be done downstairs. She made coffee in her tiny kitchen. There was plenty of work. She would soon feel better with her lists and her estimates and her schedules. But she dressed more carefully than before, in slim cotton pants and a loose lemon yellow blouse, and clipped back her hair with a tiny yellow flower, as she had seen the Malay women do, instead of tying it crudely into a rubber band.

The first person she met was Amal Malik, and his first expression was a frown. 'You had better wear uniform from now on, Sister. The tradespeople will not respect you dressed like that.'

'Am I seeing tradespeople again?'

'I wish you to go into town for me. Please change your clothes.' The sharp black eyes scanned her appearance with a grudging admiration, and Annabel

realised that, crosspatch though he was, he was quite
right about dress—the strict Muslims disapproved of
women showing their bodies or their hair. She went up
obediently and put on her white overall and cap. She
didn't want to go to town, but on the other hand, she
might be as well keeping away from Dr Christie until
they had both been able to forget their meeting that
morning.

'Right, Dr Malik. Am I to take you car again?'

'Yes. Pagodi's and the gardening centre. Here is what
I need.'

'I can't carry pot plants.'

'There is no need.' His cold dry voice grated, but it
was less disturbing than Gabriel's at that moment.
'Bring the folders from Pagodi's and leave the order for
plants for them to deliver this afternoon—and no later,
or I go elsewhere.'

Annabel paused at the front of the Jacaranth. The old
building had indeed been transformed, with gleaming
white paint, dark green louvred shutters, and a tidy
lawn edged with shrubs of hibiscus and bougainvillea.
Wrought iron gates had been fitted, with a wrought iron
sign over the top, the letters 'Jacaranth' picked out in
gold. Inside the entrance hall was a cubbyhole for
Percival, with an 'Enquiries' sign beside him, and a
further window marked 'Receptionists' where a row of
chairs already proclaimed the first waiting area. Yes, as
soon as the potted plants, ferns and dwarf palms were
here, it would look the part—the Jacaranth had been
born. All that it needed now was its official christening
by the senior Cabinet Minister next Wednesday.

Annabel found the streets crowded, and had to park
some distance from Pagodi's. It was tempting to stop
and gawp like a tourist, for the open shops contained
local woodcarvers and goldsmiths and weavers, potters
and bakers. But there was no time, and she made her
way along the narrow street, conscious that in her
uniform she attracted curious glances. She picked her
way past little old ladies selling hand-crocheted baby

garments and beautiful embroidery, and strode a across
a wide monsoon drain, empty now but still dangerous to
fall into. The air was hotter here, away from the seaside,
and she began to feel thirsty. Finally she succumbed to a
coconut-seller, who chopped off the top of a green
coconut for her, gave her two straws to suck out the
refreshing milk, and a long spoon to eat the soft flesh.

She was soon at Pagodi's tin fence, feeling better. The
BMW was not in the yard, but she greeted the pretty
receptionist and produced her list. While she was
scanning it, there came a sudden loud deep bark, and a
huge Alsatian leapt into the office and paused,
growling, at the door. The white teeth looked very sharp
as they caught the glint of sunlight. The little
receptionist called sweetly, 'Be quiet, Susan. Good
morning, Mr Pagodi.'

But the figure who ran in was obviously not the boss.
He was raggedly dressed in a sarong and old vest. 'Fifi,
call the doctor—Mohammed has fallen in the stock-
room—his leg is broken!'

Annabel thought fast. The Jacaranth was functional.
She was here. The fastest treatment the man could get
would be from Dr Malik at the Jacaranth. She said, 'Let
me see him. I can call the ambulance from our hospital.'
And she followed the man to a second ramshackle
building, where a man had fallen from a ladder and lay
with his leg folded beneath him.

There was little she could do on her own, except make
him more comfortable. 'I'll call the ambulance.' She
phoned the hospital from the desk. 'Phyll, is Dr Christie
there?'

'No. He is still seeing patients at his old surgery in
Jalan Hicks.'

'Then please call Dr Malik. There's been an
accident—a broken leg. You'll need to get X-ray
functional right away, the Theatre One. Send the
ambulance to Pagodi's place.'

'Malik here.' Annabel explained the situation. 'Yes,
naturally we can take him. And under the circum-

stances, the folders can wait until Pagodi delivers them.
Please just bring a few to be going on with.' Dr Malik
sounded more human suddenly. Perhaps he had realised
that Annabel could still cope with her elementary
Malay—or perhaps he was only happy when he was
working.

'Is Cherry there to do theatre?' Annabel decided that
it would be a generous gesture to give pride of place to
Cherry for the very first operation in the new hospital.
When Phyll assured her that they could cope, Annabel
breathed a sigh of relief. She waited for the ambulance,
and saw the patient into it before turning back to the
girl, and going over the list with her. She took two
packets of a dozen patient folders—they could surely
not get more than twenty-four patients before the
proper delivery. 'I'll see Mr Pagodi tonight, then.'

''Bye, Annabel.' Fifi already treated her like a
regular. Annabel felt pleased as she retraced her way to
the side where she had left Dr Malik's Mitsubishi. She
would have liked to see the theatre during its very first
operation. But tact had won, and she hoped Cherry
appreciated her gesture.

She had paused in front of a jeweller, attracted by the
glittering twenty-three-carat gold bangles strung up like
Christmas decorations. It was on the way to the nursery
where she was to see about ordering the indoor plants.
Then a voice in her ear sounded suddenly familiar.
'Good morning, Sister Browne. How many gold bangles
does the Jacaranth need?' and she looked up into
Gabriel's face. It was cool and amused, with no trace of
emotion or memory of the morning. He went on, 'Was
that one of my ambulances that passed? It looked very
new.'

'Yes, it was.' Annabel began to explain.

'So we have our first patient? Well done! Let's have
lunch to celebrate.'

'But the folders—Dr Malik wanted them right away.'

Gabriel Christie stopped and looked keenly at her.
'You mean he sent you to collect them in person?'

'Yes.' Annabel saw he was displeased. 'I think he's trying to imporve my Malay.'

'Hmmph.' He took her arm gently and steered her across the road. 'Well, he definitely doesn't need them right away. The information can go on the computer, and Phyll can write up anything he wants later. Lunch, my girl.'

'Is there time?'

'I have no patient till two. You need lunch, don't you?' He was his usual forceful self. She didn't bother to disagree with him. She only opened her mouth, but when he said, 'Don't argue,' she shut it again, and walked up the stone steps with him, past the empty shell of St Paul's Church. As they passed it, Gabriel said, 'There's a wishing well in there. Want to see?'

There were several tourists round the well, which was covered with a metal grille. They waited until they were alone, then Gabriel took out a fifty-cent piece. 'Here, Annabel. Wish to go back to your beloved Singapore if you like. But not till I say so!' He was smiling. She tossed the coin, closed her eyes—and her mind went blank. She couldn't say what it was she wanted most in the world at that moment—or perhaps she knew in her heart, but dared not admit to her consciousness.

She opened her eyes—Gabriel was looking at her, amber eyes impenetrable. 'I made a wish too—I hope we're allowed two for the price of one.' He took her arm gently, although there was no need, and they walked the last few yards round the corner of the steep path to the West Malaysia Club. They went to the same table they had used last time, overlooking the beach. Annabel gazed out, fascinated by the beauty of the scene, and by the flickering lightning. Gabriel said, his voice low, 'Well, do you think you like it here any better than you did at the beginning?'

'I have to admit——'

'That's very grudging. Tell me about your parents.'

It was unexpected, but she was quite happy to tell him

about Cheltenham—except the bit about her parents
needing money, and the sudden need for her to take a
well-paid job. Gabriel proved to be a good listener. He
took off his tie and slung it over the back of the cane
chair as they ate salad and seafood. Annabel wondered
if she would ever get to know the real Gabriel—the one
she had only heard by accident that very morning.
Today he was affable, almost chatty—yet still imposing,
still a little aloof. Something stirred in her heart as she
recalled the strength of his arms about her. How much
easier it had been when she lived in Singapore, and
didn't meet men with gruff voices and disturbing amber
eyes who had secrets out by the restless waves . . .

Gabriel asked about her friends. 'Celia and Martin
will come over the first weekend I'm free,' she told him.

'No boyfriend?'

'No.' Why should that concern him? There was a
silence.

'You don't say much, Sister Browne.'

'Neither do you.' But she quaked a little at the
impertinence. However, it was rewarded with a twinkle
in his eyes, a genuine twinkle, heralding the arrival of a
smile.

'I've been my own boss for too long—I forget that
manners are—well, needed now and then.'

'All the time, surely?'

'My dear, I didn't get my reputation by smiling and
making polite conversation. I got it by darn good
work—good medicine and good results. That's the way
I see it, Annabel.'

'Yes—I do know.'

He smiled again. 'You're very independent.'

'It's essential when one is alone in a foreign country.'

He nodded. 'True—but never confuse independence
for pigheadedness, will you?'

She pushed away her plate. 'Thanks for the lunch. I
didn't know it was going to be a lecture as well.'

'Oh, sit down, woman. Tell me, when would you like
to swim here? I don't want you going in the sea again.'

'I don't want to trouble you.' There was another silence—Annabel was trying to make her heart stop thumping like that at the very memory of that morning . . . And as Gabriel looked at her across the table, there was that look again she had noticed in the morning—an intense, almost hungry look. And she began to feel threatened. He was too forceful a personality for her. He could probably make her love him if he chose. They very thought began to frighten her. Involvement in Malacca was the very last thing she wanted. And then she remembered the wishing well—just exactly what had she wished for?

'Where's your car?' His question was gruffly abrupt.

'Jalan Hicks.'

'I'll walk along with you.'

'But——'

'You love arguing, don't you, Annabel?'

She said no more. He drained his coffee cup, and they walked together out of the Club, the waiter bowing and smiling. The shouts of children drifted up the cliff as they walked down, plus the smells of the roasted nuts and the satay trishaws along the side of the road. They walked to her car, and Gabriel waited until Annabel was inside, opening the windows to cool it down a little after being parked in the sun. Then he lifted a hand in salute, and was lost among the bustling shoppers and tourists. She watched where he had been, with a sudden sense of loss. What a compelling man! They had talked for over an hour, yet she felt she knew him even less than before.

There was a tap on her window. 'Sister Browne?' She nodded. It must be quite clear from her uniform and her face that she was a nurse. 'I am Amir Pagodi. Please come to my office. I'd like to go over your requisitions, if you have the time.' He was a smallish but very handsome man, with sparkling black eyes, curly hair, and dimples in his olive cheeks. Annabel liked him at once. She got out and locked the car, before turning to shake hands with the young businessman. They went back to the tin fence. The Alsatian and the secretary

were gone. 'Lucky I spotted you,' Amir Pagodi smiled.
'I wanted to thank you for the invitation to the
Opening.'

'Don't mention it.'

'Well, business first——' he took a small calculator
from the pocket of his immaculate cream suit. 'Now, I
make the total so far——' he wrote down the figure.
'The goods are satisfactory?'

'Yes, we're pleased. But we'd like them very soon.
The hospital is already being used.'

'I will be delighted to bring everything round myself.
Now, can I offer you a cold drink?'

'No, thank you. I ought to return Dr Malik's car. He
might be needing it.'

'Well, I will see you this evening, I hope. You are very
young to be in such a position of trust. I—I hope—we
can be better friends.' They shook hands again, and he
saw her to the car with an extra two cartons of supplies.
'Gabriel Christie and I are old friends too. Same club,
same barber, that sort of thing.' He smiled again, and
Annabel thought he must be one of the best looking
men she had ever met, with the gaiety in his dark eyes,
and the fire that showed a zest for life and a clear
honesty. His skin was smooth, the colour of dark
honey, and his smile was boyishly bewitching, inspiring
an equally genuine response.

Cherry Ho was waiting for her. Annabel wondered if
she was in for another dose of Cherry's jealousy. But
she was pleasantly surprised when the other woman
said, 'The operation went very good. You want to see
the patient? He wants to thank you for getting him seen
to so quickly.'

'Yes. Thanks for being there. Was it a clean break?'

'Simple fracture. Dr Christie has seen him. Dr
Christie wants to start seeing patients here from
Monday morning.'

'That's fine.' Annabel felt a weight off her mind, if
Cherry had stopped being unfriendly. 'Let's hope things
keep on going smoothly.'

Cherry said with a glint of a smile, 'Medicine is not like that, *lah.*'

'Let's see Mohammed. I have to see Phyll about the office supplies that Mr Pagodi is bringing tonight.'

Cherry said, 'Mr Pagodi himself? That very strange. That man a millionaire—that man never deliver things himself.'

'Nice man. I like the dimples.' Annabel led the way to the ward.

Cherry said, her voice sour again, 'Thinks he God's gift to the ladies of Malacca. He own ten houses, and an antiques business as well as this office equipment business. No fool, Pagodi—steer clear.'

'Antiques?' Annabel paused a moment, but went on quickly, knowing that there was no time to think of other things till the Jacaranth was launched.

After they had chatted to their first patient, the two nurses went together to the common room, where they made a pot of Chinese tea, and sat talking together, reminding Annabel of all she missed in Singapore.

Cherry had the list of guests for the grand opening. 'The Minister is a devout man, so no drink must be served near him. Some of the doctors also do not drink—but the other doctors drink a lot, so one must be very clever to keep them separate. But we have many parties here—they get together for many reasons.'

'That sounds nice. There isn't much socialising in Singapore—everyone is too busy making money.'

'You sound sad when you talk of Singapore—you mean it that you want to go back?'

'Very much, Cherry. Very much. It was home for five years.'

'Why you leave, then?'

Annabel had rehearsed the answer to that question. 'Personal reasons.'

Cherry looked knowing. 'A man.' She smiled. The ice was broken. But Annabel was well aware that Cherry wanted her job—there was steel behind her smile. She must always be very cautious when dealing with Cherry

Ho.

She changed the subject. 'Now, how do we cater for these people on Wednesday? Tables and chairs?'

'Buffet. Row of tables, plates of food all along them—chopsticks. Simple.'

Annabel smiled. 'I think the secret is not to worry about anything. Malaysia is a country where it's bad manners to worry.'

'You live longer that way.'

'Right, Cherry!' It was Gabriel, looking tired, though still elegant in his pale trousers and striped shirt. His mop of fair hair was even more ruffled than usual, giving him a rakish appearance. He looked at the teapot, and Cherry poured him a cup. 'Thanks. I'm here to stay now, Cherry. My things will be coming round tomorrow. It will be easier that way.'

Annabel said, 'You realise that will mean you're on call all the time?'

He smiled at her lazily, and sipped the tea. 'If I'm asleep, I'm not on call—it's as simple as that. Cherry was right, you know. You live longer that way.'

Annabel felt they were laughing at her. 'My Singapore ways don't suit you, then?' She collected the papers on her desk with a brisk movement of her hands, tapping them until they were straight. She was very conscious of Gabriel's ironic stare, and of Cherry's look of triumph to have the chief sitting beside her drinking tea.

Mia called them all to the dining room with a single strike of a bronze gong that had come from Dr Malik's house. Annabel had showered and changed, and had given herself a talking to about not letting the set-up at the Jacaranth get to her. She was there to do a job—the salary was good, even if nothing else was. Just as she told herself that, there was a particularly vivid stroke of lightning in the night sky, and she jumped, startled. The gong saved her from further conjecture. She ran down the inner staircase, joining the other residents, who now totalled almost thirty, and needed seven tables. Mia and her staff coped as though they were the parents of a large family. Annabel thought the foundations were there for a comfortable future—only individual personalities and individual prides and prejudices could spoil things now.

Gabriel came down to join them, demanding no special privileges. He took the nearest empty place, which was at a table where the junior doctors sat with Cherry Ho's deputy, Sister Low. Annabel tried not to notice him—wich wasn't successful—she felt his presence as one felt the presence of a tornado. However, she managed to keep a simple front, talking naturally to her nurse colleagues, and asking their advice about the nuances of the Malay language.

The outside bell rang. Several people jumped up, but then Mia told them her husband was on duty at the door. Within moments, Percival came in. 'Mr Pagodi is here with supplies—want Sister Browne.'

Annabel excused herself and went to the door of the dining room. She heard Sister Low saying to Gabriel that Pagodi was a rogue. But she didn't turn her head as she left the room, though she knew Gabriel was watching her. She smiled with relief when she saw the handsome and totally uncomplicated figure of Amir Pagodi—resplendent in a white tuxedo, standing in the foyer. She said, 'It's very good of you to come.'

'No problem. The supplies have been unloaded by your man. You wish to check the manifest?' Annabel stood close by him while they both checked the goods. He said, 'You are pleased?'

She gave him a warm smile. 'You've been so very helpful, Mr Pagodi.'

'My name is Amir to my friends.'

'Mine is Annabel.'

'How pretty—Anna-bell. You like Malaysia, Annabel?'

'It takes a bit of getting used to.'

'You like some help? You would like to see something of the countryside—maybe have tea on a rubber plantation? It is an honour to me if you say you come.'

Annabel hardly hesitated. 'I'd love to learn more about the place. Thank you for asking me. As soon as the Grand Opening is over, perhaps? She warmed to the gentle Malaysian, so polite and gently spoken. Instead of probing her private thoughts, he chatted about himself, about Malaysia, about world events. They sat in the foyer, lit only by a table lamp, talking quietly, the conversation hardly faltering.

There was the sound of a door opening. 'Hello, Amir—you still here?'

Amir Pagodi stood, went to Gabriel with outstretched hand. 'Hello, old chap. What a way to greet an old friend!'

Gabriel said shortly, 'I'm not one for manners, as well you know. I asked you a question. Why are you still here?' His rough tones, with a trace of his Scottish origins, contrasted strongly with the Malay's velvet voice. Annabel thought there could seldom be characters so opposed while still being both honourable and likeable in their own way. The two men chatted with casual familiarity. Amir caught her eye with his constantly mobile face, his dimples. And during his conversation, he turned, and finding her looking at him, seemed to accept it with pleasure and pride.

He left, with a large gesture which took in both of them. Gabriel turned to Annabel for her opinion, and she said without hesitation, 'He's vain, that's clear. But he's very agreeable, and I'm glad he's asked me out.'

Gabriel looked down at his fingernails and said quietly, 'He's married. Maybe he omitted to mention that fact?'

Annabel felt as though he had struck her. But she regained her composure. She turned away from the door. 'It's only as friends, you know.'

Gabriel took her shoulder and swung her round to face him. 'Sit down, woman. I've got to talk to you, seeing you're on your own in my country.'

'What about?'

She waited until she sat opposite him. 'You've heard of a Dutch uncle?'

'Of course.' She saw his eyebrows beginning to show authority. 'Well?'

'That's me.' He paused for a moment as the thunder rumbled outside, reminding Annabel of her employer's own voice. The waves crashed and roared, louder than usual as the wind whipped them even higher. 'Someone has to tell you, Annabel. Amir Pagodi eats young women.'

Annabel laughed at his serious face. 'Doctor, I'm not a silly kid. I've been warned. I do know what I'm doing.' Inwardly, she was angry with Amir Pagodi for leading her on, but she couldn't admit that to Gabriel Christie.

Just then the night nurse came out of the ward on the left side of the ground floor. Gabriel and Annabel were still sitting in the foyer in the waiting area, outside the consulting rooms which were situated in the right half of the hospital. The light was dim, and their faces were in shadow. The nurse said, 'Dr Christie, is it? Oh, Doctor, the patient Mohammed—he is running a temperature. Would you see him, please?'

Gabriel nodded. 'I'll be along.' The nurse went back to the ward, and Gabriel turned back to Annabel. 'Look, the whole town will find out if you go out with Pagodi. He's an amiable devil, but one to keep at arm's length, believe me.'

Annabel saw the nurse come to the ward door and look for Gabriel. She stood up. Her feelings were in turmoil, as she recalled Gabriel and his lovely Malay girl. She said, 'Perhaps we should get one thing straight—you can control me as much as you like when I'm doing my work, but when I'm off duty, I can do as I please. What makes you think you're any wiser than me in matters like this? For all I know, you also might be meeting someone who's bad for you.' She bit her lip. She knew she had said too much. The nurse still hovered, and Gabriel turned and spotted her.

He also got to his feet, torn between his duty and his desire to make sure Annabel got his message. 'You're stubborn, Annabel—I've never met a woman like you, that's for sure,' he snapped.

The waves outside broke on the sand, receded and gathered themselves for another onslaught. The electricity in the night quivered between them. Gabriel took one step towards the ward, stopped and looked back at Annabel, then turned and strode off to see his patient. Annabel, relieved to see him go, felt deprived, and knew that however painful the converation, she still wanted it to go on.

CHAPTER FOUR

ANNABEL knew that Dr Christie's flat was next to hers, but that night she was suddenly very much aware of it. Not that she heard him—all the staff were too weary not to sleep well. But she knew just where his bed lay in relation to her own. She had supervised the choice of curtains, and the colour of the light cotton sheet that would be drawn over him against the invasion of the odd mosquito through the protective mesh over the open windows. And as her own fan swirled round over her, she imagined his sending cooling waves of air over him—and she wondered just what he was thinking, and if he ever gave her a thought when they were not arguing during the day. She wondered, in short, if he would ever spend so much time thinking of her, as she couldn't help thinking of him.

After lying staring up at the fan in the moonlight, listening to the crickets outside, the waves, and the nightjars and the occasional delicious trill of a nightingale, Annabel decided she had a bad case of insomnia. She crept out of bed, pulled on cotton shift, and went downstairs as silently as she could, to pass a few neighbourly minutes with the night nurse, on duty in the ward. But she was dozing, her head leaning against the wing of her chair, and the patient too was deeply asleep. Annabel entered the ward quietly. Gabriel must have given him something.

Nurse Kau jerked her head upright, but Annabel patted her shoulder. 'It's all right, I only came down for a breath of air.' And the other girl smiled and leaned back in her chair. She would wake if she was needed. Annabel went to the back door of the clinic and turned the key, letting herself out, in bare feet, to the cool dark garden. The peace was refreshing, and she sat down at a table, hearing the cicadas now so close around her bare feet, and wondering why they always made such a noise.

Just then she heard a rustle at the bottom of the garden, where the path led down to the beach, and a figure came up the path, a tall figure, walking with great deliberation. At first Annabel froze, her first impulse being to call Percival by ringing the bell. But as soon as she saw the silhouette of the stranger, she knew there was no need. The wild mane around his head said it all. Gabriel had been for a midnight stroll. Or perhaps it had been another assignation? Annabel coughed, to show there was someone there. He stopped beside her. He was wearing a long Malay sarong fastened round his waist. His chest was bare, and the gold chain glinted in the moonlight.

'What's the matter? Thinking about Mr Pagodi, are you?' He was brusque. Perhaps he was embarrassed to be discovered.

Annabel tried to keep her temper. Coolly she replied, 'Just thinking. I didn't expect it to be so crowded at this time of night.'

He scratched his head. 'Damn these mosquitoes! Sorry I snapped. Join me in a nightcap? I've got a lot on my mind.' And though Annabel had hardened herself against his rudeness, a single apology was enough to melt her completely. She understood what he had on his mind—a beautiful Malay woman with a problem he was supposed to be solving.

'All right. I couldn't sleep either.'

He went inside, and returned with two glasses. 'Whisky—the best. Do you mind?'

'Is it diluted?'

'With Highland water.'

'Thanks.' Annabel sipped it, and said, 'You start consulting here tomorrow. You think the transfer will go smoothly?'

He breathed out very slowly. 'You know, I've taken on rather a large project. Was I in my right mind, do you think? I've carried everyone with me so far. We have one patient, but that won't pay the bills.' He stood up and

paced restlessly. 'It's far too late now. But it's a
risk—suppose no one wants hospital treatment for the
next six months?'

Annebel said quietly, 'I won't pretend you have nothing
to worry about. I've been thinking exactly the same thing,
but we've been so busy we had no time to worry. It would
be sad if all our hard work came to nothing.'

'You could go back to Singapore.' Gabriel's voice was
neutral.

'That's not on my mind just now.'

'Really?' He sounded pleased.

'I've worked since the moment I came here for the
success of the Jacaranth,' she said, raising her voice. 'It
matters to me—and to the rest of the staff. It's not just the
job—losing a job, I mean—it's loyalty. These few weeks
we've come together, worked and discussed and argued—I
think you have the basis of a good team.'

He sat down again. 'That's just the point—so many
people depend on me.'

Annabel said, looking across at the outline of his shaggy
head, the pale features in the moonlight, 'Time to start
looking on the bright side—you and Dr Malik will still
have the income from your regular patients, right? And
the new gynaecologist when she comes?'

'True—that will pay for the downstairs rooms.
Anything else?'

Yes, there certainly is. There's your reputation. You've
been here for years, Dr Christie—everyone knows
you——'

'Make it Gabriel, please—the senior staff should be
acting more like friends by now, don't you think?'

'Acting?'

'Getting to know one another?'

'All right.' She kept quiet about her conviction that
Gabriel Christie was impossible to know. 'If we're friends,
then I can tell you that everyone I've met in your little lazy
toytown of Malacca speaks of you very highly.' She
allowed herself to sound like a headmistress she had once
known. A great flash of silent lightning lit up the sky, and

her chief's wild hair. She waited for the thunder before she went on, 'I know you'll get people coming to you—you've told me yourself that you have a reputation for good medicine—and for honest fees. Add to that your total lack of humour or manners, and the fact that you never have your hair cut, and you have a recipe for complete success.'

Gabriel burst out with a great shout of laughter. He stood up against the sky, against the music of the breakers and the cries of the seabirds. Yes, she thought, this environment suits you. You're a giant of a man, and this great theatre of thunder and lightning suits you—you have no petty thoughts, only great ones, apart from the pretty Malay . . . And you're too big to think of going to the barber.

He leaned forward and grasped her shoulder. His voice was gentle suddenly, giving it more force when he said, 'You're becoming invaluable to me, Annabel Browne. Remind me tomorrow. I can't do anything about the manners, but I'll have my hair cut, if you think it will help.'

She took that as a sign that it was time to go in, and set down her glass. He said, 'Are you tired?'

'You need some sleep.'

'Not yet.'

For a moment they both waited, silent in the electric night. Then she remembered that his apartment was next to hers. She didn't want to go up with him. She said, 'Pleasant dreams. Don't make a noise or Percival will think we have burglars. Goodnight, Gabriel.'

She went lightly past him, up the outside staircase in the moonlight, the wind whispering gently in the full fronds of the palm trees. She heard Gabriel walk down the garden again, lock the little wicket gate, and return to test the back door, checking that it was bolted. She lay awake for a while, staring at the rotating fan, listening to the waves, wondering why her mind was so alert and excitable after such a long day. Sleep wouldn't come. She spent the hours going over in her mind all the things that Gabriel had said, the way he had treated her like a friend . . .

But the following day the curtain was down again. Gruff and uncommunicative, Gabriel crouched at his desk, poring over papers and case notes before going off in his car to the town. Annabel wondered if she had dreamed last night. But when Amir Pagodi arrived at the front gates in his shiny limousine, she was glad that her disapproving boss wasn't around. Amir pretended he had come on business. 'Has my man delivered the typewriters and the shredder?'

'Yes, thank you.'

Amir paused. He looked around and said, 'This place is pretty good now.'

Annabel was busy, but to be polite she said, 'You've helped. We're grateful.'

'Would you care for some lunch? It's a hot day. Maybe you'd like a swim at the Club before lunch? I often go about now because it is so quiet.'

Annabel was very conscious of Gabriel's disapproval, though the sound of a swim was almost irresistible. But she decided that lunch with a married man might be nothing, but swimming was too much. 'Another day, perhaps. I'm terribly busy.'

Amir Pagodi looked at her, silent for a moment, his amiable face suddenly dark, as though he were not used to being turned down. Then he forced his sunny smile, revealing the dimples. 'Of course—selfish of me. You have to get the Jacaranth in running order before anything else. Keep up the good work, Anna.' And with a cheery wave, he walked out into the bright sunlight to his elegant BMW.

Annabel watched him go, thinking that he wasn't such a bad chap after all. Surely no harm could come from being friendly. He was a business acquaintance, nothing else. At the back of her mind was the idea, when the hospital was running smoothly, of looking into Mr Pagodi's antiques business—she might just be able to help the family business into an interesting sideline in Oriental goods. Amir was someone she wanted to keep on good terms with

just now. It would be silly to brush him off just because
Gabriel thought him undesirable company.

The hospital bell rang, and two people came into the
foyer cautiously, looking around with curiosity. Percival
went to the door from his little alcove, but before he could
say anthing, Annabel recognised the 'Celia—Martin! How
wonderful to see you. Why didn't you tell me you were
coming? Come on in. Yes, I'm busy, but it's almost
lunchtime anyway, and there's such a cute little restaurant
just along the road.' Mia would not have minded extra
guests, but Annabel suddenly wanted the chance to get out
of the Jacaranth, to study it from outside. She had been
wrapped up in its affairs for so long she had almost
forgotten there was an outside world. She shook them
both joyfully by the hand. 'Come on, prove to me that
there's life after Malacca.'

Martin said, 'I'll just unload the van first. We brought
your pictures and ornaments. You did say you would be
here for a year, so why leave them? Hold on—it's only two
cartons.' And he came back holding two cardboard boxes
with all Annabel's worldly goods. They went up to her
flat, where she provided cold drinks, and pleaded for news
of the Mount Olivia, the Club, and all their other friends.

'They envy you. After all, you must be getting twice the
salary here—and money goes further in Malaysia,' Celia
said.

'It must do, because I haven't even thought about it.
Mia cooks for the staff, and I haven't had any time for
shopping or anything really. You've no idea how hectic it
is, starting from the very beginning. I've learned so much!'

Martin was at the window, looking out at the sea. 'This
is some hospital. I wouldn't mind a job here, Annabel. To
wake up to that view of the Straits!' He turned back. 'Any
patients yet?'

'We have one, in spite of not being officially open yet.
Come on, let's go for lunch.'

Celia said, 'You mean you can take lunch any time you
want?'

Annabel laughed. 'Right! I'm senior staff.'

The three friends went downstairs and walked along the road towards a small restaurant Annabel had noticed on her first day, and always wanted to try. Celia was still amazed at the advantages in Malacca. 'I can't see why you want to come back to the city. You have everything here.'

Annabel agreed. 'Except privacy. We all know all about each other, and if I go out, the whole hospital knows.' She grimaced. 'And half of them try and stop me too.' She explained a little about Amir Pagodi. 'He's a married man, so everyone is acting like my uncles and aunts. All I'm interested in is finding out about his antiques business, so that perhaps I can put him in touch with my father. I'm sure Oriental antiques would sell well. I'm just waiting till I have some free time.'

'What about the great Dr Christie? Is he as frightening as you thought?'

'Oh yes,' Annabel agreed. 'He's like a great bear, woolly and gruff. He's outspoken too—says what he thinks, whether it hurts anyone's feelings or not.'

Martin said, 'It sounds as though you've had an argument or two.'

Annabel didn't answer, and Celia drew conclusions. 'It would be a pity if you let personal differences ruin a good job, Annabel.'

Annabel said shortly, 'Just keep on looking for places in Singapore. As soon as my year is up, I want to get out of Malacca for good. I mean it.'

Celia understood. 'OK, rely on us. We'll look out for any theatre jobs going, and send them to you after the first seven or eight months?'

'Wonderful! I knew I could rely on you.'

Celia said innocently, 'This Gabriel Christie—good doctor, is he?'

Annabel agreed warmly. All she had seen of his work had been good. 'I have to hand it to him—he knows his stuff. The patients love him. If there's a choice between Dr Malik or Christie, they always go to Gabriel.'

There was a silence, and Annabel looked across the table at her two friends' faces. 'All right—we do use

Christian names. But it means nothing.' The atmosphere crackled with electricity, and she went on, 'I can't stay here, the lightning upsets me.' And she knew here face had reddened as she sought excuses for admitting she knew Gabriel just a bit better than she had owned. She turned her attention to a particularly tasty piece of crab in her plate of noodles.

Celia said casually, 'Nurses have been known to marry doctors, you know.'

Annabel said rather quickly, 'I'd hate to be married to one. Just imagine doing what they tell you all day at work, and then going home to exactly the same thing. You'd have no independence at all.'

'They might be quite different when you get them alone.'

Annabel tried to laugh off the conversation. 'I learned enough about doctors from Ken Lu Sen. Forget it, Celia. No matchmaking, please.'

Martin asked, 'Do you really see marriage as a sort of trap?'

'For me, it would be imprisonment.' And she saw her friends give each other a look which made her say quickly, 'Not for others, maybe.'

Celia said, 'I'm glad you added that. I—we—were going to ask you to be a bridesmaid.' Her cheeks were flushed suddenly, and she looked very beautiful.

'Celia, that's wonderful! I'm so sorry for saying things about marriage. I'm thrilled for you both, I really am, and I'd adore to be a bridesmaid.'

Martin said with a knowing smile, 'Don't worry, your outburst was quite clearly nothing at all to do with us. I'd say it sounds very personal—and something that time will sort out. Now, how about trying this mango ice-cream?'

The three walked back along the beach after lunch. Annabel knew she had a lot to do, but she was unwilling to lose her friends after such a short time. They went up the pretty garden, past the tables and their umbrellas overlooking the breakers and the sand. Just then one of the junior nurses came to the back door. 'Sister, thank

goodness you're here! Dr Christie is on the phone. I think
he has another admission—surgical. He sounds——'

'Bad-tempered, no doubt. I'm on my way.' Annabel
knew how Gabriel barked his orders when he was
working—impatient with anyone who didn't work as
efficiently as he did himself. She ran to her office and
picked u the phone from where the nurse had left it on the
desk. 'Gabriel?'

She was surprised that his voice was cool and calm. But
there was no disguising its urgency. 'Thank goodness,
Annabel! Where were you? Never mind. I'm with a
patient now—yes, at his home in Sungei Road. It's an
ulcer—bleeding already, and getting worse. His pressure's
very low. Can you have Theatre ready before I get there?
I've already told Hassan to bring the ambulance.'

'I'll see to it at once.' Annabel checked the list on the
wall to see who was scheduled to be on call in an
emergency. She rang through to make sure they were
available, then she stood up to make her way to Theatre.
Celia and Martin were standing, fascinated by the sudden
activity. Annabel started to apologise.

'No problem. We'll see you soon. And I promise to
keep my eyes open for Singapore jobs for you, Annabel.
Good luck with the patient.' Celia kissed her. Annabel had
time to give them a quick wave before getting back to her
task of being super-ready when the patient was admitted.
The only problem was his blood group. She couldn't have
blood ready for transfusion until she knew his type. And if
his pressure was low, he would need it right away. She laid
out the sterile instruments and dressings, and waited for
the ambulance to arrive.

Gabriel Christie marched in with the finesse of a tidal
wave, straight to the washbowl, and started to scrub his
hands while issuing orders with the speed of a machine-
gun. 'Is Malik ready? It's blood group O, by the way.
Ring for extra supplies, I think we'll need them. I must get
at the source of the bleeding fast.' There was the sound of
the trolley being wheeled along from the elevator. 'Right,
prepped, is he? Get him on the table. Here, Annabel, tie

this wretched gown, will you?'

Quietly, without fuss, she fastened his gown and helped him on with his gloves, noticing that his hair was even more unruly than usual. She said, 'It isn't very common in Singapore for a doctor to diagnose an illness and then rush back to do the operation himself.'

He pulled on his cap and mask, saying as he did so, 'The first time I did it I was a GP on the Isle of Skye. I also had to bring the patient to Broadford Hospital in my own caxr. You people are spoiled in Singapore. No challenge!'

And in spite of the controlled chaos as the anaesthetist and the nurses hurried to get into their places, and the junior surgeon was called to assist, Gabriel paused before entering the theatre, and gave Annabel a direct look with a strange light in his amber eyes, clear and true. He was teasing her. And even as she returned his look, she felt stimulated and excited to have the opportunity of working with such a man, so skilled and so dedicated. Yet it was exhausting too, because Gabriel never allowed his own standards of excellence to slip, and he expected the same from his staff.

The laboratory technician came in with eight packs of blood. 'Is that enough?'

Gabriel turned. 'I want more. Send for another six. If I can find where the bleeding is coming from, I won't need them, but I want to be sure. Get on to them right away.'

Annabel asked, 'Has he had an X-ray?'

Gabriel said shortly, 'Six months ago I sent him for a barium meal. The ulcer is hidden in a fold of the jejunum.'

Dr Malik came in, ready masked and gowned. 'Ready, chief.'

Gabriel said, 'Right, let's get started. Wheel him in.'

Annabel positioned herself at Gabriel's right hand, the instruments ready. She was so accustomed to the routine that even as she provided the correct scalpels and retractors at the right time, she still had time to look around the shining new theatre and contrast it with the old colonial building of the Mount Olivia, which no amount of modernising would make into new. It was in the

Mount Olivia that she had first noticed the brown eyes and wild hair of her chief, then an anonymous giant at the back of the theatre. He must have been planning this at that time—the gleaming chromework, the clean pure light, the brand-new gowns and masks.

'Scalpel, Sister.' Gabriel was about to excise the ulcer. There was a gush of blood, and both surgeons worked fast to mop it up and clear the area for him to work in. He muttered, 'It's hiding—worse than I thought. How's the pressure, Malik? Suction, fast, over here! Malik?'

'Falling.'

There was no need for further talk. They worked with a quiet intensity but without panic. The powerful lights shone on the bright instruments as they were passed from gloved hand to gloved hand, the latter tipped with blood. More blood spurted as Gabriel sought with urgent fingers the loop where the ulcer was situated. 'Got it!' Annabel was ready with the cutting instrument. She tried to hide her sigh of relief as Gabriel's capable fingers worked with dexterity to tie off the trouble spot. No one spoke as he drew back the retracted skin into position and started the long perpendicular suture from sternum to umbilicus. Gabriel straightened his back and stretched his arms. 'If we'd waited another hour, he wouldn't be here. Keep a watch on the drainage tubes, Chan. And watch the pressure.' And he strode from the theatre.

The patient was wheeled to Recovery, while Annabel checked the instruments and swabs, and cleared the theatre. There were only two packs of blood left. The bleeding point had been found only just in time. She took her time, knowing that the worst was over. The patient was a fit man in his fifties—he ought to recover with careful nursing. The clock said six—they had been in theatre all afternoon.

She heard the door pushed open, but didn't look round form her work. Then Gabriel came round and stood on the other side of the table. She stood motionless. He said quietly, 'I don't know about Wednesday—I think *this* was our Grand Opening.'

Annabel pulled down her mask and laughed. 'Wednesday will be very tame after this.'

He seemed relaxed—the eyes were readable again. 'Well, our second patient—and the first time I've worked with my poached Theatre Sister. You see what I mean about standards? This man would be dead by now if we hadn't had Jacaranth at the ready. Reputation is what I'm depending on. Not fine words and expensive show—reliable medicine is what counts.'

She was generous in her praise. 'You gave it today.'

'You were superb, Annabel. I knew we could work together. I hope in time that you stop hankering for the Mount Olivia—this is where you can use your talents better.'

He seemed to be waiting for her to admit she had made the right move. But she couldn't—part of her still longed for the carefree life and vigorous play she had enjoyed in the big city. 'May I reserve judgement?' She saw disappointment in his face, and added, 'The theatre is super. I'm so glad you bought Mayo lights. We both know that Mount Olivia is grubby by comparison.'

Gabriel was enthusiastic. 'Grubby—there's no other word for it—but it isn't just that, it's our whole new venture. The spirit is there to make it a success. You know it, Annabel—you feel it, don't you?' And while she sought for words to answer him, he went on impatiently, 'Get rid of the gown, lass, and let's go and see our first patient.' And as she walked alongside him, their footsteps quietly padding on the brand new tiles, she thought it flattering that he wasn't counting the man with the broken leg, Mohammed, as his first patient, but the one whom both of them had operated on together. What had he said before——? Poached? Had he poached her, then? She had assumed herself dismissed, and with no alternative.

But there was no time for conjecture. The houseman, Chan, was adjusting the drip, while Cherry Ho checked the blood pressure. 'It's low.'

Annabel said, 'Cherry, you weren't supposed to be on duty. If you like, I'll take over.'

But she was surprised and pleased by the response. 'No, I want to be here. I want him to get better. I know his wife, Siay. This has been such a shock to her.'

The patient lifted a hand. 'Dr Christie, you save my life.' Her voice was weak but clear.

Gabriel stood, a tower of strength, the epitome of reliability, and his face showed nothing but concern. 'You had the common sense to call me, man. I have a team that's ready for calls like yours. You saved your own life. We only did what we're here for, didn't we, Sister?'

Annabel nodded, pleased to see Mr Dan had a good colour. 'You're doing well, Mr Dan. You must get some rest now.'

'My wife?' The man struggled to speak through the oxygen mask. 'She is here, no?'

Annabel hurried out of the Recovery Room and down the stairs to the room at the back that she herself had insisted on for relatives. Sure enough, Mrs Dan sat like an ivory statue, waiting with her hands on her jade prayer beads, her small head poised, waiting for news. Annabel hurried over to her. 'Mrs Dan, your husband is out of surgery. He's well.'

'Is all right to see him?'

'I'm sure Dr Christie won't mind for a couple of minutes. Come along.'

The little woman gasped at the sight of her husband smothered by drainage tubes and masks and drips. She turned away with a little moan, but Annabel put her arm around the thin shoulders. 'It's all right—just helping him along. Look—he can take off the mask so say *salaam.*'

The patient himself lifted the mask and spoke a few words in Malay. Apparently reassured, she managed a tremulous smile, and spoke to her husband in low tones, their hands clasped together. Then she turned to Annabel, who led her gently from the Intensive Care room to the hospitality suite. 'Make yourself at home here. Try to rest. The bell is there if you need anything.'

She waited while the little lady made herself comfortable, then took a glass of water from the cooler.

She would not have this sort of time with every patient, but Mr Dan was special. Annabel waited, chatting for a few minutes, before leaving her to rest.

Annabel sat at her desk, feeling drained of energy, but soul-satisfied. There was no need to move for a while. Everything had gone well, and a life had been saved. She heard the waves in the background. Funny, that they were not conscious of the waves when concentrating on operation. She went over the operation in her mind. Slowly she began to realise that she was hungry, but perhaps not hungry enough to go down to the dining room and call Mia.

She stood up and pushed open her office door. Then she smiled, as Celia Lau came forward, and she saw Martin in the background. 'We thought we would take you out for a meal. How is your patient?'

Annabel smiled in relief. 'I didn't want to eat alone. How lovely of you to stay.'

They were soon feeding scraps of prawns to the cats under the table at the restaurant they had lunched at. The bright-coloured lights glinted over the swimming pool, and a couple of children played in the water. Annabel asked, 'By the way, how's Ken?'

'Ken Lu Sen is well.' Celia grinned. 'Once a playboy, always a playboy. He's dating a model right now.'

'His father has ruined him.' Annabel blamed her dismissal on Ken's father. Without his interference, she would still be in her wonderful position at the Mount Olivia. 'His father ought to make him settle down.'

Celia said, 'You think fathers ought to rule their children?'

Annabel smiled 'Touché, Celia. My father never made me do anything.' She was silent for a while, wondering what her parents were doing at that moment. Cheltenham seemed a very long way away. When Celia spoke, she hardly heard her. Then she said, 'Sorry—I was just dreaming of home.'

'Homesick?'

'Not entirely. I love my parents. But after living in

Singapore, I think I'd stifle to death if I went back to Cheltenham.'

Martin said, 'And how about Malacca?'

Annabel smiled. 'Malacca is only a temporary episode in my life.'

He shook his head with a wink. 'You don't think it will grow on you?'

There was a particularly loud crash of thunder just then, and Annabel said, 'I don't think so. I can't take the extra electricity—it makes one so super-active. You can never get away from the sea and the sky. They won't let you forget them.'

The restaurant was crowded, but as the three friends stood up to leave, Annabel's gaze was drawn to a corner table, where the candle had been blown out for extra privacy. It was Gabriel Christie, his hand holding the hand of the beautiful Malay in the darkness. Annabel turned away quickly, sick suddenly at the sight. How could he be an angel at work, while living this secret life of deception away from it? It didn't seem right.

The image of Gabriel with the lovely woman wouldn't leave her mind, and Annabel was absentminded in her farewells, as Martin started up the engine of his van, and Celia waved vigorously from the passenger side. Annabel went in slowly, pausing as she saw a light in the corridor outside the Intensive Care room. She walked along the corridor to see what was wrong. Surely the corridor light should be off—it was after ten at night.

'Annabel!' A sudden bark. She knew who it was, and went quickly to him. Gabriel sat at the bedside. 'He'll have to go back to theatre—BP's still falling. There must be another site that's bleeding. He has no chance unless we open up this minute.'

She stood for a moment. In those amber eyes she read a prayer. It was addressed to her alone. 'I'll get the theatre ready.' She went in, and silently took her place.

CHAPTER FIVE

ANNABEL felt the heat from Gabriel's body as he took his own place at the operating table, and checked that the stand for the drip was in the right position. He didn't speak, but she sensed the tension in him, the sense of disappointment that his first operation had resulted in failure. Her thoughts had been with her friends, as they started their journey back to Singapore. She wanted to go with them, to return to the bustling city and leave this strange flickering place with its tensions and undercurrents. Yet as Gabriel turned to her, she forgot Celia and Martin, and only tried to show him by her confident manner that this time the operation would succeed.

Dr Malik sat, his face impassive, his sharp dark eyes narrowed as he concentrated on his instruments at the head of the table. No one spoke, although Gabriel shook his head when the nurse showed him six pints of blood, and she went away, bringing back a further supply. It was clear that the bleeding had not stopped internally, and poor Mr Dan looked very weak and pale, his blood pressure obstinately rufusing to rise in spite of the packed cell drip.

The others seemed to have complete faith in Gabriel Christie—only Annabel knew how afraid he was. As they all stood motionless under the bright lights, their heads bent over the table, Gabriel held out his hand, and Annabel handed him the scalpel, looking up at him with a clear signal from her eyes to his amber-coloured ones that all would be well. He paused for a moment, both of them holding the scalpel. Then he seemed to take deep breath, turned to the patient, and drew the instrument with a single controlled stroke along the line of the previous incision. The only sound in the theatre was the breathing pump of the patient.

In spite of the air-conditioning, Annabel saw Gabriel begin to sweat, and as he turned to her, she wiped away the small drops that started again along his forehead, the wild hair controlled for the moment by the cap. She tried to instil confidence in him through her gloved fingertips, as he turned away and very carefully exposed the stomach and began to feel with his right hand fingers for the site that was still gushing blood when the original site of the ulcer had been sutured. They all looked up at once to check the blood in the drip, and the nurse replaced it without a word with a full pack.

Gabriel muttered, 'I think I have it. He has an extra curvature behind the duodenum. No wonder it didn't show on the X-rays!' Very gingerly he inched the organ to the surface, while Annabel worked as fast as she could to keep the stomach free from blood. Gabriel hissed, 'Suture,' but Annabel had it ready close to his groping fingers, and with infinite care he tied off the wound, cauterising the tiny blood vessels to stop the seepage. As he closed the wound, drawing the edges of the skin tightly together, he said, his words sounding more like a prayer, 'He shouldn't have any more trouble from that fellow.' He pushed the bloodstained needles back to Annabel, who put them into the disposal tray. He said, 'He'll have to be watched like a hawk, Sister—make sure he's monitored constantly, please.'

The entire staff hovered around Mr Dan as he lay in Recovery. Mia brought them all Chinese tea, but Gabriel waved his away. Cherry kept patting the patient's cheek, and saying gaily, 'Wake up, Mr Dan, wake up!' Dr Malik kept the cuff on the arm, taking pressure readings every few minutes. The green plastic of the oxygen mask rose and fell with his even breathing, but the eyes stayed obstinately closed. The clock in the hall chimed eleven at night, the notes echoing through the almost empty hospital. Annabel knew they all prayed the same thing—don't let their patient die, just a few days before the actual Grand Opening of the hospital. This man of all men must recover. It was Chan, the junior doctor, who said what some of them were thinking. 'Do you think he might be better in the General Hospital?'

Annabel saw Gabriel draw in his breath—but he didn't explode. 'We have the necessary equipment here—and a good team.'

Even the taciturn Dr Malik said, 'He is in God's hands now. We can pray just as well as the General Hospital staff.'

Cherry tapped Mr Dan's cheek again. 'We are waiting to congratulate you, Mr Dan. Come, wake up, lazy man!'

Just then Annabel looked out of the room and saw the lonely little figure of Siay Dan in the corridor, her narrow shoulders hunched, her head bent. She went out of the room, her heart touched, and put her arm round her. 'It's fine, Siay—the operation was a success.' But there was fear in the woman's eyes, and Annabel knew she would need to see her husband before she believed all was well. She sat with her, holding her as she would a child, as they both waited for some sign from that silent room.

Then Gabriel himself came out, and began explaining very gently about the abnormality, and how he had corrected it so that Mr Dan would have no more trouble. But tears collected in Siay's eyes and dribbled sadly down her cheeks. Gabriel looked at Annabel over the top of her head, and Annabel could have wept herself at the despair in his face. But at that moment Cherry came out, and Annabel could tell by the lightness of her step that all was well. 'He's awake and orientated, sir.'

Gabriel sprang to his feet. 'Pressure?'

'Almost normal.'

Gabriel turned and shook Mrs Dan's hands. 'Come on—would you like to wish your husband good morning?' It was indeed almost midnight. Annabel watched the two of them return to Recovery. She was no longer needed. She sat for a while, the relief of the moment filling her with warmth and gratutude. Outside the tense little hospital, the wind was getting up, a warm, playful wind that whistled in the trees, and brought with it the salt smell of the wild sea.

Cherry came back. 'What for you sit here, woman?'

Annabel looked up. 'You know very well. Don't pretend to be hardboiled, Cherry.'

Cherry sat beside her, and no one would have dreamed the two women had been enemies only two weeks before. 'Vagotomy and pyloroplasty is a simple operation—thousands done every day, *lah*. But how many surgeons are on the spot if anything go wrong huh? This man fortunate he come to Jacaranth.'

'It's a good omen. I think this team is a caring one. And Dr Christie cares—more than any other surgeon I've ever worked for. I can't help feeling proud of the Jacaranth, Cherry. I never felt proud of the Mount Olivia like I do about this.'

'You only a nurse there—here part of team, *lah*.'

'That's it—part of the team.'

'You still want go back to Singapore?'

Annabel smiled at her, as the wind howled and whistled and the breakers crashed on the rocks outside. 'Maybe not this minute.' She lifted a hand in salute as Cherry made her way to bed. She heard Gabriel talking to Siay Dan, and recalled the light in the woman's eyes as she had realised her husband had been saved. Annabel wondered what she really thought of Gabriel Christie. Saviour of lives, no doubt—and caring person. Gruff and uncompromising with colleagues—but loyal. Impossible to know, perhaps—yet that evening in the hushed theatre she had felt close to him—just for a few short minutes. The Malay damsel with the sloe eyes for a few minutes didn't matter to Gabriel—all that mattered was a nurse at his side who he could work with to save a life.

She felt the unsettled feeling of the other night—the weather and its erratic electricity wouldn't let her sleep. She wandered out into the night and stood for a while on the beach, where the water writhing and flailing reminded her of some huge beast awakening from a disturbed slumber, awakening in wrath. It still seemed strange and unnatural to see such voilence in nature—and yet still with a warm sweetness, a complete contrast—Malacca had a strange excitement about it, something unsettling that no other place had ever possessed. Her hair, which had been neatly pinned back during the operation, blew around her face, blinding her at times, while the lightning shimmerered against the stars, and ragged clouds danced across the face of the moon like dervishes in a frenzied trance.

And then she sensed she was not alone, and turned to see Gabriel, his hair like an unruly halo on end around his darkly brooding face. She watched him—he had not seen her—and reflected that he fitted this place, being as roughly disturbing as the unpredictable weather. For a moment Annabel wondered if he were here to meet the woman. If so, she must make her presence known before any there were any embarrassing encounters. She called across the sand, her voice caught and blown away by the wind, 'You're surely not out here for pleasure?'

He spotted her, and didn't seem surprised. Walking towards her, he said, 'It's less noisy out here than inside.' They stood for a while saying nothing, then he said, 'It's going to rain, you know. You haven't been here during a real monsoon, have you?'

'I don't mind rain. It means no harm.' Neither of them spoke of what was really in their hearts this time. The operation had gone well—this time there would be no boasting or rejoicing until they were all sure that Mr Dan would survive his second ordeal. They stood watching the waves and listening to their incessant voices along the shore.

Gabriel said, having to speak loudly for his words to be heard, 'You still miss Singapore?'

Annabel looked up to find him regarding her with narrowed eyes. She tried to keep back her unruly hair as it was tossed round her face. Somehow it was important not to give a superficial answer. 'Yes, I do—but maybe I'm lucky to be too busy to think about it.'

'I thought that you felt as pleased as I did—that the operating team worked together so well. I had a feeling you felt the same.'

She nodded. 'I do.' She smiled into the teeth of the wind. 'You know very well I do—because when you took me on, there was no one else. We started with nothing. Do you remember saying we'll see what we can do with such unpromising material? I'm as proud as you tonight.'

'You must stay by Malik and me at the Grand Opening. Wear you name badge with pride. We're still starting small—but I intend to be big. I don't brag, Annabel, but I do know we'll have something in the Jacaranth that will be known for good medicine and fair dealing. That was my dream. Tonight perhaps has been a perfect starting point. You'll stick with us?'

She looked out again, the horizon hidden by rolling breakers. The thought of her 'home' in Singapore, her friends, the security of life in a lively city that she had grown to love—it still tugged at her heart. She said without looking at him, 'For a year, of course.'

Gabriel said nothing, but turned suddenly on his heel and began to stride out along the seashore away from the Jacaranth. Annabel watched him, conscious by the set of his shoulders that she had displeased him. But that made no difference to her. He had a powerful personality, but she had made up her mind not to be steamrollered by it. And so far she had stood her ground. Gabriel was almost lost in the darkness now. She took a step after him, but then told herself firmly that there was no point in being too close. He had a way of being distant the next day, and confounding her hopes of one day being really in his confidence.

At that moment the rain started. And as always in Malaysia, it was not just a shower, but drenching slabs of water knocking her fiercely with every second she stayed out. Bracing herself, she turned and began to stagger back through the wet sand. She heard Gabriel's footsteps behind her, stronger than her to breast the force of the wind. They arrived at the back door of the clinic together, taking off their sodden shoes, and gasping for breath.

The hospital was hushed and asleep. They stood for a moment on the doormat, facing each other, then Gabriel smoothed back his hair and smiled. 'I never knew drowned rats could look so pretty.'

Annabel stood allowing her dress to drip, and wrung out her hair. 'I've never known you to pay compliments.'

He looked at her hard, drops of water falling from the tip of his nose, a suggestion of a twinkle in the amber eyes. Then he said, the twinkle gone, 'I've lived alone for too long, maybe. My finacée used to remind me to pay compliments.' He answered Annabel's upspoken question. 'It was a long time ago—she died of cancer. There was nothing they could do for her . . .'

'I'm sorry.' But as if he had already said too much, Gabriel's jaw tightened, and he wiped his feet once more on the mat and set off with his long legs towards his own apartment.

Annabel went up the stairs very slowly, the sound of the rain thunderous on the roof. She had not asked Gabriel to talk about himself. She felt he regretted the confidence. Yet somehow that smile he had given her, the compliment he spoke and the look in his eyes gave her an enormous feeling of pleasure. He could be so very vulnerable . . . that woman on the beach must see him like that all the time. It must make her feel secure and treasured, to be loved by such a man . . .

The entire population of the Jacaranth rose early next morning to see how Mr Dan was progressing. Even the other patient was bobbing about in his bed, and had to be told off by Cherry. 'Now, Mohammed, do that and you break the other leg, *lah!*'

Siay Dan was holding her husband's hand. It was clear that the night nurse had told them both that temperature, pulse and blood pressure were all normal, because the little woman could not hide her big smile every time she looked at her husband. The nurses were describing how they would decorate the room for the Grand Opening, and that the two patients would be dressed like sultans for the day, and treated like honoured guests.

The weather was perfect, warm and gentle, and the wind that last night had threatened to raze the hospital to the ground was this morning only a playful zephyr. The waves lapped musically on the silver sand, and the sun shone with a wondrous benevolence. Already Mr Pagodi's van had arrived with two men to assist Percival in putting up the coloured bunting, and fresh green garlands. Gabriel and Dr Malik came to the ward at lunchtime, having finished their morning surgeries. Annabel noticed that Dr Malik managed a smile at the sight of the two patients sitting up—if painfully—and joking with the nurses.

Gabriel gave the staff a briefing. 'No need to tell you to make sure your uniforms are perfectly pressed. Please wear your name tags prominently—be proud to be part of the Jacaranth staff. Percival and Ali will clean your shoes if you leave them out tonight. Now, who'll be on duty in the ward?'

Annabel offered, but he chose Cherry. Cherry was delighted, but Gabriel said quietly to Annabel later, 'I need you up front to do the talking. Don't worry—most of the GPs will speak in English. It's only the Minister and his staff who will speak Malay—and they won't ask much about the hospital anyway. It's the doctors I want to see around.'

'Very well.' Their relationship was back to its strictly businesslike footing, and she was glad. It saved embarrassment for them both. Gabriel knew where he stood with her—twelve months only out of her life was committed to the Jacaranth. She—well, she perhaps understood his gruffness better. But she tossed her head—it didn't matter. She would do her job for him, and the then say goodbye without any regrets on either side.

The sunshine they had all prayed for persisted on the morning of the Grand Opening. The entire staff positively shone with brushing and polishing and pressing and starching. Name badges glistened, carefully coiled hair gleamed and scrubbed faces glowed. The garden, so recently a wilderness, was beautiful with lawns, hibiscus and bougainvillea, and garlands of flowers and leaves and streamers slung between the palm trees. As Dr Malik said drily, 'It might be someone's wedding, instead of yet another private health clinic.'

Annabel said warmly, 'Not just any old health clinic—the Jacaranth, if you please,' and they all laughed as the wind gently stirred the wind chimes in the front foyer. Annabel was wearing her silver-buckled belt, which she rarely did because of the heat. She knew it set off her slim waist and neat hips. She was quick to compliment Cherry on her appearance. Cherry Ho was well aware that Annabel was younger, prettier and more important than herself. On such an occasion it was easy to fan the flame of jealousy, and Annabel had to hope that their relationship was on a stronger basis after the work they had done together. 'We have to be polite to the doctors' wives, Cherry. Do tell me what to say to them.'

Cherry said dourly, 'Just flatter them. And make sure they have enough to eat. They dress up like Christmas tree, so you can always praise their earrings and their diamonds.'

'Will they be real diamonds?'

'Oh yes—the Malacca Medical Association know their diamonds—and their gold.' Cherry tossed her head. 'If you want, come and meet Dr Malik's wife. She come early, see?'

'Malik's wife?' Annabel had forgotten that he was married. 'Where?' The two nurses went out to the garden, where a long gleaming car had just drawn up at the gate. Out of it stepped a vision in pale blue sequins. It was the lovely Malay woman. 'That's Mrs Malik?'

'Right. Very beautiful, but she knows it—vain, *lah*.'

Annabel's heart was doing strange things behind her ribs. The memory of that morning—the passionate way the woman had spoken, the fraught voice of Gabriel Christie, the silence when she knew they had embraced—it all took on a whole new meaning now. How could Gabriel deceive his own partner? It was appalling, the way the two men worked so closely together. She felt sick suddenly, as the slim shape of the surgeon's wife walked gracefully along the drive, looking around her, smiling and waving and greeting the staff who were outdoors.

There was no sign of Gabriel nor Dr Malik, so Annabel felt duty bound to go to greet the newcomer. 'I'm Annabel, Mrs Malik. Welcome to Jacaranth.' The woman was even more beautiful close up, her complexion perfect, her dark eyes lustrous, fringed with thick black lashes. In spite of her initial disgust at Gabriel, Annabel thought briefly that perhaps the poor man couldn't help falling in love. Perhaps this beauty gave him no choice.

'Annabel—my husband has told me about you. My name is Sukeina.' They shook hands. Sukeina was wearing Malay dress, a long slim skirt with a tunic top shimmering with sequins. Cherry had been right about the diamonds too.

'You speak English so well, Mrs Malik.'

'I teach it, you see. Please call me Sukeina. I have wanted to meet you. You must come and call on me. I have a wide circle of friends who call on me for afternoon tea.' Her teeth were perfect when she smiled.

'I'd love to.' But calling on Gabriel's mistress was not at the forefront of Annabel's desires.

'My number is ex-directory, so I'll make sure I leave you one of my cards before we go.' She shimmered on past Annabel, greeting the nurses. Annabel stood stock still, heart thumping. Here was perfectly respectable teacher and a highly thought of medical man, with spotless reputations, sharing an illicit and tearful affair. She waited to see if they would speak to each other, or whether they would avoid being seen too close together.

She didn't have long to wait. As more doctors with their wives arrived, and were greeted and given glasses of cool fruit juice, Gabriel himself emerged from the clinic, wearing a cream suit and shirt with a slim crimson tie. He stood, dashing and almost debonair with his hair almost controlled today, though still giving him—to Annabel—the look of a slightly tamed Viking.

His keen eyes searched the throng from the clinic steps. She saw him catch sight of Sukeina, then his gaze found Annabel—and a smile came to his lips as he strode down and came straight to her side. 'Well, what do you think? I took your advice and went to the barber.'

She couldn't help smiling. His artless approach had taken away the disgust she felt about Sukeina. But as the rest of the guests now realised that Gabriel was here, there was a spontaneous round of applause. Annabel joined in, seeing the affection and respect on the faces of his staff and of his friends alike. He was drawn away to shake a hundred hands and answer a thousand questions. Annabel made an effort, and began to do the same.

However, because of his height, she knew where Gabriel was in that sunlit garden, and she could see Sukeina's sequins from the corner of her eye. When they moved closer, she excused herself and went blatantly to the edge of the lawn to see exactly how they greeted one another. Surely one of them at least would be shy. But no—— Sukeina walked straight up to Gabriel and brazenly took both his hands, gazing up into his eyes. Annabel's heart lurched as he did not take his hands away, but looked down at her, speaking normally, shaking his head as though giving some sad news. Annabel could scarcely believe it—that they should stand so openly in the middle of all their friends and colleagues. Except that no one took the slightest notice except Annabel. And she soon looked away, when Gabriel suddenly looked up and caught her staring.

With a sudden amused smile, he excused himself at once from the lovely Sukeina and began to make his way through the throng towards Annabel. Surely he wasn't going to accuse her of staring? Her heart started to thump—he looked very determined as he shouldered his way across the lawn. He ignored small greetings and comments from the people he passed—just made straight for Annabel, his eyes fixed on hers so that she could not look away . . .

There was a burst of applause, and the small three-man band started to play in the corner of the lawn. A dark green Mercedes drew up, a government flag flying from it, and a chauffeur jumped out to open the door for the Minister. Gabriel, thwarted, turned at once and edged his

way to the front of the throng, making it to the car as the
Minister emerged. He bowed and shook hands, then the
two men walked slowly along the drive, followed by a
small entourage of bodyguards and secretaries. A red
ribbon had been tied between the pillars of the front
entrance, and after a brief speech in Malay, and a few
words in English, the ribbon was cut, and there was a
general squeeze to see inside the Jacaranth.

Annabel decided she had done her bit. There were
enough staff to answer questions. She had been presented
briefly to the Minister, and now the caterers were laying
out huge vats of rice and piles of skewered chicken satay.
A savoury smell drifted through the scent of the flowers
and leaves. Annabel knew that today she could eat
nothing, that if she stayed she might be ill. She ran round
the back of the clinic and up the stairs, where she changed
into cotton pants and top and ran down unnoticed to the
beach. At least she thought she was unnoticed. But as she
found herself a grassy spot under some trees, with a good
view of the small islands and the deep blue Straits, she
heard running footsteps, and saw a slim male figure in
white trousers and cerise satin shirt coming towards her. It
was Mr Pagodi.

His handsome face flowed with pleasure at finding her.
'I came late. You are tired of the ceremony?'

It was nice to see his boyish face, hear his lighthearted
tones and be with someone who was totally unthreatening
as a man. 'I wasn't hungry.'

He sat beside her without asking. 'I also will not eat. We
will sit here and talk, yes? I enjoy talking with you. You
are different from other women.'

'Because I don't throw myself at you?'

He beamed. The sun was very hot, and they were both
too warm to talk much. 'I attract women, yes. I do not
boast, Annabel—it just happens to me. Why do you think
that is? Your opinion I value.'

He was waiting for an answer, so she tried to give it. 'I
think a lot of women like a handsome man as an
additional part of their outfit—and accessory, if you like. I

don't think like that. I only like men whose characters I like.' But where her employer fitted in that statement, she hoped Amir Pagodi would not ask.

'That is a straight answer. So you like me for my character, not my beauty? His grin was disarming.

'Amir, I've travelled alone. I've seen women taken in by men. I decided never to allow my senses to decide who I make friends with—only my intelligence, if you like the word.'

Amir was preoccupied with an iridescent seashell. He said without looking up, 'But if an intelligent man was also good-looking, you would not hold it against him?'

Annabel sat still as a stone, her thoughts immediately going to Gabriel Christie, although she had resolved not to think of him. HE was intelligent, he was handsome, distinguished—and there was something else, some inner quality that drew her to him even while disliking his affair with Sukeina. She wondered what to call it. And in the shimmering heat of the Malaysian day she felt herself recognising it—Gabriel's soul spoke to her soul. She shivered as she admitted it as true. Amir had spoken to her twice before she recalled his question. 'Sorry—I was thinking.'

'About me, I hope?'

She laughed. 'Really, you ought not to ask leading questions. But you've been very kind and helpful over the Jacaranth, and we all appreciate your help and encouragement. You ought to be in there shaking hands with the Minister.'

Amir shrugged. 'The Minister is jealous of me because I have more money, bigger cars and am better-looking.' He handed her the beautiful shell. 'Here, Annabel—keep this in memory of your friend from Malacca.'

She took it, but she thought of Gabriel, not Amir Pagodi. She stifled a sigh. 'One day soon, Amir, we must talk business, but not yet. I'm tired with all the effort of the last few weeks—and the operation two days ago that went on till midnight. I think I shall ask for a few days off to sleep.'

He put his hand on her arm. 'Perhaps you allow me to show you my country? I know all the villages around here. I will drive you where you like, stop where you tell me to stop—buy friuts from the side of the road, mangosteens and rambutans and starfruit. I will introduce you to the *bomohs* and the wise women, the priests and the peasants. Amir Pagodi goes where he wishes.'

'Where are *bomohs*?'

He smiled, his dimples deep in his cheeks. 'Witch-doctors, my dear. But only good ones. Bad magic I will not show you, I promise.'

'Magic?'

'My country is magic. Allow me to drive you? Please? I will give you a day you will never forget.'

'Let me decide after I've rested.'

He knelt beside her suddenly, 'Oh, my dear, you are so very beautiful a lady.' Annabel froze. Amir saw at once that his advances were inopportune. 'Annabel, tell me about your country. Do you see much of your Queen? And the great processions they have? I have seen pictures of your Buckingham Palace, and it looks so boring—not a bit like the place where our king lives in Kuala Lumpur. Now that is a palace! Why does your Queen not have such a home?'

Annabel had regained her composure, but she felt that the handsome Mr Pagodi must be discouraged. She said with a smile, 'Amir, imagine that I'm sixty years old, with straight grey hair, round glasses and a figure like a water buffalo. But my mind is still my mind, and I'm keen to discover the East. Would you still offer to take me around your country?'

He laughed. 'Of course not. Or—perhaps—who knows? Just now I am young, and I like to spend my time with young ladies.'

'And with your wife?'

'Of course with my wife.' But he didn't sound very serious. 'Come, it is only two o'clock. Let's go now—right away from the Jacaranth for an hour or two.'

In the background the small band was playing pop

music, and the sound of voices raised in laughter was carried on the breeze. With it was the sight of Sukeina and Gabriel, hand in hand, gazing at one another in the middle of the lawn, oblivious of the other guests. Annabel looked up at Amir Pagodi, and saw only a lighthearted friend—just what she really needed just now, someone with whom to share a few hours of peace and quiet and beauty. 'All right, Amir, let's go and find your *bomohs* and your magic. I'm giving myself the afternoon off.'

He laughed with delight. 'OK, OK, so let's go.' He pulled her to her feet. 'Come, this way—up the path, then we avoid going through the clinic gardens.'

'But I want my camera.'

'No, you don't. Next time, perhaps. Today—we just go, OK?' And he pulled her back by the hand. She stumbled and fell into his arms. 'Steady—you all right?' His brief embrace had not been deliberate, then. His grip tightened as their eyes met, and he tilted her chin so that she could not avoid his look.

She had no time to struggle, before footsteps sounded on the path and Gabriel Christie appeared, tall and noble against the deep blue of the sky. Amir slowly let his arms fall to his sides.

'I'm sorry I interrupted you,' said Gabriel, his eyes almost hidden under dark brows.

CHAPTER SIX

AMIR PAGODI strode to Gabriel's side and held out his hand with his usual open smile. 'Well done, Doctor—Grand Opening, and you must be very pleased.'

Gabriel allowed his hand to be shaken reluctantly. Annabel was very conscious of his disapproval. He said, 'You both seem to have tired of the company.' His voice was acid.

Amir said at once, 'Not a bit. But Annabel has been working hard. She needs to rest this afternoon. You keep your staff too long hours, Doctor——bad for productivity, you know.'

'None of your business, Pagodi. I must get back—excuse me.' Gabriel swung on his heel. Annabel felt cheated, that he had not thought fit to speak to her—possibly even to congratulate her on her hard work for the hospital. He just walked away—she felt anger rising as his elegant back disappeared inside the Jacaranth.

Amir touched her shoulder. 'Come—let's go. You must get away. It will do you no good at all to hang around here, will it?'

She faced him, suddenly determined. 'Right, I'm ready.' She led the way along the path, muttering to herself, but within Amir's earshot, 'There was no need to look at me as though I were a criminal! He has his women friends—why can't I have friends too?'

'Woman friends?' Amir caught up with her. 'Not Dr Christie, surely? He is a loner—always was. I've never seen him in love, not even a tiny bit.'

'I've seen him with Sukeina Malik.'

'Oh, that Sukeina—she chases him, Annabel. But I do not think he can be caught. She is beautiful, yes—and intelligent. But I am sure you are mistaken——'

Annabel realised she shouldn't be discussing her chief

like this. 'You're probably right, Amir.' Privately she
decided that Amir saw Gabriel very little, and only at the
Club. This affair could have started more recently.
Perhaps that morning on the beach she had been its first
witness? Whatever it was she saw, Annabel was positive
that the passion in that conversation that morning was
proof enough for her. 'Anyway, you don't see much of Dr
Christie, do you?'

He was blatantly truthful. 'Only in passing, usually. But
I know Sukeina. She is very vain. If someone refuses to
fall for her, she makes it a matter of pride to pursue him
until he does.'

Annabel was silent as she reached Amir's Mercedes,
parked some way from the Jacaranth, as the road was
lined with the visitors' cars still. They set off towards the
paddy fields, both quiet. Annabel stole a look at her
companion's classic profile. 'Have you ever . . .?'

'Yes.' He said no more. But, aware of her continued
perusal of his face, he relented and said, 'We are both
rebels from the Islamic ideal, perhaps. I hope you are not
shocked.'

Annabel was shocked and worried. 'Rebels? You're
complete traitors to be married to someone else, and quite
happily admit to adultery!'

They were entering a dappled jungle road. Amir braked
and drew in to the side. He turned to her and said,
'Annabel, my friend, I have only one sin to confess—I am
not married.' He didn't allow her to speak. 'It was a
simple ruse to prevent my name being on the lips of all the
matchmakers in Malaysia. I invented a wife. Do you
forgive me?'

'I suppose I must. I do know how predatory mothers
with marriageable daughters can be—it's the same in
Singapore. But how many people know this?'

He said simply, 'I have told no one else. I trust you, you
see.' He started the engine again. 'We go to see the
beauties of Malaysia, no?'

Her mind in a turmoil, Annabel said, 'I don't want to be
away long. They might need me.'

'My friend, I promise.' And as the sun twinkled through
the high rubber trees, Annabel felt her conscience giving
up. She liked Amir, while knowing that he was a bit of a
rogue. She was gambling on him being enough of a
gentleman to keep his promise. He went on, 'Come, surely
seeing the sun and the trees and the flowers does not make
you so gloomy?'

She took a deep breath and straightened her back
against the soft seat of the Mercedes. 'I'm not gloomy. It's
as magical as you said.'

It was hotter now, as they left the shore. She made sure
her window was closed, so that the air-conditioning kept
them cool. But soon they rounded a bend, and there was a
village ahead, complete with roving goats and chickens,
playing children, and a village store where the men
congregated and ate *nasih limak* and drank Japanese beer.
'Oh, Amir, can we get out?' begged Annabel.

'Of course. There is a stall selling mangosteens.' By the
side of the road two laughing children dressed in shorts
and shirts presided over a thatched bench covered in piles
of the purple fruit. It was clear they must have helped to
pick them themselves from the family trees that grew
profusely along the edges of the jungle. Amir said with a
dimpled grin, 'One thing I cannot resist! Come—I want
many.'

The children produced a plastic bag, and Amir
proceeded to pick out a large bagful one by one. There
were no scales. The children estimated by the size of the
load, and charged him five ringgit. He hoisted it on his
shoulder, well pleased. They drove on, still sweating from
that brief encounter with the heat of the forest. When they
came to a shady spot, he drew in to the side. 'We stop here
and eat. See? The monkeys will come to see what we are
doing.' He spread a cloth on the grass, and laid some fruit
on it. 'I bought a *nyiur* for you too.' He produced a
coconut, which he sliced with a sharp knife that was under
the driver's seat. Annabel was slightly uneasy about the
knife, but very grateful for the cool coconut milk.
Meanwhile Amir attacked the fruit with eager fingers,

splitting the hard shells of the mangosteens and skilfully slicing out the segments, each with its hard stone in the middle. The milky pulp was delicious.

'This beats eating in the garden with a hundred others!' smiled Annabel.

'You are glad we came away?' His face was innocent, like a boy playing truant from school.

She couldn't help smiling. 'I'm glad.'

'You liked the village? There are more on the highway to Seremban.'

'Not so far—you promised.'

'OK—we turn back at the next. But you want to see a *bomoh*? Maybe he is there—you are not scared?'

By this time Annabel had all but forgotten the tensions and suspicions that had beset her at the Jacaranth. She ran back to the car. 'I'd love to see one. Do they wear bones and feathers?'

Amir followed her, laughing. 'Not all the time. Only when on duty—like your doctors wear white coats!' He started the car, and they drove rather fast round the winding narrow road edged with spiky jungle grasses and exquisite white flowers. They came to a palm-oil estate, where the trees were all squat, the leaves fringed and graceful.

But at the next village she was forced to stop laughing. The entire population appeared to be hypnotised by a tall Malay dressed in an animal skin, with white chalk round his eyes and mouth. Amir grabbed Annabel's arm. 'I could never have planned this! I know this *bomoh* is one of the big ones. But to see him in action—well, do you want to get out? Go and listen?'

Annabel stared, her eyes and her mouth open. 'Is it allowed?'

'No. But it we stay at the back . . .'

'Let's go and listen for a minute, then?'

'*Baiklah*.'

She knew that meant 'all right'. She opened her door carefully, and they both went to the edge of the throng of villagers. The *bomoh* stood by a heap of smouldering

chicken bones. His eyes were surrounded by a broad band
of white. Even his ribs were delineated by white, and
round his neck was a string of monkey skulls. Annabel
controlled a shiver. This was not a show they admitted
tourists to. She looked at Amir. He gave her a thumbs up,
put his finger to his lips.

They were too far away to see everything. But there was
a great deal of moaning and groaning, and the villagers
joined in as though rehearsed. The woman in the middle
of the throng did more groaning and crying than the
others, who seemed to encourage her. She flung her arms
out and proceeded to gyrate around, uttering low moans,
her arms outstretched to each villager in the front row,
who touched her with a murmured blessing of some sort.

The *bomoh* threw something flammable on the embers,
and there was a flash of blue that made everyone cry out.
Amir grabbed Annabel's hand. 'Better go. That's the
end.'

As they drove away, she asked, 'Do these people go to a
real doctor?'

Amir said with a smile, 'They might be Gabriel's
patients! Malacca is the nearest bit town. They go to the
town when they need Western medicine. But when it is a
matter of fertility, or infidelity—or even an aphrodisiac,
the *bomoh* does very well.'

Annabel shuddered. 'But how can they?'

'It is natural to them. Come, Annabel. Too much magic
is not good. I take you back to the world you know, *lah*.'
And he took her hand for a moment, but didn't retain it.
She felt comforted. He was trustworthy after all. She had
been right to trust him, to go along with him when she felt
so upset by Gabriel Christie and his flaunting of his
woman.

'Maybe we can come again?' she queried.

Amir seemed delighted. 'Sure, sure, whenever you like.
But you cannot be guaranteed a ceremony like this. That
lady is now free from the demon of frigidity.'

Annabel stared at him. 'But we couldn't hear what they
said.'

Amir smiled as he steered skilfully round the bends. 'I
know.' And they wound past idyllic villages, mountain
waterfalls, and by towering rubber plantations tended by
women in bright sarongs, lit by shafts of sunlight through
the regimented rows of tall grey tree-trunks. Annabel
gazed, wondering how many of these country people
believed in the magic they had just witnessed. She longed
to get to know the people, to be trusted by them, so that
she knew just how they thought and what they really
trusted.

Then Amir slowed up. They didn't seem to be back at
the main highway, but he was drawing in to a tall white-
walled garden, stopping the car and turning off the engine.
There was a profusion of hibiscus flowers over the wall,
and climbing geraniums. Banana trees gave large areas of
shade, and were laden with hand upon hand of green
bananas. He said, 'I thought you would like to see my
house.'

Annabel wasn't sure. Now that she knew he had no wife
at home, there seemed no need to stop here. But Amir
Pagodi had proved a good companion. Whe she sid, 'Just
for a moment, then,' he gave her a thumbs-up, as though
their stay would be minimal.

'Let's just take a cup of tea. I'd like to show you my
garden.'

The scent of the garden was already obvious—carefully
chosen to appeal to all the senses, the frangipani trees
surrounded the well-trimmed lawns with their fragrance
and their beauty. As the pair walked across the grass,
ignoring the gravel paths, a yard-long iguana took fright
and scuttled into the shrubbery. Annabel had never seen
such a size. She was reassured when Amir made no
attempt to protect her. 'That is one of my regulars.' His
ready smile set her mind at rest.

A long window was open on to the grass, and inside was
a polished wooden floor scattered with exquisite Chinese
rugs. The room was furnished with antique furniture.
Annabel stopped in amazement. She had seen some pieces
like this in her father's shop—dark wood inlaid with brass

and painted with gold and silver. The cost must have been enormous, yet Amir treated the entire room with familiarity, flopping on one of the embroidered settees and ringing a small brass gong. He patted the place next to him, but Annabel still stood, wondering at the beauty before her, wanting to see everything before she sat down.

A white-coated Malay in a turban entered and bowed. '*Thé, tuan*?' He saw Annabel and bowed again. Amir nodded, and the servant left the room, his bare feet making no sound.

'We will take English afternoon tea, *lah*? You seem to be fascinated by my Babar furniture. You like antiques?'

'Very much.' Annabel paused by a magnificent cabinet. 'Is it still possible to find this sort of thing outside museums? My parents would be willing to buy any of this style. I promised myself I'd start to look around as soon as my work at the Jacaranth became less demanding.'

Amir was by her side at once. 'I can get it for you—it is becoming more scarce, but I have many contacts throughout the country.' Casually he put his arm around her shoulders as he pointed out the detail in the design. 'You must come again. I can bring you objects you might like to send to the UK. Are your parents interested in modern Malay craftsmanship? I have a team of goldsmiths working for me, and two woodcarvers who are geniuses.'

The butler brought in tea on a silver tray, and then, as though used to it, laid two glasses of what looked like fruit juice beside the delicately sliced lemon by the silver teapot. Amir waved him away, and poured pale fragrant tea into china cups, placing one—with one of the glasses—on the small inlaid table in front of Annabel. They talked of antiques, so that she hardly noticed drinking the tea or the juice.

Then there was a lull in the conversation, and she realised he was looking at her, his dark eyes full of meaning. She felt a shiver. She was here in the house of one of the most powerful men in the State. She had been warned to keep away from him—yet he had been nothing but charming so far. And suddenly she felt faint. 'What—what was that in the glass?'

He stood up. 'Don't fear me, beautiful Annabel. I have explained why I pretended to have a wife. But you understand, surely—if one is young, wealthy and not completely ugly—women chase me frantically to marry their daughters.' There was a silence between them, broken only by the sounds from the jungle that surrounded the house. Annabel had no idea how far away they were from the main highway to Malacca. Charming and harmless Amir Pagodi had appeared—but now she was alone with him, and feeling definitely weak and faint.

'What was in that juice?' she asked again.

'A little Malay tonic. Your hands are shaking, Annabel.' His eyes were still on her, and they seemed more menacing now.

'I ought to be getting back.' Already the shadows in the garden were long across the lawn. There was a sudden harsh cry outside, and a pair of peacocks walked from the shadows into the remaining sunlight.

'No hurry. You have worked hard today.'

'Gabriel might need me.'

'You run after that man too much.'

'It's what I'm paid for.'

Amir was still talking quietly, but now every sentence sounded like a threat. 'Don't you want to sample Suleiman's cooking? It is excellent.'

'I'm not hungry.' Annabel's walked to the window, panic making her heart beat faster, though the gardens outside were innocent and peaceful in the rapidly deepening twilight. She put her hand to her head, recalling the strange smells and sounds as the *bomoh* in the village made his magic . . . Amir came up behind her and gently put his hands on her shoulders. She felt his breath ruffle her hair. She snatched them away and swung round. 'Take me home. Now!'

He seemed hurt. 'I'm not thinking of hurting you.'

She tried to be rational. 'Sorry for shouting, but——'

'It is *baiklah, baiklah*.' His voice was tender, smooth.

'You know I value your friendship. I would hate anything to spoil it.'

'Then please can we go?'

Without a word he led the way to the car. A nightjar was croaking its unlovely song in the palm trees above them. Annabel's heart had not stopped thumping unpleasantly in her ears. They drove in silence. It was not very far, after all. As Amir drew up outside the Clinic entrance, with its bunting still hanging, and its garlands still fragrant in the evening air, he said calmly, 'Well—safe and sound.' He looked sideways at her. The engine was still running.

Annabel bit her lip, feeling foolish for panicking. 'Amir, I——'

'You enjoyed the day, *lah*?'

'Very much.' It had been good—until the last bit. 'I'm grateful.' The atmosphere was heavy between them. She opened the car door. 'Goodnight.'

'See you soon?' She nodded tremulously. Suddenly Amir drew her into the circle of his arms and crushed her to him, kissing her lips with his soft warm mouth. Annabel sat as though frozen until he released her. With a smile that seemed suddenly full of cunning, he let out the clutch, and the car glided away.

The sound of the waves was so welcome to her now that she just stood waiting for her senses to calm themselves, thankful to be home. She had been scared, out there in the jungle, alone with Amir Pagodi. She felt in her bag for the key. The lights were on inside the Clinic; they must be eating together in the dining room at the back. She took a very deep breath of the familiar salty air, and walked to the front door.

But it was opened for her by someone who must have seen her coming. She had expected to see Percival, but when Gabriel's shaggy head showed up against the dim corridor lights, she wasn't surprised. He must be very angry with her. Yet at that moment he represented safety and security, all that was trustworthy and familiar in this disturbing country.

Annabel found herself in his arms. She was sure she had never thrown herself at him—yet there she was, firm and safe against his chest, feeling how strong and reliable his arms were, how warm and inevitable . . . She clung to him for some moments, seized by a fit of trembling that was slowly soothed by his closeness, and the steady beating of his heart. Slowly she drew away. She looked up, knowing that she must look bedraggled and fraught. 'I'm ready now. You can tell me you told me so.'

His eyes were hidden in the shadow of his eyebrows. For a moment he said nothing, perhaps trying to read in her voice what had happened that night. Then he said, 'Have you eaten anything today?'

'No.' She wasn't thinking of food.

'Then it's high time you did. Go along now, and eat properly.' He turned her in the direction of the dining room and gave her a gentle push. She turned to protest, but gave in at once as she met his look, and went towards the lights and the laughing chatter.

As she ate, and listened to the talk about the Grand Opening and how well it had gone, Annabel realised that Gabriel had represented a rock to her that night—that she trusted him entirely, in spite of his having an affair with his colleague's wife, and in spite of the fact that he had forced Professor Singh to send her away from the Singapore home she loved. How could she feel so strongly for a man who had done all this? She shrugged, and turned back to the conversation. It was suddenly normal and homely. Even Amal Malik's narrow eyes and Cherry Ho's jealousy were normal now, and nothing to fear. Amir and his jungle, his villagers and *bomohs* and dark magic were past and gone. Annabel had learned an important lesson that night. Never would she allow herself to be at a disadvantage again.

The following day the entire hospital started in earnest. That very night three new patients were admitted—from doctors who had been to the Opening. The nurses began to realise that rotas were now serious and must be kept. And to make the Jacaranth complete, the third doctor arrived—

a lady gynaecologist called Asha Santasi. She soon found her way to Annabel's office—a plumpish Indian in a homemade Crimplene dress, not a bit glamorous, but steady and talkative, exuding confidence and motherliness.

'I was reluctant at first—I had a steady practice in Johore Bahru. But I was fourth partner there—here I am to be an equal after an initial period of six months while Dr Malik and Dr Christie and I decide if we can work together. Tell me about your routine, Sister Browne.'

Annabel explained that the other doctors had their consulting rooms on the ground floor. 'They see patients every morning. There's a room for you if you wish to do this. Operations are in the afternoons, and so far we have no regular schedules. You would need one afternoon a week to start with, and then we would reorganise as and when necessary.'

'You sound very efficient, Sister.'

'I've been here since the beginning.' And suddenly Annabel realised she was proud of the fact. To have started with a broken-down building and only three staff . . . she smiled and said, 'Yes, from the very beginning—almost like a midwife.'

Asha Santasi smiled a plump smile that showed her two chins. 'Then I hope your baby grows up big and strong.'

'It's showing signs of doing just that. But it still needs careful nursing. Come upstairs, and I'll show you the operating suite.'

'May I see what instruments you have?' Dr Santasi inspected everything closely, and decided that she needed further supplies, even though so far she had no patients. The two women therefore drove into Malacca together, and spent the afternoon spending money. It was only when they returned that Dr Malik met them in the hall.

'You needed more surgical instruments? You did not gain authority from myself or Dr Christie?' The narrow eyes grew narrower.

Annabel spoke up. 'Dr Santasi was right—we had no gynae forceps and no speculum.'

Dr Malik said sourly, 'It could have come at the end of the month. We have no gynae patients.' He turned to Dr Santasi. 'You will be on duty tonight, Doctor. You have seen your apartment?'

The Indian woman said coolly, 'I shall be staying in my own house—it isn't far. Sister Browne has the phone number.'

Dr Malik shook his head. 'That is not safe. A cardiac arrest needs a doctor on the spot.'

'You have two housemen.'

'Housemen!' The two doctors faced each other, and Annabel could think of nothing to get them apart. It was true that in most hospitals the junior staff dealt with emergencies, but Gabriel wanted the Jacaranth to be one step better than most hospitals. She tried to explain this, but was talked down by the formidable Indian woman, and soon excused herself from the arguments.

Mia came in with a cup of Chinese tea. She pulled a face. 'Not so far has there been any shouting. You think this lady will stay?'

Annabel smiled. 'She likes the hospital—and she seems to me to be someone who always gets her own way.'

'It will be pity if they fight.'

Annabel nodded. But she knew that Dr Malik seemed to enjoy putting people's backs up. 'His bark is worse than his bite.'

But by the end of the day, Annabel was worn out. The combination of a busy day with the emotional strain of the previous night was too much for her, and she went upstairs as soon as six o'clock came, changing out of uniform into a housecoat and throwing herself on her bed, drained of all energy. 'If only I could just go to the Club with Celia and the gang!' She missed that, the way they could shake off the day's stresses by a swim and a carefree meal together. In the Jacaranth they were all so close to each other that any tensions rubbed off on the others. It would not be a comfortable dining room tonight.

There was a gentle tap on the door. She sat up sharply, and pulled her robe around her. 'Come in.'

It was Gabriel. Annabel pulled the robe tighter, holding the neckline together. He said quietly, 'Is Asha on duty?'

Annabel sighed. 'According to the schedule she is. But you'd better ask her yourself.'

To her surprise he shook his head. 'No—let them sort it out. I'm going to the night market for some satay. Want to come?'

She stared at him. Deserting the Jacaranth? 'Are you sure?'

'Of course I'm sure. They can manage without us now. Let's go out and leave them to it.'

Apart from the meals in the dining room, the last time she had eaten with Gabriel was at his club. She knew him better now, and was still enough in awe of him not to refuse an invitation made in a voice that was milder than his usual gruff growl. 'I'll be a few minutes.'

They drove out of the town to what seemed to be an open road, lit only by the stars. Then suddenly round a bend she saw lights—hundreds of them, flickering into the night sky, sending up plumes of smoke that blotted out the stars. And the smell—the splendid smell of cooking over charcoal, of roasting nuts and sizzling satay chicken. '*Pasar malam*.' Gabriel appeared glad to be out. 'You have them in Singapore?'

'Not like this,' breathed Annabel, gazing at the haphazard stalls covered with vivid batiks and silks, prayer mats and kitchen utensils shining like Christmas decorations in the gas lights.

'Want to walk round before we eat?'

'I'd love to.' People were laughing and gossiping, young folk were listening to pop music on transistors, while older men listened to traditional flute music and played cards. There were fruit stalls, brasses, souvenirs and sarongs. And there was a dark-skinned Malay with his satay grill on the front of his trishaw, juggling the ready-browned meat with amazing skill while turning the underdone ones on their bamboo skewers. Around him were other trishaws, selling Coke, Seven Up, coconuts and Milo. The entire scene was lit only by the tall gas lamps on each stall, so that

FREE BOOKS CERTIFICATE

Yes! Please send me my **4 Free romances** together with my **2 glass dishes and surprise mystery gift.** Please also reserve a special Reader Service Subscription for me. If I decide to subscribe, I shall receive 6 Brand New Romances every month for just £7.50 post and packing free. If I decide not to subscribe I shall write to you within 10 days. The free books and gifts will be mine to keep in any case. I understand that I am under no obligation whatsoever - I can cancel or suspend my subscription at any time simply by writing to you.. *I am over 18 years of age*

1A9R

FREE GIFT

Return this card now and we'll also send you this 2 piece glass dish absolutely Free together with...

A SURPRISE MYSTERY GIFT.

We all love suprises, so as well as the FREE books and glass dishes, there's an intriguing mystery gift especially for you.

POST TODAY!

NAME _____

ADDRESS _____

_____

_____

POSTCODE _____

Mills & Boon
FREEPOST
P.O. Box 236
Croydon
CR9 9EL

The right is reserved to refuse an application and change the terms of this offer. Offer expires Dec. 31st. 1989 You may be mailed with other offers as a result of this application. Readers in Southern Africa write to: Independent Book Services Pty. Postbag X3010, Randburg 2125, South Africa

mps MAILING PREFERENCE SERVICE

their flickering gave the *pasar malam* a sense of impermanence, as though it might fly away at any moment.

There was a shout from one of the stallholders. 'Hey, Doctor, nice to see you, *lah*!'

Gabriel replied in Malay, grinning broadly. He introduced Annabel—'my friend' and the man grinned back, showing a missing tooth, as though he saw more than friendship between the two. Annabel was glad of the dim lights and flickering shadows that hid her blush.

To cover her embarrassment she said to another stallholder, holding up a piece of silk, '*Berapa*?'

'*Lapan belas ringgit.*'

Annabel smiled. '*Lima.*'

'*Sangat mura!*'

'Baiklah, lapan ringgit. I could get two for that in Singapore.'

'*Dan lima puluh sen.*'

Annabel smiled again, and took out an extra fifty-cent piece. 'I give you a very good price. *Terimakasih*,' She took the cloth, which was worth much more than the eight ringgit.

Gabriel came up behind her as she strolled away. 'You bargain well.'

'Practice—it makes shopping more fun.' And she felt a warm happiness in wandering with Gabriel, a feeling she had not felt in Malacca until now. They approached a stall selling patent medicines and vitamins by the bottle. Gabriel called to the owner, 'You try to put me out of business, *lah*?'

The man came round to the front of the stall to shake hands vigorously. 'Doctor, tell me what you think of this?' He spoke as man to man, as though they were both in the same business. He held out a bottle of pills. 'They have been good for slimming in America.'

'Osman, Osman, my friend, you know nothing works for slimming except eating less food.'

'So—these take the appetite away.'

Garbiel shouted with laughter. 'In this place—with all

these smells of food? The only way would be to live on a
desert island and live on coconuts.'

The man said seriously, 'But they would lack many
essential vitamins.'

'So they would. But it would be better than buying your
pills!'

They were both laughing as Osman grabbed his arm,
whispering, 'Hush, man, I have a living to make.'

They strolled away, Gabriel assuring Annabel that the
man's wares were harmless. 'I keep an eye on them to
make sure he doesn't sell anything unethical. The herbal
stuff does no harm—and perhaps better than spending
money on cigarettes, eh?'

They had made a complete circle of the magic market,
and had arrived back at the satay seller. 'How many do
you think we need, Ahmed?' asked Gabriel.

The man grinned. 'You have a friend with you—two
dozen at least. Here, it very good tonight. I give you
discount.' He managed to hand over a hot-looking sauce
in a plastic bag, while still juggling his bamboo sticks over
the glowing charcoal. The smoke rose from his grill as high
as they could see above the yellow light of the gas flares,
up into the still night.

At that moment there was a sickening screech of brakes,
a scream and a scraping of metal. Then total silence just
for a moment except for the sizzling grill, before an
outbreak of human voices, and chaos as everyone ran
towards the road. They made way for Gabriel and
Annabel, who got to the front of the crowd to see a big
Mercedes, headlamps full on, though one was smashed,
illuminating the figure of a skidded motor-cyclist, his
machine and crash helmet yards away from his still body.
A trickle of blood was already congealing on the road.

Gabriel knelt by him, practised hands feeling for
fractures. 'Nothing broken. Please God it's just
concussion. But he'll need skull X-rays. Annabel, get on
the phone for our ambulance.'

The driver of the car came forward, a wealthy Chinese
with a gold watch and gold bracelets glinting in the

headlamps. 'Look at him! How he hear any traffic coming with those bloody headphones on? It his own fault.'

Gabriel looked up. 'Maybe. But he is hurt, and we're those whose job it is to care for him.' His voice was grim.

'Silly devil, he ask for it!' The man was furious. 'I have important meeting!'

Gabriel said harshly, 'Push off, then. I'll take care of him.'

Annabel said, 'He's coming round.' And Gabriel tested his eyes and ears until the ambulance arrived. There was no shortage of helpers to lift the limp form, once Gabriel had given permission. He made sure that the lad's relatives would be told where he was, before he and Annabel drove back in silence after the rushing ambulance.

As they followed the stretcher in, Gabriel said briefly, 'You're a handy girl to have around when someone decides to have an argument with a Merc.'

'Don't thank me.'

'Right. Then take the satay and keep it warm in your kitchen till I come up.'

'Asha's on call.'

Gabriel said gruffly, 'I'll let her off this one,' and strode off towards the examination room. There were two nurses there, so Annabel did as she was told and went upstairs. The night had been still, with no wind and only a very soft splashing of the waves. But as she waited for Gabriel lightning lit up the sky its jagged glow through the open shutters. The thunder began to rumble. Suddenly she didn't want Gabriel coming to her flat. She took half the satay and put it in his own room, then came back and ate a little, before locking her door and going to bed naked under the whirring fan. Gabriel had his own life. No point in intruding. Only ten more months, and they would be saying goodbye for good.

CHAPTER SEVEN

GABRIEL said nothing to Annabel about her leaving his food in his room the previous night. Again, as so often when she had chatted with him, there was a curtain down over his inner self the following morning, and he spoke only of business. 'Do you want to come on the ward round?' he asked.

She did. Now that they had many patients, she felt that she must keep up with their problems, and know what was going on. The first two patients, Mohammed and Mr Dan, were very much better. The newer ones she had to get to know. And the young man who had come off his motor-bike was sitting up, eager to thank the kind doctor and nurse who had saved him.

Gabriel led the procession, with the houseman at his elbow. Dr Santasi seemed interested too. Cherry Ho went next, while Annabel walked at the back with the junior nurse. Cherry had asked Annabel where she had been last night. 'You missed a big ding-dong argument—Malik and Santasi. All during the meal they argue. In the end, they both saw that they could not win—two people with equally stubborn ideas.' She smiled. 'Life is getting interesting. With two doctors at each other's throats, and the other doctor out with the senior Sister—I tell you, the Jacaranth is buzzing this morning!' And before Annabel could defend herself, Cherry had repositioned herself at the front of the procession.

Annabel didn't want her name linked to Gabriel's. It could lead to jealousy among the staff, and suspicion from the other doctors. So that afternoon when Gabriel decided to have a board meeting she refused to take part. 'I'm not a board member—I only work for you. Phyll can take notes. But I ought not to be there.'

Gabriel barked, 'Suit yourself, woman,' in his familiar tones, and she could tell that he was annoyed at her lack of full co-operation. But she treasured her ability to distance herself from them—only ten months to go now, and Celia was already keeping her eyes open for theatre jobs in Singapore. Gabriel called after her, 'We can always co-opt you to the board.'

She said primly, showing her reluctance, 'That's your privilege.'

At that moment Phyll came out of the room. 'Oh, you are there, Sister Browne. There's a telephone call for you.'

Annabel's heart sank. Surely not Amir Pagodi? 'Who is it, Phyll?'

'I think it is Mrs Malik.'

It went very quiet, as though the entire hospital stopped breathing for a moment. Then Annabel realised it was only her own breathing that had stopped. She let out her breath slowly, and said as calmly as she could while her thoughts did somersaults, 'I'll take it in the office.'

She saw that her fingers were shaking as she reached for the receiver, and waited until she had more self-control. She had not dared to look at Gabriel as she left him. But her mind was full of the memory of the two of them holding hands, gazing into one another's faces in full view of the entire staff and guests. 'Hello? Sister Browne here.'

'Annabel, when are you coming to take tea with me?'

'We're very busy. How are you, Sukeina?'

'Fed up.' Perhaps she hadn't seen enough of Gabriel that week. Perhaps she had heard that he and Annabel had gone out together last night, and was ringing to find out what happened.

'Dr Malik must have explained that we're getting new patients all the time now,' said Annabel.

'Yes, he did, of course. But you—your hardest work is over. Once you have arranged the work schedules, you will have much more time, surely?' She was no fool, was Mrs Malik. She knew what Annabel's job was.

'That's true. It's very kind of you to invite me. Perhaps next week. I think I can have Wednesday afternoon off.'

The Malay woman's laugh was high and merry. 'Oh, I know you can. You are as important as the doctors, Annabel, I know you are.'

Annabel tried to explain. 'I can take it off, of course. But if there's any problem, I might have to stay, if you see what I mean.'

'I do, Annabel. But come anyway. I will invite some of my friends to meet you.'

The thought of meeting other bored society housewives wasn't too jolly, but Annabel had no choice, and agreed to go. All the same, she rather hoped there might be an emergency admission, where her skills as Theatre Sister would be needed. Unfortunately, nothing turned up, and the following Wednesday she changed from her uniform into her green silk trouser suit and walked the half mile or so to the Maliks' house.

She paused at the elegant front door. It was open, and she could see the well-decorated hall, and the expensive clock and wall hangings. Then she hesitated. Someone was crying. She took her hand away from the doorbell, but then decided that she didn't intend to stand at the door all afternoon, and gave it a good push. Tinkling chimes brought her hostess to the door, handkerchief in hand, but no sign on the Dresden china face of any distress. Sukeina was wearing a Malay outfit in clinging georgette, her glossy hair tied up in a dashing turban of matching material, the end draped becomingly over her shoulder. She wore drop earrings of several seed pearls, and as always, her eyes were lustrous and her cheeks delicately tinged with pink. Her voice was a little shaky as she said, 'Do come in. I'm so glad to see you.'

Annabel obeyed. Was it really Sukeina who had been weeping? She was still clinging to the lace handkerchief. She remembered that morning on the beach. Sukeina had been tearful then too. Did this lovely and fragile person really have such a serious problem? 'I hope I'm not early.'

Sukeina shook her head. 'I asked you a little before my friends. I hoped we might get to know one another better. The hospital is busy?'

'Very. All three doctors are working now. Just as it ought to be.'

'I wonder—this new lady doctor—she is good-looking?'

Surprised at the question, Annabel said, 'Not bad. Quite handsome, I suppose—slightly overweight. Very pleasant, though—talks a lot.'

Sukeina showed her into a graceful living room with a view down a pretty lawn edged with flowers. Two small white poodles played with a ball, and then sought out the shade of a large jackfruit tree in the corner. Sukeina draped herself on a small sofa. 'Tell me—do you think my husband could possibly be—having an affair?'

The question was so silly that Annabel laughed at once. 'No.'

'My dear, you sound so very sure.'

'They're far too busy . . .' Annabel's voice trailed off. Gabriel too was busy, yet he had found the time to meet Sukeina Malik on more than one occasion. 'Perhaps I don't really know him,' she suggested quietly. 'I'm not terribly observant in matters like that.'

'So it might be possible? I see so little of him these days, you see.' Sukeina touched a corner of an eye with the handkerchief.

Annabel tried to be realistic. 'I can't see Dr Malik doing anything underhand, Sukeina. And certainly not with Asha Santasi—they fight like cat and dog.'

'Perhaps to throw you off the scent?'

Annabel shrugged. 'Is he cold towards you?'

'No—he is even kinder than usual. He brings me flowers and presents. It makes me suspect, you see.'

Annabel said firmly, 'Dr Malik knows very well he has the prettiest wife in Malacca.'

'Then why do we meet only at mealtimes? Perhaps he

would be happier with another medical person who can live with these irregular hours and long lonely evenings.'

Annabel began to understand Sukeina Malik. Intelligent, beautiful—she was simply bored. And as Amir Pagodi had hinted, she filled in her days by chasing men. 'You have your school work, surely?'

Sukeina sighed. 'Yes. But I only work in the mornings, and my preparation takes little time. Come, Annabel, try some angel cake. The baker on the corner makes it freshly every morning.'

Out of politeness, Annabel ate the cake, which tasted like sawdust as she thought of the way Sukeina was chasing Gabriel and catching him up in her fairy-story plots. She was glad when two other teacher friends arrived, and the talk could become less harrowing. As Sukeina saw her to the door, she whispered, 'You will let me know if you suspect anything?'

Annabel nodded, although she felt like a traitor. It wasn't her job to spy on her colleagues. But if Gabriel could meet a woman on the beach, then there was no basic reason why Amal Malik could not—except that she was sure he wouldn't. She walked back to the Jacaranth feeling very unhappy. Sukeina might be genuine—in which case she was sorry for her. Yet she was still married—and it could not be right for a married woman to chase after men, even if she believed Dr Malik unfaithful too.

The ambulance was not in position at the side of the clinic. As Annabel went up to her flat, she heard its siren coming along the road, and ran down to see if help were needed. She almost collided with Dr Malik, who was waiting at the foot of the stairs. He explained, 'It is a patient of mine. She is haemorrhaging.'

A voice behind him said, 'It sounds like a case for me, Malik,' and the shapeless form of Asha Santasi came out of the dining room where she had been taking afternoon tea. Annabel watched the thin Dr Malik, his keen black eyes fixed on the door waiting for his patient, and the plump round-faced Asha—an unlikely

Romeo and Juliet, but Sukeina had made it sound possible. Annabel turned away with a shake of the head. Her job at the Jacaranth was proving more complicated than she had bargained for.

Dr Malik was saying, 'I have done enough cancer surgery . . .'

Asha didn't allow him to finish. 'It is a gynae problem. Why hire me if you want to do them yourself? It is in all probability a fibroid.'

Malik allowed himself to throw Asha a glance. 'You can assist me, then.'

'But you always anaesthetise.'

'Chan can do that.'

Annabel suggested timidly, 'Maybe we ought to discuss cases like this afterwards.' The patient was being wheeled in now, with Ali holding up a saline drip. The two doctors followed her, Asha saying, 'We already settled it this afternoon. Some people forget what has just been agreed.'

Annabel asked, 'Is Cherry on duty?'

'Yes. You won't be needed.'

Annabel turned away, as the party followed the trolley up in the lift. If those two had any affection for each other, then they hid it very well! Annabel knew that Sukeina was manipulating her, in the same way that she did Gabriel, and had tried with Amir Pagodi. But it didn't alter the fact that Gabriel was the one she was currently meeting and using as she wished. Annabel couldn't understand how he could allow himself to be trapped—except perhaps that Sukeina Malik was beautiful, lovely to look at and graceful and charming when she wanted to be.

She went outside into the back garden, looking up at the lighted windows of the operating suite. Again she wished with all her heart that she could just get on the next express bus back to Singapore, where the happy badinage of her friends and the fragrant waters of the Professional Club swimming pool would wash away all these troublesome thoughts. Then she heard a shout and looked back at the hospital.

Gabriel was at his window on the top floor. He called out, 'Don't forget the jellyfish!'

Annabel turned back to the path. Jellyfish indeed! There were times when she found her employer totally infuriating. Then the thunder growled exactly like Gabriel's voice, and she ran down further so that she should not be visible from the hospital. She stayed out on the beach a long time, watching the waves and listening to their roar. Nature was wild, but it was less hassle than humans. Only hunger drove her in, and the delicious smell of Mia's cooking.

Dr Malik had gone home. Gabriel was in the dining room, but he was sitting with the houseman. Annabel sat by Cherry. 'You look tired. Was it a fibroid?'

'Yes. She's OK now—in ward seven. I must agree that Dr Santasi is an excellent surgeon. I think if we can keep her from murdering Dr Malik, things might settle down, just as Dr Christie hoped. He always said Dr Santasi was what we needed.'

'We didn't see it at first. Neither did Dr Malik.'

Cherry smiled. 'Well, Dr Christie is on tonight. And I'm going to bed. Anything urgent, you can have it, Annabel.'

The wind was getting up again. 'I won't sleep anyway. I never do when it's windy. It unsettles me.'

'Well, I hope you have a quiet night.'

'Thanks.'

But within the hour Annabel was scrubbing up alongside Gabriel Christie. He briefed her as she helped him on with his gloves. 'A tree fell on his car. Looks like the spleen that's damaged. I'm surprised this doesn't happen more often on these jungle roads when the wind is as wild as tonight.' The went into the theatre. 'You were communing with nature yourself for a long time.'

She said drily, 'It's less quarrelsome than people.'

'Remember my warning and don't swim.'

'I'm capable of remembering good advice.'

'I'm sure you are.' And suddenly, in the middle of the

preparations, was his amber look, that look of a private shared joke, that always made her feel special.

The junior doctor was giving anaesthetic. 'He is shocked, sir.'

Gabriel nodded. 'Yes. Keep him alive till I get at that spleen, Chan.' He made an incision, while Annabel kept the area free from blood. He checked the liver and pancreas. 'They seem OK. Yes, I'll have to take this out.' His hand encircled the spleen, whose outer covering was seeping blood. 'How's the pressure now, Chan?'

'Low but stable.'

'Keep me briefed.' Gabriel began to cut carefully, pushing the stomach to one side while he sought for and found the splenic artery. 'That tree has given him a hell of a blow. This must have been part of the steering wheel that gave him all the bruises. Poor devil! Still, I've got it now. Scalpel, Annabel. Forceps. Cautery, quick!'

'Pressure's down.'

'Hold on—I've got it now. Have to be a bit brutal here.' He gave the damaged organ a good heave, and laid it in the dish Annabel held, turning back at once to check that nothing else in the area was bleeding.

At last Gabriel was satisfied that the abdomen was now clear of damaged tissue. 'Suture, Annabel.' It was difficult to stitch, as the skin was bruised and torn also by the tree and the ragged ends of the steering wheel. 'He isn't going to be very comfortable when he comes round.' He tied the final stitch. 'Get him to IC right away. Who's on Recovery?'

'I'll stay. I'll be glad of something to do.' Annabel was almost glad to stay up. It stopped her having to go to her own room and staring wide awake, at the ceiling fan.

'I'll stay too.' Chan wanted to keep an eye on the blood pressure, and administer the morphine in measured doses. Between them they watched the patient all night. By seven in the morning she was very tired indeed. But at least the patients had come round, and in spite of the discomfort, was very grateful for the care he had been given.

Gabriel had come in at intervals. Now, as the sun shone through the curtains, he said, 'Bed, woman. I don't want to see you until tomorrow morning.'

'Right.' Annabel couldn't help smiling at Gabriel. His eyes were ringed with black, but he still sounded alert and fresh. He seemed to thrive on crises. His blond Viking locks were tousled round his head, and reminded Annabel again that they and his clear brown eyes were the first thing she had ever noticed about him. He smiled back suddenly. 'We don't work too badly together, do we?'

She brushed off the compliment. 'You work well all the time.' And she managed a bleary smile as she passed him and made her way up to bed. She did indeed sleep all through the day and most of the night, waking at five the following morning. The day was delicious, warm and gentle. The eastern sky was rosy and yellow through the dark palm trees, the shadows from the hospital long over the garden. The sea sparkled like diamonds, and it was too inviting to ignore. Annabel took her towel and putting it over her bathing suit, ran down the outside steps, her skin feeling warm and caressed by the fresh morning air.

It was only after an hour, in which she swam out a little and was tossed back by the waves many times, that she gave in and went to lie down on the vey rock where she had overheard Gabriel and Sukeina. The sun was hot now, and she lay like a sand lizard, warming her whole body, motionless in the kind glare. Malacca wasn't Singapore—but it wasn't a bad place to be, when you had little choice in the matter.

'Good morning.'

She jerked upright, knowing at once that only one man could roar like an angry lion. 'Good morning, Gabriel.'

'You've been swimming.' He definitely was not pleased.

'Very carefully.'

'I've warned you more than once.'

He strolled to the rock, as she lay on top of it on her stomach. Their eyes were on a level, and Annabel was suddenly annoyed at his constantly treating her like a child, while still expecting her to be his equal in the hospital. 'Please let me make my own decisions occasionally. You brought me out here. You might at least leave me alone.'

'To get poisoned? Why? I have a responsibility——'

Stung, she said, 'Go and look after Sukeina, then. She doesn't mind.'

His eyes blazed. She waited for an angry retort, but his voice was very quiet. 'What sort of answer is that, Annabel?' His body was stiff, his fists clenched and his jaw was tight.

Annabel said briefly, 'I'm sorry, your private life is none of my business.' She caught her towel, and slid quickly down, turning to go towards the hospital.

Gabriel's long strides prevented her, and she stopped again. He said, 'You were accusing me of being involved with another man's wife. I want to know why you said that. It isn't the sort of thing you dreamed up. Did she say anything when you were there? If so, it was a lie.'

Annabel looked down at her own bare feet in the sand. She hated being told off like a schoolgirl, but on the other hand she couldn't let him get away with what was almost a downright lie. 'I saw you, Gabriel. I saw you both walking on this very beach, and you were definitely not walking as casual acquaintances. You'd arranged to meet. Can you deny it?' He started to reply, but she said, 'I'd rather not talk about it. All I want to say is that while I'm here, I want you to stop telling me what to do unless it's Jacaranth business. I have nine months and three weeks left here. Let's get it over without quarrelling any more.'

He said, still standing solidly in her way, 'You aren't jealous, by any chance? I don't deny I met Sukeina. She phoned and said she had something to tell me. Why does it make you so angry?'

'I'm not jealous and I'm not angry. I just want to be left alone.'

The waves crashed and ebbed and crashed again. Gabriel said, still very quietly, 'And to think I only came out to wish you good morning!'

Annabel said, in a small voice as her anger faded, 'I've offended you now. Do you want me to leave? The hospital can do without me now.'

'For heaven's sake, woman—first you insult me and now you want to leave me in the lurch, just when I need you more than ever! How selfish can you get?'

'Me selfish? How dare you——'

'Don't look for another job. You owe me nine months and three weeks.' And he turned and walked rapidly into the clinic. She waited until he had disappeared inside. Her anger had gone as quickly as it had arrived, and she now stared after him. 'Don't look for another job.' Was he really begging her to stay? She knew they worked well in theatre, but she wasn't irreplaceable, as Cherry had told her several times. She began to walk slowly up the garden, and round to the outside staircase. Would she ever know this man? Unaccountably, as she climbed the stairs to her own front door, tears stung her eyelids. She shoved open the door—only to find Gabriel standing inside. The sight of her tears made him draw in his breath. He caught her for a moment and held her very tightly, while she managed to control her sobs before they took hold of her.

'We've been through a lot,' he said gently. 'You've been invaluable to me, Annabel. Let's just try and carry on. I think you need a few days off. I didn't realise just how much time you've put in. This morning didn't happen, all right?'

'Right.' Her voice was a whisper, and she was glad he left her then. He was trying to be nice. She showered and changed into uniform. She didn't need a holiday yet—but she would ring Celia, and go and spend some time in Singapore as soon as Celia could have a few days off. She ran downstairs after a light breakfast, and tried to pretend that nothing had happened.

Asha was seeing her first patients. Afterwards she went to Annabel's office. 'I think I ought to keep some contraceptives here, my dear. Could you arrange it?'

'Of course. Can you give me a proper list?'

Asha said sharply. 'No need to get Dr Malik to authorise it either. I'm a partner, and what I need I get!'

'Yes, Doctor.' Annabel kept out of the private quarrel. What rot, to think these two could ever be in love. Sukeina was indeed a bit of a witch at getting people to believe her. She took the list from Asha, and said, 'You'll be doing sterilisations?'

'I am ready if I am asked, but only in the husband and wife are both in favour. Vasectomies, no. I can only advise them to have it done elsewhere.' The two women talked for a while before Annabel telephoned the suppliers for Asha's requirements. Then she checked the rest of the stock, and realised that they would need more dressings too, and another stock of office stationery. Wryly, she picked up the phone and dialled Amir Pagodi's number, unsure how he would react. But he was bright and charming. She had forgotten how pleasant was his light tenor voice.

'Good to hear from you, Annabel.'

'Another order, Amir.'

Immediately he said, 'How fortunate—I was coming in your direction anyway.' So he had not given up his pursuit of her. She wondered if perhaps she was flattered. But no—even though he wasn't married, no one else knew that, and would think Annabel cheap if she allowed herself to be drawn into a deeper relationship. So she thanked him, and at once made arrangements for Phyll to receive the goods, while she herself went off to help Asha in the ward.

'This poor lady came in while you were busy this morning.' They had stopped by a bed where a young women, her long hair tangled around her head, lay sleeping, her eyes very red. 'Her baby died this morning—cot death. I'm afraid there is so little we can do to console her.'

They stood for a while, Annabel trying to think how she would feel if her only child died at a few weeks old. Later Asha said, 'Half the women I see want babies and can't have them, while the other half have too many. Life is strange, Annabel. When you get married——'

Annabel interrupted, 'Married? Me? No, you haven't heard. My ambition is to be rich and success-ful.'

Asha walked with her to the end of the ward. She said quietly, 'My dear girl, think twice before you say that.' She was quiet for a moment, busy with her own thoughts. Then she said, 'I wasn't a pretty child—which meant I wasn't a good catch for any mother organising an arranged marriage. None of the boys wanted me—yet as soon as I graduated, there were offers to my parents for my hand.'

'You refused them?'

Asha said, her lips hard, 'I wasn't going to marry someone who didn't want me for myself. So now—I am rich and successful. But who knows? Perhaps things might have been very different . . .'

Annabel went back to her office, where Amir Pagodi had left a note—'I have found some small tables and trifles you might like for your parents.' She toyed with the paper, yet she delayed phoning him. She decided to leave it for the day.

Just then the telephone shrilled, and she picked it up. 'Sister Browne.'

The voice at the other end of the line was very English. 'Well, well, young Annie! Remember me? Tony Holland?'

'Tony? Where are you?' A whole world of forgotten memories flooded back.

'I'm in Kuala Lumpur, working out here for a few months. When can we get together, old thing? Make it soon.'

CHAPTER EIGHT

ANNABEL got ready for her first meeting with Tony Holland with special care. It was not that she was delighted to be meeting an old flame. In fact, she had some embarrassing memories of him during their amateur dramatics days in Cheltenham, when she had had a teenage crush on him because he was so much older than her, and at a public school. She was fascinated by his accent, and thrilled when he asked her out. But she soon found that there wasn't a personality to go with the accent, and by the time she left the Board Walkers, he had finished at Cambridge and was working in the City. Which sounded good, but to Annabel, knowing Tony, it was probably very boring.

And now Tony was in Malaysia, and sounding lonely. Annabel hadn't told anyone except Celia, by telephone, about Tony's arrival. Since her last rather emotional meeting with Gabriel, they had been on good but entirely unemotional terms. And as she worked away in her office day by day, assisting in theatre at Gabriel's operations, she soon recognised the simple fact that she had no real friends at the Jacaranth. So when she was going to meet Tony, there was really no one who was interested.

He had not told her what car he drove, so she was uncertain what to look for—because she didn't want him walking in and asking for her. She stood at the front upstairs window, hoping to be first to spot him. But when he came, there could have been no other—a scarlet Citroën estate car — a vehicle that would have taken two families and their camping equipment. Trust Tony to make himself bigger by outward show! Smiling, she ran down the stairs, hoping to get to the drive before he actually made it to the hospital.

He had once been what they call well made—meaning that he played his full part in the rugby forwards. But middle age had set in, with resulting loss of waistline and hair. All the same, as he stepped out of the car, he looked every inch a gentleman, and his blue eyes under pale brows still had a youthful vitality and interest in his surroundings.

Annabel was wearing a simple flowery summer dress with short sleeves and a low back. She wore her hair piled on top of her head, but loosely, rather than the tight bun she used for theatre. It was far too hot to have hair around one's neck. She didn't bother with make-up, as her dark brows and lashes needed nothing against her tan, but she did go to the trouble of putting in a pair of pretty silver filigree earrings. And from the expression in Tony's eyes, it was a total success. 'Annie, you're looking gorgeous!' was the first comment. Then he took her by both hands and kissed her cheek very positively. 'How long have we got?'

'I don't have to be back today.'

'How super. Then I can show you the estate where I'm working——'

'What as?'

'Accountant, sweetie. One of these bigwig planters who can't be bothered to do his own sums. Not far, actually. We can lunch there, and then dinner at my club in KL. How does that sound?'

'Fine.' It would be different. She looked at him, trying to think of something complimentary to say. 'You do look successful,' was the best she could do.

They made small talk as he drove into the hills, the roads winding round the very villages that Amir Pagodi had taken her to. But with Tony, they skimmed through the villages and ignored the people, as he waved his hand at the palm oil and rubber estates, seeing them only as units of profit. It was fairly clear that he had not had much time for marriage. Unless he had no success with girls. Yet materially he was well off. Annabel was surprised that no one had snapped him up.

The planter himself was absent from his mini-palace in the hills, but the butler made them welcome, on a terrace overlooking the sea of palm trees, and brought them Martinis, followed by smoked salmon, roast duckling and bombe surprise. Over liqueurs, served in large glasses over crushed ice, they reminisced. Then Tony said suddenly, 'And now, Annabel—secrets time. Who's the man who's been so fascinating as to keep you from visiting your parents all this time? They asked me to find out.'

Annabel looked at him in amazement. 'They didn't! They wouldn't.' But as she looked again into those familiar blue eyes, she began to see that her parents might well have encouraged Tony, thinking that marriage to him might be quite a good idea. She collected herself, and gave him a superior smile. 'There's no man—but I'm totally committed to the idea of being rich and successful.'

Tony blotted his copybook for ever when he gave a hearty laugh. 'You? My dear, leave that sort of thing to the men.'

Nettled, she said, 'In fact, I already have a business partner in mind. I'm seeing him—tonight——' she did some quick calculations. She could still telephone Amir Pagodi after she got home tonight. 'I can't see Daddy complaining about that—fellow can get me antiques at a fair price. All I have to do is act as the Malaysian agent, and ship them home.'

'Honestly?'

'Cross my heart.'

'Any chance of getting in on this?'

Annabel laughed. 'I thought you were rich and successful already.'

'One can never be too rich.'

'I know—because you pay it all back in taxes,' she laughed. 'When are you going home?'

'Christmas, for two weeks.'

'Then you'll be able to tell them. Maybe take a couple of small things with you?'

By the end of the day, Tony was convinced of Annabel's business prowess. They drove to the capital for dinner at the Selangor Club. It was one of the most famous of all colonial landmarks, and Annabel thoroughly enjoyed the experience of drinking sundowners overlooking the old *padang* where cricket was still played. But she refused brandy, with the excuse that she had a business meeting.

It was ten by the time they returned along the main highway from Kuala Lumpur to Malacca. The moon was bright, almost full, low over the rolling Straits. Lightning flickered in the clouds. And as Annabel turned to thank Tony for a lovely day, he caught her in his arms without warning, and kissed her hard. 'You don't get rid of me so easily, sweetie.'

Breathless, she said, 'I wasn't trying to get rid of you, Tony.'

'Then may I come in for a nightcap?'

'I told you—I have a meeting.'

'But I don't believe you.'

Her eyes sparked fire. 'Don't you? Too bad.' And she wrested herself from his embrace and ran round the side of the building to the back door, which she knew Percival would not have locked if he was still in the back. It was open, she went quickly in and turned the key behind her. Then she went to the phone in her office. The patients were settled for the night, with only the dim corridor lights on. No one was about. Annabel picked up her phone and dialled Amir Pagodi's office. At first there was no answer, but then an answering machine gave a second number, in Malacca. A woman answered, but Amir was there.

'Annabel? Anything wrong?'

'I just wanted to fix a date for seeing the merchandise. I take it you're busy tonight?'

'No. I'll be round.'

Her heart was beating rapidly, as she hoped he would not think she had called him out of affection. She said briefly, 'Over the phone will do.'

'I think we'd better talk.'

'All right—round the back. I'll wait in the garden.'

She went back to the garden, unlocking the door silently. There was no sign of Tony. She waited another ten minutes, then slipped out and sat at one of the wooden tables. Within minutes she heard Amir's smooth limousine draw up, and he was soon opposite her in the moonlight. She said, 'Thanks for coming, Amir, but there was no need. We could have arranged a meeting.'

She saw his dimples in the moonlight. 'Believe me, I was overjoyed to get away.' He saw her eyebrows rose and said, 'Yes, a lady friend, but a very self-centred one. I wanted to get away without hurting her feelings.' He produced a list. 'Now, here are some items—I have priced them for you. If you want them all, fine. If only some, ring me tomorrow. I'll have them ready at the house.'

'The house?' She was unsure. 'Not the office?'

She saw him grin again. 'OK—it will be more hassle, but I'll get the van. Call me tomorrow. The prices, by the way, are rock bottom. No haggling. Take it or leave it.'

They shook hands. Amir paused, but Annabel said no more, feeling rather out of her depth, to have got into business so quickly with no experience except working in her father's shop. Amir left, and she went indoors, fingering the paper. Was this her first step to wealth? Or all a silly mistake? Only time would tell.

The following morning she was tired. She wasn't used to long days outside the safe environs of her hospital. But somehow her confidence had grown, and she felt ten feet tall as she coped with her day-to-day clinic correspondence. The staff would come in and chat. Dr Malik even popped his head in to congratulate her on working out the duty lists so well. 'You do not miss nursing? You make an excellent administrator.'

'I do. I'd like some extra sessions in theatre if nobody minds.'

'Bring it up at the next board meeting. Oh—you won't be there.'

Annabel smiled. 'I might reconsider sitting in.'

'Fine. I think you ought.' He leaned over the desk. 'You can draw up the schedules if you like—I'll definitely back you in advance.'

He was in a good mood. Annabel thought it was time to tackle him over neglecting his wife. 'Dr Malik—you do know that you're doing more night sessions than anyone else?'

'Of course.'

'May I reschedule so that everyone does equal? I feel sorry for your wife.'

Dr Malik looked at her with raised eyebrows. 'One does not feel sorry for wives after fifteen years of marriage—they are glad to have their husbands out of the way. You'll find out.'

Annabel said stoutly, 'I'd never want to be left to my own devices three times a week. That's too much.'

'The schedules are fine. Don't interfere.' His good mood had gone. Annabel went back to her desk, suitable chastised. Clearly there was little love left in the Malik household.

There were no operations for that afternoon. Annabel drew up the following month's paperwork, and walked along towards Gabriel's office. She was slightly apprehensive about meeting him face to face, after so many weeks of distant politeness. She tapped on the door and looked in. He was on the telephone, but beckoned her in.

'Sit down, please.' How very formal! He returned to his phone conversation. 'I'll do my best. What more can I do?'

Annabel heard the woman's voice quite clearly—it was bell-like and beautiful. 'Please make it very soon, darling. I can't bear it!'

'Don't worry. I give my word.' And he hung up, his eyes unreadable under his brows. But then, as though challenging Annabel to mention Sukeina's name,

Gabriel swung round and faced her across the desk, his chin on both hands. 'Now, what can I do for you? Next month's agenda? Right, let's see.' he drew the sheets of paper towards him. His voice was gruff as he said, not looking at her, 'You seem to have been hiding from me.'

'No, sir. I've been busy running your hospital.'

'I'm not complaining.' A neutral reply. A lock of hair fell across his eyes, and he said, 'You haven't reminded me to have a haircut. That seemed to be one of your duties once.'

She looked down and said in a low voice, 'I'll make a note of it.' The sight of his hair reminded her of their earlier meetings, when they seemed to be close, when his wild looks matched her feelings in the wild beaches and the storms . . . How fortunate that she no longer reacted to her surroundings in the same naïve way . . . Then she added, 'I wonder if you agree that the doctors ought to take equal night duties.'

'Of course. You know that in the beginning I said equal shares and equal responsibilities.' He put the paper away from him suddenly. His tone changed. 'You know, Annabel, I don't think I was cut out to be an accountant.'

'But we're beginning to do well—very well in the past three weeks. Now that there isn't so much equipment to buy, we're showing a profit.'

He looked her in the eye. 'You know what we started with. What I didn't tell you was that only half of it came from the bank. The rest came from a private loan—and instead of having the money back, this person wants a seat on the board.'

'And don't you want him?'

'Her. No.'

Annabel didn't answer. There was nothing she could do to help. But form his expression, she guessed that Mrs Malik wanted to be on the board alongside her husband—and her lover. Annabel could do nothing—except offer to be there too. 'I thought I'd sit in at the next meeting.'

'Really?' And for the first time that afternoon, Gabriel's amber eyes showed their usual clear confidence. 'I'm glad, Annabel. I think it will help.' If he loved Sukeina, he clearly didn't mind Annabel seeing it. But she was not going to keep either of them if she behaved so childishly. He sat up straight. 'I'll have a look at these and get back to you later this afternoon.' He swivelled his chair again, and said, 'Annabel, I think you're seeing too much of Pagodi. People notice these things. Your good name ought to matter to you.'

She snapped back immediately, 'You mean it's fine for me to see him on hospital business—but not on business of my own?'

His voice was deep and low. 'When you go on hospital business you wear uniform. When you see him alone, you wear attractive clothes, and you wear your hair loose.'

She didn't answer straight away. Gabriel must have been watching her. That alone was irritating. Amir was a friend—he had made no more advances. She said in a calm but cold voice, 'Do I keep watch on you and tell you when you are improperly dressed?'

'I don't dress improperly.'

'That's a matter of opinion.'

For the first time his eyebrows relaxed, and a hint of a smile showed in his eyes—a reminder of the man she had once started getting to know. 'Then you must tell me. I want to know if I haven't polished my shoes, or worn a tie.' He leaned back in his chair and gazed out of the window, fingers together, then he swung round and looked at her. 'No, perhaps you're right—I'm a rotten old chauvinist. Forgive me.'

Annabel was taken aback by his sudden admission. It disarmed her, and she felt a rush of tenderness that was totally unexpected. And he was staring at her, and recognised her sudden lack of all defences. She saw it in his face. She waited for some other quip at her expense, but none came. Hesitantly she stood up. 'There's nothing else, then?'

'Not really.' As she got to the door he said, 'I don't mean to spy on you, you know. I'm just here most of the time, that's all. After all, you didn't mean to spy on me—but we both happened to walk past the same rock.'

Annabel almost ran out of the room. Embarrassment, anger and that small knot of tenderness vied in her heart. She went straight to her room. How she wished she were back at the Mount Olivia! Dear Professor Singh had never been so exasperating. All this couldn't be good for her blood pressure—this verbal sparring, at once gentle, sharp and downright rude. She put her finger on her pulse and looked at her watch to check her heart rate. There ought to be a health warning on Gabriel Christie—beware, this man is bad for your health.

'Annabel?'

She looked up. Gabriel had entered without knocking, and was watching her time her pulse. 'Getting hypochondria?'

She faced him, her face pink. 'You ought to have knocked.' She marched to the door, brushing past him. His hands came out and caught her shoulders, and for a moment she drew in a breath sharply. She had forgotten how safe and comfortable and right she felt when she was so close to him. But he shouldn't have done it just then—not when she was mad. She said in a bitter whisper, 'Save all this for your fancy woman!'

His fingers tightened, hurting her. She sensed the warmth of the full length of his body parallel with hers. He said, 'That wasn't fair.'

'It seems to me that not much is fair around here any more.'

'Is Mr Pagodi? Or the fat gentleman in the Citroën?'

Annabel struggled to free herself then, wanting only to be very far away from the Jacaranth. But instead of letting her go, Gabriel bent down and found her lips. She shook him off, but he sought them again, and this time she had no strength of will to pull away. She felt his warm breath on her cheek, and the softness of his mouth, gentle, now that she wasn't fighting him. His arms tightened around her, and she had no will to stop herself from holding him closer, so close that for a moment they stood as one person, locked together as though nothing else mattered in the whole world.

And then he released her gently, looked into her eyes for a moment, and was gone. She held on to the doorframe for a moment, then turned back to her desk like a robot. She sat down. All acrimonious thoughts had gone, all memories of Sukeina Malik had vanished. She touched her mouth, as though somehow it might feel different. She had been kissed before, but as she sat there, the afternoon sun vivid against the office walls, she knew that this was the first.

There was a tap at the door and Mia came in with a cup of Chinese tea. 'Dr Christie said you wanted it.'

'Thanks, Mia.' Bother him—wasn't it bad enough to have a chief like a grizzly bear, without him wanting a kiss and a cuddle that felt as though he was trying to hug her to death? Annabel's heart still beat fast. She might have liked him—except that his personality was too powerful for her. Anyone who had a relationship with Gabriel would find themselves swallowed up—just as she had been in that kiss—the first and very definitely the last. She had vowed in Amir Pagodi's house not to allow this to happen to her. She renewed her vows as she sipped the welcome tea. No man unless she herself could control him.

The phone rang, and she looked at it, hoping that nothing more was going to hurt her that day. 'Hello? Sister Browne.'

'Hi, Annabel!'

'Celia, how wonderful! I'm so desperately glad to hear you.'

'Is something wrong?' asked Celia.

'Not wrong exactly—no, nothing's wrong. When are you coming to see me?'

'I've some free time next week. Why don't you come

here?'

'I've never heard anything more beautiful said in my whole life!'

Later that afternoon the papers from Gabriel were returned to Annabel's desk, though she didn't see him. She picked them up, noting his scribbled remarks. And she thought again about his confidences over Sukeina. She had lent him money and now wanted it to buy her a stake in the Jacaranth. Surely, if he loved the woman, he wouldn't mind that—unless, of course, he wanted the affair kept quiet. Having her around could be embarrassing for him. Annabel smiled. In a way Gabriel had been niïve to allow Annabel to know so much. It must mean he trusted her completely, though—which was nice.

Tony Holland called her again at the weekend, and she was able to tell him quite truthfully that she was going to Singapore for a short break. She didn't tell Gabriel where she was going—only that she would take four days off. He had nodded gravely, and agreed that it was time she got away from the hospital. 'Have a nice time,' he said.

'Thank you.' She turned at the door. 'I might come back!' she attempted a joke.

Gabriel looked up, solid, sure of himself at that moment. 'You owe me nine months, two weeks and four days.' And he smiled broadly at her astonished look. So they parted on good terms. And as the grey bus sped along the road towards Johore Bahru and across the Causeway to dear old Woodlands Road, Annabel was able to smile to herself. She hadn't known what sort of creature Gabriel Christie was when she drove the opposite way to her new job. Now she knew—there couldn't be anyone else in the world as intelligent, as skilful, as kind—and as utterly exasperating.

She alighted from the bus near the mosque not far from the hospital. Celia would still be working. Annabel walked along the street, filled with a strange elation to be back in her beloved city. It was even busier than she remembered it. She was jostled and pushed by people all in a hurry, hooted at and almost run down by long Cadillacs and Mercedes and BMWs. The smells were there, the brilliance of the clothes, the sophistication of the people.

She paused at the imposing entrance to the Mount Olivia. No, she didn't want to go in. She would wait till Celia came out. Just then a dapper figure came out, running down the steps like a young man. 'Well, how are you, Annabel?'

'Professor Singh, how lovely to see you!'

He shook her hand warmly. 'I have an urgent case, my dear. But do tell me how you like Malacca—and my old friend Gabriel.'

'It's—fine, Professor.' Why bother to complain? 'The hospital is off the ground, and we find we're quite popular already.'

'I'd be happy to come along and do any orthopaedic work for him some time. You like Christie, then?'

For a moment the traffic roared by and the city rolled on while Annabel looked into the wise eyes of her old chief. She knew she couldn't fool him. 'Yes, I do,' she said simply. 'But he had no right to make you fire me. He should have asked me fair and square to join him.'

The Professor looked at his watch. 'Good luck, my dear. Give him my kindest regards.'

He had driven off in his limousine before she had collected her thoughts. Why had he made no answer to her comment? She would dearly love to question him, but one did not chase after eminent medical men in the street. Just then there was a gentle tug at her sleeve, and she turned, expecting to see Celia. Instead, Tony Holland stood there, the typical expatriate in his tropical trousers and bush shirt. 'Tony!' Annabel exclaimed.

'Hope you don't mind, old thing. Had some time free—thought it might be fun to see Singapore with you. Followed the bus, parked on a yellow line, and here I am.'

Annabel stared at him. 'I suppose we'd better sit ᴅown and have a cold drink.'

'You don't sound overjoyed.' They walked to a small pavement café. 'Wrong man? Meeting someone?'

'No, Tony, nothing like that. I'm meeting my best girl friend—and to be honest, our tongues can't wag when there's someone else around, that's all.' They sipped tall glasses of cream soda and ice cream.

'OK—I'll check in somewhere. Maybe I could take you both out for a meal?'

Her heart went out to him. After all, they had been friends, and she was sure he would be generous to anyone from home in the same position. 'I'm staying at my club. If there's room, you can stay there—it's very reasonable compared with hotel prices.'

'OK, it's a deal. In return, I'll make myself scarce when you want to gossip.'

So it turned out that the party at the Professional Club that night was four instead of just Annabel and Celia. Martin had come along as well, and when Celia showed her sparkling diamond, there was no reason at all for not having an impromptu engagement party. Tony fitted in happily, grateful to have the chance of seeing Singapore through the eyes of its residents. Afterwards, the men went swimming, while Celia talked about the wedding, and about what Annabel was to wear as chief bridesmaid. It was getting on for midnight when Celia said, 'And what about Malacca, Anna? I forgot—you sounded upset on the phone, *lah*. What happened?'

There was so much that had happened in the few weeks since they had parted. Yet Annabel couldn't put it into words coherently. 'Yes, Gabriel is a good boss. The work has been very successful. The hospital is already showing a profit, and it's great living so close to the beach.'

'So where's the problem?'

'There isn't one.'

Tony came up to ask if anyone wanted a nightcap. As he and Martin went to bring them, Celia asked, 'Tony is close friend?'

'No. I told you about him once, remember? We used to do amateur dramatics together. But he's a nice chap. Nothing between us, though, and I intend it to stay that way.'

After Celia and Martin had left, Annabel and Tony sat outside until the early hours, chatting about old friends, whose names Annabel had forgotten until now. Tony said, 'Time to turn in?'

'Right.' She had booked a room for Tony as her guest, suggesting one at the other side of the building. But the clerk had obviously thought that rather unfriendly, and had put them side by side. Annabel paused at her door. 'Goodnight. I'll show you the sights in the morning—but not too early, please.'

Tony paused, but it was quite clear that Annabel was sleeping alone. He said ruefully, 'I can't work out if it's Pagodi or Dr Christie.'

'What does that mean?'

'This man you're in love with.'

Annabel knew he wanted her to be riled into a reply, but she simply said sweetly, 'His name is Success. Sweet dreams, Tony.'

'There's a verandah outside our rooms. Maybe we could do the balcony scene?'

'My acting days are over.' She closed the door with a smile. It had been a good evening, and tomorrow she would enjoy seeing all the old places with Tony. She was glad he had come. Then she realised with a little twinge that perhaps Singapore wasn't quite the paradise she had once thought. Noisier, ruder, more pushy, full of hard-nosed people intent on amassing money . . .

But she wanted to come back. How very much she

wanted to come back and make a career here, where all
was excitement and fun, where one never need wander
on a beach for the sake of something to do . . .

CHAPTER NINE

ANNABEL tried not to admit to herself that she was glad to get back to Malacca, but when she awoke the morning after her return, she listened to the waves as though to some magically refreshing music. She was up at once, showered and dressed and at her desk before the hall clock struck. She dealt with the papers that had piled up, made some telephone calls, and noted with a smile that her name was on the list of those to be present at the next board meeting at the end of the week.

Then came the phone call she didn't want. 'Sukeina here. Annabel, I have started a small group of ladies who wish to hold events in aid of your hospital. They will be coming to tea later in the week, and I want you to come and speak to us. They are sure to want to ask questions.'

Annabel felt annoyed and suspicious. The Jacaranth was not in need of funds. The receipts were adequate, in spite of Gabriel's tendency to charge people more modest fees than those on the price list. There was no doubt in Annabel's mind that Sukeina was yet again trying to muscle in on the hospital, not content with pursuing poor Gabriel. Yet Gabriel could take care of himself. Surely he would not allow himself to be used— even by a very lovely women.

The day lost its splendour. Irritation set in again, the annoyance of living in a small community that had no one else to think about but itself. Annabel made a noncommittal reply, and banged the phone down as she turned to see who was knocking at the door.

It was Gabriel, in his white coat, looking very concerned. 'Annabel—Mrs Madan. Please would you speak to her? She's been in for two days, and I don't know what else we can for her.' He went away quickly, visibly upset. Annabel went to the ward at once. She was shown the little Indian woman who had been due to have an operation first thing in the morning. She was leaning back against her pillows, her face drawn, her cheeks sunken.

Annabel sat quietly beside her. 'Is there something you want to tell me?'

The big eyes widened in their dark rings. 'Has Dr Christie sent you?' There was an expression of dull resignation in those eyes. 'There is no hope. He said he will operate—he told me so two months ago when he first found this lump in my side. But it has been there too long.'

'Are you in pain?' There was no point in pretending; the patient herself had decided that her life was almost over. 'Can I get you anything?'

The patient shook her head, as though the very movement was an effort. 'I have told Dr Christie that is was not his fault.'

Annabel nodded, knowing now why Gabriel looked so sad. 'Illness isn't choosy. It's no one's fault.'

'Yes, Sister, it is my fault. It is Karma. There is nothing anyone can do. In a previous life, I must have sinned grievously.'

Annabel stared down in pity. 'My dear, if you have something the doctor can cure, you must allow it to happen.'

'I must endure what Karma decrees.' The woman's face was saintly.

'Mrs Madan, you're not being fair. Dr Christie's Karma decrees that he must save you. Can you deny him this right?'

'My religion tells me that my illness is my fault.'

'I respect that.'

'I pray every morning for one hour, and every evening for thirty minutes.'

Annabel put out her hand over the woman's thin wrist. 'Then how can you think that you deserve to be ill?'

'In this life I have been faithful. Perhaps I will be rewarded in the next reincarnation. Perhaps I should seek it as soon as I can.' The prolonged conversation had exhausted her, and Annabel realised there was little point in going on. She patted the wasted hand. Mrs Madan had closed her eyes, but she opened them to say, 'I do not wish Dr Christie to be sad. He is so kind to me and my family over many years.'

Annabel attempted a smile. 'Rest now, my dear. I'll come and talk later, when you've eaten.'

'You have started me to think, Sister. Perhaps it is wrong for me to stay here when I do not permit operation?'

Annabel looked down at her, tears biting at the back of her eyes. The wind sang softly outside the walls, and the waves lashed the shore with gentle regularity. 'Listen to the waves on the shore. Listen to the seabirds calling. They make no conditions in their lives. They accept what they have to do. They live and die with no problems and doubts. Listen to nature, dear, and relax. The right message will come to you.' Annabel was whispering now, and the patient closed her eyes, and soon her breast rose and fell rhythmically. Annabel sat with her, still holding her hand, wondering why her own heart was sad when there were people who were so unfortunate in life. Then she went away silently, her thoughts grieving for a woman whose scruples were such that she didn't believe she was worth saving.

She returned to her accounts and her schedules, but somehow she couldn't get back to work. She called Phyll to take over the routine work. Mrs Madan, with her quiet dignity, wouldn't leave her thoughts. What must it be like to believe that one was worthy of nothing but pain and death? It was too much to comprehend.

There was a sudden bang on her door, and a pale anxious Malay woman came in, tears in her eyes. 'This is doctor, *lah*?'

'No, my dear. Did you just walk in? I'll take you to the waiting room. Which doctor would you like?'

The woman hesitated. She was heavily pregnant. 'I see doctor soon?'

'Your pregnancy—is there a problem? Would you like me to see you? I'm a midwife.'

'Yes.' The voice was nothing but a whisper. And then the woman slipped heavily to the floor, her face pallid and her eyes tightly closed. She was sweating, and her limbs were jerking out of control. Annabel called at once for a trolley. 'Ali, is Dr Santasi in the hospital?'

'She went shopping, Sister. She say she will not be long.'

Annabel swore quietly. 'Call any doctor, then—the sooner the better. Tell them it's eclampsia.' The trolley came, and the nurse helped her lift the woman up and place her on her side, her neck stretched to ensure a clear airway. 'How on earth she reached this stage——' Annabel soothed her gently, and wrapped the cuff round her arm. The blood pressure was sky-high. Annabel looked up wildly. 'Where's the doctor? Please hurry!' She checked the woman's legs. Yes, they were swollen in the typical pattern. There was nothing she could do herself except check the unborn child. It was fortunate that Asha Santasi had demanded the correct instruments even before she began practising. Annabel found the trumpet to place on the distended abdomen. For a moment she couldn't hear the child's heartbeat, then faintly it came through, regular so far.

She knew from her former training what drugs would be needed, and went to bring the phials. She set up the drip, ready for the doctor to insert the drugs: saline, Hydrallazine and Diazepam. Where was everyone? Annabel took the pulse again, and listened again to the child, lying in such great danger. She knew very well that delivery of the child would cure the woman's condition, but if the child wasn't ready to be born, it could be a long process. Another look along the corridor showed no sign of a doctor. Annabel went back to the stock cupboard and brought out a prostaglandin pessary. That might hurry up labour—though she dared not insert it herself.

The woman's breathing was harsh. Annabel sat by her for a moment. 'Hold on, my dear. We'll look after you.'

Just then Gabriel appeared, his long strides making his white coat fly out behind him like a cloak. 'No sign of Asha?' He was already putting on a glove. 'No time to take a history. The baby isn't ready. I'll have to rupture the membrane. But the head isn't engaged. Have you a——?' Annabel handed him the pessary. 'Great! OK, here goes.' He stood up. 'Stay with her. Call me at once if there's any change in the foetal heart.'

'She hasn't passed water.'

'Don't force her.' Gabriel looked down at the distressed woman. 'The diagnosis isn't in doubt, but if there's the slightest worry about the baby, prep her for Caesar. And please God bring Santasi back before I have to do it.' He hurried back to the ward, where, the nurse whispered he had been busy counselling a woman who was threatening suicide.

Staring after him, Annabel saw him go back to Mrs Madan's bedside. Her admiration for him grew. He would never give up on anyone, even if they seemed to have given up on themselves.

Annabel's eyes were drooping. It was after eight in the evening, and she had not moved from the patient's side. There was a tap on her shoulder, and Gabriel was standing there. 'Go and eat—I can't have you passing out on me.'

'Has Dr Santasi come back?'

'Not yet, but we've located her by phone. I'm putting up an oxytocin drip. Go and eat, Annabel. If this doesn't start labour, you may have to go to theatre with her, and I don't want you passing out.'

She leaned over and felt the woman's forehead. It was clammy. 'I think——'

'Then stop thinking and do as I say.'

'Yes, Doctor.' As she passed him, he put a hand on her shoulder. It was a simple gesture, but it said a lot.

She turned and said, 'You won't be very angry with Asha, will you?'

Gabriel's handsome face relaxed for a moment at her concern. He said, 'I'll say what needs to be said.'

She nodded, and went off to the dining room. She didn't feel hungry, but she knew Gabriel was right, and that she must eat something. When she returned, it was to hear the woman crying out, and for once, her screams were a good sign—they meant that labour was established. And to her relief, the white-gowned figure of Asha Santasi stood at the side of the bed, her capable manner making up for her former absence. Annabel took her place beside her without need for words. Asha said, 'I think it will be a normal delivery. But this is her first, it may go on a long time.'

'Epidural?'

'We'll see. It's all right, my dear,' Annabel said to the patient. 'You're doing very well.'

The patient was not the quiet type. She screamed and shouted and called for her husband. But Asha wasn't ruffled, soothing her, cajoling her, and finally providing her with just enough painkilling injection not to harm the new life within her. And in a rather noisy three hours, an equally noisy, purple little boy was born. Asha was laughing with delight. 'Just look, Annabel—six weeks premature, and with lungs like that! He'll be all right. I'm sure of it!' She wrapped the child in a blanket after examining him, and laid him in his mother's arms. She was smiling happily, happily, not even noticing as the nurses checked her carefully, and found that she was rapidly getting back to normal.

It had been a traumatic day. Annabel was going to bed when she saw Mrs Madan beckoning her. Stifling a yawn, she went to her bedside and explained what had happened. 'It is a blessing.'

Annabel shrugged. 'That's what we're here for.'

On her way through the hall, she heard voices—Gabriel and Asha! Hoping to avoid fireworks, Annabel decided to take the other stairs. But she couldn't help overhearing Asha saying, 'I want to apologise . . .'

At the same moment Gabriel said, 'I'm sorry . . .'

They both smiled. It was clear that the successful outcome had mellowed them both. Asha said, 'I will make sure you can always get hold of me when I am away from the hospital.'

'Thank you. I'm sorry I was so abrupt.'

'I understand. You have high standards.' Annabel smiled to herself and slipped up to her room, well satisfied with her day.

The sound of the breakers woke her next morning. She found herself listening with pleasure, feeling sorry for people who only woke up to the noise of the rush-hour traffic. She went down to her room promptly at nine, only to find a note from the night nurse—'Mrs Madan wants a word.' She went straight to the ward. The little wasted figure was on her mind.

Mrs Madan reached out a thin arm, so weak from not eating that she couldn't hold it still. Annabel it. 'You wanted me?'

In a weak voice, she whispered, 'I think God is telling me that I should listen to what the doctor tells me. That little baby yesterday—so innocent—he just allowed himself to be born. I must just allow whatever Karma brings me—and he has brought Dr Christie. I will obey him now.'

Annabel gazed into the black-ringed hollow eyes. If only she had agreed to operation earlier! But now? There could surely be no hope. She went at once to find Gabriel. He was taking a clinic, but he stopped at once when he saw Annabel's face. 'What's the matter?'

She explained. 'What do you think?'

He shook his head. 'Too late—far, far too late.'

'What shall we do?'

Gabriel said, 'I'll speak to her husband. Perhaps I can bypass the primary lesion and give her a few pain-free months. Who knows?'

'Karma?' suggested Annabel, rather sadly.

'That too. We'll do our best. Can you get the husband's telephone number for me? I'll do it tomorrow if he agrees.'

Annabel went back to her office. She had accepted life's tragedies as part of any nurse's life. But they still hurt. Each patient becomes a friend for a short time, and Mrs Madan was a kind and good woman. Annabel sat for a while, staring into space, until she was summoned shrilly to attention by her phone. 'Hello?'

'Annabel? You havn't forgotten my party today? I am expecting you.' It was Sukeina. Annabel felt distaste at the voice of the social butterfly intruding on to her private thoughts. 'You said you would speak to the ladies who want to support the hospital.'

'I'll do my best.' She put the phone down. She knew she was scathing of Sukeina's superficial attitude to life. But also, she knew, deep down she was very jealous of her hold over Gabriel Christie. How he could find her company congenial—beautiful though she was . . . And she recognised that in her eyes, Gabriel was some sort of superman, and his weakness for the lovely Malay woman only showed him up as far too human. Annabel gave a deep sigh, and settled down to dealing with the paperwork in her In-tray.

Gabriel spotted her when she was on her way out of the clinic wearing a blue silk dress and white sandals. 'So—business meeting with Pagodi?'

Annabel prevented herself with a big effort from losing her temper. Sweetly she said, 'I'm taking tea with Sukeina.'

'Oh—that group of women who are going to be Friends of Jacaranth?'

He had obviously been told of Sukeina's intentions. Annabel said gravely, 'You like her very much, don't you?'

Gabriel faced her, amber eyes clear and honest. 'She's lonely, pretty, and very sweet. And she doesn't have a very happy home life.'

Annabel turned away, muttering, 'You could have

fooled me.'

'What did you say?'

'Nothing. I must go. You have her phone number, no doubt, if you should need me back here.' And she sailed out without looking back. Gabriel reached the door before her. She looked up at him. Surely he wasn't going to defend Sukeina again?

He said softly, 'Tell me, Annabel, are you happy here? Has it turned out as you expected?'

'I'm very happy here.'

'Are you sure? You seem to have reservations. Is it Singapore? You really do want to go back?'

Their eyes met. Something stirred inside her, reminding her that she did have a soft spot for him. She tried to think of something to say. Suddenly there was the sound of a car screeching to a halt, and they both went to the front door to look out. Annabel gasped, 'It's Tony!'

'Tony who?'

'Holland. A friend of mine.'

'Oh yes—I noticed. 'Gabriel had sounded rather acid up to then. Suddenly he said, 'He isn't well. Quick, call a trolley.' And he rushed out to the drive, where Tony Holland had collapsed on the hot tarmac and lay with his arms and legs spreadeagled, his face pale and sweating profusely.

They got him to a room. Annabel said, 'Is it malaria? He's been working out in the plantations near Seremban.'

'There aren't any malaria mosquitoes there.' Gabriel was examining him. 'Could be dengue fever. Ask Asha if she's free—she lived in a dengue area for a while, she'll have more experience of it than I have.' He entered the high temperature on the chart. 'Get a sample of urine when he wakes.'

Annabel stood by the bed, hardly believing that the ill-looking form was really that earnest young man she had once idolised. But it was quite likely that he had picked up a fever—the jungle areas were noted for mosquitoes, and Tony had been plunged into the worst areas as soon as he arrived in Malaysia. Gabriel had started to walk out of the room, but he came back to say, 'Don't look so worried.'

She said, 'But when will we know what's wrong?'

Gabriel said, 'You've forgotten your tropical medicine? In malaria the fever is intermittent. In dengue, it won't ease up. So make sure he's carefully supervised.'

'There's no treatment, is there?'

'No. It's a viral condition. Careful nursing—you ought to be good at that by now.' And he walked away. Annabel watched him for a moment. Did he really care about her interest in Tony? There was no time to consider the point. Tony woke, and groaned, and Annabel had to be there to hold his hand and soothe him. She took a bowl of iced water, and sat beside him, administering cool pads to his forehead.

Phyll came in, her neat bun and white shirt proclaiming her efficiency. 'Annabel, there's a call for you. It's Mrs Malik. She says she is expecting you.'

Annabel stood up. 'I'll speak to her.' She went to the nearest phone. 'Sukeina, I'm very sorry, but we have an emergency admission, and I can't get away.'

'Later, perhaps?'

I'm afraid it's out of the question. I'll be needed here all day.' Sukeina was annoyed. Annabel repeated, 'There's nothing I can do. We're really very busy today.'

Tony was awake when she got back to him. 'Sorry to be a pest.'

She smiled. 'Not your fault.'

He said, his voice weak, 'Your mother asked me to find out if your boss really was as marvellous as you describe.'

'I hardly mention him in my letters.'

'Somehow, she seems to think you're smitten.'

'What utter rot!' But Annabel felt her cheeks growing hot, and turned away to reach for the thermometer,

to hide her face. Smitten . . . surely not Annabel
Browne? Love, as far as she was concerned, was
nothing but a nuisance that got in the way of one's
career . . . She was relieved when Tony drifted off into a
disturbed sleep again. She watched him patiently. There
was no sign of his fever abating. So Gabriel must be
right—not malaria but dengue fever, a haemorrhagic
fever that could at times be very serious indeed. She
touched his cheek. 'Tony dear, keep fighting. You
mustn't give in.'

She sat for a long time, thinking of home. Perhaps
Tony being here reminded her that Malaysia wasn't
really her home. But what would she do in Cheltenham
now? As though in reaction, Annabel looked out of the
window at the late sun. Sukeina's party was over. She
would probably be annoyed with Annabel for turning
her down—she was such a petty woman. Annabel rose
and went outside at the back, sat at one of the small
tables and listened to the wind in the palm trees. A small
monkey scampered down the trunk of the nearest tree
and grabbed a banana that had been left on the table.
He seemed unafraid, nibbling at the skin before biting it
in the middle and extracting the flesh with nimble tiny
fingers.

Annabel laughed at him, as he turned away, looked
over his shoulder at her once more, then ran off, leaping
three yards from the table to the tree. Monkeys were
cute—but she also knew that in the jungle they carried
the dengue fever virus that was so easily transmitted to
man by affected mosquitoes. Poor Tony—he could
have been incubating the fever while they were in
Singapore. Annabel had never suffered from any of the
tropical diseases, though she had nursed some before
taking the theatre job in Mount Olivia.

A voice said, 'Don't worry, Annabel.' She turned to
see Asha Santasi, dressed in a shimmering silk sari that
fluttered in the breeze. The sun glinted on the vivid
peacock blue and gold borders, and on the sapphires she
wore in her ears. She had swept her hair up into bun

instead of ringing it with a rubber band as she usually
did. She smiled and said, 'Don't worry, your friend will
recover. Dengue isn't so serious in adults as in children.'

'But people do die—of kidney failure.'

'Very rare, my dear. I myself have had it twice. Now
come and let me see your friend.'

'But—you are looking so lovely—you must be going
out.'

Asha laughed. 'Yes, I do not often dress up to the
nines, do I? Perhaps it is perverse of me, because my
mother always dolled me up so that I should look
attractive for any prospective husbands—I grew to hate
my saris, and my jewels and my gold.' She jingled her
seven narrow bangles. 'Perhaps now I am too old for all
that, I can do it now and again.'

'You're going out?'

'Only to visit some friends of mine for dinner. I am in
no hurry.' The two women went in together. They
thought Tony was sleeping, but he opened his eyes as
they approached. Annabel wiped his face with a tissue.
Asha said, 'Now, tell me how you feel. Hot, I know.
What else?'

Tony said weakly, 'Are you a doctor?'

'Yes—take no notice of this old sari—I do not always
dress like a Christmas tree!' She smiled down at him,
and Annabel saw with a smile that his bleary eyes
brightened a fraction at the sight of the delicate beauty
of the sari—and the cheerful pleasantness of its wearer.

'Can you cure me, Doctor?' Tony's voice was only a
shadow. 'I'm so weary—so terribly weak. It isn't like
me to be so helpless.'

'You will get well.' Ash's tone was positive. 'The
weakness is diagnostic—it is definitely dengue—and it
didn't catch me, although I have suffered from it twice.'
She turned to the nurse. 'Was there haematuria?'

'Yes, quite heavy.'

'So. We will keep Mr Holland quiet and calm, give
him lots of liquids and tender loving care, and he will
recover within—two, three weeks. There is no treat-

ment, Mr Holland—only allowing your own body to develop its own antibodies. Have no fear. Relax, and try to enjoy being cared for.'

'I must let Mr Osman know.'

Annabel put her hand on his hot one. 'I'll do that. Rest, Tony.' She went to the phone, leaving Dr Santasi with the patient. When she looked in again an hour later, he was fast asleep. She checked his temperature herself before leaving him for the night. It was very high. But Asha herself had warned that it might take three weeks for Tony's body to be able to fight off the illness.

Gabriel was sitting at a table by himself when she entered the dining room. She sat opposite to him, knowing that he, like her, was completely drained by the day, and would not want to talk. Mia brought them plates of *wanton mee* and short bamboo chopsticks. Annabel started to eat, tempted by the smell. Gabriel smiled at her hunger, and followed suit. 'So you've met a friend from home?'

She said simply, 'Singapore is my home. I'd stifle in Cheltenham. Where is your home, Gabriel?'

He held his chopsticks suspended, a curl of *mee* between them. 'Home? Where the heart is, Annabel—did nobody tell you that? Here, right in the heart of the Jacaranth. But if you mean my birthplace—that was a long, long way away, in the heart of Glasgow. You've heard of the Gorbals?'

'Yes, I have.'

Gabriel paused. She looked at him—and frowned as she saw his face suddenly grimace in pain. Involuntarily she put out her hand, but he shook her off. After a moment, he want on as though there had been no interruption. 'I loved Glasgow—but like generations of Scots before me, I wanted to see more. I never meant to stay . . .'

'Neither did I.'

He looked at her kneenly. 'But you still long for the city, Annabel. This lovely place is only a provincial town to you. Right?' A jagged streak of lightning lit up the entire sky as he spoke. Gabriel stood up. He seemed to sway, and put his hand to his head, but almost at once straightened his back and said gruffly, 'I'm going to the beach.'

He hadn't invited her, but he hadn't said he didn't want her company. She stood up. 'I'll come too—if you don't mind. The breakers—so endless—they relax me—I don't know why. Maybe because they make me feel how very small and insignificant human beings are . . .'

He nodded, apparently not wanting to talk just then. They walked slowly along the shore, the moonlight turning the sand to spun silver. As the lightning flickered, Annabel felt the strange excitement it always brought—even more as she walked at the side of the restless Viking who had—whether she wished or not—dominated her life for the past ten months.

He said suddenly, 'You're glad to see your Mr Holland?'

She nodded. 'Of course. Very glad he came to the Jacaranth. I know he'll get the best treatment.'

There was a silence, during which the thunder grumbled far away, and the rollers murmured their ceaseless song. The grandeur of nature dwarfed them. Then Gabriel stopped, and leaned against a tree. Annabel stopped too, but he said after a moment, 'He—isn't special, then?' She shook her head, somehow glad that it mattered enough for him to ask.

They made their way back, and up the stairs together, Gabriel pausing more than once to look back on the splendour of the Straits and the sky. When they stopped at Annabel's door, the thunder rumbled again, and without a word, she went into his arms, and held him as though she never wanted to let him go.

CHAPTER TEN

FROM THE DEPTH of Gabriel's embrace, Annabel heard the phone. He released her slowly, their breath disturbed and their hair dishevelled. 'Hello? Annabel here.'

'Annabel, is Dr Christie there? He isn't answering his phone. There's a problem with Mrs Madan.' Annabel handed the phone to Gabriel, her eyes following the line of his jaw as he sat on the edge of the bed to speak. She saw him scrape his fingers through his hair as the night nurse gave her story. For a moment he put his face in his hands.

'Then we have no choice. Prep her—I'll be down in two minutes.' He put the phone down and turned to Annabel. 'She's developed obstruction. Can you get theatre ready?' He looked tired, worried.

Annabel stood up. 'Right.' Like an automaton she straightened her dress and put on her sandals, leaving Gabriel to compose himself. Perhaps it was just as well the phone rang. Yet as she ran downstairs, Annabel felt a great sense of loss—as though perhaps such a closeness might not ever happen again. She knew now that she loved him—she had willingly given herself when he asked—yet his love was not so easily gained. He still supported the lovely Sukeina. He was still unknowable, although she knew him well enough to be sure no one else could dominate her whole being as Gabriel did. She had been weak to give in so easily. She would have to guard against such a situation occurring again. It would be pointless.

They scrubbed and gowned themselves, pulled on masks and caps and gloves. It was a routine action—yet tonight extra poignant as the patient was liked by both of them. Dr Chan was anaesthetising. He was already with Mrs Maden. 'I have informed her husband,' he told Gabriel.

'Right, then let's start. Poor lady—her scruples have been her worst enemy.' Gabriel had sat down for a moment, but he stood up, alert.

The hall clock downstairs could just be heard, striking twelve very faintly. For a moment Gabriel looked at Annabel. It had become part of the procedure for them to exchange a look, and this time it was fractionally longer than usual. She knew without any need of words just how he felt. There was already sweat on his brow. 'There's a chance,' she said. 'There has to be, or why are we here?'

'OK, let's do it.' He held out his hand for the scalpel, and she placed it on his gloved palm, no sound in the theatre but the patient's breathing. Gabriel made the incision right over the lump in the thin side, in the ascending colon. There wasn't much bleeding. He went straight for the edges of the tumour, then he seemed to sway back, and the knife fell from his hand.

'Gabriel!' Annabel went to steady him, her heart pounding.

'It's all right. Bring that stool here. I hope I'm not getting fever.' He shook his head and waited a moment, then went back to his work. She heard him breathing rather heavily behind his mask. They were all staring at the wall of the gut as Gabriel exposed it, and Annabel could tell that everyone thought what she was thinking—the tissue looked far too healthy to be cancer. Gabriel finally said it. 'By all that's wonderful—it's mobile! Look, Chan—look, Annabel—it isn't deep in the skin at all, only attached by all these tough adhesions. I rather think we've just witnessed a miracle. If I can cut round it, this fellow can be rushed to histology. But I'm ninety-nine per cent sure this is only a hardened polyp.'

The tension round the table relaxed, and as Gabriel eased the lump from the wall of the colon and anastomosed it with small neat sutures, the junior nurse

removed the excised tissue for analysis. Gabriel stitched the skin taut over the iliac crest. 'This is one lucky
lady.'

Annabel said, 'She'll be happy more because she
knows she hasn't been sinful in her previous life.'

Gabriel said, leaving the theatre, 'You can tell her the
good news in the morning, Annabel.' He seemed in a
hurry suddenly, and Annabel saw beads of sweat on his
face again. He brushed aside her concern. 'I'm
exhausted, that's all.' But he swayed against the door as
he left the room, and she watched him leave with a
worried frown. Surely dengue wasn't infectious? Yet
Gabriel's face showed every sign of a fever, the eyes
unusually bright and a spot of red on each cheek. She
watched him go up the single flight of stairs, heard him
close his door. Poor man, perhaps all he needed was a
decent night's sleep.

Later she lay in bed listening to the sound of his fan,
turned up high. She slept at last, weary herself from the
long day. But in her dreams she thought she heard
Gabriel moaning, and she felt helpless because as in all
nightmares, she was incapable of moving to go and save
him. In the morning she woke early, only to hear the fan
still going fast. She lay for a while, not knowing whether
she ought to go and see if he was all right.

It was when he vomited that she knew he was ill.
Pulling on her robe, she went to his apartment. The
door was not locked, and she pushed it open. Gabriel
lay on top of his bed, his body curved and his knees
drawn up. She put her hand on his forehead. It was very
hot. He wore only underpants, and she was able to see
the abdominal muscles drawn tight. 'Gabriel, is it
appendix?'

He groaned. 'Yes. Call Malik. He's at home.'

She hastily tapped out Dr Malik's number, saying,
'You must have felt ill last night.'

'Yes. Hoped it wouldn't get worse.' He grimaced with
pain, but attempted humour. 'Tell him sorry to call on
his day off.'

Sukeina answered the phone. Annabel was brief. 'Gabriel has bad appendicitis. Could your husband come at once?'

Sukeina screamed. Annabel looked down to see if Gabriel had heard, but he lay sweating, his eyes closed and his hands covering his stomach. Dr Malik grabbed the phone. 'Gabriel?'

Annabel asnwered, 'Appendicitis. I'm preparing theatre in twenty minutes, if that suits you.'

'I'll be there.' Dr Malik rang off, but not before Annabel heard Sukeina having hysterics in the background. She turned back to Gabriel, stroked his forehead. 'I'll just prep you. Stay here, I'll bring the things up.'

'Ask how Mrs Madan is.'

'For once, leave the Jacaranth to me!'

He didn't answer. Annabel hurried back to her room to splash her face with water, and pull on briefs and a cotton dress. Then she ran down to theatre, so recently the scene of great triumph, and began to get out the sterile packs, the instruments, the dressings and the drugs that might be needed, and put them on the trolley, ready for Dr Malik to operate on their most important patient ever—their chief.

Dr Chan was there, his eyes showing the strain of last night's long operation. 'Better if I do the anaesthetic—I am already on the spot. It will take time for any other doctor to come.'

Annabel agreed with him. 'Thank you.'

'Anything I can do for Gabriel, I will do. He has helped me very much, taught me much.'

'Have you seen Mrs Madan, Dr Chan?'

'She is deeply asleep. So tiny and thin, she was—the strain of the gas will take some time to get over. But she is stable. She will make it, I think.' Just then there was the sound of hushed voices, and Gabriel was wheeled, sleepy from the pre-med, into the operating theatre. Chan and Annabel went to him at once, Annabel's heart weeping as she looked down on the usually tall and

confident man. Chan gripped his hand first, before
gently taking it and inserting pentathol into his vein.
Gabriel looked so boyish, the blond hair escaping from
the white cap, no sign now of the gruff voice. Annabel
put a strand of hair back, and no one mocked at her as
she stroked his cheek tenderly for a second.

He was asleep. Annabel walked beside him as he was
placed on the table. Dr Malik was already waiting, the
piercing black eyes even sharper than usual over the
white mask. She positioned herself just behind him,
ready to supply the instruments as he needed them.
Gabriel's body was covered by a sheet now, but she
knew how it looked, so perfectly proportioned. How
tragic to cut into such health-looking skin! But better do
it quickly. Dr Malik took the scalpel from her and made
a confident incision in the iliac fossa.

Chan said in a whisper, 'We should have known he
was ill last night. He was sweating, and couldn't always
stand upright.'

Dr Malik said, 'You should have sent for me.
Rectractors, Annabel. Suction.' Then he gave a
strangled cry. 'My God—it's perforated! Suction,
quick—over here! Nurse, ring Mr Low to scrub and
assist this minute. I need another pair of hands. Here,
Annabel, hold these.' He worked feverishly, trying to
clean the area so that he could remove the affected
appendix. 'Antibiotic, Annabel. Here, pour a little
down here and swab.' He sutured the gut where the
ruptured appendix had been, and then began to clear the
peritoneum all round the site. In the hushed theatre they
all heard the clock strike nine in the morning. And their
chief, who was usually down and ready to start his ward
round, lay stretched on the table before them all.

The houseman came hurrying up, gowned and
masked, and took his place opposite Dr Malik. Annabel
was able to go back to her own job of providing the
surgeon with all they needed to do their work properly.
She knew very well that Mr Malik would be wondering
if he had removed all the diseased tissue. He checked

and rechecked the entire area, before drawing back the peritoneum across the abdomen, and then pulling the skin back together. His sutures were very neat and regular. It would make a neat scar eventually—unless he had to re-open in case of a recurrence of infection.

It was ten o'clock when Gabriel was stitched, and the anaesthetist began to give the gas that reversed the action of the muscle relaxant. Then he lightened the halothane, and as Gabriel took over his own breathing, removed the tube altogether. Annabel held the drip aloft as he was wheeled to Recovery. It was there that the first hazard stood, in the shapely form of Sukeina Malik. The porter stopped, but Annabel said, 'Go on, get him into the room.'

Sukeina stood in the way. She looked down dramatically at the prostrate form, seized his hand and burst into tears. Gabriel stirred, and said with his eyes still closed, 'Don't cry. I love you.' His voice was only a harsh whisper, but Sukeina heard it. And Annabel heard it. They faced one another across the helpless form on the trolley. In the silence that followed, the cry of a seabird could be heard in the hushed corridor.

A mask of steel welded Annabel's features together, and she carried on with her work as though nothing had happened. Carefully she wheeled the trolley to the bed, and Gabriel was lifted off gently by the male staff. She fixed the drip, and almost at once inserted the thermometer under his arm, then wrapped the cuff of the sphygmomanometer round the hard muscle of his upper arm. The routine helped. There were things to be done, and Annabel did them, thankful that she could keep busy, and didn't have to sit and think.

Dr Malik came in, having got rid of his theatre gear. His usually composed face showed stress. 'Everything all right?'

'Yes.' What a lie! Gabriel, in his anaesthetised condition, had just declared his love for Dr Malik's wife. 'Yes, he's OK.'

Dr Malik looked directly at her. No longer was there any malice in his eyes—only concern. 'I know I can trust you to call me if there is the slightest need. But I have to operate this afternoon, so I think I'd better try to get some rest.'

'Of course. You'll have extra work. Can you get a locum consultant?'

'Possibly. We can afford it, huh?'

'If it means you shouldering all the work and getting sick, I think we have to afford it.'

'You're right, Annabel.' She watched him go, all her pent-up feelings going with him. He wasn't a charmer, but he was a good man, and the more she knew him, the more she felt he was too good for his vain little wife. She had married him for the status of being a surgeon's wife—not thinking that along with the status goes a hell of a lot of responsibility.

Sukeina tried to follow her into Recovery, but Annabel said coolly, 'I'm sorry, Sukeina, he must have complete rest for at least twenty-four hours.' She tried to keep her voice from trembling, but it was impossible to pretend she hadn't heard Gabriel say those words. 'Better go home, and phone me before you come. I'll let you know how he is——' the shakiness came back, and she paused before saying, 'The operation was more complicated than normal. He'll need a lot of rest.'

Sukeina looked at the other nurses and the houseman. They were all looking at her, and she had the grace to realise that it was not seemly to have hysterics over a man when her own husband had only just left the room. She turned away, twisting her graceful body for the maximum effect. The young Dr Chan went gallantly to escort her to her car. There was no doubt she was genuinely upset, but then so were all the staff. There was no one in the Jacaranth that morning who did not feel desolated and distressed at the illness of the man they all owed so much to.

And it was Annabel who was left alone with the inert form that was Gabriel Christie. She stood for a moment looking down at him, feeling wave upon wave of affection, dread for his safety, and total desolation at the way he had spoken to Sukeina, even while still under the influence of the gas. His love must be very deep. She sighed a shuddering sigh, lifted her head, and took a thermometer from the locker. 'I'm just going to take your temperature,' she whispered.

'Thank you.' His own voice was so low she could scarcely hear it. 'It's still up, I think—I feel cold.'

'It is up.' She didn't tell him how high. Dr Malik had inserted an antibiotic drip. There was little they could do but wait. If the peritonitis had spread before Dr Malik caught it in time, then there was a very real danger of losing him. She caught back a sob as she looked at him, and restrained herself from grasping his hand, that lay, so strong and tanned, helpless now on top of the sheet. She put a second coverlet over him, drawing it up to his chin to stop him shivering. Then she took a tissue and wiped his forehead where the small drops of sweat started as quickly as she mopped them away.

A nurse looked in. 'Sister, Mr Holland is asking for you.'

'I can't come. Is he bad?'

'Dr Chan says he's very weak, but not dangerously ill.'

Annabel felt torn. Tony was alone in a strange land. She ought to go to him, but she knew that she couldn't leave Gabriel. 'Tell him to rest. I'll come when I can.' But even as she spoke she knew she was not leaving Gabriel's side until she knew he was going to be all right.

Gabriel's hand moved, and he whispered. 'Go and see him. And find out how Mrs Madan is.'

'Impossible, Gabriel. I'm not leaving you.'

'It's an order.' And even as he lay, eyes closed and breathing faint, his powerful personality overwhelmed her, and she beckoned the other nurse.

'Ask Sister Ho to come if she's free.'

Gabriel whispered. 'Well done! If Mrs Madan is awake, tell her the tumour was benign, will you?'

'I will. I won't be long.'

'Thanks.'

Annabel turned at the door, unwilling to leave him. But Cherry was there, and he did want to know about Mrs Madan, even in his weak state. She ran along the corridor, first to Tony. She sat on the chair close to him and took his hand. 'Oh, Tony, you look awful! His face was pasty and sweating, his eyes sunken.

'I'm not going to make it, Annie.'

'Dr Chan says you are. You're nearly over the worst.'

He was shaking his head when the door opened and Asha Santasi came in. 'Now, what has been happening while I have been off duty? Is it true?'

Annabel nodded. 'I'll get back to him now. Peritonitis, and he had it while he was operating on Mrs Madan. Fool!' She was half crying in her anger with Gabriel and her anxiety about him.

Asha saw with wise eyes what she was gong through. 'Now, you get back to him. I'll nurse this young man. You are looking well, Mr Holland. Soon have you back with your facts and figures, or whatever it is you accountants do.' And she patted his hand cheerfully. Annabel breathed her thanks, and turned to go back to Gabriel. She paused in the ward, only to see Mrs Madan still unconscious.

'She hasn't come round, Sister.'

Biting her lip, Annabel hurried back to the Intensive Care room, where Cherry was giving Gabriel some iced water through a straw. 'Temp still up,' she mouthed, nodding at the chart. Annabel grabbed it—and choked back another sob. He would never make it. The antibiotic wasn't working. She was loth to disturb Mr Malik, but knew she must.

He made no bones about it, coming down from his room at once. 'I'll change the antibiotic—no point

in waiting and hoping. We must have results soon, or he
has no hope.' Feverishly they unfastened the plastic
pack, and replaced it with a stronger wide-ranging drug.
'Let us pray he can tolerate this one—some people are
allergic to it. Please watch him very carefully for signs
of allergy, and have some hydrocortisone ready in
case.'

Gabriel's lips were dry, and Annabel put some lanolin
on her little finger and touched them gently. Gabriel
muttered, 'Mrs Madan?' And Annabel pretended she
hadn't heard. The mental picture of the tiny woman,
her little face half hidden by the oxygen mask, her eyes
tightly closed, her chest rising and falling with the
delicacy of a bird, the blood pressure still painfully low
. . . how could she tell him that?

Instead she rearranged his sheets and smoothed his
pillows. For the first time he opened his eyes, and they
looked so sad and lifeless as Annabel met his gaze from
only a few inches away. He said through tortured lips.
'Do you believe in Karma?'

She sat up slowly, his eyes still fixed on her. She said,
'I'll tell you that when your temperature comes down.'

He whispered, 'It's a patch of pneumonia, I
think—the pain is when I breathe.'

'I'd better X-ray.'

'Don't bother—I can't breathe in deeply to get a
decent picture. Just turn me, would you? I haven't—the
strength——'

Annabel closed her eyes for a moment. 'Oh God, help
him, please help him . . .' Then she reached and held his
beloved body in her arms as she turned him on his side.
Dr Malik came back as she did so.

'Augmentin working?' he asked.'

'Not yet.'

Gabriel said, closing his eyes as he spoke, as though it
took too much effort to hold them open, 'Work your
way through them.' He sounded too tired even to suggest a
suitable drug for himself. Dr Malik sat on the bed and
checked the temperature and blood pressure himself.

'Don't worry, my friend. At least your condition is stable. Sleep now, and perhaps when you wake, the worst will be over.'

Gabriel said weakly, 'Let this be a lesson to you—never overwork.'

'Go to sleep, man.'

'When I wake I'll be up and about!' But the faintness of his voice made even Dr Malik turn his face away to hide the sudden brightness in his eyes. Annabel was left alone with him, and soon she was relieved to hear his breathing deepen to show he had fallen into a fairly comfortable sleep. She crept to his side and took the limp hand in hers. There was no alteration in the regular breathing, the steady rise and fall of his chest. She lifted his hand to her lips, and pressed against her breast, held in between both hers, willing her own strength to pass to him and help him fight the infection. She leaned her head against his pillow, tears squeezing through her closed lids . . .

She woke with a start, feeling very guilty. She could tell by the shadows outside that the afternoon was drawing to a close. She looked up at Gabriel's head, lying so still on the pillow. His eyes were open. He smiled weakly. 'Go and see how Mrs Madan is.'

'In a minute.' She took his blood pressure again, feeling the skin under her fingers less hot. Please God the temperature would be down. Her hand was shaking as she entered a normal blood pressure reading on the chart. Then she picked up the thermometer. The atmosphere was very still in that small air-conditioned room. She could hear the waves as though in the very far distance. She slowly withdrew the thermometer and tried to read it with eyes that were blurred with unshed tears. She turned it from side to side, finding difficulty in reading it. Then she saw the thick line of mercury—it had fallen. 'Oh, praise God!'

She shook it down, and put on the small bedside light. 'You could eat something now?' she asked Gabriel.

'Mrs Madan.'

'Very well.' Annabel called a nurse to sit with Gabriel
while she went through to the other ward. There seemed
to be no change in the comatose form. Annabel moved
in silently, and sat at her side. 'Mrs Madan?' No sign at
all of consciousness returning. Annabel leaned over and
whispered in her ear, 'My dear, Gabriel is very sick. I
think it would make him well if I could tell him that you
are all right—your Karma has taken care of you.'

She stared for a long time. There appeared to be a
sudden change in the breathing—and then the dark
eyelids flickered, and the black eyes opened. 'I am well,
Sister?'

Tears flooded into Annabel's eyes and down her face,
so overwrought was she at the sight. 'You're well—and
you'll stay well. Your tumour has gone and you'll
recover—you'll recover!'

'Please tell Dr Christie my whole life I will pray for
him.'

Annabel hesitated. Dashing the tears from her eyes
with the back of her hand, she blurted out, 'Pray for
him now! Oh, please pray!'

As Annabel returned along the corridor, the clock
chimed eight. For the first time she realised just how
long she had been on duty. The hall seemed to swim
before her eyes, but she knew she must stay well long
enough to tell Gabriel the good news. She got to the
door, and saw him looking anxiously, waiting for her.
She fell on her knees at his bedside. 'She's well, Gabriel.
Now you must get well too.'

'God be praised! He lay back, his shaggy hair spread
out over the pillow. Annabel looked up, their eyes on a
level with each other. She remembered smiling, and
seeing his amber eyes regain some of their former
clarity. But then she remembered nothing else. When
she awoke she was in her own bedroom, and the
morning sun was streaming in with a glorious
brightness, accompanied by the crashing of the waves
that told her she was at home, in her own little flat in
Malacca, which she loved and always would.

Her heart sank as she looked out at the front and saw Sukeina's limousine already at the door. She had come to claim her love—in the full glare of the hospital's publicity! It sickened Annabel. To flaunt their relationship like that—Gabriel would never permit it were he well enough. But he was in no position to control the woman. Annabel could only hope that Dr Malik himself would come to realise just what was going on.

Downstairs, Annabel approached Gabriel's room cautiously. She knew that if he was no better, she would be unable to hide her feelings—just now particularly easily bruised after seeing Sukeina's car. She heard voices inside. Pushing the door slightly, she could see Gabriel leaning back against his pillows, holding a cup in both hands, sipping from it and at the same time chatting to someone in the room. He turned and spotted Annabel. At once he put the cup down and held out a hand to her. 'Here's the heroine. Come on, Annabel. Come in and I'll try to say thank you.'

She went in, seeing that the other occupants were Dr Malik and Sukeina. Gabriel was still attached to his drips, but his face was alive now, eyes alert. The other two were smiling. The worst *was* over. Annabel took Gabriel's hand—and found herself pulled down towards him, receiving a brotherly kiss on her cheek. Her heart turning somersaults, she tried to hide her rush of emotion. 'I see the night nurse hasn't combed your hair properly. Shall I send for the barber?'

Amid laughter, Gabriel said, 'I thought I might be allowed to be untidy just for a day or two?'

'Not in my hospital you can't.' How she wished the others would go away! But she knew their joy at seeing their friend getting better was perhaps almost as great as her own. Gabriel, alas, didn't belong to her and never would. 'Has Asha seen you?'

'Yes, bless her, she was in at the crack of dawn. She's taking my clinic this morning, and Malik has arranged for a locum to come in and help out for a couple of

weeks.' Gabriel winced then, and it was obvious he was
still very weak, and the pain of the wound must be
troubling him.

'You want analgesics? You're allowed them post-
operatively.'

'No, no.' Gabriel's lips turned a little white, and
Annabel went to him and held the cup while he drank.
He looked up at her. 'You'll understand, Annabel. How
many surgeons get to know how it feels to come round
from oblivion and feel totally helpless? Oh, we arrogant
doctors know know to operate, how to give them drugs.
But when we actually know how it feels to the patient,
only then can we treat them with the respect they
deserve.'

They finally left Gabriel to sleep, though Sukeina
insisted on hanging around. 'I can make myself useful,
I'm sure, Annabel,' she said sweetly, with a special sly
look from her lovely sloe eyes that emphasised that they
had both heard Gabriel declare his love for her.

'Of course.' What else could Annabel say? 'You
could make sure nobody wakes him—he needs as much
total rest as possible, to allow the antibiotics to work
properly.'

'He's out of danger now?'

'Better ask your husband. He saved his life.' Annabel
looked at the beautiful face for any sign of remorse.
Sukeina looked down briefly, her long silky lashes
brushing her cheek. She moved away without saying
anything.

Annabel went to her office and tried to concentrate
on the paperwork Phyll had loaded on her desk. There
was a note to phone Amir Pagodi, but she put that
aside. Somehow the thought of making lots of money at
import/export had lost its charm. She was a nurse, and
that was where the rewards were, although sometimes
one had to endure awful disappointments and tensions
to counterbalance the rewards.

She had been working without raising her head.
When Mia brought her a cup of Chinese tea at eleven,

she had reduced her work and was sitting pondering about the future board meeting. It was due next week. Gabriel would be up by then. Sukeina would insist on being there. Annabel quietly put a tick by her name, confirming that she should sit in on this one—if only to make sure Sukeina didn't try to use her charm too blatantly. Asha would be on her side too. But the men were only men, and therefore susceptible, whatever Gabriel pretended, to the lovely Malay's perfect looks and musical voice.

There was a knock at her door, then a face from the past showed round it. 'Sister Browne? May I come in? I believe I have to report to you first. I'm doing a locum for Dr Christie.'

Annabel swallowed hard. Then she straightened her back, stood up, and held out her hand, forcing a welcoming smile. 'Dr Sen, how very kind! I'm pleased to meet you again.'

CHAPTER ELEVEN

KEN LU SEN'S handshake was firm, his gaze straight and honest. 'I am glad I could help. I am between jobs—I go to take up a consultant post in Kuala Lumpur next month.'

'Congratulations,' smiled Annabel.

'Dr Christie is ill. You wish me to start work at once?'

'I'll call Dr Malik.' She explained what had happened, while Dr Malik was on his way round. 'Professor Singh is well?'

· 'Fine.' Ken was still looking at her, with no attempt to be clever or pushy. 'We must talk, Annabel. I have some apologising to do.'

'That doesn't matter now. You're free to take all Dr Christie's clinics?' She showed him the schedules for the next month.

'Yes, I'll do it. Annabel, you are happy here?'

'I don't see why that matters, but yes, I love it here. I never want to leave.'

A look of great relief crossed his handsome golden face. 'I'm glad.' But then Dr Malik arrived, and the two men left the office, for Dr Malik to take their new locum on a ward round. Annabel went back to work, inserting Dr Sen's name in her lists and making out a neat doorplate for him. It was a coincidence, seeing him again after so many months. He seemed to have changed a lot. That was good. But there was no need for them to become friendly again. A normal working relationship was all that she expected, nothing more.

There was a sudden burst of voices near the back door, and Annabel went to the corridor to see what was happening. Percival and Mia were both trying to pull back a tall figure who had burst in, and was demanding to see 'the woman—the evil woman!'

It was the *bomoh*, complete with white rings around his eyes and his necklace of monkey skulls. He spotted Annabel, and pointed a sharp speare-like stick at her. *'Perempuan!'*

'I am a *perempuan*,' she said calmly. 'So?'

The *bomoh* was dressed, underneath his necklace, in a singlet and grubby sarong. His large feet were bare, and he had a gold chain around each ankle. He fixed his eyes on her—an expression which he must have calculated would strike terror in her—and said in a low throaty whisper, 'I want my patient out of this cursed place. You take her in, I say no, but she still come. I take her back now. Now!'

Annabel said calmly, 'If you are talking about Mrs Kan, she is in no state to be removed. But if she had stayed with you, both she and her child would be dead by now.'

'You are a foreigner, not know about such things. She come back to village with me.' He was not cowed by the atmosphere of clinical sobriety all around him, the lack of fear of his horrible appearance. But Annabel began to see that possibly he might be deranged. Amir Pagodi had told her that most *bomohs* were good, simple men, who genuinely cared about the people in their village. This man was different.

Annabel put on her best Sisterly accent. 'I see you don't understand. Only the patient's husband can take her away without our consent. He is happy for her to stay until the baby is stronger.'

'Ho, kawan!'

All eyes turned at the loud Malay greeting. Annabel gasped and wanted to run to him, as Gabriel stood there, holding on to the doorway with one arm, garbed boldly in a short crimson robe. His hair stood out round his head, and his height was accentuated by him standing on an upper step. He waved Annabel back. In Malay, he went on, 'You care for your patient—so do we. In a day she will return to your village, and they

will all rejoice that she has a fine son. Come with
her husband, and you can all three return together.

The *bomoh* appeared tempted by the offer—he would
himself share the glory. Gabriel had been clever.
Annabel's eyes were on Gabriel and not the *bomoh*,
seeing the strain in his face of the pain of his wound. As
soon as the *bomoh* gave in, nodding his agreement,
Percival bundled him from the hall, while Annabel
reached Gabriel, pushing a wheelchair towards him as
he collapsed in a heap. They got him back to bed, and
Dr Malik was called. As Gabriel lay gasping, his face
white under his tan, Dr Malik said sourly, 'Kill yourself
if you want to, but for God's sake wait until I have
cured you!' He inserted the drips again, and called
Annabel to check the temperature. 'I shall have to insist
that you are watched every minute, in case you do such
a foolhardy thing again.'

It was Sukeina who said gently, 'My husband, I am
the only one here with nothing to do. Let me be the
gaoler and I promise he won't leave his room again.'

Dr Malik nodded. 'Right. Annabel can't really spare
the time anyway. Sit with him and call me if he tries to
get up again.'

Gabriel opened his mouth to protest, but Dr Malik
shook his head. 'Go to sleep, man. Let us hope your
fever does not return. A double dose of tranquillisers if
you so much as dare to sit up!' His affection for his
partner was obvious in the sharpness of his tone. He
patted Gabriel's shoulder as he went out. Annabel
stayed for a while, watching Sukeina. But she was soon
called out by the telephone, and was forced to leave
them together. Her deep love for Gabriel was still
troubled by the fact that he had allowed himself to be
duped into loving a woman who was not free. In every
other way he made no mistakes. His judgement was
immaculate. Yet in this one thing he had no control over
his own feelings. She stifled a sigh as she pushed open
the office door.

Asha was there, dressed in a fashionable long skirt and tunic top, her glossy hair looped up, giving her an aristocratic air. Annabel smiled at her. 'Why are you looking so beautiful lately, Asha?'

Asha smiled. 'Perhaps because I have nursed your young man back to health.'

'Wonderful! He's over the worst, then?'

'Yes. It will take some weeks for him to regain his full strength. But he wants you to phone his employer to give a date for his return.'

'I'm so relieved.'

'Yes—after four emergencies in one day, they are all on the road to recovery.'

Annabel made the call, then she sat back in her chair and said, 'Asha, it's just so good to be part of this hospital. To have been there at its birth—it's my child, in a way, and I'm as proud as any parent of the way it's growing up so strong and full of integrity.'

Asha smiled knowingly. 'And what about your yearning for Singapore?'

Annabel said innocently, 'What yearning is that?'

The both laughed, before Asha said, 'Are you coming for some lunch? I have three operations this afternoon.'

'Fine. I'll come now, then.' Annabel put her things away and straightened the desk. At that moment Ken Lu Sen came in, and paused when he saw Asha. Annabel said, 'Ken you haven't met Asha Santasi—but no doubt you've heard how brilliant she is?'

Ken said tactfully, 'Famous in all medical circles.' He shook hands with Asha. Annabel again wondered at the way he had improved. He was so much more attractive as a person when he wasn't posing and showing off.

Asha said, 'We can all three go for lunch, then. How did you find the clinic, Dr Sen?' and they walked along the corridor together. Annabel excused herself to go along to see Gabriel. Sukeina Malik still sat reading a glossy magazine, while Gabriel slept peacefully.

Annabel checked temperature, blood pressure and heart rate. They were all slighty raised, but that was an almost inevitable result of his heroism that morning. She looked down on him with a smile.

Sukeina said, 'You are fond of your boss.'

Annabel said quietly, 'Who isn't?'

'True. He is a good man.'

'I think so.' Annabel wondered if this was the time to pursue the conversation. Something made her ask, 'Do you think it's right for you to be so friendly with him? You don't mind what people say?'

A look of triumph glinted for a brief moment on the smooth face. 'Can I help it if men pursue me?'

Annabel said sourly, 'Yes, you can,' and walked out of the room, her cheeks hot and her heart thumping with rage and helplessness.

After lunch, when the gentle unemotional chat of Ken and Asha had calmed her down, Annabel joined Dr Malik for a ward round. Mrs Madan was sitting up, drinking a bowl of soup made for her by her mother-in-law, who sat beside her beaming with delight that she had finally got her appetite back. After a few words with each patient, Annabel paused a while with Tony. He lay on his back, having kicked off the sheet, wearing only pyjama trousers. He smiled as she came in. She bent and kissed his cheek, as there was no one around. 'It's good to see that twinkle back in your eye.'

He stretched his limbs indulgently. 'I feel as though I've been dropped from a great height on to a hard floor.'

'Just try to live with it. You must admit the Jacaranth food is up to five-star standard.'

'Yes. Asha said I have to stay here for another few days. This is the part of being ill that I enjoy—getting better.' He turned to her. 'I must say, old thing, that it's a relief to know that your chief is over the worst. It must have been quite a tough time for you.'

She grinned. 'Yes—if you've been dropped from a great height, I feel as though I've been through a tumble-drier.'

'We must get together when all this is over. I'm
aiming to go home for Christmas. If you want any
antiques taken, I'll do my best. And your folks will
want to know if you're thinking of getting married or
joining any harems. You will let me know, won't you?'

'No chance of either,' she said drily.

Tony said confidentially, 'I say, do you think I dare
ask Dr Santasi out for a meal? She isn't married, is
she?'

'That's a nice idea.'

'She's a good sort, Annie—you've no idea how much
care she gave me. A first-class doctor—and a very kind
woman as well.'

'Well, you'll be treading on no one's toes, if that's
what you want to know. She has no ties—she thinks she
isn't attractive enough.'

'What utter rot!'

Annabel didn't go straight back to work. It was a
warm, lazy day, when even the waves seemed too sleepy
to crash on the shore too roughly. The sun was warm,
and bees buzzed in the flowering clemetis round the
back door, and blue dragonflies swooped and danced
near the water's edge. She walked down the garden and
out on to the beach. She went as far as the white rock
where she had once listened to Gabriel declare his
support to Sukeina, and heard her swear she had no one
else but him . . .

She took off her shoes and walked along the edge of
the water, the waves sweeping in over her knees, and
then far back into the Straits to gather in volume again.
Crazy place, crazy people—yet now she loved them all.
Even as she thought, the lightning flickered in an empty
sky, and she looked up and smiled at it.

'You look happy, Annabel.'

She swung round. It was Ken. He said, 'Do you mind
if I walk along with you?'

She shook her head. 'But you'll get your expensive
suit wet.'

'I'm not so bothered about my appearance as I was.' He stopped. 'Let's sit down.'

They moved to the shade of a palm tree, and Annabel saw in his face that something was on his mind. He said, 'First of all—I have to admit my behaviour was very bad. I was furious, of course, when you walked out on me. But it was later, when I met Martin—he was nursing a relative of mine, and we began to talk, and later we became freindly. You know he and Celia are to marry soon? They told me what a good person you were. And I became very sorry for the way I treated you.'

'It's all over, Ken, really.'

'Not quite. It was my fault that the Professor fired you. I told my father to do it, and Professor Singh had no choice. I have been feeling great remorse about that. That is why I am so relieved to see you here, so successful and so happy.'

Annabel smiled. 'It wasn't your father, Ken. It was Dr Christie who requested me. Apparently he'd seen me working at the Olivia, and thought I would be a suitable person to help organise the Jacaranth.'

Ken was shaking his head as she spoke. 'If that is what he told you, he was trying to save your pride, perhaps. I was there. My father was there, insisting that you be sacked. Professor Singh was there, swearing that you were too good to lose. And Dr Christie was there, taking no part in the conversation, until the Prof asked him if he could use you in Malacca.'

'The Prof asked him . . .' What did he say?' Annabel's voice had gone very husky all of a sudden.

'He didn't say anything at all at first. Then he spoke, in that deep growly sort of voice. He said that you worked well in theatre, but he doubted very much if you had the character or the experience of life to take full charge of a new hospital.'

'I know why.'

'You know?'

'Yes. To get away from you, I hid in the Prof's room—and Dr Christie was there. He looked very angry and very superior. No wonder—I was right when I thought he despise me a bit. He found me asleep in Malacca, the day I went for interview, too. What an idiot I've been! I honestly thought he chose me for my skill. He took me because the Prof made him! No, don't deny it—it's the truth, I know it is.'

Ken said in a low voice, almost lost as the breakers roared towards them and broke over the white sand, 'So I was the villain again? Annabel, if I didn't see you contented here, I would insist that Father take you back. But you would have been pleased to hear what the Prof said about you.'

'He had to say something nice, if he was forcing Gabriel to take me.'

'It was nice.' Ken looked at her, and with his right hand smoothed a strand of hair gently from across her face. 'He said you were as dear to him as his own daughter, and he trusted you as much. That was enough for Dr Christie. He agreed, and they shook hands.'

Annabel sighed. 'It's a bit awful to hear how one was bartered and sold. I suppose I can't complain now—but I shall be very embarrassed now when I see Gabriel— to think he only took me to please his old friend.'

'I think it was more than that.'

'How can it be? You were there. You heard him doubt my ability. Don't try and tell me now that he really wanted to take me all the time!'

Ken shook his head. 'If he didn't, he could have refused you at interview. Why didn't he?'

Annabel didn't know. 'Why didn't he? I hadn't proved anything to him. But he didn't hesitate.'

'Then don't worry about it. He realised he had a good bargain, and Malik was telling me how the entire staff come to you with their problems, and you put everything right. If he didn't want you at first—I tell you, Annabel, he doesn't want to part with you now.'

She sighed. 'You may be right.' She looked up with

a smile from the patterns she had been tracing in the sand. 'You did say you could get me back at the Olivia if you wanted?'

Ken nodded. 'Yes—my father still believes what I say—he is only a businessman, but I am a consultant. He will take you back if you want to go.'

Annabel looked at her watch. It was time to get back. As they walked in the shade of the trees, she said, 'Perhaps I'll ask you to do that for me—one of these days.'

Ken said, 'I'll do it—but think carefully before you throw all this away. Why not wait until after the wedding? You'll be coming to Singapore for that, won't you?'

'Yes. I'm bridesmaid.'

'Then I'll see you there. I'll be working in KL, but I promised Martin that I'll fly down for the wedding. We'll talk then.' They had reached the wicket gate. Ken put out a hand and let it lie on her shoulder. His voice was friendly and warm as he said, 'Meanwhile, forget what I said. Does it matter if he wanted you or not? You know he wants you now.'

Annabel watched him go, his slim figure lithe and healthy. Then she walked in slowly, still deeply shocked by the way she had actually been foisted on to Gabriel. She had been able to work well, thinking that her chief admired her work. Now she knew he had only the picture of the dishevelled nurse, lost for words in the Professor's study. And when she had come for interview and got lost—what sort of impression had that given? She tried to remember his words as he woke her, that first day by the rocks on the beach . . .

Mia came along the corridor with a tray. When she saw Annabel, she said, 'You wish to take Dr Christie's tea?'

'Is he awake?'

'I think so.'

Annabel took the tray from her and went to Gabriel's room. He was sitting propped up, his face a little strained. Sukeina wasn't there, but her magazine and her purse lay on the chair, so she was definitely coming back soon. His face brightened when he saw her. 'Annabel! How has your day been? You still can't have caught up on your sleep, my dear.' His deep voice now sounded nothing but concern. There was no hint of the grumpiness she had noticed in him when they first met. Now she understood a little of that grumpiness.

She put the tray on his table and removed the cloth. Without being asked, she poured his tea and buttered a piece of bread. She looked up to see him watching her face. She said drily, 'I've just been talking to your locum. He remembers chasing me into the Prof's room when you were there. Do you remember a nurse rushing in like a terrified rabbit?'

Gabriel's eyes were soft. He put his hand over hers that still held the butter knife. 'How could I forget?'

'You certainly looked furious. He didn't mention this to you later? No, of course not. How was he to know you were in the room? He was there when you refused to take me, though—and had to be persuaded by Professor Singh.'

Gabriel pushed the tray away. 'I refuse to eat until you stop talking like that.'

'Like what?'

'As though I was reluctant to take you.'

'But you were, Gabriel, you were. If the Prof hadn't made you, you would never have chosen me.'

'I would, I would. I had no other replies!' His brown eyes were twinkling now. 'I had to take you. How could I manage with no Theatre Sisters? Annabel, promise you'll never refer to that again?'

She pushed the tray back. 'Drink your tea.'

Sukeina came in. 'Oh, let me do that.' She pushed Annabel bodily from the bed. 'You are much too busy to bother with little things like this. Come, Gabriel dear—I'll hold the cup for you.'

Annabel stood as Sukeina took over. But Gabriel was having no bullying. He looked up at Annabel and said,

'I do recall that incident. I was really quite amused at the time.'

Annabel said, 'It didn't look like that from where I was standing. You showed nothing but total disdain and annoyance.'

'Well, at first, you were slightly mussed up.'

She took a breath. 'Drink your tea.'

'Yes, Sister.'

They exchanged a look, which made Sukeina suddenly very annoyed. 'Come now, do try this.' Her musical voice contrasted with Annabel's curt order. Annabel left the room, conscious of her lack of charm of the kind Sukeina exuded without any effort. What must it feel like to be so totally beautiful?

She sat at her desk. There were some packets on it, but she didn't open them, merely sitting down, putting her chin on her hands, and staring into space. A voice from the other side of the room said, 'Well, well—what is on your mind, *lah*? Don't think so hard, Annabel, or you will develop lines in your lovely forehead.'

She turned with a smile. 'I'm sorry, Amir—I was miles away. You've brought the forms I ordered to be printed? That's very good of you.'

'Your *tuan* is well? I heard of his sudden illness.'

'My *tuan* is going to be all right, Amir—but we've all been through a terrifying few hours. His temperature was so high—Malik thought he was going to develop septicaemia. It was touch and go.'

Amir came round and sat in front of the desk. 'Your *tuan* must be blind as a cave fish.'

'Blind? What do you mean?'

'Not to see how you are in love.'

Annabel retained her composure, though she knew her cheeks were reddening. 'You must guard against jumping to conclusions, Mr Pagodi.'

He smiled, his eyes sparkling like the sea outside, his cheeks dimpling. 'I've known you a long time, Annabel. It is seven months since I first met that innocent girl in my office, and decided she was one of the most

beautiful women I knew. You have grown so much, in
composure and in confidence. And you have a
protective shield round you—one that is guarding you
from all men.'

'You're so good at talking, Amir! Come now, what
do I owe you for the cards?'

He laughed. 'See what I mean? The Jacaranth and
Annabel have grown together. And Annabel is the more
beautiful of the two.' At the look on her face he
produced the bill. 'There. And what shall I do with the
box of goods for your father that you haven't been to
see?'

'Oh, Amir, I'm sorry. Can I put you in touch with
Tony Holland? He'll be going back to the UK for
Christmas—he can deal with everything—he's a friend
of the family.' She had thought she could combine two
careers, but she knew now that she couldn't be a good
nurse if she did.

'I think it might be good if I went to the UK with him.
Would your father like it if we met?'

'That's a good idea. He believes in meeting the people
he does business with. You must be well travelled,
Amir?'

'To be honest,' Amir confessed, 'I have never been
further than Penang.'

Annabel watched him as he left. His open admission
surprised her. Yet she was pleased too, because it
showed he was no longer trying to impress her with his
wealth, but accepted her as a friend. She leaned back
and silently agreed with him—the Jacaranth had been
good to her, good for her. However much of a mistake it had been in the beginning, it had been worth-
while.

And Amir knew that she was in love with her boss.
Did it show so very much? She went out into the
corridor, aware that her feet took her in Gabriel's
direction. She paused at the door, her hand raised to
knock. Then something stopped her, and she gently
pushed the door ajar. Sukeina was sitting on the bed,

holding Gabriel's hand between both her dainty ones. Her head was very close to his.

Annabel backed away. Anger welled up in her. Surely Sukeina couldn't be so blatant about her infatuation when her own husband was in the same building? Sukeina was very wrong—but then so was Gabriel Christie. How could a man of his qualities have such a large flaw in his character? Annabel ate little that evening, and went to bed early, exhausted both mentally and physically. The last thing she did as she drew the mosquito curtain over her open window was to look down into the dark garden, alive with the shrilling of the cicadas. There, where it had been all day, stood Sukeina's car. Annabel lay awake for a while, praying she would hear it drive away, but she fell asleep before she heard anything.

Sukeina was not there the following day. Had Dr Malik perhaps put his foot down? That was good—Annabel hoped he would keep it up. But she was busy most of the day, dealing with administration, and at the same time doing ward rounds, and twice a week working in theatre with Asha. At one of these sessions Asha said hesitantly, 'Your friend is to go back to the jungle tomorrow?'

'Tony? Yes, he's survived his first taste of tropical disease. He'll go home and boast about it, no doubt.'

'Suture, please, Annabel. You know he has asked me to go out with him?'

'He has?' Annabel pretended not to know. 'And why not?'

'No reason. It is just that I am surprised that someone asks me who isn't after my money or my status. He asks me as a—friend, Annabel. Forceps—thanks. It is a long time since I was asked out as a friend—not since med school.'

'That's nice.'

'Yes—very nice. It is almost like a first date, somehow. I am most touched to be asked. Scissors, Annabel. Swab.'

Afterwards they walked down together. Asha confided, 'Even though I am Indian, I believe in love—I must be a romantic at heart. You think so?'

Annabel said warmly, 'You're a wise woman, Asha, and we all love you.'

'You think it is wise to be romantic?'

'Definitely!'

Just then Ken Lu Sen came along the corridor. 'Your cook is so good, I do not wish to leave your Jacaranth.' He fell into step with them. 'I have just been speaking with Mrs Kai. She wishes to call her baby after Dr Christie. Do you think Gabriel Kai sounds all right?'

Annabel said, 'It sounds fine—but Gabriel is the name of an angel, and Mrs Kai is a Muslim. Perhaps his second name might be better. It's Alistair. If she calls him Alistair, he'll be called Ali—which sounds much more suitable.'

'I'll go and tell her at once.' Ken ran back. He had fitted into the swing of the Jacaranth now, and they would be sorry to see him go—but they would rejoice when Gabriel was back at work. Things hadn't felt right without him.

Gabriel was on his feet when Mr Kai and the *bomoh*, without his monkey skulls, came in a battered *teksi* to take the mother and son back to the village. He joined Annabel and Asha at the front door as the grateful family gave their thanks and waved as they were driven away. Annabel found herself alone with Gabriel, conspicuous in his crimson silk robe. Their eyes met. She said, 'Yes, I do believe in Karma.'

'Totally?'

'Especially when there's a jolly good doctor to give it a helping hand,' Annabel smiled.

'Help me back to my room.' There was no need for him to put his arm round her shoulders. But she allowed it, while her heart wept. At the door she detached his arm, and helped him into bed. He said, 'What have I done to deserve this cross face?'

'Cross? Me? She attempted to joke, but knew he wasn't taken in.

He said drily, 'Well, your long year of purgatory in provincial Malaysia will soon be over. You clearly can't wait to get back to Singapore. Has Ken Lu Sen been making you feel homesick?'

She said bluntly, 'He's promised me a job if I want it.'

'So your troubles are over.' Gabriel leaned back on the pillows, his face drawn. The illness had taken a lot out of him, and she couldn't help feeling for him. He said, the deep voice somehow vulnerable, 'I must have kidded myself—I was beginning to think you liked it here—might even reconsider your decision to end your contract?'

Annabel didn't answer. She did like it here. But knowing as she did that Gabriel had to be persuaded to take her on, she no longer felt quite as happy. 'You've been—very good—to me. I've enjoyed the work very much.'

Gabriel looked into her eyes, his amber flecks catching the light as she had seen them that first day in the operating theatre of the Mount Olivia Hospital. 'Then what a pity you're already speaking in the past tense, Annabel. Have you already applied to Singapore?'

'No. I shall be visiting again before my year is up. I'll let you know in good time to find a replacement for me.'

'How do you know there is a replacement for you?' he growled. 'How do you know you aren't irreplaceable?'

'No one is.' But Annabel felt a pull at her heart. The silence between them grew. She was conscious that the thunder was active tonight, rolling ominously out over the wild waters.

Gabriel said, 'I was wondering—do you think your Mr Holland might be willing to give us some financial advice?'

Pleased, she said, 'He would—I'm sure he would. He's having dinner with Asha—she can mention it.'

'With Asha?' And though his voice was still gruff, he looked very slightly happier.

CHAPTER TWELVE

SO THE OCEAN rolled and roared, and the thunder grumbled and occasionally crashed. Day succeeded day, and Annabel dreaded the day when she would have to leave the Jacaranth. Yet what was the point in staying on, only to be unhappy? She was working for a man who was quite obviously a confirmed bachelor, content to carry on a rather sordid affair with his partner's flighty wife.

Dr Malik came into the office. 'Have you been to see Gabriel this morning?'

'Yes. He's very well. A man of his constitution can soon rally after surgery.'

'Go and take his stiches out.'

'Me?'

'I can't send a junior, and Cherry is off duty.'

'Maybe a junior doctor should do it.'

Dr Malik wasn't given to chitchat. But at this he put one foot on a chair, leaned his elbow on his knee, and his chin on his hand. 'Let me know when you have finished with the excuses.'

Annabel had the grace to apologise. Why should she let her own sadness prevent her doing her job properly? 'I'll go and take his stitches out.'

'Thanks.'

'I take it your wife isn't there?' She watched his face. He must be well aware how may times Sukeina had called, sat with Gabriel, brought him titbits, curry puffs, candies and half-bottles of wine.

Dr Malik said calmly, 'Annabel, my wife is a very intelligent woman. She is also one of the most beautiful women in the country. It would be naïve of me to expect her not to know this—and not to know that she is extremely bored when she isn't working. I either lose her, or I allow her to have a fairly open marriage. I prefer not to lose her.'

'But—with Gabriel . . .?'

'I trust them both.'

'But Amal, they see so much of each other.'

'Trust—you should try it some time. It is so much better for the digestion.' And for the first time she detected a slight smile on the thin lips. 'I do not have friends I do not trust. You may think my wife is frivolous—but I believe I can count her as one of my friends. You see now, Annabel? So go and take his stitches out.'

Annabel walked along the corridor to fetch the pack of equipment. Amal Malik had made her think. Trust—yes, it was a nice, comforting word. It was distrust that was causing her own heart to twist itself into painful contortions. Amal Malik, the man she had pitied, now appeared as sensible, realistic, philosophical. She stopped. She had arrived at Gabriel's door, and her hands had suddenly started to tremble. She closed her eyes for a moment, prayed that she could disguise her feelings, and pushed open the door that was already ajar. Then she stared. 'Gabriel!'

He was standing at the open window, dressed only in grey silk pants, doing arm exercises. He turned—he had never looked so like a Viking. All he needed was a pair of animal-skin trousers and a helmet with horns. He smiled. 'Just getting fit.'

Annabel said primly, 'That's quite enough. If you'll get on the bed, I'll take your stitches out.'

Unembarrassed, he walked back to his bed. 'There's no need to sound so delighted.' He stretched out, so that she couldn't help admiring his body, the broad shoulders, flat stomach, long strong legs.

'I'm delighted to see you looking so fit. Don't forget when we opened you up, we thought you were finished.' She had been trying to sound confident, breezy, but suddenly the memory of that day overcame her, and the sentence ended in a sob.

Gabriel sat up. 'Hey, hey, it's all right!' His voice was low, tender, and he put his hand on hers as she sat on the edge of the bed. 'It's nice of you to care.'

She swallowed, and controlled herself. 'It was the temperature—I was frightened—I've never seen such a temperature . . .'

'It's all right,' he said again. 'Here, take these damn things out, then I can get back to work.' He lifted the pad that was fixed with a couple of pieces of tape to his body. The wound was well healed, already losing its redness. He smiled. 'That's not a bad scar. I'm proud of that.'

Annabel had recovered enough to say sharply, 'It's nothing to do with you—it's Malik who should be proud of it.'

'It's my skin!' he grinned.

She smiled slightly as she took the small stitch cutter and the forceps and deftly removed each stitch separately. Then she doused the area liberally with iodine, which he bore stoically. 'There. Would you like a shower or a bath later?'

Just then there was a tap, and Mia looked in. 'Telephone from Singapore for you, Annabel. Your friend Celia, she ask if you will ring back.'

'OK, thanks Mia.' Annabel turned back to Gabriel. 'Is there anything else I can do for you?'

'Stay and talk for a while?'

'All right.' She sat still on the bed.

'Tell me about Asha and Mr Holland?'

'He's grateful to her, that's all. They like each other.'

'Is he coming to the board meeting?' asked Gabriel.

'Yes, he'll try to be in town that day.'

'And how are you getting on with Pagodi these days?' Gabriel was no doubt remembering the state she had been in after that disastrous day when Amir had made a pass at her and she had become ridiculously upset.

'We—are business friends only. He's selling antiques to my folks.'

'Handsome devil, isn't he?'

Annabel had to smile at the way he led the conversation. She had to tease him a little. 'Handsome, yes, and charming. And so deliciously rich—one never knows when one is to be picked up in the Mercedes, the BMW or the Porsche!'

Gabriel said thoughtfully, looking at her with deep unreadable eyes, 'You're quite a sophisticated lady these days. I know you're joking about Pagodi now—but once you were terrified of him. Now you can cope with his type, can't you? You've come such a long, long way . . .'

There was a silence between them as they both remembered how far she was from the tousled kid who had rushed into the Professor's consulting room. Then Gabriel reached out and put his hand lightly over hers. 'Tell me, Annabel——'

But at that moment Sukeina Malik put her lovely head round the door. 'May I come in?' She wore her hair down today, loosely swinging almost to her waist. The very sight of such beauty made Annabel curl up inside, knowing that she couldn't compete with perfection.

She jumped up at once, picked up the bits of dressing and tape and put them on the trolley. 'I've finished, Sukeina. The stitches are out, so I suppose he'll be even more disobedient.' She gave them both a smile, and stood up, her heart sadly wondering what else Gabriel would have said if they had not been interrupted.

Sukeina laid a bouquet of orchids on the bed. 'Don't go, Annabel, unless you are busy.' She glided round the room so that the lines of her graceful figure in its Malay dress could be well appreciated. She said to Gabriel, 'Darling, it's so nice to see you looking so handsome.' At her entrance he had modestly covered himself with the sheet. She went on, 'See, I've brought you a papaya straight from the tree. Here, I'll peel it for you—I have brought a knife.'

Annabel looked at the pearl-handled fruit knife and thought evil thoughts. Then she said, 'You must excuse me,' and turned towards the door.

But Percival was just coming in, and they almost
collided. 'Sorry, Sister. Gentleman left this for you.'
And he handed over a glittering gold pendant, set with
sapphires and lapis lazuli.

Sukeina said at once, 'It is so beautiful—my, what it
is to have such an admirer!' The stones glinted and
sparkled in the sun.

Annabel said, 'It can't be for me,' and wheeled the
trolley out of the room, giving no opportunity for
further discussion. Sukeina's tinkling laugh reminded
her that Gabriel wasn't the same Gabriel when he was
with her. It was so blatant of her to come so openly—yet
Malik trusted her . . .

Annabel went back to her office, wishing that Gabriel
Christie didn't have so much power to hurt her.

She sat for a long time looking at the pendant—a gift
from Amir, of course. Was she happier here, where she
could at least talk with Gabriel? This illicit affair might
even peter out . . . Oh dear, love was a very painful
thing to suffer from; much more serious than shingles,
say, or varicose veins . . .

Annabel changed from her uniform, and went back
to the office to catch up on business. There were letters
to write, and a new provisions store to be investigated,
to see if its vegetables were fresher and more reasonably
priced than the present one. As she sorted out her work,
and made appointments for later in the week, she
dangled the pendant in her hand, and wondered if she
ought to have refused it. She stared in the direction of
Gabriel's room, wondering if they were trying to guess
who sent it.

Someone knocked at the office door, and Annabel
was glad to stop her painful thinking and do some real
work. It was Mr Madan. 'My wife—we have come to
bring her home.' And behind him were several relatives,
all smiling and cheerful, and full of praise for the
hospital.

Mrs Madan was stitching. 'I make a dress for Mrs

Kai's baby.' The thin face was alive now, glowing with the certainly of good health. It would take some time to bring back some flesh on her little skeleton, but her appetite was already improving.

Annabel sat on the bed. 'I'll miss you here in the corner—but I'm so happy for you, to be going home.'

Mrs Madan saw her family, and almost wept with delight. 'I'll never forget you, Sister.'

'I won't forget you either. Or your Karma.' The little group prepared, and made their way to the door. Annabel felt a sudden rush of tears, and called after her, 'Don't forget your vitamins!' as a way of saying that she cared. As the little procession vanished round the corner, Annabel felt a deep rending sense of loss. If she left this hospital, she would leave all she had built up. She had worked so hard and so long to make the Jacaranth. Did she really want to see someone else running it? But Gabriel had never really asked her to stay—never begged her. He had expressed a wish that she had settled down. But he had hardly got down on bended knee and said, 'Please stay.'

Annabel prepared the agenda for the board meeting. She wasn't looking forward to it, but she felt so strongly about the hospital by now that she knew she had to be there. She was just about to telephone Tony Holland, glad that someone so reliable was to be advising them on money matters. At that moment the telephone rang. It was Celia. 'I've got some lovely patterns for bridesmaids' dresses. Can you spare the time to come, or shall I send them? Don't forget my tailor will need your measurements.'

'I'm so busy—but send them, Celia, send them all. I can't wait to see them. Are they all suitable for me?'

'They're lovely.'

'I'm really looking forward to it. Are you?'

'Too busy to know how I feel. I'll put these in the post, then—don't forget to measure your skirt length to just above the floor.'

'I won't forget. I'll be looking out for the Singapore

post now.' Annabel went back to her work, cheered by
the thought of the wedding. It would be the first time
she had met all her old friends since the day she had
hidden from Ken Lu Sen and encountered the fierce Dr
Christie face to face . . . She knew now that she wanted
to stay. Singapore was a stage in her life. But in Malacca
she had grown up. She added a note to her own copy of
the agenda—agree to a renewal of her contract, which
only had another two months to run.

Someone said, 'Everything all right with your
friends? That was Celia, wasn't it?' Annabel looked up
to see Gabriel, fully dressed, looking slightly thinner,
but definitely well. 'I didn't mean to listen.'

'It doesn't matter. Yes, she's fine. I did let you know
the date of her wedding, didn't I?'

'You did.' He seemed distant, as though uninterested.
With a nod he said, 'The Singapore post comes mid-
morning.' And he strode off, where Dr Chan was
waiting for him. Annabel shook her head. He ought not
to be doing a ward round yet. But she knew there was no
holding him back. When Gabriel decided on something,
no one succeeded in changing his mind.

The board meeting was to take place in Gabriel's
consulting room, which was large and airy, and had a
veiw over the neat lawn at the front. Annabel went in
first with Phyll to make sure there were enough chairs,
and that everyone had a pen, pad and carafe of iced
water handy. Phyll giggled as she stood back, admiring
the official look of the room. 'Do you remember the
first meeting? Only Dr Malik and Dr Christie? You and
I took notes and we all wondered if we would ever make
it.' She smiled. 'I think I'll bring some flowers in—it's
more of a celebration than a meeting.' Annabel watched
her, knowing exactly how she felt. She was glad she had
decided to stay. She went to the window, where the
garlands of fragrant leaves placed there by Mrs Madan's
grateful family were still strung between the palm
trees.

It was afternoon, allowing the doctors to take normal

morning clinics. As Amal and Gabriel came in, they
were laughing together, and it seemed more like a party
than an official meeting. Tony Holland came in,
wearing a white tropical suit, and bore the jokes of
'Expat!' with a grin. Asha was with him, and they had
obviously lunched together, and were in the middle of
an intimate chat, which they seemed reluctant to stop.
Tony turned to Gabriel. 'You said Mrs Malik would be
here.'

It was Amal Malik who said, 'I think she has found
herself another hobby, Mr Holland. She will be quite
happy to have her loan back if we can afford it. She got
a little tired of the way we all paid more attention to the
patients than to her.'

Tony said, 'Well, you can certainly afford it—or you
will by the end of the financial year. You wish me to
delete her name?'

Annabel felt a great load off her mind. So Dr Malik
has been right to treat Sukeina's posturing with
aloofness. She looked at Gabriel. He was showing no
emotion whatsoever. She would have thought he didn't
care—except that she had heard him tell Sukeina that he
loved her. She and she alone had overheard it—and he
could easily say he had been under the influence of the
anaesthetic—but it wasn't for nothing that it was called
truth gas . . .

Gabriel picked up the agenda. 'I'd better begin by
thanking you all. In some companies the thanks are
formal—mine are heartfelt. You all remember our
beginnings—what doubts and what ignorance we
shared—but within the time scale we set ourselves, we
have, in fact, made it.' The rest of the company clapped
spontaneously, and Gabriel smiled. 'I'll ask Mr Holland
to explain the treasurer's report. He's the only one who
understands it—except that we can all see there are no
red figures on it.'

In good humour, and helped on by Mia's tray of
Chinese tea, the agenda was covered. Annabel was
tensed, ready to request a renewal of her contract.

But Gabriel beat her to it. 'And now—Annabel!—I'm sure you all agree that Sister Browne is the law around here?' He was playing for laughs and he got them. 'Her contract was for twelve months—and I've decided that we won't renew it. Of course, you can all vote on it, but what I propose is—I know she had feelers out in Singapore, and I'm taking that into account——'

They had heard the town ambulance in the distance for some time, but when it suddenly blared out at their very gate, and turned in, headlights full on, and screeched to a stop in the drive. The two men in the front scrambled out, one hurrying to ring the bel while the other went round to open the doors. 'Accident! Road accident!'

Gabriel said shortly, 'Business adjourned!' and ran for the door, followed by Amal Malik and Asha. Annabel had screwed up the agenda in both hands, hardly able to comprehend what she had heard. Even without asking her, Gabriel was terminating her contract. 'Feelers in Singapore?' He had overheard her talking to Celia. Yes, he had heard her saying it to Celia, 'I can't wait to see them.' Did he think they were jobs she had found in the newspaper? Was that why he said scathingly that the Singapore post comes mid-morning?

Annabel followed the others slowly, her heart numb. She could explain to Gabriel, of course, that she had no other jobs in mind. But it was the way he had said no definitely, 'I've decided we won't renew it . . .' He didn't say 'reluctantly' or 'unfortunately'. In fact, he sounded quite relieved. Annabel took a deep breath. Perhaps it would be better if she went quietly. Better than making a fuss. The Jacaranth was well on its feet now. She had succeeded beyond all thier hopes, and done her work more than competently. Perhaps Gabriel was right—time to bow out gracefully, perhaps even get a small cheque in gratitude from the Jacaranth?

The accident victims—two of them, both in the same car, apparently, that had swerved to avoid a motor-cyclist and hit a tree—were being taken to theatre.

Cherry was on duty, so Annabel wouldn't be needed. She was glad—she wanted time to herself. Time to make new plans, to cope with this sudden change in her future. Her heart felt like a stone in her chest, her legs almost too heavy to move. But she took herself out to the back garden, and sat for a moment at one of the tables. The baby monkey came running down, expectant for some pickings, but Annabel shook her head sadly at him, his funny little face so appealing, his big eyes hopeful. He looked solemnly at her, then imitated her, shaking his little head from side to side.

Somebody put a letter of the table, and flung a piece of papaya to the monkey. Annabel opened the blue air-letter as she had so many times before, knowing the familiar feel of being in touch with that small antique shop so many thousands of miles away. Unseeing at first, the words began to form, and for a moment she was taken out of the lonely, lost world Malacca had suddenly become, 'Dearest Annabel—things have picked up so well, we can scarcely believe it. Those Malaysian trinkets you sent have proved highly saleable, and we already have repeat orders, so we do hope you can keep up the supply!'

Annabel felt pleasure for her parents. The supply of 'trinkets' would become even more profitable when Tony and Pagodi arrived to co-operate with father. She smiled mirthlessly. She had succeeded in her aim to be a businesswoman—succeeded very well, from the tone of the letter. Yet she allowed the blue paper to drift to the ground, suddenly so very aware of how pointless material success was when one's whole future had been shattered in one single statement. 'I have decided we won't renew the contract . . .'

She heard voices, and decided she wasn't in the mood for company just then. She walked down the path and out on to the beach. She didn't stop walking for a long time, just walking and listening to the waves. Only when the sunset became so glorious, setting the whole world on fire, did she stop, realise she was tired, and lean

her back against a slim palm trunk. She looked
reprovingly at the waves. Usually their repetitive music
soothed her, allowing her to return to calmer mood. But
not tonight. Tonight something had snapped inside her,
a thread she had hoped would grow and become
something steady into the future, her future in Malacca.

She could go back to Mount Olivia. She looked
around at the enormity of the beauty, the magnificence
of the sky, and sighed deeply. She used to be a good
actress, in those early days when she was in the Board
Walkers with Tony. She would need her acting skills
now, because her heart would not settle back in the city,
where there was no ocean, no sunset to speak of, no
Gabriel . . .

She slid to the sand, her back still against the tree, and
leaned her forehead on her knees, her arms clasped
around them. She had walked farther than usual, and it
was a long way back. She couldn't be bothered to go
back—not yet. Because back there was the
Jacaranth—and Annabel Browne no longer belonged to
the Jacaranth. She had once. She had nursed it when it
was a tiny idea, she had tramped round suppliers,
arranged cleaners, bargained for contracts, tended the
sick, and rejoiced at those who recovered.

Slowly she began to be angry with herself. 'It's your
own fault. If you hadn't been so blatant about missing
Singapore—if you hadn't insisted on a twelve-month
contract, you wouldn't be crying now.' Slowly her anger
grew, until she stood up suddenly and ran to the water's
edge, gazing out at the horizon, now navy blue and
purple streaked with orange, lit by a strange and
wonderful light. Looking far out, she felt the tears
trickling down her cheeks, as she pleaded silently with
Eternity. 'Have I been so bad? Have I been foolish? I
did try . . .'

There was a low rumble of thunder. It reminded her
of Gabriel's voice, and she turned away from the Straits
and started very slowly to walk back along the sand.
Somewhere she had mislaid her shoes. It didn't

matter. Then someone caught her roughly by the shoulders. 'So this is where you are!' Gabriel's face was lit red by the sunset, sweated with the exertion of walking so far, so soon after his operation. His wild hair was blown around his face and his eyes were hidden by the shadow of his eyebrows.

She faced him uncertainly, her mind in a sudden turmoil so that she couldn't think of the right thing to say. 'Yes. Does it matter to anyone?'

His voce low and husky, he said, 'I had no idea where you were!'

Something inside her responded—he sounded so lost, desolate—just the same as she felt. Was he possibly feeling as deeply hurt and alone as she was. In a wondering tone she said, 'Gabriel——'

In a second they had caught each other in an embrace so spontaneous that Annabel wasn't sure if this was what she had intended. But there was no escape. The look on his face, the tears in his voice made her go to him, hold him as though nothing else mattered in the whole world. He would understand—Gabriel had always understood, always known her inner thoughts, always been there when she needed him. She clung to him as though for her very life, as though this was their final embrace, that she would vanish into the night air if he let her go. 'I love you, you see,' she explained to his shirt pocket, and his grip tightened as he stroked her hair, held her very still and very tenderly, as though she might fall to pieces if he let her go.

'And I love you, so very much, Annabel—so very much.'

She heard the words, but they had no place in her expectations. Her cheek was still pressed close to his beating heart, she said, 'But you love Sukeina.'

He tangled his fingers in her hair so that it hurt, and drew her head back so that he could see her face. 'That's a damn silly thing to say.'

Looking into the shadows where the amber eyes searched her face as though for the first time, she said,

'You told her—when she made a scene as we were wheeling you to Recovery. You said, "Don't cry—I love you." '

'I said that to *you*. How was I to know there were others there? I knew you were beside me, holding the drip. I said it to you!'

Annabel took a deep breath. Still looking up at him, she said, 'I can be quite stupid sometimes, can't I? Yet you've always been so nice about it. Even taking me on to please your friend.'

They turned and began to walk back, arms tightly about each other's waist. Gabriel said, 'Singh knew what was good for me. I was turning into a recluse—refused to ask women out, because I never thought I'd ever meet anyone I could love again.'

'And now?'

'Now—a great peace has come to me, that fills my whole being, and leaves no part of me with any room to be angry or sad about anything.'

The beauty of his words brought tears, and they both stopped while she mopped them away. 'I don't really deserve to be so happy. Are you really going to terminate my contract?'

'Of course. You won't need a contract if you're on the board.'

Night was falling now, and the cicadas had started their piercing chorus all around them. Annabel leaned her head against Gabriel's shoulder, and they said nothing for a while as they walked, close together, the enormity of love enveloping them in a cocoon made of stars and radiance. After a while, she said, 'Sukeina——'

'Why do you go on about that butterfly? I never asked her out—she used to follow me and sit with me. I never kissed her, though she used to cling on in hope. She used to imagine herself in love, but it was only something she dreamed up to make her boring life more interesting. I soon learnt how she lied to get attention. Malik advised me to say nothing and just wait until something else turned up to take her fancy.'

The familiar landmarks began to show, the very rock where Annabel's doubts had first happened loomed ahead. She looked up at Gabriel again, put up a hand to try to tame his mane of hair. She said gently, 'You've walked too far, you know. You must rest now, straight after dinner. My poor Gabriel, I would never have walked so far if I'd thought for a minute you would follow me.'

He smiled, taking her hand in his and kissing her palm. 'So you see, darling, I can do stupid things too.'

Annabel said softly, 'It's a good job we have each other to look after us.'

They closed the wicket gate and locked it. They could hear voices in the dining room. Just before they went in, Gabriel said, 'I shall need a hand to help me to bed, Annabel. We convalescents can't manage alone.'

'I'll come with you.'

They stood at the door, locked together in an embrace that promised making love that night. Annabel felt like crying at the sheer glory of the whole world, at the fire of the flickering lightning, the hidden energy of the thunder and the ceaseless reliability of the waves on the sand.

STORIES OF PASSION AND ROMANCE SPANNING FIVE CENTURIES.

CLAIM THE CROWN – *Carla Neggers*_____$2.9
When Ashley Wakefield and her twin brother inherit a trust fund
they are swept into a whirlwind of intrigue, suspense, danger an
romance. Past events unfold when a photograph appears of Ashle
wearing her magnificent gems.

JASMINE ON THE WIND – *Mallory Dorn Hart*_____$3.5
The destinies of two young lovers, separated by the tides of wa
merge in this magnificent Saga of romance and high adventure se
against the backdrop of dazzling Medieval Spain.

A TIME TO LOVE – *Jocelyn Haley*_____$2.5
Jessica Brogan's predictable, staid life is turned upside down whe
she rescues a small boy from kidnappers. Should she encourage th
attentions of the child's gorgeous father, or is he simply actin
through a sense of gratitude?

These three new titles will be out in bookshops from January 1989.

WORLDWIDE

Dare you resist...

Mills & Boon romances on cassette.

TWO CASSETTE PACK
ONLY
3.99

A WIDE RANGE OF TITLES AVAILABLE FROM
SELECTED BRANCHES OF WOOLWORTHS, W.H. SMITH,
BOOTS & ALL GOOD HIGH STREET STORES.
*SUGGESTED RETAIL PRICE

Mills & Boon

WINTER COMPETITION

How would you like a
year's supply of Mills & Boon Romances ABSOLUTELY FREE?
Well, you can win them! All you have to do is complete the word
puzzle below and send it into us by 30th June 1989.
The first five correct entries picked out of the bag after that date
will each win a year's supply of Mills & Boon Romances (Ten
books every month - **worth over £100!**) What could be easier?

```
C W A E T A N R E B I H
H R I C E R W O L G M Y
I F R O S T A O E L U Y
L N I B O R U D R I V Y
L B L E A K B W I I N F
T O G L O V E S E A R R
S O S G O L R W I E T E
T T C H F I R E L R O E
S K A T E M Y C I K S Z
I Y R R E M I P I N E E
N A F D E C E M B E R N
N C E M I S T L E T O E
```

Ivy	Radiate	December	Star	Merry
Frost	Chill	Skate	Ski	Pine
Bleak	Glow	Mistletoe	Inn	
Boot	Ice	Fire		**PLEASE TURN OVER FOR DETAILS ON HOW TO ENTER**
Robin	Hibernate	Log		
Yule	Icicle	Scarf		
Freeze	Gloves	Berry		

How to enter

All the words listed overleaf, below the word puzzle, are hidden in the grid. You can find them by reading the letters forwards, backwards, up or down, or diagonally. When you find a word, circle it, or put a line through it. After you have found all the words the remaining letters (which you can read from left to right, from the top of the puzzle through to the bottom) will spell a secret message.

Don't forget to fill in your name and address in the space provided and pop this page in an envelope (you don't need a stamp) and post it today. Hurry - competition ends 30th June 1989

Only one entry per household please.

Mills & Boon Competition,
FREEPOST,
P.O. Box 236,
Croydon,
Surrey CR9 9EL.

Secret message _____

_____

Name _MRS M HARDMAN_____

Address _64. WESTERN ROAD_____

_____GOOLE_____

_EAST YORKSHIRE_____

_____ Postcode _DN14 6QL_

INTERNET

ELECT

File Edit View Options

From:
To: Subject:

michael coleman
WEB TRAP

| OPEN | SEND | FORWARD | REPLY | DELETE | SAVE | PRINT |

★★★★★   Mail:

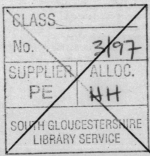
A WORKING PARTNERS BOOK

MACMILLAN CHILDREN'S BOOKS ▷

First published 1996 by Macmillan Children's Books
a division of Macmillan Publishers Limited
25 Eccleston Place, London SW1W 9NF
and Basingstoke

Associated companies throughout the world

Created by Working Partners Limited
London W6 0HE

ISBN 0 330 34739 X

Copyright © Working Partners Limited 1996
Computer graphics by Jason Levy

9 8 7 6 5 4 3 2 1

A CIP catalogue record for this book is available from
the British Library.

Printed by Mackays of Chatham plc, Kent

CHAPTER 1

Manor House, Portsmouth, England.
Monday 2nd September, 8.25 a.m.

'Rob!' shouted Mr Zanelli angrily as he saw his son's specially-designed screensaver popping up randomly on the screen. 'Are you using this PC?'

Hearing his father's shout, Rob Zanelli gulped

down the piece of toast he'd been eating at the breakfast table in the kitchen.

'Yeah, I am,' said Rob, swallowing the last mouthful. 'I mean, I was. I was on the Internet earlier.'

'Then turn it off! I haven't got money to burn!' came a shout from the hallway. 'You spend too much time on that system, Rob. Did you see how much our last telephone bill was?'

'Sorry,' began Rob, 'I …'

Mrs Zanelli appeared at the top of the stairs and called down. 'Paul, what is all the noise about?'

'Wasting money, Theresa!'

'I left my PC on,' said Rob.

'Paul, really!' said Mrs Zanelli, hurrying down. 'Is that all?'

'I'll see you at the office later!' Mr Zanelli said angrily as he stomped out through the front door.

'What was all that about?' Rob asked his mother.

Mrs Zanelli took a seat opposite Rob at the table and shrugged. 'Oh, don't mind your dad. He's under a bit of strain at the moment.' She gave Rob a weak smile. 'We both are, to be honest.'

'Why? What's the matter?' asked Rob.

'Sales,' said Mrs Zanelli. 'They're down. The last couple of months have been disappointing.'

Rob felt a knot in his stomach. His parents ran a computer games company called GAME-ZONE. If the company was in trouble then it was no wonder his Dad had been in a bad mood.

'Sales are down?' he echoed. 'Why?'

'Oh, lots of reasons,' said Mrs Zanelli. She smiled. 'The Internet, for one. There are plenty of free games on there. Maybe kids are downloading them instead of buying ours.'

'But the games on the Net are nothing like as good,' said Rob. 'That's *why* they're free!'

A thought suddenly occurred to him as he remembered an e-mail he was going to send to his friend Tom in Australia. 'Anyway, things'll pick up when Speed Surf comes out, won't they? Tom wants to know when he'll be able to buy a copy.'

Mrs Zanelli laughed. 'I don't think one sale in October will help us much!'

'October?' said Rob.

'Afraid so. That's when Speed Surf is being released in Australia,' said Mrs Zanelli. Her mood had already become solemn again. 'We could certainly do with it being sooner. Advance orders for Speed Surf are down in the UK. Even after all the advertising we've paid out for.'

Speed Surf was GAMEZONE's latest product, a virtual reality game in which the player had to sail a racing yacht single-handed round the world. Apart from plotting a route and sailing the yacht, the player had to handle everything from hurricanes to shark attacks! Complete with the sounds of howling winds and the crashing surf, the game even had action video shots taken on a real yacht that the company had sponsored in a Transatlantic race.

'But why are orders down?' asked Rob.

'If we knew that,' said Mrs Zanelli. 'We'd know what to do about it. Anyway, I don't want *you* worrying about it.' Looking at her watch, she snapped into action. 'And this sort of talk won't get you to school, will it?'

Rob threw his cup and plate into the dishwasher. 'Can I send that e-mail before we go?' he said.

'If you're quick,' called Mrs Zanelli.

'I will be,' called Rob.

Moments later he was in front of his keyboard in his room and typing his message to Tom Peterson.

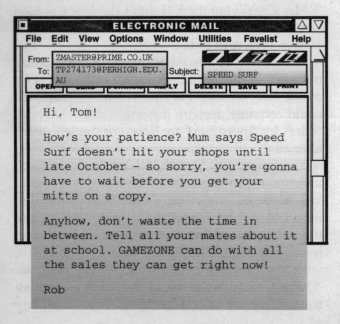

```
┌──┬──────────────────────────────────────────┬──┬──┐
│■ │          ELECTRONIC MAIL                  │△ │▽ │
├──┴──────────────────────────────────────────┴──┴──┤
│ File  Edit  View  Options  Window  Utilities  Favelist  Help │
├────────────────────────────────────────────────────┤
│ From: ZMASTER@PRIME.CO.UK                            │
│  To:  TP274173@PERHIGH.EDU.     Subject:             │
│       AU                                 SPEED SURF   │
│  OPEN    SEND   FORWARD   REPLY   DELETE   SAVE   PRINT │
├────────────────────────────────────────────────────┤
│  Hi, Tom!                                            │
│                                                      │
│  How's your patience? Mum says Speed                 │
│  Surf doesn't hit your shops until                   │
│  late October - so sorry, you're gonna               │
│  have to wait before you get your                    │
│  mitts on a copy.                                    │
│                                                      │
│  Anyhow, don't waste the time in                     │
│  between. Tell all your mates about it               │
│  at school. GAMEZONE can do with all                 │
│  the sales they can get right now!                   │
│                                                      │
│  Rob                                                 │
└────────────────────────────────────────────────────┘
```

Rob stared at the words on the screen. *Why are sales falling?* he wondered. Was it simply that kids weren't buying so many games nowadays? Or could there be another reason?

He shrugged. Either way, as his mother had said, there was nothing much he could do about it. He had to hope that his parents sorted it out themselves.

Switching his PC off, he turned towards the door. *What a great way to start the new school year!*

Abbey School.
Monday 2nd September, 1.45 p.m.

'Welcome to your first English class of the new school year.' Ms Gillies gave a broad smile. 'And your first piece of homework!'

The room was filled with groans. After a gentle morning spent in extended registration finding out all about their new timetables, this was school work for real.

Josh Allan turned to Rob and gave him a thumbs-down. 'I was going to suggest some Net-surfing tonight,' he whispered. 'Bang goes that idea!'

Behind them, Tamsyn Smith leaned forward, her short dark hair framing her face. 'Hey, it's not the end of the world, guys – it's gonna be *English* homework!' English was her favourite subject.

Josh pretended to slump lifeless in his seat. 'That *is* the end of the world,' he moaned. English was *not* his favourite subject.

At the front of the class, Ms Gillies called for attention.

'English isn't just about reading and writing. It's also about listening and speaking ...'

'So how come she's always telling me to be quiet!' Josh whispered.

'Be quiet, Josh!' shouted Ms Gillies. 'This term,' she went on, 'we will also be looking at writing for the mass media. That is, the different methods used to spread news and information to the general public such as the newspapers, television, radio ...'

Josh suddenly jerked up in his seat. 'Hey, don't forget the Internet, Ms Gillies. That reaches zillions of people!'

The teacher nodded. 'I thought you'd find a way of getting that in, Josh! But, you're right. The Internet, like satellite television, is an excellent example of one of the many new and developing forms of mass media. So, for your first homework, I want you to choose one type of information and examine how effective the different mass media are at disseminating that information.' She put her hands on her hips and looked round the class. 'Any questions?'

Slowly, Josh put his hand up.

'Yes, Josh?'

'Er ... this being English, Ms Gillies ... could you possibly say that again? In English?'

The teacher tried not to smile. 'Perhaps it might help if I give you an example. Take advertising. Every newspaper carries adverts. So does the television—'

'And the Net,' said Josh. 'So you want us to look at where it's best to advertise?'

'That was just one example. You could look at how we receive international news, or sports results ...'

She rambled on. But, as far as Rob, Tamsyn and Josh were concerned, their teacher could have stopped talking there and then. Each of them had already decided which topic they would be examining ...

Technology Block. 3.45 p.m.

'Advertising,' said Rob. 'That's the one for me.'

Tamsyn nodded. Rob had already mentioned GAMEZONE's falling sales. 'You reckon you'll come up with a better way of advertising computer games?' she said.

Rob shrugged. 'I doubt it. But it's worth a go. What are you going to look at?'

'Photographs,' said Tamsyn at once.

'Photos?' echoed Josh. 'What have photos got to do with English?'

Tamsyn laughed theatrically. 'Haven't you ever heard of the saying, "a picture is worth a thousand words"?'

'Of course I have,' said Josh, pulling a face and putting on a daft voice. 'You fink I'm an ignoramus?' He held up his hands as Rob opened his mouth. 'No, don't answer that!'

'Newspapers are full of pictures,' said Tamsyn. 'But so's the Net. And the ones on the Net can get round the world fastest of all.' She smiled. 'Anyway, it'll give me an excuse to surf the on-line encyclopaedias!'

Both Tamsyn and Rob turned to Josh. 'So, what are you going to look at?'

'Well …' he said, 'I thought I'd keep that a secret for the time being.'

'Josh!' cried Tamsyn. 'You know what *we're* doing!'

'Too right,' grinned Josh. 'But that doesn't mean I've got to tell— Yee-ow!'

'Looks like you *have* got to tell,' laughed Rob. Tamsyn had leapt to her feet and grabbed Josh by his dark spiky hair. 'Unless you want to end up bald, of course!'

'All right, all right!' cried Josh.

'I thought you'd see it our way,' said Tamsyn, letting go.

Josh rubbed his head. 'Just don't laugh, OK?'

'Laugh?' said Rob. 'What could you be looking at that we'd laugh about?'

'Kelly Rix,' said Josh.

Rob and Tamsyn exchanged glances. As each saw the other trying to keep a straight face, they burst out laughing.

'I'm serious, guys!' yelled Josh. 'This is a serious English project!'

'Serious English?' cried Tamsyn. 'Studying a TV soap star and pop singer? Come on, Josh, this I've got to hear!'

Josh leaned forward, counting off points on his fingers as he went. 'One. Pretty much the whole universe has heard of Kelly Rix – right?'

Tamsyn and Rob both nodded. Kelly Rix, although still only in her early twenties, was fast becoming a household name. Starting out as one half of a pop duo called Ambush, she'd become world famous after joining the cast of a TV soap called *New York, New York*. It was a series about the lives of different characters who lived in the city and was currently being shown on TV in dozens of countries. The programme had a large cast, but it was Kelly's role – as a junior newspaper reporter – that had captured the public's interest. Everybody wanted to know what sort of scrape she was going to get into next.

'Two,' Josh continued. 'Stars need the media to keep them in the public eye, don't they? Y'know, publicize what they're doing and all that?'

'Like bringing out their latest single,' said Rob.

Kelly Rix was making successful records, too. She and her Ambush partner, Jeannie Corrick, had split up to pursue solo careers some eighteen months before. The newspapers had tried desperately to prove that the split had been the result of a bust-up, but they'd failed. Although Jeannie Corrick had been nothing like as successful as Kelly Rix, the two girls had continued to be seen together, laughing and joking.

'And to keep their fans happy,' said Tamsyn.

'That was point number three,' said Josh,

popping up a third finger. 'Contact with their fans. How do they do that?'

'Fan clubs,' said Rob. 'You pay your subscription to get on their mailing list ...' He stopped, even as he said the words. 'Mailing lists? Is that what you're going to look at?'

Josh shook his head.

'You're not going to try e-mailing Kelly Rix?' said Tamsyn, wide-eyed.

'I've said enough,' grinned Josh. He stood up and grabbed his bag as Tamsyn took a step towards him. 'And you can torture me as much as you like but I won't say another word!'

CHAPTER 2

Hoy Street Market, Perth, Australia.
Tuesday, 3rd September. 7.50 a.m.

Tom Peterson yawned as he cycled. Out on the road before eight o'clock! What was he doing?

Getting back into his mum's good books, that's what he was doing!

It had been an accident. He hadn't meant to smash her glass-topped coffee table with his cricket bat. He'd just wanted to practise the sort of flashing cover drive he was hoping would get him picked for the All-Perth cricket team.

And if it hadn't been raining, he wouldn't have been inside anyway. But it *had* been raining, accident or not he *had* hit the coffee table for six, it *was* in pieces, and now he was paying for it by having to get some stuff for his mother in Hoy Street Market.

Turning into the street, he skidded to a halt. Ahead of him, the market stalls stretched out along both sides of the road as expected. What he hadn't expected was that the area would be so crowded at this unearthly hour of the morning. Shoppers with bulging bags of fruit and vegetables hurried past.

Dismounting, Tom chained his bike to a lamp-post. Unloading the empty rucksack from his back, he began wandering along. In his hand was the $20 bill he'd been given to pay for the things he had to buy.

Making for the nearest vegetable stall, Tom joined the queue. That was when he saw it. Tucked behind the vegetable stall was another – but this one wasn't piled high with apples and oranges.

It wasn't really a stall, either. A trader had placed a large suitcase on some old crates and spread out his wares around it. Attached to the wall above them there was a hand-written sign: *Tapes, CDs, Computer Games – Bargain Prices.*

Leaving his place in the queue, Tom wandered across for a closer look.

'All good as new, son,' said a man, from behind. 'You won't get 'em cheaper anywhere in Perth.'

Tom could believe it. The trader's stock of second-hand music tapes, CDs and computer games were all on offer at much cheaper prices than if they were new. There was even a Kelly Rix CD there at $12 that Debbie Levitt in his class had been talking about buying for $25. Tom picked it up. And it did look as good as new!

'Never let it be said that Nick Pereira don't give you a fair deal,' said the man at once. 'You can have that one for $10.'

'Ten?' said Tom.

Looking at the $20 bill in his hand, just as Pereira had done, Tom's plan took quick shape. He could buy the CD now, sell it to Debbie for $20, then come back to the market after school. Ten dollars profit!

But what if something went wrong? He was in enough trouble already. Turning up with a $10 CD instead of the family vegetables would just about finish him off.

'Interested?'

Tom shook his head. 'Nah. Another time.'

As he turned to go, Pereira bent down and plucked a CD-ROM from a box to one side that Tom hadn't noticed. 'I'm a fool to meself,' said the trader. 'Here you go, I'll throw a copy of this in for free.'

Tom looked at the title on the CD-ROM he was being offered. 'You're on!' he said immediately.

Minutes later, he was unchaining his bike and pedalling furiously in the direction of school. Talk about a double triumph! If this worked out he'd more than be in profit. He'd have made money *and* got a game he'd really wanted.

It was the CD-ROM that had persuaded him. The moment he'd seen the title Speed Surf on it, he'd been hooked. It was the game Rob's note had said wasn't going to be released in Australia for another month.

Tom laughed as he swung round the corner and raced for school. What a dumb-head! Fancy not knowing when a game your own parents produced was going to hit the streets! He'd certainly give Rob a hard time when he e-mailed him!

Perth High School. 1.00 p.m. (UK time: 5.00 a.m.)
'All yours, Tom!'

As the clock on the wall flicked over to one o'clock, the boy sitting at the PC closed down his work.

Tom moved into his seat with a sigh of relief. Having only one PC in the school connected to the Internet was a real pain. He'd have to have another go at his dad about buying a PC for himself – that Tom could use of course! The situation at school was becoming desperate.

He hadn't been able to get near the thing after arriving that morning, and even the first thirty-minute slot in the lunch break had been booked. He'd had to wait until now for his chance.

Still, it hadn't been time wasted. The moment the lunch bell went, he'd searched out Debbie Levitt. She'd nearly ripped the Kelly Rix CD from his hand.

'Twenty dollars?' she'd squealed. 'You bet!'

Living just round the corner from school, Debbie had raced home and grabbed her money. The deal had been done in moments.

He pulled the banknotes from his trouser pocket for another look, gave them a quick kiss, then put them back again. It was time to check out the other part of his morning's business.

Slipping the Speed Surf CD-ROM into the drive, he set the demonstration part of the game into motion. It was as good as Rob had described it. Every shot, from the graphic of the yacht's cockpit through to the video clips of the swirling sea, made it feel as though he was actually there, racing across the turbulent ocean.

And that Nick Pereira guy had *given* it to him, just to make a sale on something else!

Still wondering how the street trader could do that sort of thing and still make a profit, Tom clicked into MAIL. His note to Rob was brief …

Manor House. Tuesday 3rd September, 7.55 a.m.
Rob saw the note not long after he got up. Hearing the beep from his PC as it arrived in his mailbox, Rob had gone straight to it.

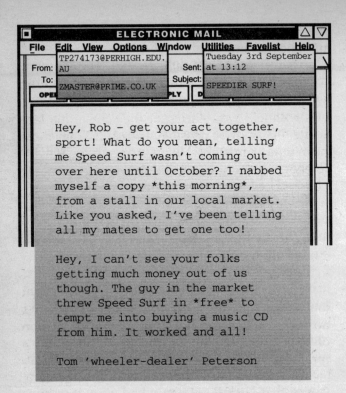

ELECTRONIC MAIL

File   Edit   View   Options   Window   Utilities   Favelist   Help

From: TP274173@PERHIGH.EDU. AU   Sent: Tuesday 3rd September at 13:12

To: ZMASTER@PRIME.CO.UK   Subject: SPEEDIER SURF!

OPE   PLY   D

Hey, Rob – get your act together, sport! What do you mean, telling me Speed Surf wasn't coming out over here until October? I nabbed myself a copy *this morning*, from a stall in our local market. Like you asked, I've been telling all my mates to get one too!

Hey, I can't see your folks getting much money out of us though. The guy in the market threw Speed Surf in *free* to tempt me into buying a music CD from him. It worked and all!

Tom 'wheeler-dealer' Peterson

'Hi, son,' came a voice from the doorway. 'Look, about yesterday. I'm sorry …'

Rob spun round. 'No sweat, Dad.'

'I shouldn't take it out on you because the company's having a few problems.'

'Yeah, Mum said.' Rob turned back to the screen. 'Maybe you shouldn't let people give your software away.'

'What?'

'I just got this note from Tom. Didn't you tell

INTERNET DETECTIVES

me Speed Surf wasn't being shipped overseas until next month?'

'It isn't,' said Mr Zanelli, drawing closer.

'Tom bought a copy this morning. Actually, he was *given* a copy!'

Mr Zanelli was staring at the screen, his face white. 'That's not possible,' he said. 'Tom must have made a mistake. He must have bought a different game.'

Rob shook his head. 'Not Tom, Dad. If he says he has a copy of Speed Surf, then that's what he has ...'

Mr Zanelli ran a hand across his eyes. 'This is part of our problem,' he murmured.

'What is?' asked Rob.

'Pirate copies,' said his father grimly. 'Rob, I look after software distribution myself. There's no way that Tom's disk can be a genuine version of Speed Surf. The only explanation is that it's a pirate copy.'

'You mean somebody's got hold of a genuine Speed Surf and copied it?'

'Possibly thousands upon thousands of times.' Mr Zanelli nodded. 'Yes. It's a problem every software company faces. But I can't believe ...' His voice tailed away.

'That one of the GAMEZONE programmers is responsible?' said Rob. 'Dad, it's happened before.'

'I know,' said Mr Zanelli.

They were both remembering a programmer named Brett Hicks who had been sacked for trying to hack into the GAMEZONE development computer and steal software.

'My staff have all been with me for years,' said Mr Zanelli. 'They have shares in the company. If *we* do well, *they* do well. I can't believe any one of them is responsible.'

'Somebody must be,' said Rob. He looked at his father. 'You want me to e-mail Tom for anything more he can find out?'

'Please,' said Mr Zanelli. He sighed. 'And I'll take another look at our security. If we've got it wrong, this could be just the tip of a very big iceberg.'

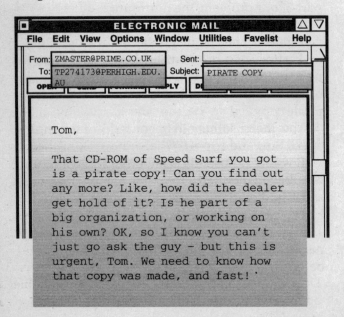

ELECTRONIC MAIL

File   Edit   View   Options   Window   Utilities   Favelist   Help

From: ZMASTER@PRIME.CO.UK   Sent:
To: TP274173@PERHIGH.EDU.   Subject: PIRATE COPY
AU

OPEN   SEND   REPLY   DE

Tom,

That CD-ROM of Speed Surf you got
is a pirate copy! Can you find out
any more? Like, how did the dealer
get hold of it? Is he part of a
big organization, or working on
his own? OK, so I know you can't
just go ask the guy – but this is
urgent, Tom. We need to know how
that copy was made, and fast!

Rob's note arrived too late for Tom to see it. He'd cycled out of school the moment the day had ended, heading for Hoy Street Market and the final transaction of his day's business.

Chaining his bike to the same lamp-post he'd used that morning, Tom headed for the vegetable stall and bought the things his mum had asked him to get. He glanced over towards the spot where Nick Pereira had been – and saw nothing but an open space. The trader had packed up and gone.

Feeling like a successful trader himself, Tom went back to his bike and pushed off for home. Errand completed, ten dollars profit, and a Speed Surf game! The end of a perfect day!

Turning into his front drive, he leapt from his bike and raced indoors.

'Hi. It's me ...'

He stopped as he saw the girl sitting at the kitchen table, talking to his mum.

'Debbie,' said Tom. 'What are you doing here?'

It was Mrs Peterson who answered. 'Returning shoddy goods to the person she bought them from,' she said.

Debbie Levitt held up the Kelly Rix CD she'd started playing the moment she'd got home. 'It's useless, Tom. Total rubbish.'

'She wants her money back, Mr Wheeler-Dealer,' Mrs Peterson said with an unmistakable edge to her voice. 'And *I* want an explanation!'

CHAPTER 3

Library, Abbey School.
Wednesday 4th September, 12.45 p.m.

Tamsyn was having second thoughts. Logged in to the Net on the library PC, she'd spent half an hour checking out some of the on-line encyclopaedias. Then she'd connected to the NASA site in Florida, downloading some pictures from the space shuttle that were on file.

She looked at the image of the Earth on her screen – and sighed. It was wonderful, and she could access it instantly. But what she was after was something a little different. Nowadays a newspaper could do the same thing she'd done almost as quickly, printing the same pictures in its next edition. What *couldn't* a newspaper do?

'Turn that thing off, please!'

At the sound of the school librarian's voice, Tamsyn turned. Over by the door, a boy had come in wearing a personal stereo that was on so loud that even she could hear its tinny squeaking sound from where she was sitting on the other side of the room.

Sound! That was it!

The school's Technology Block had recently been extended and, as part of the expansion, many of the PCs had been upgraded with multi-media equipment.

'Video, sound, *and* computer power!' Mr Findlay, the school's Head of Design and Technology had crowed during his initial demonstration to the whole class. 'What more could you want?'

Nothing! thought Tamsyn. *Just so long as they're connected to the Net.* Moments later she was hurrying towards the Technology Block to check it out …

Technology Block. 12.50 p.m.

Josh had been sitting at one of the new multi-media PCs for the past twenty minutes. The first thing he'd done was to e-mail Lauren King, their friend in Toronto.

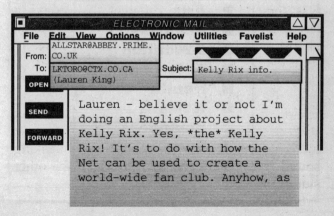

ELECTRONIC MAIL

File Edit View Options Window Utilities Favelist Help

From: ALLSTAR@ABBEY.PRIME.CO.UK

To: LKTORO@CTX.CO.CA (Lauren King)   Subject: Kelly Rix info.

OPEN SEND FORWARD

Lauren - believe it or not I'm doing an English project about Kelly Rix. Yes, *the* Kelly Rix! It's to do with how the Net can be used to create a world-wide fan club. Anyhow, as

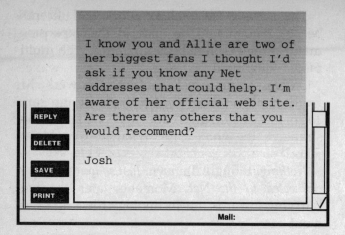

I know you and Allie are two of
her biggest fans I thought I'd
ask if you know any Net
addresses that could help. I'm
aware of her official web site.
Are there any others that you
would recommend?

Josh

REPLY
DELETE
SAVE
PRINT

Mail:

After this, he'd switched to the Net Navigator
home page with its menu list.

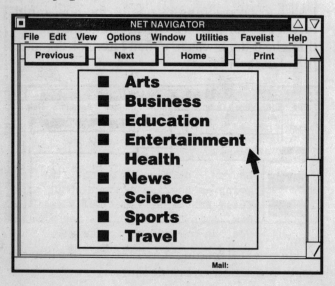

NET NAVIGATOR

File   Edit   View   Options   Window   Utilities   Favelist   Help

Previous   Next   Home   Print

■ **Arts**
■ **Business**
■ **Education**
■ **Entertainment**
■ **Health**
■ **News**
■ **Science**
■ **Sports**
■ **Travel**

Mail:

From there he'd clicked on ENTERTAIN-
MENT, then moved the cursor down to the panel
at the bottom of the screen marked SEARCH
FOR? He typed in KELLY RIX and waited.
Moments later a surprisingly long list of matches
came up on the screen. But, seeing the entry at the
top of the list, Josh didn't bother to look any further.

```
1. Kelly Rix - official world-wide web
   site
```

Clicking on the entry, he brought up the TV
star's home page.

He was still reading it as Tamsyn came into the
room and sat down beside him.

'What on earth is a "biovox"?' muttered Josh.

'Will it get you off this machine any quicker if I tell you?' said Tamsyn.

Josh grinned. 'It might. Then again, it might not. Try me.'

'Well,' said Tamsyn, 'a biopic is a filmed biography, so at a guess, a biovox is a sound biography.' She reached for the mouse. 'Only one way to find out,' she said, clicking on the first menu item.

The screen changed. 'Half right,' said Tamsyn as she saw it.

Kelly Rix's biography had been laid out in the form of a question and answer interview. Josh and Tamsyn read the opening questions:

KELLY RIX'S MANAGER, STEVE DENNISON, ASKS THE QUESTIONS MOST FANS WANT ANSWERED. Opening question, Kelly. Which came first, acting or singing?
Singing! I went to the same university upstate as Jeannie Corrick – we were both studying computer science would you believe! We started singing together while we were there, did a few university gigs, and decided we wanted to be singers, not computer boffs.
Why did you call yourselves Ambush?
Because that's what we'd do to anybody we thought could help us get into the music business! We even went as far as to call our first song Stand And Deliver! Our first tapes were solos and duets. We recorded them in my garage! They were awful, but we gave copies to every pop

group manager we could discover. That's
how come you got picked on, Steve!

**Thanks! Yes, Stand And Deliver was bad,
but I could see you had talent. And the
Ambush successes proved it. So, tell us
about the split.**

I was happy enough as we were, but Jeannie
wanted to try a solo career. I could
understand that. But it was never a bust-
up like the papers tried to make out.
We're still the best of mates. You should
know, Steve – you're Jeannie's manager
too!

How did you get into TV?

It was something I'd always fancied and,
after the Ambush thing ended, I thought it
was a good time to try. When I heard about
a new TV soap being made about New York, I
went along for an audition. Nobody was
more surprised than me when I got a part in
it! I always thought that New York, New
York would be a smash hit, though.

What's your next project?

A very exciting project which means a trip
to England. I can't say any more about
that one right now.

**You're a TV star, and your solo recordings
are selling well. How do you handle two
careers?**

With difficulty! The team here are really
great – you, Sadie Mulkern your PA, and
Shep Ahlberg who produces my records –
they've sure helped a lot. But I can see
the time coming when I'll have to decide
whether I want to concentrate on singing
or acting.

And which one do you think it will be?

I'm not saying!

'So where does the "vox" bit come in?' said Josh.

'There,' said Tamsyn, pointing. Down in the bottom left-hand corner of the screen was a small check-box.

❏ Download recorded interview

'Click on that and you actually hear Kelly Rix answering the questions, I suppose,' Tamsyn said.

Josh shook his head. 'Not as simple as that according to the manual.' He held up the slim booklet that Mr Findlay had given him that morning. 'What you get is a file that can only be translated into sounds by the right sort of software.' Josh took over the mouse again from Tamsyn. 'So let's give this interview a miss and have a look at what else is on here.'

He clicked on the PREVIOUS button at the top of the screen. Immediately the Kelly Rix home page popped up again with the starting menu they had seen before. This time, Josh selected the item MUSIC SAMPLE – 1.

'Hey, it's transferring something!' said Tamsyn as the red light on the computer's hard disk began to flicker on and off.

They watched as the transfer finished. Then, quitting Net Navigator, Josh switched the computer over to its sound player system. Moments later, having selected the Sample file, the husky voices of Kelly Rix and Jeannie Corrick –

otherwise known as Ambush – were blasting out through the computer's twin speakers.

'Hey, quicker than going to a record shop!' said Josh. 'And cheaper!'

'Famous last words,' said Tamsyn as the singing stopped suddenly.

Josh looked confused. 'Hey, what's happened?'

'Maybe that's why it's called a sample, eh?' said Tamsyn. 'On account of you only get a sample. If you want the whole thing, you've got to go down to the record shop with your money in your sticky little hand and actually buy it.'

Glaring at the PC as though it was all its fault, Josh slid the cursor over to the icon for MUSIC SAMPLE – 3. Downloading that, he set it playing.

But this time the music was of a vastly different quality. The smooth, professional voices were gone. In their place was a solo voice which sounded squeaky and amateurish.

'Who is *that*?' cried Tamsyn. 'She sounds dreadful!'

Josh listened hard. After a few more bars of singing he was amazed, but in no doubt. 'That's … Kelly Rix.'

'You sure?' Tamsyn listened until the sound file came to an end. When it did, she looked at Josh. 'You're right. It *was* her. But – it was awful!'

'Maybe it was a practice tape,' said Josh. 'But why has she put it on her web site? Her fans sure aren't going to be impressed by that!'

Perth High School. Wednesday 4th September, 9.24 p.m. (UK time: 1.24 p.m.)

Tom slumped in front of the PC and groaned. He might have known. After the nightmare few days he'd had, coming into school for some Net-surfing while his mum did her cleaning job was bound to be a bad idea.

Only a lot of persuasion, plus helping her out for an hour, had made Mrs Peterson agree to him coming at all. Now he wished he hadn't bothered. On the screen in front of him was Rob's note, sent more than twenty-four hours earlier.

'That CD-ROM of Speed Surf you got is a pirate copy,' read Tom aloud in a funny voice. 'Rob, that is *all* I need!'

If this is what happens when you try to go in for a bit of wheeling and dealing, thought Tom, *you can forget it!* His whole day had turned into nothing less than a disaster.

Debbie Levitt had started the ball rolling, of course, turning up at his house.

'It's useless, Tom. Total rubbish,' was what she'd said.

And, when she'd played a snatch of the CD, he'd had to agree. It was the voice of Kelly Rix, all right, but not singing the songs off the album. Instead the CD had been full of songs which sounded as though they'd been recorded in a cave rather than a proper studio.

In the circumstances, and with his mother breathing down his neck, he'd had no choice but to give Debbie her $20 back. *That*, of course, hadn't been so simple.

So, he'd then had to give her the full story about what he'd done and about how he'd used her money. Of course, he'd then had to borrow from her to pay Debbie back, leaving him even further out of pocket.

And then his dad had come home. Mr Peterson, a detective with the Perth police, hadn't minced his words.

'You bought a CD from one of those fly-by-nights?' he yelled. 'You idiot! How many times have I told you? If one of those guys is selling you something for next-to-nothing then it's because that's what it's worth! Next to nothing!'

'I can take it back, can't I?' Tom had argued. 'The market's there again on Friday. I'll ask for my money back.'

'Ask for your money back?' Mr Peterson had laughed. 'You can't ask somebody who isn't there! He won't be back there again in a hurry. Forget it, son. You've been done.'

The only consolation in the whole sorry business had been the fact that he'd got a copy of Speed Surf out of it. And now here was Rob telling him it was a pirate copy.

He placed the CD-ROM in the computer's drive and clicked into the game, just as he had the day before.

Pirate copy or not, it worked yesterday, Tom told himself. But, inside, he couldn't shake off the nagging fear that he'd only tried the demonstration sequence of the game. What would happen when he tried to get right into it?

He quickly found out. No sooner had he entered the first level than the screen went blank. As he watched, horrified, the 'busy' light on the hard disk started flickering madly.

Tom didn't know what to do. Should he turn the machine off? No, that would surely only make things worse. He waited. The disk light was still going on and off. Suddenly, it stopped flickering. With his heart in his mouth, Tom turned the PC off.

Perhaps it would be all right when he powered it up again. He pressed the button, and heard the whirr of the hard disk.

But all he got on the screen in return was a message that made his blood run cold:

FATAL DISK ERROR

Abbey School. 3.36 p.m.

The idea had come to Tamsyn in the middle of the afternoon. Instead of showing how useful the Net could be for *storing* and transmitting sounds and pictures, why didn't she use it for doing even more – by *collecting* some sounds and pictures of her own?

Straight after her last lesson of the day, she'd hurried across to the Tech. Block. and logged in. She needed some help for the particular idea she'd had – and Tamsyn knew just where to get it from. Moments later she was composing an e-mail for Mitch Zanelli.

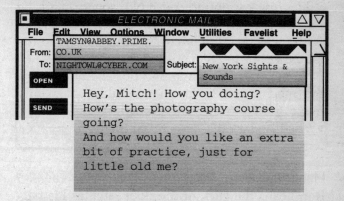

From: TAMSYN@ABBEY.PRIME.CO.UK
To: NIGHTOWL@CYBER.COM   Subject: New York Sights & Sounds

Hey, Mitch! How you doing?
How's the photography course
going?
And how would you like an extra
bit of practice, just for
little old me?

Mitch lived in New York. He was studying photography at college and, to help pay his way, worked part-time in a special café called Cyber-Snax that offered its customers Net surfing time as well as cups of coffee. The computer gear in the café was really up to date, so if anybody could help her it would be Mitch.

I'm trying to come up with
something different for an
English media project, and I've
had the idea of showing how the
Net could be used to write the
sort of travel article you see
in the newspapers – except that
my one's going to have pictures
and sounds in it!

So...is it possible? I know
you've got stacks of photos of

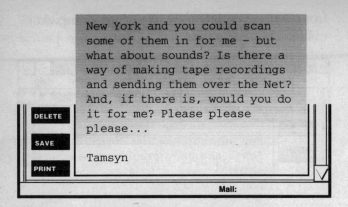

New York and you could scan
some of them in for me – but
what about sounds? Is there a
way of making tape recordings
and sending them over the Net?
And, if there is, would you do
it for me? Please please
please...

Tamsyn

DELETE

SAVE

PRINT

Mail:

Manor House. 7.50 p.m.

Rob heard the click of the door latch as his parents came home from work. Since he'd got in from school they'd telephoned half-a-dozen times to say they'd been delayed.

'Busy time?' said Rob.

'You could say that,' said Mrs Zanelli. She tried to smile at him.

Mr Zanelli took off his jacket and threw it over the banisters. His collar was undone and his tie loosened. He looked as if he'd had a terrible day.

'Fill me in, huh?' said Rob. 'I'm part of the family business too, y'know.'

His father paused, then nodded. 'Sure,' he sighed. Seating himself on the stairs he opened up.

'Tom was right,' he said. 'There's a pirate copy of Speed Surf out there.'

'But it's not just Australia. We've had calls from Canada, New Zealand, USA ... all over.'

'Calls?' echoed Rob. 'Who from? Saying what?'

'Complaints,' said Mrs Zanelli. 'From people who've got hold of it.'

Rob felt his blood begin to boil. 'Complain? We should be having a go at them for having a pirate copy of our game! They're the ones using stolen property!'

Mr Zanelli shook his head. 'I know that, Rob. But they don't see it that way. And after what's been done to it ...'

'What? What are you saying?'

'The pirate copy's been spiked,' said Mrs Zanelli quietly. 'That's what the people were calling to complain about. When they ran Speed Surf, it corrupted their hard disk.'

Rob was struggling to understand what his parents were telling him. 'You mean ... whoever's responsible hasn't just copied the program? They've changed it?'

'Right,' said Mr Zanelli. 'The demo part works fine, but the minute you try to run the game ... bang. Down goes your system.'

'But – that's not your fault! The proper GAME-ZONE version doesn't do that, does it?'

'Of course it doesn't,' said Mrs Zanelli. 'But that doesn't help us. If word is going round that corrupted versions of Speed Surf are on the market then our reputation is bound to suffer.'

Mr Zanelli looked hard at Rob. 'And whether our versions are good or not, people *will* be scared away from us. It costs a fortune and many months of development to produce a game. And if we don't sell them, we're in trouble.'

'That's another reason we're so late, Rob,' said Mrs Zanelli. 'We've been working out if we can afford to carry on with our next game.'

'What's that?' asked Rob.

His dad smiled for the first time since he'd come through the front door. 'It's a multimedia game. We've given it the working title of Smash Hit. You're a singer. It comes complete with backing music. You start by going into a virtual reality studio and making your own recording. Then you have to try to get it to the top of the hit parade by fighting off villains like crooked promoters and DJs who want bribes to play your record. In the final virtual reality sequence you get to find out what it feels like performing on stage at a packed open-air concert.

'Sounds brilliant!' said Rob.

'I think it still needs something extra,' said his dad, 'but we're working on that. The immediate problem is whether we can afford to go on with it.'

'We don't have much choice, Paul,' said Mrs Zanelli. 'We're in too deep. The contract's been signed.'

'Contract?' said Rob.

His mother answered. 'We want to be really different with the music and video part of this game – not just have it as graphics, but using a real star in it.'

'Singing a brand new song,' added Mr Zanelli.

'That way, the record sells the game and the game sells the record.'

'Cle-ver!' said Rob.

'That's what we thought. So we went ahead and signed contracts. If we pull out now, her management will sue us for sure.'

'Her?' said Rob.

'Kelly Rix. You've heard of her?'

'Heard of her?' cried Rob. 'The whole world's heard of her!'

'That's what we thought,' said Mrs Zanelli. 'That's why we're paying her the earth to appear in Smash Hit.'

CHAPTER 4

Perth High School. Thursday 5th September, 3.42 p.m. (UK time: 7.42 a.m.)

'That … should … be … it!'

The technician pressed the drive button and ejected the final systems diskette.

'You reckon?' said Tom.

'Just so long as you don't bring that duff CD-ROM within a mile of this machine again,' growled the technician.

Tom breathed a sigh of relief. If anything, the past twenty-four hours had been even worse than the twenty-four hours before. Thankfully his FATAL HARD DISK error hadn't been *totally* fatal, but the school's PC had certainly been pretty sick. The technician had been forced to take it out of service, leaving Tom as the target for the complaints of every kid in the school who'd wanted to use it – and that, to Tom, had felt like every kid in the school!

'Don't worry, it's stashed away in my drawer,' said Tom. It was, too. Tom kept a crime drawer, in which he saved souvenirs of mysteries that he'd been involved with.

'What did it do, exactly?' asked Tom. 'Was it a virus?'

He'd heard about computer viruses, which could spread from one disk to another, causing havoc on the way.

The technician shook his head. 'Nothing so smart. It had just been doctored with a crude bit of programming that rubbed out as much of the hard disk as it could.'

Tom looked up sharply, as the full meaning of what he'd just heard struck him.

'Doctored? Are you saying that Speed Surf program was deliberately changed?'

'That's what it looks like to me?'

'But why? Who by?'

The technician looked at the screen with satisfaction as the PC booted up successfully.

'Why?' he said, answering Tom's first question. 'I haven't got a clue. Why do vandals wreck anything?'

He clicked into the File Manager to check that the files had all installed properly, then replied to Tom's second question. 'As to who ... All I can say is, it wouldn't have been the company that developed the program.'

'GAMEZONE,' said Tom. 'They're based in England.'

'Well, like I say. It wouldn't have been them. That piece of code couldn't have been in there when the program was released. Even the most basic testing would have found it.'

'So – it was added after?'

'Sure was,' said the technician, standing up. 'There you go, all yours. And try not to wreck it again, Tom, OK?'

As soon as the technician had left, Tom connected to the Net. Moments later, he was typing a note to Rob …

Abbey School.
Thursday 5th September, 8.41 a.m.
Tamsyn read Mitch's reply to her request with a broad smile. What he was suggesting sounded brilliant!

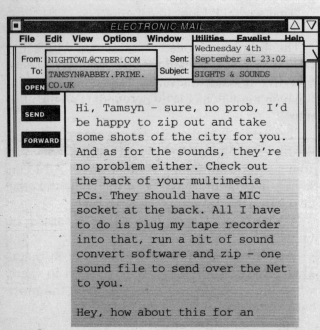

Hi, Tamsyn – sure, no prob, I'd be happy to zip out and take some shots of the city for you. And as for the sounds, they're no problem either. Check out the back of your multimedia PCs. They should have a MIC socket at the back. All I have to do is plug my tape recorder into that, run a bit of sound convert software and zip – one sound file to send over the Net to you.

Hey, how about this for an

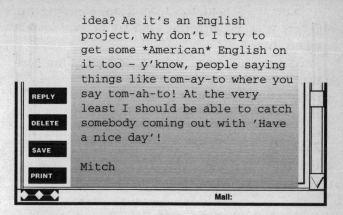

idea? As it's an English
project, why don't I try to
get some *American* English on
it too - y'know, people saying
things like tom-ay-to where you
say tom-ah-to! At the very
least I should be able to catch
somebody coming out with 'Have
a nice day'!

Mitch

REPLY
DELETE
SAVE
PRINT

Mail:

She looked up as the door swung open and
Rob pushed his way in. He looked serious.

'What's up?' said Tamsyn.

'I got a reply from Tom at last,' said Rob. 'I saw
it first thing this morning. Look.'

Moments later, they'd brought it onto the
screen.

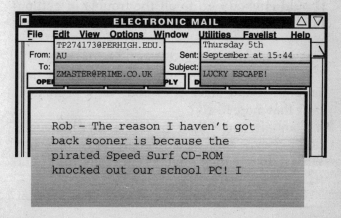

ELECTRONIC MAIL

File Edit View Options Window Utilities Favelist Help

From: TP274173@PERHIGH.EDU.AU   Sent: Thursday 5th
                                             September at 15:44
To: ZMASTER@PRIME.CO.UK   Subject:
OPE   PLY D LUCKY ESCAPE!

Rob - The reason I haven't got
back sooner is because the
pirated Speed Surf CD-ROM
knocked out our school PC! I

```
am *not* flavour of the month
round here, I can tell you.

Anyhow, I can't fill you in on
too many details right now
except to say that the technician
who fixed it reckons the program
was *deliberately* doctored by
some computer vandal.
```

'Not just pirated,' said Rob, 'but *doctored* as well.'

Beside him, Tamsyn frowned. Rob had told her about the pirated software and about how Mr Zanelli was looking into the possibility of it having been down to a GAMEZONE employee.

'That doesn't make sense,' she said. 'Why should anybody go to all the trouble of getting hold of a program like Speed Surf, and then mess it up?'

'Vandalism,' shrugged Rob, 'like Tom says.'

'Come on, Rob. Selling pirate copies of that program could make somebody a lot of money. Isn't that more likely?'

'Vandals make their money as well though, don't they?' said Rob. 'People only find out what it does to their systems after they've bought it.'

Tamsyn still wasn't convinced. 'But ... that

would ruin their chances of doing it again, wouldn't it?'

'Doing it again?'

'Ripping off another GAMEZONE package. If they get their systems wrecked by this spiked version of Speed Surf, people will think twice about buying GAMEZONE again, won't they?'

Rob nodded. 'That's what Mum and Dad are so worried about,' he said angrily. 'Their company's reputation is being hit hard and they've done nothing wrong.'

'So why should a pirate copier do it?' said Tamsyn again. 'Surely it's in their interest for GAMEZONE to stay in business, isn't it? I mean, they'll have nothing to steal and sell if the company goes bust!'

'Unless …' began Rob, trying to keep his voice steady as a chill fear enveloped him. 'Unless whoever doctored Speed Surf did it because they're *trying* to wreck GAMEZONE's reputation …'

'That's what I'd say it looks like,' said Tamsyn, looking serious. 'Which means it can't be somebody inside GAMEZONE. They'd be doing themselves out of a job by wrecking the company. That wouldn't make sense either.'

'So Dad's looking in the wrong place!' cried Rob.

Tamsyn pointed at the rest of Tom's note, still glowing on the screen. 'But maybe we're not,' she said, trying to sound cheerful. 'Let's hope detective Tom can get his man!'

Take it from me, though, I'm
going to sort this bloke out!
He's caused me more grief in
the last few days than I've
had in my whole life!

Market days are Tuesday and
Friday. So, come tomorrow, I'm
going to be there waiting for
him...

Tom 'good and mad' Peterson.

Mail:

Hoy Street Market, Perth, Australia.
Friday 6th September, 6.15 a.m.

Tom rubbed the sleep out of his eyes. Tuesday
had been bad enough, but this was worse. Just
after six in the morning! He wondered if he
should pinch himself to see if he was having a
nightmare.

Then the feeling of grim determination
took over. He didn't have to pinch himself. He'd
had his nightmare; it had been going on all
week. That was why he was here – to get his own
back.

Around him, the market was coming alive.
Lorries were growling into Hoy Street, crates
were being unloaded, stall-holders were beginning to lay out their wares. Tom, trying to look
unobtrusive in a nearby shop doorway, could see

the vegetable stall he'd called at on Tuesday. Behind it, the entrance to the alleyway was completely clear.

There was no way Nick Pereira could turn up there and Tom not spot him at once. And when he did …

When? In the cold light, his dad's words came to mind. *He won't be back there again in a hurry! Forget it, son. You've been done.* What if Pereira didn't turn up? Pushing the thought to the back of his mind, Tom settled down to wait.

8.15 a.m.
Two hours later, Tom was still waiting.

The market was nothing like as busy as it had been on Tuesday. What was more, there'd been no sign of Nick Pereira.

Now what was he going to do? Another fifteen minutes, and he'd have to be on his way to school. After the week he'd had, a detention for being late was the last thing he'd want to have to go home and explain to his dad.

Tom kicked angrily at the ground. His dad – he'd been right about Nick Pereira, of course. *He won't be back there again in a hurry!*

Back there? Back *there*? Cursing himself for being so stupid, Tom darted out from his hiding place and raced across to the man running the vegetable stall he'd been queuing at when he saw Pereira on Tuesday.

'Excuse me,' said Tom breathlessly. 'Do you

remember the guy who was in that alleyway the other day? Guy selling CDs and stuff?'

The man sniffed, then nodded. 'What about him?'

'Is he a regular there by any chance?'

'Regular, yeah,' laughed the stall-holder. 'Does a week here every three months. Just long enough for people to forget the rubbish he sold them the time before.'

'A week? Then – he'll back today?'

'Probably.' The stall-holder jerked a thumb back towards the alleyway. 'But not there. That's the one advantage of working the way he does. You can follow the crowd.'

Crowd? Tom looked around. Why wasn't it as busy as Tuesday? If anything, he'd have expected it to be busier.

'You mean there's more shoppers somewhere else?' said Tom.

'Today there is.' The man pointed away down towards the far end of Hoy Street. 'That big electronics sale starts this morning, don't it? He'll be down there somewhere. Poor suckers.'

'Cheers, mate,' said Tom and raced off down the street, leaping from the kerb to the road as he dodged between shoppers. He knew the electronics store the stall-holder had mentioned. It occupied a whole block, and was surrounded by small side roads.

The closer he got, the thicker the crowd became until, as Tom got within a hundred metres of the electronics store, he suddenly found himself at the end of a long queue. He gazed along its length. Surely, if Pereira was here he'd be squatting at the side of the road, working the crowd.

Or would he? Nearby, a uniformed policeman was keeping an eye on the crush. *Pereira wouldn't want to be operating in full view of him, would he?* reasoned Tom.

He looked along the queue – and saw, above their heads, the opening to a small side alley. Doubling back on himself, he turned left, then left again.

Yes! The other end of that alley came to the road he was now on. Tom hurried forward and peered round the corner.

At the far end, with the sale queue shuffling past him, sat Nick Pereira. As before, he was selling from his large open suitcase. This time it was on the ground, well out of the sight of the policeman.

Tom crept towards him. Closer, closer … until, just as Pereira was reaching into his case and pulling out a CD for a person in the queue, Tom was close enough. He didn't hesitate.

Yelling, 'Get the police!' at the top of his voice, he leapt forward and brought the lid of the suitcase slamming down onto Pereira's hands.

'Agh!' screamed Pereira in pain.

Tom wasn't finished yet. Before Pereira could get his hands free, he jumped on the case lid and sat there. Seeing the trader firmly trapped his face finally broke into a grin.

'I reckon you've been caught red-handed, mate!'

8.42 a.m.

'I didn't know it was spiked, I tell you,' said Pereira, ruefully rubbing his fingers.

'Who are you trying to kid?' said Tom. 'Come on, admit it. Why'd you doctor it?'

Mr Peterson looked at his son. 'Who's the detective here, eh? Leave the questions to me.'

He'd been called at Tom's insistence after the people in the queue had called the police-man on duty.

'OK, then,' said Mr Peterson to the trader. 'Let's say I believe you. But that CD-ROM caused a pack of damage and it won't take much to find something you can be charged with. So, shoot. Who'd you get it from?'

'I don't know that either.'

'Come on, Pereira! Who are you kidding?'

'I don't, I tell you. I got that one off the Net.'

Tom looked at him. 'The Internet?'

'Sure. What Net do you think I'm talking about?'

'But that game hasn't been released,' stammered Tom. 'Are you saying there's stuff on the Net that's been stolen?'

Pereira laughed. 'Now who's kidding? Sure there's stolen stuff on the Net. Stacks of it. Games, music, videos – you name it. It's all there if you know where to look.'

'And that's where you get it from?' said Mr Peterson.

'Some of it, yeah,' said Pereira.

'No wonder he could afford to give Speed Surf to you,' said Mr Peterson to Tom.

'But I didn't know that was spiked,' Pereira said. 'And I didn't know some of the Kelly Rix CD tracks were bad either.'

'Kelly Rix?' said Tom. He'd been so wrapped up in the problems with Speed Surf that he'd almost forgotten about the CD he'd bought for Debbie Levitt which had started all the trouble in the first place. 'You mean those songs are on the Net as well?'

'Sure. Like I say, if you know where.'

'And where's that?'

Pereira gave Tom a defiant look. 'Find it yourself.'

CHAPTER 5

Abbey School. Friday 6th September, 8.34 a.m.
'Hey!' cried Rob. 'Come and look at this!'

As Tamsyn and Josh left the PCs they were at and leapt across the room, Rob pointed at Tom's latest e-mail on the screen.

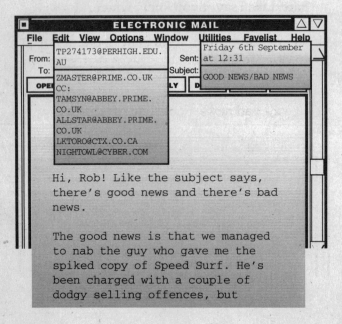

```
┌──────────────── ELECTRONIC MAIL ────────────△─▽─┐
│ File  Edit  View  Options  Window  Utilities  Favelist  Help │
│  ┌──────────────────────────┐  ┌──────────────────────┐
│ From: │ TP274173@PERHIGH.EDU. │   │ Friday 6th September │
│       │ AU                     │Sent: │ at 12:31          │
│ To:   │                        │Subject: │                │
│ OPE   │ ZMASTER@PRIME.CO.UK    │ LY │ D │ GOOD NEWS/BAD NEWS │
│       │ CC:                    │
│       │ TAMSYN@ABBEY.PRIME.    │
│       │ CO.UK                  │
│       │ ALLSTAR@ABBEY.PRIME.   │
│       │ CO.UK                  │
│       │ LKTORO@CTX.CO.CA       │
│       │ NIGHTOWL@CYBER.COM     │
│       └────────────────────────┘
│
│      Hi, Rob! Like the subject says,
│      there's good news and there's bad
│      news.
│
│      The good news is that we managed
│      to nab the guy who gave me the
│      spiked copy of Speed Surf. He's
│      been charged with a couple of
│      dodgy selling offences, but
```

nothing major. Dad says the law
still hasn't caught up with crime
over the Net.

Yeah, that's where he got the
game from – the Net! He just
downloaded it and had the CDs
made up in bulk. So *somebody*
must have got hold of a copy of
the original game, added the bad
bit of program, filed it on the
Net – then spread the word that
it was there.

'On the Net?' said Tamsyn.

'No wonder it got around the world so fast,'
said Rob. He looked at the others. 'But who put it
there?'

'Maybe we'll be able to answer that when we
find it. Where does Tom say it is?'

Tamsyn pointed them to Tom's note again.
'That's the bad news. Look.'

The bad news is that he won't say
whereabouts on the Net it is. I've
tried a couple of searches, but
found nothing. Maybe one of you
will do better. It's got to be a
biggish business. If it's any
consolation, Rob, it's not only
GAMEZONE's stuff that's being
ripped off. Maybe I didn't mention
it, but the other thing this guy

'A duff Kelly Rix CD?' murmured Tamsyn. 'Is that a coincidence, or what?'

Rob looked at her. 'What do you mean?'

Josh explained. 'I downloaded a music sample from the official Kelly Rix web site the other day. That was awful, too.'

'So what's the coincidence?'

'Only that we said it wouldn't do *her* reputation much good, that's all,' said Tamsyn. 'And here's Tom saying that not only did this guy have a screwed-up Speed Surf …'

'Which has knocked GAMEZONE's reputation for six,' said Rob, nodding.

'But he also had a duff Kelly Rix CD.'

Josh ran a hand through his hair. 'Hey, there's a big difference here. Speed Surf was *doctored.* That music sample was just plain *bad*!'

Tamsyn looked thoughtful. 'Was it? Or could that have been doctored, too?'

'I suppose it's possible,' said Rob. 'Yeah, it must be. I mean, music files can be edited too, can't they?'

'Come on, guys,' said Josh, reaching for the mouse. 'Let's get real here, eh? I bet if we can discover whereabouts on the Net this Australian guy downloaded his gear from, we'll find stacks of stuff. Just because he had a Kelly Rix CD and a GAMEZONE game in his grubby mitts doesn't mean to say the two are connected, does it?'

'But there *is* a connection, Josh,' said Rob quietly. Tamsyn and Josh turned to look at him as he went on.

'Mum and Dad were telling me about the new game they've got planned. It's going to be a multimedia job, featuring a brand new song. And guess who they've got signed up to do it?'

'Not ...' said Tamsyn, her eyes opening wide, 'Kelly Rix?'

Rob nodded. 'The one and only. And here's the both of them ...'

'Having their stuff ripped off,' interjected Josh.

'Not ripped off, Josh. Ruined. So that it makes them both look bad.'

Still shaking his head, Josh said, 'Why don't we have another listen to that sample, then? Maybe we'll be able to tell if it's been doctored or just bad singing.'

As Rob moved beside him and Tamsyn looked over his shoulder, Josh quickly went up to the menu bar and clicked on FAVELIST, his hot list of favourite Internet locations. He'd added the Kelly Rix home page to this list and went straight to it.

'Sample three, it was,' said Tamsyn as they waited.

The screen changed. Up came the same home

page they'd seen on the previous occasion. There was just one difference.

'It's not there,' said Josh. 'Music sample three just isn't there. Somebody's deleted it.'

Toronto, Canada. Friday 6th September, 2.50 a.m. (UK time: 7.50 a.m.)

As the muffled squeal broke into her dreams, Lauren King sat bolt upright in bed.

What had that noise been? She sat in the darkness, not daring to move, as she listened. For a while all she could hear was the sound of her own breathing until, suddenly, there it was again. Another soft squeal, coming from the direction of the lounge.

Gently, Lauren pushed back the covers and slipped out of bed. Padding across the floor, she eased open her bedroom door. Through the thin crack a dull light glowed. Somebody was in the lounge.

Without a sound, Lauren crept along the passageway. She'd suspected something like this was going on for ages. Now she was going to prove it.

She tiptoed into the lounge and saw the evidence at once. The computer was on. And, hunched in front of it, her grey hair tinged like a rainbow from the colours of the screen, was …

'Allie!' cried Lauren. 'Caught you!'

As her grandmother screeched, Lauren collapsed onto the sofa laughing fit to burst. She'd suspected for ages that, after telling her that computing was bad for her eyes and packing her off to bed, the grey-haired grandmother she lived with would settle down for a spell of Net-surfing herself. And now she'd seen it with her own eyes.

'Lauren!' shouted Allie. 'I could have had a heart attack!'

'Oh, I'm sorry, Allie,' said Lauren, wiping her eyes. 'I just couldn't resist it.'

She padded across to her grandmother's shoulder and gave her a kiss. 'What are you doing, anyway?'

'Just a little Net-sailing,' said Alice.

'At three o'clock in the morning!' cried Lauren. 'And you tell me I'm up too late if I'm still on-line at ten!'

'Three? It's never that time, is it?' Alice peered at her watch in the glow of the screen. 'Good heavens. Doesn't time go quickly when you're chatting.'

'Chatting?' Lauren looked more closely at the screen. It was covered with the sort of output she'd never seen before. 'Allie, what exactly are you doing?'

Alice smiled in the half-light. 'Oh! Found our old granny doing something we don't know about, have we? Well, I'm not sure I'm in a fit state to tell you. Not with my heart still pounding away like a steam hammer ...'

'Allie, c'mon,' pleaded Lauren.

'All right,' said Alice. 'That nice little man at the computer shop told me about it when I went in there the other day to get some printer paper for you. We got talking and he told me about Internet Relay Chat ...' She waved at the screen. 'It's a sort of chat line for Internet. It's so simple. You just pick a channel and start chattering!'

'A channel?' said Lauren. 'What's a channel?'

'Like a radio channel, apparently. That's what the man said. There's lots of them. You just join the one you want and away you go. Whoever else is there sees what you type, and you see what they type. It's just like talking to a dozen people at once.'

'No wonder you lost track of the time,' said Lauren as Alice stifled a yawn. 'So, which channel were you on?'

Alice seemed to receive another burst of energy. 'That's the most exciting bit about it. I found a *New York, New York* channel!'

Lauren's eyes lit up. 'Our favourite soap? With our favourite star? It's got its own channel?'

'Sure looks like it,' said Alice. 'And you get all sorts of people connecting. See?'

Crouching down beside the computer, Lauren scanned the screen. It was filled with lines, each starting with a different name in curly brackets. She read the first few.

```
{NIGHTHAWK} I'm in New Zealand. We're on
    episode 87. Anybody know how far we are
    behind?
{SUSAN} Three months, sounds like. We've
    had it from day one and we're on episode
    102.
```

'Who are Nighthawk and Susan?' asked Lauren.

'Just nicknames. You pick a nickname when you join the channel. This is me.'

Allie typed a line, then sat back. Within seconds it was duplicated on the screen, to be followed by further lines as other people joined in the on-line conversation.

```
{ALLIE} We're on 90 in Toronto. Two months
    off. Say, does Kelly Rix last until 102?
    If her reporter character gets much
    closer to that Mafia mobster I can't see
    her surviving!
{SUSAN} She's still in it. You want
    to know what happens to the mobster?
{ALLIE} No way! We'll wait until we
    see it.
{NIGHTHAWK} Did you know Kelly's going to
    miss a couple of episodes this month,
    though. I read it on her web site. She's
    off to England to take part in some
    secret project.
{SAD} It's a multimedia project with
    a company called GAMEZONE. She's
    doing a solo act with them, recording
    a single to fit in with one of their
    games.
```

'Hey, who's SAD?' said Lauren as she saw the last entry flick onto the screen.

Allie put on a face. 'A lurker,' she said dramatically.

'A what?'

'A·lurker. The man told me about them.

Lurkers connect to the channel but don't say anything for a while. Maybe not at all.'

```
{NIGHTHAWK} Sounds great! I can't wait to
   buy it.
{SAD} You won't have to buy it. It'll be on
   the Net, free. So will the GAMEZONE
   game. Connect to this channel this time
   next Wednesday if you want to know more.
```

'Free!' cried Lauren. 'Allie, who is that creep? There must be a way of finding out who it is!'

Alice reached across and turned on a table lamp, then dropped to her knees and began rummaging amongst some sheets of paper on the floor.

'There is,' she muttered. 'If I can find the bumph the man at the shop gave me ... Ah!'

She'd found a page of instructions. 'There,' she said. 'Type the command "/WHOIS SAD".'

Quickly, Lauren typed what Allie had told her. The response came back immediately.

```
*** SAD: NO SUCH NICKNAME ON THIS CHANNEL
```

'Too late,' said Lauren. 'Whoever it is has disconnected.'

Abbey School. Friday 6th September, 12.34 p.m.
'So, where does that leave us?' asked Josh as the three friends piled back into the Computer Club

room at lunchtime. 'Why would that dodgy song have been rubbed out?'

'Obvious, isn't it?' said Tamsyn. 'Somebody realized it was duff and took it off before it did any more damage to Kelly Rix's reputation. What do you think, Rob?'

Rob irritably punched the power-on button of the nearest PC. 'I think it doesn't matter,' he snapped. 'What matters to me is whereabouts on the Net that pirate software is, and who's putting it there.'

Tamsyn and Josh exchanged glances. 'Yeah. You're right,' said Josh. He pulled up a chair and sat down. 'So, come on then. Let's crack it!'

'Internet detection session in progress!' laughed Tamsyn, pulling up a chair for herself. But her smile had faded by the time she sat down and said, 'Where do we begin looking, though?'

'Use a search,' said Rob firmly.

He entered Net Navigator and took the cursor down to the SEARCH FOR? panel.

'What are you going to try?' said Josh. 'GAME-ZONE?'

'Seems a fair bet,' said Rob. He typed in the characters and waited until the search was complete.

'Useless,' said Tamsyn as they checked through the list of matches. The best reference the search had turned up was to GAMEZONE's own web site.

Josh looked doubtful. '*Is* it useless? Why couldn't that doctored Speed Surf have come from there?'

Rob shook his head. 'No way. That site's as secure as they come. Besides,' he added, 'why do it in a way that's certain to be discovered? They'd *have* to file it somewhere else.'

'But where, though?' said Tamsyn. 'Come on, Rob. Try another search.'

Rob clicked back to the Navigator home page and down to the search panel again. And again. And again. Everything they tried drew a blank.

Tamsyn stood up after fifteen minutes, deliberately stepping away from the PC in an effort to clear her mind.

'Come on, guys. Let's think this through. Put yourself in the vandal's position. You've got hold of a copy of Speed Surf. You spike it deliberately. Now, what do you do?'

Rob hammered his hand on the desk in disgust. 'How could I have been so dumb? What have I been looking at for my English project? Tell me?'

'Advertising on the Net ...' began Tamsyn, then realized what Rob was on about. 'Of course. What you *wouldn't* do is file it on the system and hope people will come and find it!'

'Which is what we've been assuming,' said Rob. 'No, you'd advertise it somehow.'

'How?' shrugged Josh. 'E-mail?' He immediately corrected himself. 'Junk. You wouldn't know who to tell. Hey – mailing lists! There are stacks of those on the Net!'

Tamsyn looked thoughtful. 'A games mailing list? Yeah, that could be it.'

'It would be a way of getting to interested people. Y'know, of spreading the news in the right—'

'News!' shouted Rob, turning for the keyboard in the same instant. 'Newsgroups! There are stacks of those, too.'

Rob knew that newsgroups were electronic bulletin boards to which people all over the world posted information. They covered just about every topic under the sun. Was it possible that one of them could be what he was looking for?

Quickly he switched to Newsgroups. Moments later he was scanning a long list. A *very* long list.

'Where do we start?'

'With a search, of course!' said Rob. He took the cursor down to the SEARCH FOR? panel and typed in 'SPEED SURF'.

Josh leaned across and stopped him. 'You sure that'll work? Won't that look for a newsgroup called SPEED SURF?'

Deleting the characters he'd just typed, Rob said, 'Yeah, you're right. So what do we try?'

'How about something obvious, like "SOFT-WARE"?' said Tamsyn.

Rob typed the word. Moments later, the screen was displaying a section of the list.

'How about that one?' said Tamsyn. 'Sneaky?'

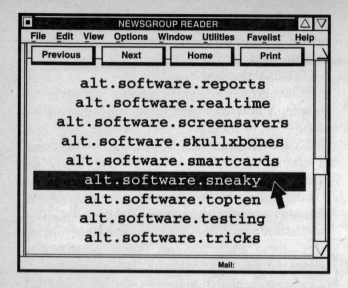

Rob clicked on the 'alt.software.sneaky' news-group line – and again, they were disappointed.

'Nothing dodgier than how to cheat your way through Dungeons and Dragons,' complained Josh. 'I worked that out *years* ago!'

Rob clicked on the PREVIOUS button to bring up the small list of software newsgroups again. 'This is hopeless,' he said.

Next to him, Josh was looking at the screen. 'A lot of these *are* junk,' he said. 'I mean, what's that one about?' He pointed at the newsgroup line:

```
alt.software.skullxbones
```

'Who cares?' said Rob, looking at his watch. 'It's nearly time to go anyway.' He started to spin the cursor up towards the menu bar to quit the system – only to find Tamsyn leaping across to grip his hand

'Go back!' she said.

'What? Why?'

Tamsyn pointed at the newsgroup name Josh had drawn to their attention. 'Skullxbones,' she said. 'That has got to be short for "skull and crossbones", Rob.' Her eyes were gleaming. 'As in piracy!'

Quickly Rob clicked on the newsgroup name. Moments later he was reading the newsgroup's introductory text.

Beneath it there was a whole list of entries.

'Look at that lot!' whistled Josh.

But Rob had eyes for one entry only – an entry a short way down the list.

14. **Speed Surf** – The latest from GAMEZONE. Why buy when you can get it for free? (posted by: ANON)

CHAPTER 6

Manor House. Friday 6th September, 7.50 p.m.

A click of the mouse and it was done.

'Stealing is so easy,' said Tamsyn.

The newsgroup item had told them exactly what to do. They'd followed the instructions to the letter and now, with Tamsyn's final mouse click, the copy of Speed Surf was being down-loaded.

'At least it would be stealing,' said Rob grimly, 'if it wasn't ours in the first place.'

The light on the hard disk stopped flickering. It was done. 'And that's all there is to it?' said Tamsyn.

Rob nodded. 'Reckon so. From here, somebody like Tom's trader could get a CD-ROM made up. Others would just be happy that they'd got some-thing for nothing and run it.'

'Not knowing that they're a few seconds away from wrecking their hard disk,' said Tamsyn.

'Blaming GAMEZONE when it happens,' said Rob angrily, '*and* conveniently forgetting that they were stealing the software in the first place.'

Rob pushed himself away from the keyboard, sighing as he did so. 'It still doesn't tell us *who* put it there in the first place, does it?'

The signature at the end of the newsgroup entry had told them nothing.

14. <u>**Speed Surf**</u> – The latest from GAMEZONE. Why buy when you can get it for free? (posted by: ANON)

'Or why,' said Tamsyn. 'Somebody must have a pretty good reason for having a downer on your parents' company.'

They were interrupted by the sound of the front door being opened. With Tamsyn following, Rob wheeled himself out of his room and down the corridor.

'Meet the next Olympic cycling champion,' said Mr Zanelli, holding the door ajar for an excited-looking Josh as he raced up the drive on his bike. 'He almost overtook my car at the top of Portsdown Hill!'

'Got to show you something,' panted Josh. 'On-line.'

'Sounds interesting,' said Mrs Zanelli.

'It is,' said Josh, still struggling to get his breath back. Looking at Rob and Tamsyn he said, 'I found it after school, when you'd both gone.'

'Found what?' said Rob.

Josh looked as though he was going to answer, then shook his head. 'Easier to show you. Come on.'

'We've got something to show you as well,' said Rob.

Josh led them all back down to Rob's room, then sat himself in front of the keyboard. Disconnecting Rob's session, he then logged in under his own ID.

'I've just received this e-mail from Lauren,' he said.

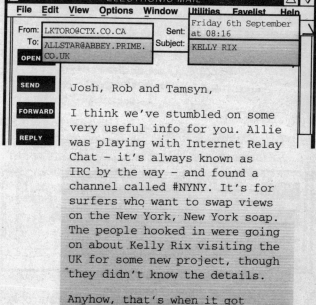

ELECTRONIC MAIL

File Edit View Options Window Utilities Favelist Help

From: LKTORO@CTX.CO.CA
To: ALLSTAR@ABBEY.PRIME.CO.UK

Sent: Friday 6th September at 08:16
Subject: KELLY RIX

OPEN

SEND

FORWARD

REPLY

Josh, Rob and Tamsyn,

I think we've stumbled on some very useful info for you. Allie was playing with Internet Relay Chat – it's always known as IRC by the way – and found a channel called #NYNY. It's for surfers who want to swap views on the New York, New York soap. The people hooked in were going on about Kelly Rix visiting the UK for some new project, though they didn't know the details.

Anyhow, that's when it got interesting. Up pops somebody nicknamed 'SAD' who seemed to know the works – like that it's a multimedia project with GAMEZONE.

'How did they know that?' cried Mr Zanelli.

'We weren't going to announce it to the press until *after* the recording,' said Mrs Zanelli. 'Being swamped with fans and TV cameras is the last thing we want right now.'

Josh cut them short. 'Read on!' he cried.

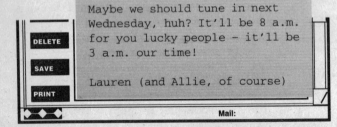

```
Then, when somebody said they
couldn't wait to buy the CD,
what did this 'SAD' come back
with? Exactly this:

    'You won't have to buy it.
    It'll be on the Net, free.
    So will the GAMEZONE game.
    Connect to this channel this
    time next Wednesday if you want
            to know more.'

Maybe we should tune in next
Wednesday, huh? It'll be 8 a.m.
for you lucky people — it'll be
3 a.m. our time!

Lauren (and Allie, of course)
```

DELETE

SAVE

PRINT

Mail:

Josh turned to them all. 'So, what do you make of that?'

'There *could* be a link, then,' said Tamsyn.

'A link?' said Mr Zanelli. 'What are you three thinking?'

'We found a bad Kelly Rix recording on the

Net, too. We're thinking there could be a link between that recording and the spiked Speed Surf.'

Rob looked up at Josh. 'And this 'SAD' character could be it?'

'Got to be,' said Josh, convinced. 'If he reckons he can put the Kelly Rix single on the Net, *and* the new game when it comes out, then somehow he must be pretty sure of getting access to both.'

Tamsyn explained to Rob's parents about the 'skullxbones' web site, then looked back at Josh. 'And to be *that* sure, he must already be in position?'

'More than that,' said Josh, insistently. 'He's *that* sure because he's *already* done it.'

'With the duff sample on the Kelly Rix web site, and the spiked Speed Surf!' said Tamsyn. 'You're right!'

Rob turned to his parents. 'So *could* it be a GAMEZONE employee? They must all know about the Smash Hit project.'

'Of course they do,' said Mrs Zanelli. 'A couple of them have been working on it for over six months.'

A memory stirred in Tamsyn's mind. 'But would they be able to change what's on the Kelly Rix web site?' she asked.

Rob shook his head. 'No.'

'Then it can't be down to one of the GAME-ZONE workers, Rob! That duff music file was on the official Kelly Rix web site. It can only have put there by one of the people who run the site!'

'You mean ...' began Rob.

'She means,' said Josh, 'it's working the other way round. Whoever's trying to do the dirty on Kelly Rix is trying to do the same to GAME-ZONE.'

The three of them looked at Mr and Mrs Zanelli. 'Mum, Dad,' said Rob. 'Is that possible? Is there any way somebody connected to Kelly Rix could have got hold of a copy of Speed Surf?'

Mr Zanelli paused – then nodded. 'Yes. When we first started talking about the project they asked for some samples. We sent them some. As we'd just cut the gold diskette for Speed Surf we sent that too, as an example of our best multi-media game so far.'

'So one of her people could have doctored it,' said Rob. 'Dad, you've got to tell them what's going on!'

'No, I can't do that,' said Mr Zanelli simply. 'I can do my best to get that 'skull x bones' web site closed down, and I will, but I can't do what you're suggesting.'

Rob looked up at his father in astonishment. 'What do you mean, you can't? Somebody in that organization is doing their best to trash GAME-ZONE!'

It was Mrs Zanelli who answered. 'We can't just accuse them,' she said, 'not without some sort of proof.'

'There's more to it than that, Theresa,' said Mr Zanelli. 'I wouldn't go to them even if we had a cast-iron case.'

Now it was Mrs Zanelli's turn to look surprised. 'Why ever not?'

'Because we just can't take the risk of them pulling out. This project *must* go ahead.'

'Even if it's going to be pirated?' said Josh.

Mr Zanelli nodded grimly. 'We're going to have to take that risk. There's too much riding on this project for the company. So,' he said looking from one of them to the other, 'none of your Internet detecting, right?'

'But …' began Rob.

'I mean it, Rob. Kelly Rix is flying in next Thursday. If anything stops that happening, it'll be a disaster. So, forget all about Speed Surf. Understand.'

Rob nodded. 'I understand. No rocking the boat, yeah?'

As she heard his words, Tamsyn wondered how on earth Rob could manage to joke at a time like this. But when she looked at him, he wasn't smiling.

Abbey School.
Monday 9th September, 8.28 a.m.

Tamsyn and Josh walked through the school gates and across to the Technology Block.

'I can understand Rob's dad not wanting us to get involved,' said Tamsyn.

'It's a pity though, isn't it?' said Josh. 'I mean, a mystery with a real live TV star. They don't come along every day of the week.'

As they pushed through the doors and headed down the corridor, Tamsyn wondered how Rob had managed to survive the weekend without trying to find out more about the mysterious 'SAD'. For Josh and herself, it hadn't been a problem. But for Rob, with his own PC and Net link, it must have been torture.

'Come and look at this!' said Rob the moment they opened the door to the Computer Club room.

'What are you doing?' said Tamsyn.

'What do you think I'm doing?' said Rob. 'Checking out this case. I can't do it at home without being seen, so I've got to do it here. I told Mum I'd forgotten to bring one of my books home for the weekend and got her to drop me in early.'

Tamsyn and Josh pulled up chairs and sat on either side of him. They immediately saw that he'd logged in to the Net and brought up the same Kelly Rix home page they'd visited before. Its short list of menu options were at the bottom of the screen.

'I thought we'd been warned off this,' said Josh.

Rob gave him a thin smile. 'A-ha. Dad said "Forget all about Speed Surf." So I have. I'm thinking about Kelly Rix's problem instead.'

'But we think they're linked,' said Josh.

Tamsyn laughed. 'Don't you see, that's what he means! If we can find out who's trying to rubbish Kelly Rix then we've found out who's responsible for pirating the GAMEZONE software as well.'

'OK, then,' Josh grinned, pulling his chair closer. 'So what you found out?'

'This,' said Rob. He pointed at the web site page he had on the screen. 'For a start, MUSIC SAMPLE 3 is back on the menu again.'

'But that—'

'Had been removed,' said Rob. 'I know. Well, it's back again and the rubbish tracks are in it again too. I've just downloaded it and tried it.'

'Why?' said Tamsyn. 'Why take it off and then put it on again?'

Rob shrugged. 'The only reason I can think of is that, for some reason, whoever's doing it can't leave it there all the time in case they're caught. They put it up for a while, then whip it off again before somebody updating the site notices it.'

'Anyhow, that's one thing,' continued Rob. He spun the cursor across to a different menu item. 'This is another.' He clicked on CONTACT LIST.

'Who are they?'

'People associated with Ambush,' said Rob. On the screen was a list of people.

Contact Addresses:
2nd floor, 992 Park Avenue at 82nd Street,
New York.
e-mail: team@dennmgmt.com

Manager: Steve Dennison
British-born Steve is the guy who recognized the raw talent that was hidden in
the tapes pressed on him by Kelly Rix and
Jeannie Corrick in their student days.
Abandoning a steady career as a computer
programmer to go full time in the much
riskier music business, Steve guided
Ambush from day one. He's now manager to
both Kelly and Jeannie as they pursue
their solo careers.

Personal Assistant: Sadie Mulkern
Girl Friday. Sadie does every job under
the sun and a lot that aren't. She's the
girl in charge of publicity. Write, phone
or e-mail and it'll likely be Sadie who
answers. Although we all do our bit on
occasion, Sadie is the one who keeps this
web site up to date.

Producer: Shep Ahlberg
The wizard who's personally handled every
one of the girls' recording sessions. Shep
is a leading exponent of synthesized and
computer-generated music and has been
responsible for the imaginative backing
tracks and mixes for which the duo are
well known.

'So you think it's this Shep Ahlberg guy?'
said Josh. 'Sound supremo. Computer-generated

music. He could have messed up that music track for sure.'

Tamsyn was shaking her head. 'Yeah, but could he be the one who spiked Speed Surf?'

'Well it's hardly likely to be their manager, is it?' said Josh.

'Which only leaves Sadie Mulkern, the PA,' said Tamsyn.

'Who's the obvious choice for two reasons,' said Rob firmly. 'One, she's the person who handles the web site, so she must know her way round the Net. It would have been a doddle for her to pull the music samples.'

'And two?' said Josh.

'Two, look at the first letters of her name. S-A-D.'

'Lauren and Allie's late-night contact ...' whistled Josh.

'The one who reckons they'll be able to supply the new Kelly Rix record and the new game with no trouble. If she's not a suspect, who is?'

'Suspecting her is one thing,' said Josh. 'But where do we go to get some evidence?'

Rob pointed at the address at the top of the screen. 'Nine nine two Park Avenue,' he said. 'New York, guys.'

The three of them grinned at once.

'Mitch!' they said together.

CHAPTER 7

Cyber-Snax Café, New York.
Monday 9th September, 10.12 p.m.

Mitch Zanelli took a bite out of a Cyber-Snax muffin, then sat back to think about what he could do with one of the oddest requests he'd ever received from his namesake in England.

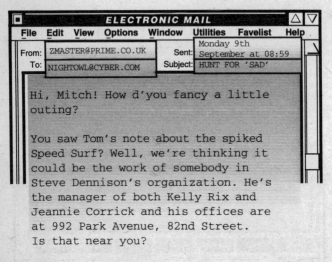

```
┌─────────────────────────────────────────────────┐
│ ■         ELECTRONIC MAIL            △  ▽          │
├─────────────────────────────────────────────────┤
│ File  Edit  View  Options  Window  Utilities  Favelist  Help │
├─────────────────────────────────────────────────┤
│ From: ZMASTER@PRIME.CO.UK    Sent:  Monday 9th         │
│ To: NIGHTOWL@CYBER.COM       Subject: September at 08:59 │
│                                      HUNT FOR 'SAD'     │
├─────────────────────────────────────────────────┤
│ Hi, Mitch! How d'you fancy a little               │
│ outing?                                           │
│                                                   │
│ You saw Tom's note about the spiked               │
│ Speed Surf? Well, we're thinking it               │
│ could be the work of somebody in                  │
│ Steve Dennison's organization. He's               │
│ the manager of both Kelly Rix and                 │
│ Jeannie Corrick and his offices are               │
│ at 992 Park Avenue, 82nd Street.                  │
│ Is that near you?                                 │
└─────────────────────────────────────────────────┘
```

Mitch didn't need to check a map. Apart from the southernmost tip, the streets on the island of Manhattan are organized by numbers, north to south and east to west. Cyber-Snax was on West 111th Street, so he was twenty-nine blocks away. Not close, but not such a giant distance on the New York subway.

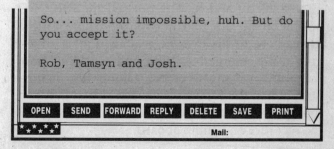

Trouble is, the only thing we've really got to go on is the nickname 'SAD'. Somebody calling themselves that joined an IRC session that Allie and Lauren were connected to and said they'd be back on Wednesday (at 3 a.m. your time!) with details of how to get a pirate copy of the recording Kelly Rix is making at the GAMEZONE studios on Friday.

The other names we took from the Net are Shep Ahlberg and Sadie Mulkern. He's a sound whiz. She's Dennison's PA and our favourite on the basis that she maintains the Kelly Rix web site.

So... mission impossible, huh. But do you accept it?

Rob, Tamsyn and Josh.

| OPEN | SEND | FORWARD | REPLY | DELETE | SAVE | PRINT |

Mail:

Mitch chewed thoughtfully for another couple of minutes. Then, he leaned forward and clicked on the REPLY button.

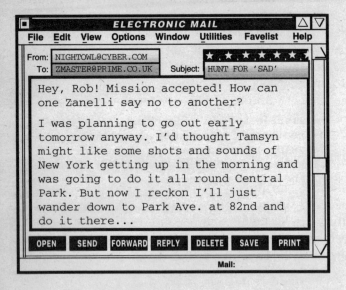

Hey, Rob! Mission accepted! How can one Zanelli say no to another?

I was planning to go out early tomorrow anyway. I'd thought Tamsyn might like some shots and sounds of New York getting up in the morning and was going to do it all round Central Park. But now I reckon I'll just wander down to Park Ave. at 82nd and do it there...

New York. Tuesday 10th September, 7.30 a.m.
As he heard the low rumble, Mitch made sure the zipper of his sports bag was holding the microphone steady and then depressed the RECORD button on the tape machine tucked inside. Lifting his camera to his eye, he waited until a silver-grey train emerged spitting and crackling from the subway tunnel, before taking his picture. Only when the train had screeched to a halt and the doors had swished open did Mitch turn off the recorder and climb aboard.

The ride took about ten minutes. From the subway station, Mitch had just a short walk to the building on Park Avenue. He spotted the office at once. The address Rob had given him referred to the second floor and there, clearly visible from across the other side of the street, was a row of windows with the bold sign 'Dennison Management' spread across them.

Mitch busied himself. With a zoom lens attached to his camera he took shots of New York's famous yellow cabs, at the same time recording the sounds of their slamming doors and, as the traffic began to build up, their increasingly furious honking.

He took more photographs of a bagel seller setting up his stall, catching him beautifully as he glared up at the dark and cloudy sky as if to tell it not to rain. Once the office workers began hurrying by, Mitch even managed to wander over and tape the bagel seller telling one of his customers to "Have a nice day!"

Throughout this, Mitch kept one eye on the building across the road. Slowly, people had begun to arrive. First were two men, at just after eight-thirty. One was tall and wore a green-grey suit and a pair of white shoes. The other man was shorter and more casually dressed, his colourful shirt open at the neck. *Steve Dennison and Shep Ahlberg?* wondered Mitch.

As he watched, the taller man punched a number into a security keypad at the side of the door. Mitch groaned. He'd been hoping to walk straight up to the offices. Now he'd have to think of how to talk his way in – unless …

Raising his camera to his eye, Mitch focused on the keypad. Yes! Through the zoom lens he could see it clearly.

He waited until the next person turned up at the door, then raised his camera again.

'Four – two – nine – six', he muttered as saw in close-up the keypad code being punched in. 'That's one problem solved!'

He settled back and watched as more people arrived, and the lights in the second floor windows flicked on. Soon only one remained in darkness.

A yellow cab pulled up. In the back seat was a young woman, her auburn hair falling loosely about her shoulders. Mitch watched as she paid the cab driver, then got out. She seemed to be moving slowly but, with the yellow cab still in the way, he couldn't see properly. By the time the cab moved, she too had gone inside.

Up above, the final light flicked on. *Time to move*, thought Mitch.

Packing his camera and tape recorder into his sports bag, he trotted across the road. He reached towards the keypad, punched in the code number and pulled at the door handle. To his relief it clicked open instantly. Moments later he was climbing the wide stairs and passing through a set of glass-panelled doors bearing the same 'Dennison Management' lettering as the outside windows.

Taking a deep breath, he went in – and found himself in a plush reception area. Soft white leather seats lined the walls, on which hung an array of glittering discs in frames.

On one side, in an open-plan office, various people were talking on telephones or tapping at keyboards. On the other, a solid mahogany door had the name Steve Dennison on it in gold lettering.

'Can I help you?' said a voice.

To one side of the reception area, as if she was guarding Steve Dennison's door, sat the young woman Mitch had seen arrive in the cab. She was seated in front of a PC, a handwritten sign, 'Hands Off – I belong to Sadie!' taped to its side.

'Er …' began Mitch, then stopped as he saw why the young woman had been moving slowly when she'd got out of the cab. Her right ankle was swathed in plaster.

'Bad news,' said Mitch. 'How did you do it?'

'The leg? In the bathroom last Friday night. Would you believe, three in the morning when I should be asleep, I'm at the hospital having this cast slapped on me.'

That's that! thought Mitch. *She couldn't have been chatting over the Net and in hospital at the same time!*

Sadie Mulkern smiled again, but there was a no-messing edge to her voice as she repeated her question. 'So, how can I help you?'

'Well … er …' began Mitch uncertainly. He'd found out the first thing Rob and Co. had wanted to know. Should he simply clear off now, or should he hang about and see what happened? He decided to hang about. 'I work at a place called Cyber-Snax,' he said finally.

'So I see,' replied Sadie Mulkern.

Mitch looked down at the Cyber-Snax T-shirt he was wearing. 'Right. So, as you can guess I'm heavily into Net-surfing and stuff …'

He was interrupted by the buzz of the intercom on Sadie Mulkern's desk. A disembodied voice followed. 'Sadie, send them straight in when they arrive. And no interruptions. We're going to get this GAMEZONE business sorted out once and for all.'

'OK.'

'Like I was saying,' continued Mitch, 'I'm into setting up pages on the Net, and … well, I wondered who set up your Kelly Rix pages. Y'know, all that sound stuff. Cool.'

'Well, we all do a bit. We're quite a high-tech bunch here, you know.'

'Right …'

Mitch was just wondering how to proceed when he was interrupted for a second time. Not by the intercom, but by the glass door opening and two girls breezing in.

He turned – and felt his mouth drop open as he saw who they were. Standing in front of his very eyes were Kelly Rix and Jeannie Corrick.

Kelly Rix, looking shorter than she did in *New York, New York*, gave the PA a wide smile. 'Sadie! How you doing? How's the peg leg?'

'Hi, Kelly! Not so bad. Soon be running round

the block.' She turned to the other arrival. 'Hi, Jeannie.'

Jeannie Corrick simply nodded. 'Steve and Shep here, are they?' she said. Under her arm she had what looked to Mitch like a flat grey brief-case.

Sadie Mulkern nodded. 'Said to go right in.'

The two girls opened the connecting door and went through. Mitch caught the briefest glimpse of the two men he'd seen arrive first – Mr White Shoes and Mr Casual – before the door was closed again.

Almost immediately the muffled, but unmis-takable, sound of raised voices starting coming from behind it.

Sadie Mulkern glanced towards the door, then back to Mitch. 'Er … we're kind of busy here today. They're all going to England first thing Thursday morning and there's a lot of sorting out to be done.'

'Sure,' said Mitch, dawdling as much as he could in the hope that the voices would get loud enough for him to make out what was being said. 'No sweat. Just called in on the off chance …'

'OK,' said Sadie Mulkern, glancing nervously towards the office door. 'Look, come back next week, yeah?'

Behind the door the voices were getting louder. *If I can only stall for just a bit longer*, thought Mitch …

Dropping to his knees he dipped into his

sports bag. 'Say,' he said, pulling a sheet of paper from the pad he'd been using to make his notes. 'I'd really like Kelly Rix's autograph. You don't think you could ...'

Mitch stopped as, from close behind the door, a man shouted, 'Listen to SA, Jeannie! The contracts are signed. We're going to England!'

Sadie Mulkern started to move painfully towards Mitch to usher him out. 'Yes, OK. Autographs are no problem. Leave it with me.'

She'd got no more than half way when Mitch was forced to leap back of his own accord as the connecting door to Steve Dennison's office was ripped open and Jeannie Corrick, still clutching her grey case, stormed out and past him.

With a hasty 'Thanks. Much appreciated' in the direction of Sadie Mulkern, Mitch clutched his sports bag to his chest and ran after her.

By the time he'd got down the stairs, through the glass swing doors and back out into the bustle of Park Avenue, Jeannie Corrick had already hailed a yellow cab.

Quickly, Mitch whipped out his camera and fired off a couple of shots. His first ever pop star!

As the cab drew away, Mitch bent to his bag again. The recording that he'd started under Sadie Mulkern's nose, turning his tape machine on with one hand while he pulled out his sheet of paper with the other, was still going. He pressed the stop button.

It would be interesting to see if he'd got anything.

Cyber-Snax Café, New York.
10.21 a.m. (UK time: 3.21 p.m.)

The moment he got back to Cyber-Snax, Mitch persuaded one of the other assistants to change shifts with him. Then, getting himself on to a spare PC, he started work. Connecting his tape player in through the MIC socket, he made two sound files. Soon, one of these was on its way across the Net with an accompanying e-mail.

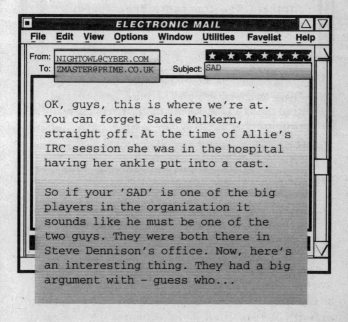

ELECTRONIC MAIL

File   Edit   View   Options   Window   Utilities   Favelist   Help

From: NIGHTOWL@CYBER.COM
To: ZMASTER@PRIME.CO.UK   Subject: SAD

OK, guys, this is where we're at.
You can forget Sadie Mulkern,
straight off. At the time of Allie's
IRC session she was in the hospital
having her ankle put into a cast.

So if your 'SAD' is one of the big
players in the organization it
sounds like he must be one of the
two guys. They were both there in
Steve Dennison's office. Now, here's
an interesting thing. They had a big
argument with – guess who...

Abbey School. 3.35 p.m.

Rob, Tamsyn and Josh had their eyes glued to the screen as they read Mitch's note.

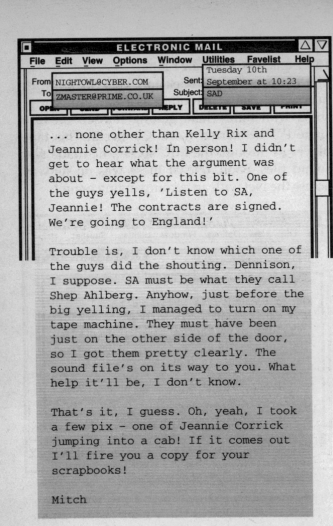

From: NIGHTOWL@CYBER.COM   Sent: Tuesday 10th
To: ZMASTER@PRIME.CO.UK   Subject: September at 10:23
                                           SAD

OPEN   SEND   FORWARD   REPLY   DELETE   SAVE   PRINT

... none other than Kelly Rix and
Jeannie Corrick! In person! I didn't
get to hear what the argument was
about - except for this bit. One of
the guys yells, 'Listen to SA,
Jeannie! The contracts are signed.
We're going to England!'

Trouble is, I don't know which one of
the guys did the shouting. Dennison,
I suppose. SA must be what they call
Shep Ahlberg. Anyhow, just before the
big yelling, I managed to turn on my
tape machine. They must have been
just on the other side of the door,
so I got them pretty clearly. The
sound file's on its way to you. What
help it'll be, I don't know.

That's it, I guess. Oh, yeah, I took
a few pix - one of Jeannie Corrick
jumping into a cab! If it comes out
I'll fire you a copy for your
scrapbooks!

Mitch

They downloaded Mitch's sound file. Rob
switched to the sound player. Moments later a
strong New York accent filled the room. 'Listen to

SA, Jeannie! The contracts are signed. We're going to England!'

Rob looked at the other two. 'That's an American.'

'Sharp!' laughed Josh. 'What did you expect?'

Rob didn't answer. Instead he clicked into the Kelly Rix web site and brought up the details for Steve Dennison they'd looked at before.

Manager: Steve Dennison
British-born Steve is the guy who recognized the raw talent that was hidden in
the tapes pressed on him by Kelly Rix and
Jeannie Corrick in their student days.
Abandoning a steady career as a computer
programmer to go full time in the much
riskier music business, Steve guided
Ambush from day one. He's now manager to
both Kelly and Jeannie as they pursue
their solo careers.

'Look!' he cried '*British*-born. What I wouldn't expect is for Steve Dennison to have an American accent!'

Josh held up his hands. 'Hang on, Rob. He could have. It all depends on when he went to the States.'

Rob looked again at the screen – and remembered something else that had been part of the Kelly Rix web site. 'The interview!' Another mouse click and it was there, on screen. 'Steve Dennison did the interview. See!'

'And there was the option to download the sound version.' Quickly, he paged down to the bottom of the interview and found the select panel.

❏ Download recorded interview

Soon their hard disk light was flashing as the sound file was transferred. Rob set it to play. After a moment's pause they heard the voice on the introduction.

'Kelly Rix's manager – that's me, Steve Dennison – asks the questions most fans want answers to.' The accent was light and neutral.

'No way is that the guy on Mitch's tape!' said Rob.

'So, if there were only two men in the room …' began Josh.

Rob finished off for him. 'Then the American must have been Shep Ahlberg – and he was refer- ring to *Dennison* as "SA".'

Tamsyn shook her head. 'Rob, what are you getting at?'

'Isn't it obvious?' said Rob. 'If somebody's call- ing Dennison "SA", then they must be his initials. "S" for Steve and "A" for his middle name.'

'Steve A. Dennison …' began Josh.

'Equals SAD!' exploded Rob. 'The guy behind all this is Kelly Rix's own manager!'

'Her manager?' said Tamsyn. 'Come on!'

'Why not?' said Rob. 'I bet he's still got the demo tapes Kelly Rix sent him – and that track sounded like what I'd have expected from an amateur tape.'

'And he's an ex-programmer,' said Josh. 'He'd have the ability to doctor a program.'

'But it doesn't make sense,' said Tamsyn. 'Why should Kelly Rix's own manager be trying to wreck her projects?'

'I don't know!' yelled Rob. 'And I don't care. I just want to know if he's responsible for what's happening to GAMEZONE.' He searched his mind for a possible reason. 'Maybe … maybe he's still sore about the Ambush split and this is his way of getting his own back.'

'But why?' said Tamsyn. 'By doing Kelly Rix down he's cutting his own throat, isn't he?'

'Maybe he doesn't care,' said Rob. 'He manages Jeannie Corrick as well, doesn't he?'

'Who's not doing half as good since the split,' said Josh. 'In fact, Jeannie Corrick doesn't get much of a mention any more, does she?'

'So that could be it,' said Rob quickly. 'Jeannie Corrick's being overshadowed, so Dennison's trying to put the stoppers on Kelly Rix's singing. That way Jeannie Corrick's got a clear run and Kelly Rix can concentrate on her acting. He wins both ways!'

Tamsyn shook her head. 'I don't know …'

It was Rob who took the initiative. Reaching

for the mouse again, he clicked into the mail system.

'We haven't got time to work out the details. They're all supposed to be arriving on Thursday. Dad said the recording session is on Friday at GAMEZONE. As far as I'm concerned, Dennison's our man. And he's going to say more about pirating the project on that chat line tomorrow. So ...' He swept the mouse firmly upwards and clicked on OPEN. '... We've got to be in on that IRC channel too. All of us.'

CHAPTER 8

Toronto, Canada. Wednesday 11th September, 2.59 a.m. (UK time: 7.59 a.m.)
Lauren watched as Allie typed in her entry command to the Internet Relay Chat channel.

```
/JOIN #nyny {ALLIE}
```

'You reckon this pirate is going to show?' said Lauren.
'I sure hope so,' said Allie.

Perth High School. Wednesday 11th September, 4.02 p.m. (UK time: 8.02 a.m.)
Tom logged in. He hadn't used IRC before, but since Rob's note had arrived he'd printed down what he could, and studied it thoroughly. The list of commands he could use were at his elbow. Referring to it, he switched to IRC mode and typed:

```
/JOIN #nyny {TOM}
```

Rob had asked him to make sure the subject didn't wander off course if and when this 'SAD' came on line. Tom's job was to bring it back to the pirate stuff.

'No problem,' muttered Tom as the message flicked up telling him that he'd joined the channel successfully. The thought of actually talking on-line to the cause of his nightmare week was something he'd been looking forward to all day.

'The problem'll be keeping my temper,' he scowled.

Abbey School.
Wednesday 11th September, 8.03 a.m.
'Ready?' said Josh.

He turned to Rob and Tamsyn, sitting on either side.

'Ready,' nodded Rob. 'Go for it.'

Swiftly, Josh typed in his entry command to IRC.

```
/JOIN #nyny {JOSH}
```

After a short delay, the response came back telling him he'd joined the channel.

```
{JOSH} you are now talking in #nyny
```

'Here we go,' said Rob.

The three of them focused on the screen,

watching as those already connected to the channel continued with the conversation they'd been having.

```
{SUSAN} Did you see the last episode?
   Wasn't it great when Kelly drove off in
   that sports car and made her boyfriend
   jump into the bushes?
{NIGHTHAWK} Fantastic. I don't know how
   I'm gonna manage without her in the next
   couple of episodes.
```

'Come on, somebody, change the subject,' muttered Rob.

'Well done, Allie!' said Tamsyn as the next line of chat came up. 'Come on, Josh, join in. We've got to take over this chat.'

```
{ALLIE} Me neither. Anyone know how long
   she's going to be in England?
{JOSH} Hi. I just joined this channel.
   What's she doing there?
{TOM} I joined, too. I thought it was some
   secret project. With a new recording
   coming out of it.
{ALLIE} That's right. We were talking
   about that the other night.
{NIGHTHAWK} Can we get back to talking
   about last night's episode?
{TOM} Let's stick to this for a while,
   huh? I heard mention of this recording
   being on the Net - y'know, *freebie*
   style?
{JOSH} Me too. And a GAMEZONE game Kelly
   Rix is going to be in. Is that right?
```

'Come on, SAD, whoever you are,' muttered Rob. 'Come on.'

As a couple of other contributors suggested getting back to discussing the programme itself, Tamsyn said, 'They won't be able to keep this going for long.'

```
{TOM} I thought somebody promised more
    details of the Kelly Rix project.
{ALLIE} Yes, they did. Somebody nicknamed
    SAD said they'd be on-line with more
    details.
```

'Time to flush him out, yeah?' said Josh. He typed his next line, and hit the RETURN key.

```
{JOSH} Probably just a poser trying to
    come across big.
```

'Yes!' cried Rob. 'Here it is!'

The next line on the screen was the one they'd been waiting for. They leaned forward in their eagerness.

```
{SAD} Wrong. Kelly Rix cuts a new song as
    part of the GAMEZONE project on Friday.
    A sample of it will be on the Net the
    same day.
{JOSH} Where?
{SAD} Check out a newsgroup called
    'skullxbones'. All the details for
    getting it will be on there.
{ALLIE} That's a newsgroup for
```

```
          pirated stuff, isn't it?
{SAD} So? You got a problem with that?
{JOSH} How about the GAMEZONE game? What's
     it called?
{SAD} SMASH HIT. That'll be on the Net as
     soon as it's available.
{TOM} You mean you can pirate that as
     well?
{SAD} No problem.
{TOM} Where you gonna put it, then? On
     that skullxbones newsgroup again, so
     every crooked dealer can get hold of it?
```

Rob read Tom's line with growing horror. 'Cool it, Tom! Don't scare him off!'

'Quick, Josh!' cried Tamsyn. 'Steer it off!'

It was too late. Tom had let his feelings boil over.

```
{SAD} I can't help that.
{TOM} And will it work? Or will it bomb out
     like Speed Surf?
{SAD} Blame GAMEZONE if their programs
     knock out hard disks.
{TOM} How'd you know that? There's only
     one way. Because *YOU* spiked it didn't
     you?
*** {SAD} quits #nyny
```

'He's gone,' moaned Rob.

Josh disconnected from the IRC system himself. 'Still, we got something out of it. We know when it's going to be done.'

'True,' said Rob. 'And if it's going to be on Friday, then Steve Dennison is going to have to work fast.'

'If it *is* him,' said Tamsyn, still uncertain. 'I can't figure out why he'd want to do all this.'

She stopped, as a bip from the PC indicated that an e-mail had arrived. Josh opened it. 'Apologies from Tom,' he said.

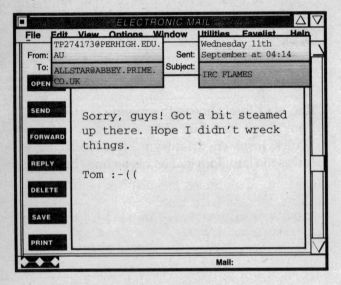

It was almost immediately followed by a note from Lauren.

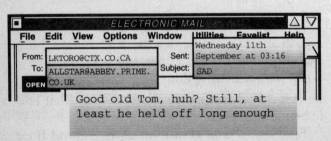

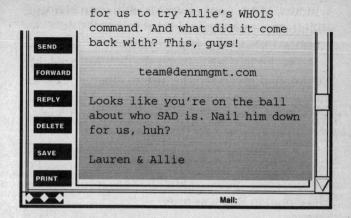

```
for us to try Allie's WHOIS
command. And what did it come
back with? This, guys!


        team@dennmgmt.com

Looks like you're on the ball
about who SAD is. Nail him down
for us, huh?


Lauren & Allie
```

SEND
FORWARD
REPLY
DELETE
SAVE
PRINT

Mail:

'Look at that! The Dennison Management ID!' cried Rob. 'Come on, Tamsyn, if that doesn't convince you that Steve Dennison's behind this, nothing will.'

Tamsyn nodded, thoughtfully. It still wasn't conclusive enough for her.

'Let's see what Mitch comes up with.'

Park Avenue, New York. Wednesday 11th September, 3.20 a.m. (UK time: 8.20 a.m.)

Mitch had never spent a more nervous half hour in his life. Waiting in the shadows of a New York street in the early hours of the morning was not something he wanted to do too often.

He checked his watch, turning it to catch the light from a street lamp. Three-twenty. That had to be long enough.

Taking one final glance up at the second floor

window, Mitch jumped on his mountain bike and didn't stop pedalling until he'd reached the safety of the Cyber-Snax rear entrance.

As he let himself in with the key his boss, Mr Lewin, had given him for use in emergencies, an electronic signal started up. Quickly, Mitch went across to the control panel on the wall and, with a second key, turned off the alarm system.

Not bothering with the lights, he then padded out into the main café area and switched on a PC whose screen glow couldn't be seen from outside. His e-mail to Rob was brief.

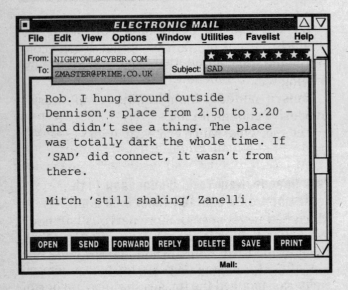

```
ELECTRONIC MAIL

File   Edit   View   Options   Window   Utilities   Favelist   Help

From:  NIGHTOWL@CYBER.COM
To:    ZMASTER@PRIME.CO.UK          Subject:  SAD

Rob. I hung around outside
Dennison's place from 2.50 to 3.20 –
and didn't see a thing. The place
was totally dark the whole time. If
'SAD' did connect, it wasn't from
there.

Mitch 'still shaking' Zanelli.


OPEN   SEND   FORWARD   REPLY   DELETE   SAVE   PRINT

                                      Mail:
```

Abbey School.
Wednesday 11th September, 1.43 p.m.
'It doesn't change a thing,' said Rob.

The note from Mitch was on the screen. 'I agree with Rob,' said Josh. 'Everything we've got points to Steve Dennison.'

'It points to *somebody* in his organization,' said Tamsyn. 'I'm still not sure it has to be him. Maybe if Mitch had actually seen Dennison there at the time of the IRC session ...'

'That would have been a bonus,' interrupted Rob. 'But, like I say, it doesn't change a thing. The guy's an ex-computer programmer. He's bound to have a PC at home. He was probably using that.'

Tamsyn shrugged. 'I suppose so.'

'Question is, what're you going to do now?' said Josh.

Rob's expression clouded. 'I – I don't know. Set a trap for him, somehow.'

'You've got to get near him first.'

'I've thought about that. They're arriving from New York tomorrow, but the recording session's not taking place till Friday at GAMEZONE.'

'At GAMEZONE?' said Josh. 'Not some swish recording studio?'

Rob shook his head. 'GAMEZONE's got its own studio. It's pretty much state of the art. Besides, the project's not just about the music, remember. There's the animation side. Doing it at GAMEZONE means they can train a camera on Kelly Rix and feed the images straight into one of their computers. That way they can see what sort of animation and morphing works best and get her to change things if necessary.'

'So they'll be there all day Friday,' said Tamsyn.

'Right. And that's where we're going to be too. Watching Steve Dennison like hawks.'

Josh coughed gently. 'Er ... haven't you forgotten one small detail? Called school? Aren't we supposed to be here on Friday – or did I miss the holiday announcement?'

'I've thought about that, too. I'll ask Mum and Dad if we can come and watch. They'll sort it all out with the school.'

'And you reckon they'll agree?' said Tamsyn.

Rob nodded confidently. 'No problem.'

Manor House.
Thursday 11th September, 8.25 a.m.

'No way, Rob!'

'But, Dad!'

'Watch my lips, son. No way! You are not going to be at this recording session.'

Rob slumped into silence. From the first time he'd asked the evening before, through to the moment he'd got up that morning, he'd tried every argument he could think of. Every time, the answer had been the same.

What he *couldn't* say was what he *wanted* to say: that he suspected Steve Dennison of being the cause of all their troubles, and that he wanted to be there to watch his every move.

'I'm not picking on you, Rob. Everybody in the company wants to get a glimpse of Kelly

Rix and Jeannie Corrick, but they're banned too.'

'Jeannie Corrick?' said Rob. 'I thought this was a Kelly Rix solo.'

'It is. But she's on the trip too. I understand Steve Dennison's lined up a couple of meetings for her to try and revive her career. But they're not until the Saturday, so she's asked to come along. I could hardly say no to her, could I?'

'But you are saying no to me,' said Rob glumly.

Mr Zanelli nodded. 'Yes. They're all due on a flight back to the States on Sunday morning. So, this recording has got to go smoothly – which means only those people concerned with it can be there.'

'There *is* going to be a small get-together afterwards,' said Mrs Zanelli, popping her head round the door. 'He could come to that, couldn't he, Paul?'

Mr Zanelli nodded. 'Good idea. It's not going to be a big deal, but you can come along for that. I might have remembered it myself if you hadn't gone on so much about being at the recording.'

Afterwards? That's when we need to be there anyway! thought Rob, suddenly realizing how stupid he'd been. Even Steve Dennison couldn't pirate something until it had been recorded in the first place.

'I'll pick you up from school,' said Mrs Zanelli. 'OK?'

'Sure,' said Rob. He was going to need help, though. 'Er ... how about Tamsyn and Josh?'

Mr and Mrs Zanelli exchanged glances. Finally, Mr Zanelli said, 'No. Not this time.'

'Why not?'

'Same reasoning as before. It's not that I think you'll cause problems together, but there's a lot to do and the fewer distractions the better.'

'But …'

'No, Rob,' said Mr Zanelli. 'And that's final.'

Abbey School.
Thursday 12th September, 3.05 p.m.

Rob had been racking his brains all day.

After meeting Tamsyn and Josh first thing and telling them about his parents' decision, their paths hadn't crossed until this final lesson.

As the bell went, and everybody else rushed for the door, Tamsyn and Josh came over to Rob. 'Had any brainwaves?' said Josh.

Rob shook his head. 'Nope. Apart from you hiding in the bushes and leaping out if I call.'

'Hey, that's not a bad idea,' joked Tamsyn. She put an arm round Josh's shoulders. 'We could call ourselves Ambush! How about that for a name?'

'It'll never catch on,' said Rob. His smile faded. 'I'm sorry, guys, I think this is going to have to be my problem.'

'What are you going to do?' asked Josh.

'Watch every move Steve Dennison makes. And if I see him so much as look at a PC …'

'Hey, that's something we *could* do,' said Tamsyn. 'Stay logged in here and monitor that

Net newsgroup. At least that way we'll spot it if something does go up. We could give you a call at the GAMEZONE offices.'

'And I can e-mail if there's anything you can do,' said Rob. He shrugged. 'Nothing like as good as having you both there, but it's better than nothing.'

'Until tomorrow, then,' said Josh. 'Friday the thirteenth.'

'So it is,' said Tamsyn. 'I wonder who it'll be unlucky for?'

CHAPTER 9

GAMEZONE Offices, Portsmouth.
Friday 13th September, 3.20 p.m.

'Rob,' said Mr Zanelli, introducing the tall man standing beside him, 'this is Steve Dennison, Kelly Rix's manager. And Jeannie Corrick's, of course. Steve, this is my son, Rob.'

Steve Dennison smiled warmly. 'Pleased to meet you, Rob.'

Rob gave him a thin smile in return. 'And you, Mr Dennison.'

He and his mother had just arrived after the fifteen minute drive from Abbey School, and were in the corridor outside Mr Zanelli's office.

'How's it going?' asked Mrs Zanelli.

'Pretty good,' replied her husband.

'Another half-hour and we'll be done I'd say,' said Steve Dennison. He indicated the plastic coffee cup in his hand. 'I just popped out to get a drink – not that they'll notice I've gone,' he added.

'You're going back to the studio, are you?' asked Rob. Surely that couldn't be where he'd do it?

Steve Dennison nodded. 'Think I'd better.' Turning, he began to walk off towards the studio.

It had to be now. He'd have to take the chance. 'All right if I come?'

The manager stopped, his expression uncertain.

'Rob!' hissed Mrs Zanelli. 'What did we say?'

'No, er … that's OK, Mrs Zanelli,' said Steve Dennison. 'I don't see any problem with that.'

Two minutes later, Rob was ushered into the darkened control room. A man was sitting at a desk, facing a battery of switches. A PC was next to him, its screen filled with images. Next to the man sat a girl Rob recognized at once.

'Rob, meet Shep Ahlberg and Jeannie Corrick,' said Steve Dennison. Sitting down on the seat nearest the PC, he turned and beckoned Rob forward.

Rob shook his head. 'It's OK,' he said, looking back at him. 'I can see exactly what I want to see from here.'

Cyber-Snax, New York. Friday 13th September, 10.27 a.m. (UK time: 3.27 p.m.)

Mitch had collected his pictures from the processing store. Undoing the packet, he'd leafed through them as he'd made his way back to the café.

'Not bad,' he'd said to himself, 'not bad at all. Mitch, my man, you're becoming real smooth with that shutter!'

Virtually every shot had come out well, from his pictures on the subway through to the close-ups he'd taken of the bagel-seller at his stall outside Steve Dennison's offices. He'd scan those in and Net them across to Tamsyn when he could.

Right now, there was one he particularly wanted to see for himself. Flipping through the pack to the end, he picked it out.

Yeah! Really good!

In spite of the hasty set-up, his shot of Jeannie Corrick climbing into the yellow cab had come out well too. He'd caught her side on, her grey case under her arm, just as she was shouting her instructions to the cabbie.

Back in the café, he'd scanned the picture in. He'd also produced the sound file he'd promised Tamsyn. Now, as he reached the end of his own coffee break, he prepared to send the package across.

Clicking on OPEN he starting typing a quick covering e-mail.

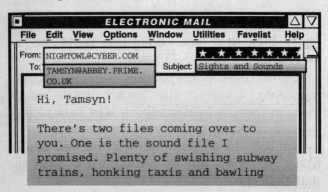

ELECTRONIC MAIL

File Edit View Options Window Utilities Favelist Help

From: NIGHTOWL@CYBER.COM
To: TAMSYN@ABBEY.PRIME.CO.UK

Subject: Sights and Sounds

Hi, Tamsyn!

There's two files coming over to you. One is the sound file I promised. Plenty of swishing subway trains, honking taxis and bawling

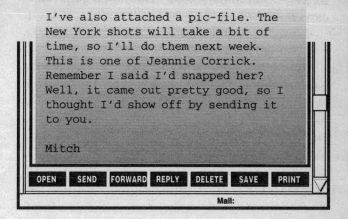

street sellers – typical Big Apple!

I've also attached a pic-file. The New York shots will take a bit of time, so I'll do them next week. This is one of Jeannie Corrick. Remember I said I'd snapped her? Well, it came out pretty good, so I thought I'd show off by sending it to you.

Mitch

| OPEN | SEND | FORWARD | REPLY | DELETE | SAVE | PRINT |

Mail:

Abbey School. Friday 13th September, 3.58 p.m.

Tamsyn smiled as she saw the note. 'The guy's just star-struck!' she said.

'Come on, let's check it out,' said Josh.

'Hang about, hang about. I want to listen to some of these sounds first.'

Downloading the file, Tamsyn played it over the sound system.

'Very atmospheric!' said Josh.

Mitch had done a good job. As she listened, Tamsyn could almost imagine being in New York. Taking a clean diskette from her shoulder bag, she slipped it into the drive and took a back-up copy. Only after putting the diskette safely back into her bag did she set about downloading the picture file.

'Good one!' said Josh as they displayed it. He looked closer at the screen. 'Hey, what's that she's carrying?'

'Looks like a briefcase.'

'Bit small for a briefcase.'

'That's because it isn't,' said a voice from behind them. They turned to see Mr Findlay, peering in at the door. 'Thought I'd just let you two know it's Friday, and that means closing up and going home for the weekend for your faithful old Tech teacher. Ten minutes, OK?'

'OK,' grinned Josh. 'Hey – and Mr Findlay.' He pointed at Jeannie Corrick's grey case as their teacher turned back. 'What is it, if it isn't a brief-case?'

The teacher shook his head. 'And I thought you were a techno-star, Josh. It's a laptop PC, of course. And a really expensive one by the look of it.'

As Mr Findlay gave them the answer, Tamsyn's mind began racing. All the niggling doubts she'd had about Rob's theory came bubbling back to the surface. She knew it didn't make sense for Steve Dennison to be the one trying to knock Kelly Rix's reputation.

But, as she looked again at the picture on the screen, it occurred to her that it *could* make sense for somebody else to have been doing it …

'Quick, Josh,' cried Tamsyn. 'Find that Kelly Rix interview again!'

'What for?' asked Josh, doing what Tamsyn had asked.

 INTERNET DETECTIVES

'Jeannie Corrick. If she's carrying around a lap-top PC, then … Yes! Look!' she shouted as the opening part of the interview flashed up onto the screen.

Opening question, Kelly. Which came first, acting or singing?
Singing! I went to the same university upstate as Jeannie Corrick – we were both studying computer science would you believe! We started singing together while we were there, did a few university gigs, and decided we wanted to be singers not computer boffs.

'Jeannie Corrick was a computer science student. They both were. She'd definitely know how to spike a program like Speed Surf. And she'd have had no trouble getting hold of it. Same goes for the Kelly Rix tracks.'

Josh looked at her. 'Hang on, hang on. Why'd she want to do that? Kelly Rix was her partner. Ambush were big stars.'

'Were, Josh. *Were!* Not any more. Since the split, Jeannie Corrick's solo career hasn't taken off at all. She hardly rates a mention. Kelly Rix has become the big star. And if the GAMEZONE project is a success, she'll be even bigger!'

'But if it goes down the tubes …' said Josh slowly.

'And Kelly Rix has her reputation dented in all sorts of other ways,' continued Tamsyn, 'then maybe Jeannie Corrick's thinking people will start taking a bit more notice of her.'

'It would explain why Mitch didn't see anything at Dennison's offices the night of the IRC session as well,' said Josh. 'With that laptop PC, she could have plugged into a phone socket anywhere.'

At the mention of the IRC session, Tamsyn turned back to the screen. 'What would really clinch it,' she said, 'is some evidence to link her with that nickname.'

'S-A-D,' murmured Josh. 'Hardly matches her initials, does it?' He grinned. 'Hey, is Jeannie Corrick her real name? Maybe she changed it. Pop people do that, don't they?'

'At the start of their careers,' said Tamsyn.

Even as she said the words, she scrolled further down the Kelly Rix interview. Could there be something …?

'Look! There!'

> **Why did you call yourselves Ambush?**
> Because that's what we'd do to anybody we thought could help us get into the music business! We even went as far as to call our first song Stand And Deliver! Our first tapes were solos and duets. We recorded them in my garage! They were awful, but we gave copies to every pop group manager we could discover. That's how come you got picked on, Steve!

'The first song they ever recorded! Stand And Deliver!'

'S-A-D!' said Josh.

'And Jeannie Corrick's at the GAMEZONE offices right now,' cried Tamsyn, remembering what Rob had told them. 'Because she *asked* to be there!'

'Even though she's not involved in the recording,' cried Josh.

Tamsyn snatched up her shoulder bag and dived for the door. 'Come on, Josh! Rob's concentrating on the wrong person!'

The GAMEZONE Studio. 4.12 p.m.

'That's it! We'll buy that one.'

Shep Ahlberg's delighted shout brought sighs of relief all round. On the other side of the glass screen separating the control room from the recording studio, Kelly Rix put a thumb in the air.

'Great. Thanks, everyone.'

As the lights snapped on in the control room, Steve Dennison leaned forward and typed a couple of commands on the control PC keyboard. Moments later he was taking a diskette out from its drive.

'There you go,' he said to Rob.

'On there?' said Rob. He looked hurriedly around the control room. Now the lights were up he realized there wasn't a tape deck to be seen. 'Is there enough room?'

Steve Dennison nodded. 'Not for the whole thing, no. For that we use the hard disk and back it up with a tape streamer.' He held the diskette up. 'But with a special audio compression system we use, we can get a fair sample on one of these.'

Making it really simple to pirate! thought Rob. Slip that diskette into a PC connected to the Net, a quick log-in – and a copy could be zipping across the world in seconds.

As everybody began to pack up, Rob's eyes were glued to the diskette in Steve Dennison's fingers.

Suddenly a cork went pop as Mrs Zanelli arrived with a bottle of champagne and, behind her, Mr Zanelli carrying a tray of glasses.

'Celebration drink, Steve,' said Mr Zanelli, filling a glass as he approached.

The manager, still with the diskette in his hands, looked for somewhere to put it down.

'Here, you want me to take it?' said a cool voice.

Steve Dennison looked at the speaker. Again he seemed uncertain.

'C'mon Steve, if you hang on to it the thing'll most likely end up being used as a drinks mat.'

Dennison smiled. 'OK. Thanks. It is kind of valuable, isn't it?'

'Sure is,' said Jeannie Corrick. She was wearing a smart trouser suit. Rob sighed with relief as he saw her take the disk from Steve Dennison and slip it into her jacket pocket.

At least he can't do anything with it while she's got it, thought Rob.

The next thing he knew, Jeannie Corrick had turned her attention to him. 'Rob, I need to call the office in the States, tell Sadie our schedule, y'know?' Her voice dropped to a whisper. 'Is there anywhere I can use a telephone?'

Even as Rob glanced towards the telephone on the studio wall, she added, 'Somewhere a bit quieter.'

The studio was becoming crowded now, as word spread that the session was over and that it was party time. In the centre of it all, Rob's parents were talking to Kelly Rix, while all around them the babbling was getting louder.

'Sure. Dad's office is just down the corridor. You want me to show you the way?'

'Would you? Thanks.'

Picking up her flat grey case, Jeannie Corrick followed Rob as he led the way out into the corridor, through Reception, and then along to Mr Zanelli's office.

'Telephone over there,' said Rob, pointing to the desk.

'Perfect.' She smiled at Rob, but the warmth had gone. 'It's kinda private. Do you mind leaving me on my own?'

'Sure,' said Rob.

He headed back towards the reception area and the studio. Behind him, Jeannie Corrick was already opening her case.

The GAMEZONE Offices. 4.16 p.m.

Tamsyn and Josh had been to the GAMEZONE building only twice before, both times during the school holidays. Like the offices of many computer games companies, they'd discovered it to be surprisingly small, just a flat broad building at the edge of an industrial estate.

What they hadn't seen on those occasions, though, was what they found now, as they rode their bikes furiously up towards the entrance.

'Where did this lot come from?' yelled Josh.

Along the front of the building, crush barriers had been erected. Behind them, jammed shoulder to shoulder, must have been nearly five hundred people.

'Looks like word's got around,' shouted Tamsyn above the noise. There was a gap between two barriers to allow cars in and out of the GAMEZONE car park. With Josh close behind, Tamsyn swung her bike through the gap and towards the building – only for a solid-looking policeman to step out in front of her.

'And where do you think you two are going?'

Slowly it dawned on Tamsyn that they were being stopped, just like all the other fans.

'Hey, we've got to get inside!'

'We've got an important message for Mr and Mrs Zanelli,' said Josh.

The policeman looked to the heavens. 'See that lot?' he said, gesturing towards the crowd behind the barriers. 'Half of 'em have said the same. Now come on, move along.'

Tamsyn didn't have time to argue. Dropping her bike on the ground, she ran.

'Come here!'

As the policeman gave chase, Josh sprinted towards the door too. If they could only get inside …

Rob saw them as he reached the Reception area. Tamsyn was ahead, with Josh close behind. The policeman caught up with them just as they reached the entrance.

'Rob! Tell him who we are!' cried Tamsyn.

'It's OK, officer,' said Rob at once. 'They can come in.'

The policeman frowned, and looked beyond Rob to the receptionist on duty. As she nodded, he sniffed and went back outside again.

'What's going on?' said Rob.

'Not Dennison,' gasped Tamsyn. 'It's not Steve Dennison.'

'What?'

'It's not Dennison. It's Jeannie Corrick.'

They saw Rob's face go pale. 'It can't be.'

'There's no time to explain,' said Josh. 'But we're sure of it. Where is she, do you know?'

'In my dad's office,' said Rob, still stunned. 'With the sample recording …'

Tamsyn didn't wait. 'Go fetch your parents, Rob! We'll go down there. Come on, Josh!'

As Rob spun his wheelchair round and headed for the studio as fast as he was able, Tamsyn and Josh hared off down the corridor towards Mr Zanelli's office. They saw Jeannie Corrick the moment they reached it, typing on the keyboard of her laptop PC.

'We've got to stop her,' hissed Tamsyn. 'Josh, think of something!'

Josh hesitated for no more than a moment. Then, snatching open the door to Mr Zanelli's office, he stepped inside. As she saw him, Jeannie Corrick stopped typing and looked up in stunned surprise.

'It … it's you, isn't it?' stammered Josh, his mouth and his eyes wide. 'You're Jeannie Corrick, aren't you?'

'Excuse me. I *am* rather—'

'You are! You're Jeannie Corrick! From Ambush. You and Kelly Rix! I've got all your recordings!'

Jeannie Corrick had stopped typing. Now, as she got to her feet she looked angry. 'Hey cool it!'

'He's your greatest fan!' cried Tamsyn, following Josh into the room as she realized what he was up to.

'I'm sure he is, but do you both mind leaving …'

Josh was pretending to be in raptures. 'Jeannie Corrick!' he screeched, louder and louder. 'I've met Jeannie Corrick!'

The singer stepped out from behind the desk and made for Josh. Grabbing him by the arm, she tried to move him towards the door.

'Jeannie Corrick! I've been touched by Jeannie Corrick!' he said, resisting her attempts to make him leave.

Nearby there came the sound of footsteps running towards them.

'Tamsyn! Josh! What on earth is going on?'

It was Mr Zanelli, rushing to his office as Rob had asked him to. The others were following him, Rob amongst them.

'It's her, Mr Zanelli!' cried Tamsyn. 'She's the one!'

'The one?' It was Steve Dennison, standing beside Mr Zanelli.

Josh turned to them. 'She took the copy of Speed Surf you were sent, doctored it, and put it on the Internet. And she's been putting duff Kelly Rix tracks up on your web site!'

Steve Dennison shook his head in disbelief. 'You're crazy! Paul, what's going on here?'

Mr Zanelli didn't get a chance to reply. Another voice cut through the air.

'It would sure explain a lot if it's true,' said Shep Ahlberg.

All eyes turned towards him as he repeated his statement. 'A whole lot. I told you about that third music sample I found on our web site by accident. I assumed it was down to a rival manager who'd been sent those tapes and hadn't seen the star potential in them like you did. But by the time Sadie got on to it, the file had gone.'

Steve Dennison looked at Jeannie Corrick. 'You didn't want Kelly to do this project either, did you, Jeannie? Kept on telling us that GAME-ZONE were a bad company until we had that bust-up in my office and Shep supported my decision to come here …'

'When all the time it was her who was making GAMEZONE *look* like a bad company,' said Rob.

Tears were streaming down Jeannie Corrick's face as she faced them, unable to speak.

'Why, Jeannie?' said a soft voice that Tamsyn, Josh and Rob had heard so often on CDs and on the television.

All eyes turned to Kelly Rix as she pushed forward to face her friend. 'Why'd you do it?'

Jeannie Corrick was struggling to find the words. When they finally came, it was in a torrent.

'Because … because it's all gone wrong! You've got a great solo career. Your records are doing well. You've got your TV work. You've got this project. And what have I got? Nothing! Nobody wants to know me, Kelly!'

'But the split was your idea …'

'I know it was! And it's the worst decision I've ever made in my life. That's why I've been …' She waved a wild hand towards her laptop PC. 'Why I've been doing everything I have. I just thought if I slowed you down a bit—'

'Knocked her reputation, you mean,' said Josh.

'And GAMEZONE's with it,' added Rob, bitterly.

'I know,' sobbed Jeannie Corrick. 'I didn't think it would do the damage it did. I never thought …'

Kelly Rix spoke again. 'You haven't answered my question, Jeannie. *Why?*'

'Because I thought … if your solo career started taking some knocks …' The words came out in a rush. 'I thought you would be ready to re-form Ambush!'

'Re-form!' shouted Steve Dennison angrily. 'You wanted the split, and just because it hasn't worked out, you want to come back again? After what you've been doing, do you expect her to agree to that?'

'I *do* agree, Steve.'

'What?'

'I've been thinking about it for a while. Singing's my first love. That's what I want to concentrate on. So, when we get back, I'll be asking to be written out of *New York, New York.*' She grinned at Jeannie Corrick. 'I picked up those awful tracks on the web site, too. But they didn't embarrass me. They just made me hanker after the old days.'

As the two friends came together Rob cried out angrily, 'Great! You're OK, then! But what about GAMEZONE?'

Jeannie Corrick turned to Mr and Mrs Zanelli. 'I … I'm sorry. I'll tell the whole story to the papers. Her voice plunged to a whisper. 'I don't know any other way of making it up to you.'

'I do,' said Josh.

He turned to Mr and Mrs Zanelli. 'When Rob told us about SMASH HIT he said you reckoned it still needed something a bit special for it, right?'

'Right,' nodded Mr Zanelli.

'So what could be more special than including the comeback of Ambush?'

Rob's eyes lit up at the thought. 'Josh! That's brilliant. Dad, you could still call it SMASH HIT but it could be a game for two players. One of the challenges they have to face is deciding whether to split or not! The final scene could be a big comeback concert!'

'It could work, Paul,' said Steve Dennison. 'And, after what you've gone through, I think the least we can do is to give you another day's recording for free. And you can be sure this one won't end up on the Net!'

As he finished speaking a look of horror crossed Jeannie Corrick's face. Spinning round, she saw the laptop PC sitting on the desk, its drive light flickering. Even as she dived across to it, the light went out.

'The recording,' she stammered. 'Your sample disk. It's – it's already on the Net ...'

'No, it isn't.' Dipping into her blazer pocket, Tamsyn pulled out a diskette. She held it up so that Jeannie Corrick could see it clearly. '*This* is the recording sample.'

The singer's face was a mixture of incomprehension and relief. 'But how ...?' she began.

'No prob,' said Tamsyn. 'I switched it while you were struggling with Josh.'

'So – what *has* been sent?' asked Steve Dennison.

'My English homework. You want to play it?'

With fumbling fingers, Jeannie Corrick typed a

couple of commands on the laptop's keyboard to bring up the sound player.

There was a pause. Then slowly, the room was filled with sounds.

The clatter of a subway train.

The swish of its doors.

The honking of a taxi cab.

And a final shout of 'Have a nice day!'

michael coleman
VIRUS ATTACK

'Oh, no!' Desperately, Rob tried
to exit the program. But it was
too late. His computer screen
was being taken over by a
huge spider's web. Words
appeared in lurid red:
'Welcome to the hourglass of
horror ...'

Rob has become the latest victim of a
computer virus. It has already wiped
out the Abbey School computers. Now it
seems to be attacking the Internet
Detectives one by one ...
Can Rob, Tamsyn and Josh use the
power of the Net to trap the sinister
Black Widow - before the twisted
hacker triggers total computer melt-
down?

Publication March 1997

Other books in the series ▷

michael coleman

ACCESS DENIED

A guided tour of a visiting US warship leads Josh, Rob and Tamsyn to a trail of bizarre and inexplicable incidents.

They begin to research the ship's movements on the Internet, and find some shocking, potentially dangerous information.
But if the Internet Detectives are to find out the truth, they need access to Top Secret files. Classified information. And suddenly, every path they take comes to a dead end:
ACCESS DENIED.

Publication April 1997